Entwined

I Found My Heart in San Francisco
San Francisco
Book Five

Susan X Meagher

To KAREN—

THANKS FOR THE

LOAN OF YOUR

SHARP EYES

Susan

ENTWINED
I FOUND MY HEART IN SAN FRANCISCO: BOOK FIVE
© 2006 BY SUSAN X MEAGHER

COVER DESIGN AND LAYOUT BY CAROLYN NORMAN
COVER PHOTO OF THE UC BERKELEY CAMPANILE
ISBN 0-977088-55-3

THIS TRADE PAPERBACK ORIGINAL IS PUBLISHED BY BRISK PRESS, NEW YORK, NY 10011

FIRST PRINTING: SEPTEMBER 2006

Acknowledgments

Many people have assisted in editing and proofreading this manuscript. I'd like to thank Catherine from France, Day, Karen, Medora MacDougall, NY, and Tracey.

As always, to Carrie.

By Susan X Meagher

Novels
All That Matters
Arbor Vitae

Serial Novels
I Found My Heart in San Francisco:
Awakenings
Beginnings
Coalescence
Disclosures
Entwined

Anthologies
Undercover Tales
Telltale Kisses
The Milk of Human Kindness
Infinite Pleasures
At First Blush

To purchase these books go to
www.briskpress.com

Chapter One

R yan O'Flaherty sat in the kitchen of her family home just after dawn on the 4th of July, sipping a cup of coffee while she thoughtfully surveyed the foodstuffs laid out in front of her. Her shoulder-length black hair was a little mussed from sleep, the long bangs that poked out from the more ordered strands giving her a slightly childlike appearance. Her father entered the room and placed a hand on her shoulder, giving it a slight squeeze. "I'm telling you, darlin', it doesn't matter how many ways you slice it, we can't get this all prepared by one o'clock. I know you're a whiz with the maths, but you can't make these numbers work for you."

She scratched her head lightly, the gesture causing the few well-behaved hairs to tumble across her forehead. Her father looked at her fondly, fluffing the long strands with his hand as he chuckled at the expression on her face. "I swear I've never seen anyone's hair get longer after a haircut."

"I don't know what that guy was trying to accomplish, but he sure as heck didn't do a darned thing to these bangs. I guess I'll have to do it myself."

A few minutes later, Jamie Evans poked her head into the kitchen, expecting to find breakfast preparation well underway. She squawked sharply when she spotted her lover sitting on a tall kitchen stool, a dish towel draped across her shoulders, and Martin O'Flaherty brandishing a pair of scissors and a comb. "What are you two doing?" She scampered across the floor, placing a restraining hand on Martin's arm just as he was about to make the first cut.

"The lass wants her fringe cut. I cut her hair until she was in high school, I'll have you know."

"I can hardly see," Ryan complained, her crystal-clear blue eyes peeking up through the glossy black hair.

Jamie took a breath, the images of Ryan from early photographs assaulting her brain. Her partner had always had fairly long hair, but Jamie had noticed in nearly every childhood picture that her bangs were perpetually off-kilter. She tried to be as diplomatic as she could, knowing that both O'Flahertys were a bit thin-skinned. "Uhm, honey," she soothed, quickly removing the towel from her partner's shoulders, "Giancarlo left them like that intentionally."

Ryan cocked her head slightly, her brow furrowing in puzzlement. She met her father's equally puzzled glance, and they turned to gaze at Jamie with identical looks on their faces. "Why would he do that?" Both dark heads tilted, waiting for an answer. *If Duffy comes in here and mimics them, I'm gonna lose it.* Willing the smile to remain off her face, Jamie explained. "He thinks the bangs detract from your features, so he wants them to grow out. He thinks you have a lovely forehead, and that you shouldn't hide it." Waiting a beat, Jamie added, "He's absolutely right on that point, by the way." She brushed the hair from said feature and placed a gentle kiss there. Grasping Ryan's chin with her fingers she tilted her head up, displaying her face to Martin's gaze. "Don't you agree, Martin?"

His eyes narrowed a bit, and Jamie could see that he was giving the question his full attention. "She's a lovely girl, that's true," he commented thoughtfully, "but if she wants the fringe cut, that's really all that matters, isn't it?"

Hmm, maybe I should get Duffy to come in here. He'll vote on my side, for sure. I know he'd appreciate more exposed skin on his mommy's face.

"Okay, let's back into this. Do you like the way Giancarlo cut your hair overall?"

"Yeah, I already told you—"

"Bear with me. Do you want him to cut it again?"

"Yeah, I said that I did—"

"Okay." She placed her hands on her hips, pleased that her argument had carried the day. "Then you can't cut your bangs."

"Huh? Why the heck not?" Ryan looked more confused than ever now, and Martin even more so.

"Because, once you cheat on him, he'll never take you back."

"Getting my bangs cut is cheating?"

"Honey, I've seen him ban somebody from the shop because she parted her hair in an unapproved fashion. He's not very forgiving."

Ryan shook her head and stood up, removing the scissors and comb from her father's hands. "Hard to believe Italy is so darned close to Ireland, isn't it?"

"I've always thought so," he agreed, looking just as confounded as his daughter.

After Jamie poured a cup of coffee for herself and replenished her partner's, she came to stand behind her and look over her shoulder at the figures and boxes she was drawing. "You look like you're preparing for the invasion of Normandy," she whispered, causing the tiny hairs at the nape of Ryan's neck to flutter while a shiver chased down her spine.

Martin was busy preparing omelets for them both, so he was distracted enough that Ryan felt comfortable engaging in some sexually charged banter. "If you keep blowing on my neck like that, you're going to be preparing for the O'Flaherty invasion," she said, blue eyes flashing in the early morning light.

"I was ready to surrender last night, hot stuff, but the allied commander fell asleep on duty." Jamie leaned over even further and took a nibble from Ryan's neck, sniffing at her always-alluring, earthy scent.

"Mmm," Ryan's deep morning-voice rumbled. "I'm on duty now, and I'm itching to see some action."

It became apparent that their banter had grown a little too loud and a little too obvious, as Martin started to hum a tune, the volume rising until their voices were obliterated.

The young lovers were so focused on each other that it took a moment for them to recognize Martin's evasive tactic. When they did, their blushes fought for supremacy, with Jamie's winning out in the end. Giggling like schoolgirls, they retreated from the kitchen to the relative safety of the dining room to continue their play while awaiting breakfast.

"Is this really the best idea, Ryan?" Jamie wondered aloud, struggling with the two grocery bags filled with mayonnaise, mustard, celery, eggs, parsley and onions.

"Do you actually think I *want* to carry a fifty-pound sack of potatoes all the way to my aunt's house?" Ryan gave her partner an aggrieved look.

Knowing Ryan, the chore might just be one of her little fitness tortures, so Jamie was aware that her complaints were mostly teasing. "I guess I shouldn't have volunteered us for the potato salad, huh?"

"I've been getting by for years with making deviled eggs," Ryan said. "Next time, don't volunteer for anything unless you check with me first. I've learned where all the land mines lie in this family." She was actually a little out of breath, unaccustomed to toting such an unwieldy load.

"It's a deal," Jamie said. "From here on in, you make all the decisions." At Ryan's amused smirk, Jamie amended her statement slightly. "About family picnics, that is."

"I suspected that blanket concession went a little further than you intended."

They sat in Maeve's sunny kitchen, peeling potatoes for what seemed like hours. "Are you sure this isn't going to be way too much food?" Jamie asked, as she dropped yet another spud into a kettle of cold water.

"I doubt it," Ryan mused. "We almost always run out of potato salad, and we usually use a fifty-pound bag. This looks like the bare minimum to me."

Jamie had never heard of people eating two pounds of potato salad each, so she politely asked, "Are a few other people coming?"

Ryan tossed her head back and laughed heartily, the vibrations echoing off the walls of the small room. "Did you think this was just for us? Oh, Jamie, that's rich."

"Well, you didn't say who was coming…"

"My bad, my bad. All of my aunts' people come to this, a bunch of Driscolls come, a raft of people from the neighborhood, some people from church. Last year we had about eighty-five, and this year I'll be surprised if we don't top a hundred."

Jamie rolled her eyes and shared in Ryan's amusement. "That makes a little more sense. But why will there be fifteen more people this year?"

"Because of you," she smiled, offering no further explanation.

Jamie pointed her index finger and twirled her hand quickly, giving Ryan the usual sign for "Go on."

Ryan grinned and said, "The boys hate the fact that I've got a girl now. I'll be the most surprised woman in Golden Gate Park if every one of the rascals doesn't show up with a date—all trying to win the contest."

"Contest?"

"Oh, yeah. Whenever there's an event like this, the fellas all compete to see who brings the best-looking woman. But just to be fair, I'm going to opt out of the game. It'll hurt morale to have me win, time and again and ag—"

Her comments were cut off by a pair of coral-tinted lips that latched onto her mouth firmly. When Jamie pulled away, she promised, "You are gonna get *so* lucky tonight."

When the Boxster was loaded with as much beer and soda as would fit, they took off for Golden Gate Park. Finding a convenient parking spot was beyond fanciful, so when Jamie spotted the poster board signs that indicated the gathering was up ahead, she double-parked so they could unload before she took off again.

Martin and his three brothers were already on the job, five full-sized Weber kettles smoking away. A tall, cylindrical smoker had been called into service also, and the acrid aroma of mesquite hit Jamie as soon as she exited the Porsche. "Wow, I'm hungry already," she said, even though it was only 10:00 a.m. They worked together to unload the car, then Jamie fluttered a wave at the O'Flaherty brothers and took off in search of a parking spot.

By the time she returned, Ryan had carted all the beverages over to the plastic tubs that held bags of ice waiting to chill the drinks. Jamie stood next to Martin while Ryan organized all the cans and bottles. Jamie had been in the company of the senior O'Flahertys several times, and all of the men had been cordial to her, but without the noise and the clamor of the rest of the family she felt slightly uncomfortable. It wasn't that they treated her any differently than they did Ryan or any of the cousins—actually, her discomfort came from being treated just like one of the family. Where this family was concerned, it wasn't necessary to keep up a conversation just for the sake of politeness.

Each brother tended his own grill, with Francis being in charge of the smoker and Martin having two kettles of his own. The grills were set in a circle with the men standing on the perimeter, arms crossed over their chests or hands in their pockets. No one said a word, since nothing was occurring that required speech. Martin slung an arm around Jamie's shoulder, looking perfectly content. She flashed him a smile and stood in silence, watching the chunks of mesquite begin to turn an ash-covered white.

Since the grills had been lit at the same time, they all reached a state of readiness simultaneously. All at once, the brothers became verbal, arguing briefly about who was to do what and when each item should be put onto each grill. Jamie stood smiling at the group, while Ryan came up behind her and snuck her arms around her waist. "Ooh, decision time," she said, placing a light kiss on her partner's cheek. "The most vital part of the day."

Jamie turned and said quietly, "Nobody said a word for the longest time. Are they angry with each other?"

Ryan considered the question for a moment, seeing the men from Jamie's perspective. "The happier they are, the quieter they are. They talk when they need to, but they're not into small talk. You'll know you're part of the family when they don't even acknowledge your arrival," she said with a wry chuckle.

Jamie laughed in reply. "Then I'm clearly a member of the family. I didn't even get a grunt."

Ryan gave her a gentle hug, holding on for just a minute longer than discretion called for. "I knew they'd love you," she whispered, clearly pleased by her uncles ignoring her partner.

By 11:00 most of Ryan's generation was in attendance, and as correctly predicted, every cousin was in the company of a woman. In fact, Brendan was the only holdout, and Jamie commented on this to Ryan. "Does Brendan date?" she asked, having never seen him with anyone, nor having ever heard him speak of a romantic entanglement.

Ryan chuckled at the way the question was framed and told Jamie all that she knew. "I don't think he's gay, and I don't think he's a hermit, but to be honest, you only know what Brendan wants to tell you, and that's not much."

"Are you serious? You really haven't met any of his girlfriends?"

"Nope." Ryan shook her dark head. "I honestly have never seen him with a woman. Bren has always valued his privacy much more than any of the rest of us. I'm not sure why, but you'll notice that he's the only one the aunts don't tease. His personal life has always been personal, and everybody knows it."

"Is that why he moved out?" Jamie's intent gaze showed her interest in hearing more.

"I suppose." Ryan thought for a moment. "There wasn't a lot of discussion about it. When he came back home from law school I'd moved into his room, since it was long past time for me to stop sharing a room with

Rory. Rory and Conor offered to bunk together since Bren was the oldest, but he said he was getting his own place, and that was that."

"Your father didn't make a big deal out of it?"

"Nope. If you try to force the issue, Bren will just blow smoke at you. Da knows better than to try to get him to say something he doesn't want to reveal. He's always been like that, Jamie. That's just Bren."

Jamie gave a short laugh. "Kinda like his uncles, huh?"

"Kinda," Ryan agreed. "We used to tease him that he should be a priest since he didn't seem to need a woman, and he'd never violate the confidences he'd hear in confession."

"Maybe that's in the offing," Jamie observed, mulling over the fact that Brendan was the only regular churchgoer of his generation.

Ryan laughed at the thought. "You could be right. All I know is that we wouldn't know a thing about it until he was wearing a Roman collar."

A short while later, Jamie found herself sitting on a small rise behind one of the softball diamonds, surrounded by at least a dozen women, most of whom appeared to be in their early to mid-twenties. On the field, seventeen men and one woman stretched their muscles in a show that reminded Jamie of taking Duffy to the dog park. All of the cousins, Ryan and her brothers, and a few of the Driscolls were among the group, and as they sized each other up, Jamie wondered if one of them might actually lift his leg on one of the bases, just to mark territory.

Ryan came trotting over, giving her partner a blindingly white smile. She wore a bright green softball jersey with "USF" emblazoned in gold block letters across her chest, black double-knit shorts, green knee socks, and well-used knee pads. Black, low-cut cleats finished off her outfit, and as usual, Jamie was more interested in getting the uniform off her than she was in watching her play, even though she enjoyed both pastimes. "Nice shorts, Tiger," she teased. "How many polyesters had to die to make those babies?"

Ryan took the teasing in stride, running her hands over the thick black material. "Not many," she said. "They're small."

"I like small," Jamie said. "I'd like to take all of your clothes and wash them on hot."

"I thought you had an ulterior motive in trying to get me to let Maria Los do my laundry."

Getting to her feet, Jamie signaled Ryan to walk over to the corner of the diamond.

Ryan followed her and cocked her head in question. "Wassup?"

"I don't really want to sit with the girls," she complained. "I want to play with you guys."

Ryan looked a little uncomfortable, and she shifted her weight from foot to foot as she considered her reply. In a move that nearly made Jamie laugh, the dark-haired woman spit rather forcefully into the pocket of her glove, rubbing the moisture into the leather, the smell of wet cowhide and dust just barely reaching Jamie's nose. "Have you...uhm...played before?" Hesitant baby blues peeked out from the dangling bangs, adding to Ryan's adolescent demeanor.

With just a touch of indignation Jamie assured her, "Many times, Ryan. I even have a position."

"What's that?" Given the look on Ryan's face, Jamie knew she was on the verge of getting zapped.

"I play second base," she said, crossing her arms over her chest.

"Tell ya what," Ryan suggested, "I normally play second because I'm the little one in this crowd. Let me play the first inning since I'm warmed up. We can alternate after that." Ryan let her eyes wander to the spot on the grass that Jamie had vacated. She slowly checked out every other woman, letting her gaze linger on a couple of them for a moment. "You're still in the lead in the best-looking-date contest, but Conor's entry hasn't shown up yet."

A quick backhand to the gut proved that Jamie's reflexes were perfectly adequate for a second baseman.

Ryan's team took the field first, and Jamie spent more than a minute watching her partner toss the ball around the infield while Frank warmed up to pitch. She was so engrossed in staring at the lean, lanky second baseman that she almost didn't notice the woman who sat down next to her. The cloying scent of *Eternity* reached her nose before any of her other senses became aware of the woman, and as she turned she was stunned to find an absolutely knock-down-dead gorgeous woman smiling at her. "That good-looking man over there told me that you could tell me where Conor O'Flaherty is." She inclined her head in Malachy's direction, and Jamie gave him a grin along with a thumbs up.

The woman next to her was tall, tan, blonde, and decidedly European. Her accent was Scandinavian, but Jamie wasn't sure which country. "I'm Jamie Evans," she said, extending a hand.

"Bindi," replied the woman, nearly blinding Jamie with her smile.

"Conor should be here any moment," Jamie said. "He's changing into his softball clothes." With a start, she looked up to see Ryan leaning into the chain link fence, blue eyes dancing.

"Everything okay, Jamie?" she asked, innocently keeping her eyes only on her partner.

"Yes, dear, everything's fine."

"We could switch now if you wanted," Ryan offered, guileless eyes blinking slowly.

"No thanks." Jamie ignored the impish grin that now covered Ryan's face. "I like it just fine right here."

"Okay," Ryan tossed over her shoulder, as she ran back to her position. "Just want to make sure you're happy." When she was about twenty feet away, she turned and added, "The votes have been tabulated. You're still number one."

"You're a generous grader," Jamie called after her, smiling sweetly at Bindi. "My lover, Ryan," she said pointedly. "She's Conor's little sister."

Bindi gave the tall woman an appraising glance. "She's not so little, is she? People are very large in this family."

A quick look at Jamie refuted her own statement, but Jamie caught the look and reminded her, "I'm an O'Flaherty by marriage."

"Oh, people of the same sex can get married in the United States, too?"

Jamie shook her head briefly. "No, not legally. We're married in every way that counts, though. Where are you from, Bindi?"

"Denmark," she said. "I'm just visiting some friends who are living in San Francisco. I'm going home next week."

"Ooh, that's too bad. How did you meet Conor?"

"I was having a drink with my friends in a little club the other night and he was just there. All of a sudden we were chatting like the oldest of friends. He's a very nice man, isn't he?"

"Yes, he is," Jamie said. "Now his sister on the other hand…"

On her way back to second base, Ryan had stopped by the bench and snagged a black baseball cap which was now pulled down low on her head.

Jamie smiled at the intense look of concentration on what little of her face she could still see, thinking it quite funny that Ryan would take a mere family softball game seriously.

Dermot was the first player to bat, and he beat out a single by laying down a bunt, catching the left side of the infield by surprise. There was a bit of grumbling from the team on the field, but they settled down and took their positions, waiting for Niall to take his turn. After letting a few pitches sail wide of the plate, he hit a grounder to short, and Kieran grabbed it and zipped it to Ryan to begin the double play. To Jamie's amazement, Dermot slid in, spikes high, giving Ryan a good shot to the knees as she leapt into the air to make the peg to first. She landed heavily atop her cousin, and he immediately took umbrage, pushing her off roughly. Ryan scrambled to her feet, her face filled with fury, and pushed him as he tried to get up. There was a very brief pause as both decided how to respond, then each gave the other a strong shove, and the melee was in full swing. All eighteen of the players pushed and shoved, their voices rising as they shouted taunts and insults at each other. A cloud of dust swirled around the group, and the noise level rose dramatically as the fight seemed to escalate.

Jamie leapt to her feet and took off, not sure what she could do, but determined to protect her lover, who was at the epicenter of the scrum. She had barely reached the edge of the backstop when a strong hand gripped her shoulder, effectively stopping her progress. She whirled and cried, "Martin! Ryan's at the bottom of that pile!"

"Don't worry about her," Martin soothed, maintaining his hold. "There's always a fight, darlin'; this one just got underway a little early." Even as he spoke the brawl was breaking up of its own accord, the players slapping each other on the back as they returned to their positions. The last two were Dermot and Ryan, and Jamie watched in amazement as her smiling lover pulled Dermot down for a kiss on the cheek. He laughed and slapped her hard on the butt, grinning as he dropped his head and trotted back to the bench.

"Wha...how did?" Jamie was sputtering, completely shocked by this development.

"They've been fighting since the first two of them were three years old," Martin assured her. "No one's ever been seriously hurt. Don't give it another thought."

She shook her head slowly, making eye contact with her partner, who waved. "I'll never understand that woman," she muttered slowly.

"Don't even try," Martin said. "It'll make you old before your time."

Jamie prudently decided that being a spectator at an O'Flaherty softball game was more her style, and she spent the rest of the game chatting with the cousins' dates. By the time the contest was over, they were all quite companionable, and Jamie had answered the thousand questions Bindi had about the United States in general and San Francisco in particular.

Ryan was, as expected, a sweaty mess, but she managed to make herself presentable in the public restroom. She emerged in jeans and a peach, French-cut T-shirt, reminding Jamie of the womanly curves that had been hidden by her oversized jersey and unfashionable shorts.

As she met and held Jamie's gaze, Ryan gave her an enormous grin and said, "Have I told you how absolutely fabulous you look today?" Her eyes trailed up and down Jamie's body, taking in her pale yellow jeans and the Madras plaid cotton blouse in bright pink, purple, and yellow.

Jamie tilted her head, considering the question. She looked toward the sky, pursing her lips as she finally gave a short shake of her head. "You haven't said word one."

"I swear I don't know how you put up with me. I was watching you sit there on the ground with all of those other…people…I'm not sure if they were men or women, you know. And I kept thinking, 'How did I get so lucky as to have such a beautiful woman fall in love with me?'"

Jamie offered up a knowing smile at the effusive compliment, patting Ryan's flushed cheek while she was at it. "Even with the fight and the obvious attempt to take a look at Miss Denmark, you're still getting lucky tonight, hot stuff, so you can stop sucking up."

Letting out a heavy sigh, Ryan gazed at her partner with a completely serious look. "I'm lucky every day of my life as long as I have your love."

It was late when they arrived back at the house, and they spent a few minutes assembling their gear for the trip back to Berkeley. After Ryan carried the travel bags out to the car, she came back in to find Jamie closing her cell phone. "Mother called to see how we were," she said, a bright smile on her face.

"That's nice. Does she still seem okay about Saturday?" It was hard to believe that it had only been two days since Jamie had come out to her parents, and Ryan sincerely hoped that Jamie's mom would remain as supportive as she had been on that night.

"Yeah, she seemed fine. She asked how you were, but other than that it was just our normal conversation."

"Normal is good," Ryan said. "Business as usual is what I'm hoping for."

Jamie felt so completely and totally loved at the end of the long day that she was honestly too excited to sleep when they were tucked into their bed in Berkeley that night.

"I can't tell you how good it felt to have you parade me around introducing me all day," she said, her childlike enthusiasm bubbling out.

Ryan looked a trifle puzzled. "Why is that surprising for you? I introduce you everywhere we go."

Jamie didn't answer with complete candor, since she didn't want to bring her own family into the discussion, but she knew that Ryan would never be offered the same level of complete acceptance that she felt from the O'Flaherty clan. "I guess it's not that it's surprising," she said. "It just feels so darned good that I want to thank you for making me feel so special."

Ryan began to nibble down her soft, smooth neck, pausing to whisper, "If you're that thankful for a few introductions, you're gonna build a shrine to me when I'm done with you tonight."

"I already worship at your feet," Jamie gasped out with a quavering voice as a spine-tingling jolt of desire shot down her body. "Ooh, yeah, I can picture the shrine already."

Chapter Two

The holiday weekend over, Ryan was back into her routine on Tuesday morning, leaving for her weight lifting session while Jamie was still trying to pry her eyes open. When Ryan returned home, she was pleased to see that her partner was dressed and waiting for her, an expectant look on her face.

"Good morning, princess. Sleep well?"

Ryan looked relaxed and happy, and Jamie realized that it was the first time in days that there were no signs of tension on her face. "I did indeed," she said, a sunny smile lighting up her features. "My fabulously talented lover put me to sleep nice and early, she let me sleep in this morning, I've had breakfast, read the paper, and listened to the news. I'm ready to rock."

"And just where do you plan on rocking?" Ryan asked, bending over to greet her with a proper kiss.

"It's time to pay a little visit to the bank."

"Aw, gosh," Ryan said in her most adolescent manner, her lower lip sticking out. "Do we really have to?"

"Honey," Jamie said as she got to her feet and scratched Ryan's belly in a soothing gesture, "my parents know about us now, so there's no reason not to start acting like what we are—permanently partnered. I want you to be able to write checks for things around the house and for emergencies. And I want you to have an ATM card so you can get cash when you need it."

"But I never need it. I like the way I have things set up now. I know how much I can spend, and that's what I keep with me."

"Ryan, you're going to be traveling all over the country with your team. You need to have an ATM card. I'll travel with you as much as I can, but if I make the golf team I'm sure our schedules will conflict. I'll worry about you if you don't have the ability to get money in an emergency."

Letting out a sigh, Ryan sidestepped her partner and sank into the cushions of the loveseat. She looked tired and a little defeated, making Jamie's heart start to race. "There's one little detail of my discussion with your father that you need to know about."

Jamie sat next to Ryan and scanned her face for clues. "What is it?"

Ryan's knees were spread, and as she leaned over, her hands dangled between them. Slowly, she slid her hands together, fingers interlaced, and stared at them for a moment. "I told your dad that I was going to start paying rent, since I was taking Cassie's spot in the house. He thought that was a good idea," she added quietly.

"No...no...no. That's unacceptable." The obviously perturbed blonde hopped to her feet and paced across the redwood plank floor. "You are not a tenant. You are not a roommate. You are my spouse and I won't tolerate your being treated with this kind of disrespect."

The lines of tension appeared once again on Ryan's forehead. "Don't make a big deal about this. Let's see where things settle and revisit it in a few months. I can easily pay the rent until I quit my job. Heck, if I tried, I could probably work another five or six hours a week, and that would give me a little breathing room."

Jamie turned and stared at her for a long minute. "You don't need breathing room. I have enough money to support your entire family for the rest of their natural days. My father makes close to a million dollars a year in salary, so he doesn't need your rent money. He's just trying to make it clear that he's withholding his approval of our relationship." Her tone was calm, measured, but there was a steely determination to her voice that Ryan had no interest in trying to break.

"Sweetheart, we both knew this would be hard for one or both of them to accept. I think they both behaved really well and we need to support that by giving in a little now. Let's just pay the rent and let this rest."

Jamie sat down next to her on the loveseat and grasped Ryan's hand in both of her own. They sat in silence for a few minutes as Jamie slowly traced each of the tendons and veins. "I know you don't want to cause trouble. And I know that you wish I didn't have this much money." She looked up and caught the acknowledgment in the clear blue eyes. "It's going to be a struggle for us to figure out how to live in a way that makes both of us happy."

Ryan nodded, leaning over to kiss the top of Jamie's herbal-scented hair. She detected a note of lilac and decided that the fragrant flower was a perfect complement to Jamie's natural scent. With a start, she realized that she had completely zoned out, and she shook her head a little to renew her concentration. "I uhm, I know that it's gonna be hard. That's why I think we should wait."

"I understand that, but here's another way of looking at it. Taking a few small steps toward merging our lives makes it clear to everyone that we're in a partnership. If we treat each other like roommates, it makes us guilty of diminishing our relationship. I don't want that. I want to take a stand on this one small thing. I want to add you to my checking account, get you an ATM card, and tell my father that I don't want you to pay rent."

"And if I don't want to do any of those things just yet?"

Jamie hated to have to give in, but she knew she couldn't push Ryan too far. "Then we wait. I only want to do this if you agree."

"Damn." Ryan leaned her head back against the back of the loveseat, and let out a heavy sigh. "I was hoping you'd be stubborn and insist we do it your way. Then I could refuse to go along with it and feel like I was justified." Her eyes held a hint of mirth, but Jamie knew there was an equal measure of sincerity in their depths. "Okay," Ryan said, in clear, measured tones. "I see your point, and I guess I agree with it. I don't really want to throw away $1,500 a month if I can avoid it, and I can understand that you want me to be able to write checks for things around the house. I give." She held her hands up in surrender, and Jamie grasped her around the neck and pulled herself onto Ryan's lap.

"That was a longer, more involved discussion of finances than I had in three years with Jack," she murmured, placing whisper-soft kisses all along Ryan's salt-flavored jaw. "I really appreciate that you try to see my point of view."

"Well, I think I understand your position better. It's gonna take us a long time to agree on everything, but as long as we keep talking about it, I'm sure it'll work out." She pressed a kiss onto Jamie's lips and patted her on the butt. "Hop off, babe. I need a shower if we're gonna go to the bank."

With a final nibble on Ryan's neck, Jamie slid off. "I guess not everyone likes you sweaty and salty, huh?"

Ryan grabbed her nose between two fingers and gave it a tug. "Not many are among that number, sport, and it surprises the holy hell out of me that you are."

"That's my goal," Jamie said, grasping Ryan's hand to accompany her upstairs. "I like to keep you guessing."

When Jamie entered Cal, she had visited the local branch of Bank of America to introduce herself and to switch her account from the San Mateo branch to the Berkeley office. The pleasant young man who had been assigned as her account manager had recently left the bank and his replacement, Richard Merriman, now gazed across the desk at them. "Okay, now what did you want to do today?" he asked in a slightly distracted tone.

"I want to add my partner to my checking account," Jamie repeated.

"Okay. You *do* understand that by making her a joint signer you, in essence, would allow her to close the account by withdrawing all of the money for her personal use if she so chooses?" He looked at Jamie to make sure she understood the ramifications of her actions, ignoring the rather outraged look from the blue eyes that bore into him.

"Of course I understand that," Jamie said. "She's my partner, Mr. Merriman, no different than if we were married."

"Right. Well, let's see," he mused as he looked at his computer screen to find her accounts. "Hmm, is this your only account with us?"

"Besides my trust, yes, the checking is all that I have here."

He looked at her face, then back at his screen. "Are you the Jamie Evans who is the income beneficiary of the William A. and Phoebe Dunlop Smith Trust?"

"That would be me," she said with a small smile.

"Pleasure to meet you, Ms. Evans," he said, now sitting up straight in his chair and gracing her with a broad smile. "Is this the only thing I can do for you today?"

"Yes, just add Ms. O'Flaherty to the checking account."

"Well, that will take a few minutes," he said. "And then you'll need to order more checks. Would you like me to bring the paperwork to your home so you don't have to wait?" His now eager face reminded Ryan of Duffy's need for approval when he performed one of his few tricks.

"We have time."

He pushed a big binder in her direction. "Here are the styles of checks you have to choose from, Ms. Evans. I'm sure you'll find something you like."

"The account is now for both of us," she reminded him.

"Right, right, no offense, Ms. O'Flaherty," he said as he now smiled eagerly at Ryan.

She gave him a cross between a smirk and a smile and looked through the book while Mr. Merriman went to find the papers they had to sign.

"Are people always like this?" Ryan whispered when he was out of earshot.

"Like what?" Jamie asked in an intentionally obtuse manner.

Ryan chuckled. "Like they want to lick your boots. He jumps to attention faster than I do."

"I wouldn't go that far," Jamie playfully scoffed. "You'll get used to it after a while." She sat back and looked at Ryan for a moment, then said, "It'll probably be disconcerting at first. It seems natural to me, but you're gonna have to learn the rules."

"Rules?"

"Yeah. Like if they personally benefit from pleasing you, they act like you're a goddess, but if they don't benefit, you often get the very cold shoulder."

"That's so odd," Ryan said as Mr. Merriman came scampering back.

"Okay, Ms. Evans and Ms. O'Flaherty," he obediently addressed them both, "you need to sign these new signature cards and then I'll need I.D. from both of you."

They followed the instructions, then Ryan informed him that they had chosen the "High Tech" series of checks. He put all the papers together and promised that the new checks would be delivered in a few days. "I could have them sent by messenger to your home."

"The usual delivery will be fine," Jamie assured him. "Ryan will have an ATM/debit card, too, won't she?"

"Absolutely," he said. "Do you need me to expedite delivery for you, Ms. O'Flaherty?"

"No, not at all," she assured him hastily. "No big deal."

As they walked to the door, Mr. Merriman offered them CDs, money market funds, lines of credit, and every other possible product the bank had to offer. Jamie practically had to close the door on him, but he finally waved good-bye, looking after them rather longingly.

"This is a whole new experience for me, and it's not one I think I'm gonna like," Ryan said quietly as she got in to drive the Boxster home.

Jamie's gentle touch upon her arm caused her to make eye contact before she drove off. "Are you okay with this?" she asked softly. "I had a long time to get used to it, but I'm asking you to just jump in as an adult. I know it's hard."

Ryan smiled over at her. "Thanks for understanding. It's gonna take me a while."

The reassuring touch continued as Jamie lightly ran her hand up and down Ryan's leg. "Do you want to start using this account to deposit your paycheck and things like that?"

"Nah. I'll stick with my normal way."

"You haven't explained what your normal way is."

Ryan gave her a smile and said, "It's quite simple and very low-tech. I take the checks I get during the week and go to the bank on Saturday. I just keep the amount that I need for the week and deposit the rest into my savings account."

"Okay," Jamie nodded, seeing that such a process could work as a general rule. "But what do you do when you need more? Isn't it a drag to have to go to the bank to make a withdrawal?"

They were at a stoplight, so Ryan was able to turn slightly to face her. "If I want to do something or buy something and I don't have the cash, I wait until the next week when I get paid again. There's rarely anything that's that urgent."

"Don't you ever charge things?" Jamie asked, still stunned by this nineteenth-century style of finance.

"Don't have a charge card."

"Not *any* charge cards?" They were inundated by offers for charge cards at school, and she personally knew several people who were already tens of thousands of dollars in debt from the readily attainable credit. It seemed incomprehensible that Ryan had never succumbed to the lure of the credit card companies, but Jamie didn't want to show just how odd she thought it was.

"Nope. And if Da finds out you got me one, he'll throw a fit."

"But it's not a charge card. It's a debit card."

"Won't make any difference. It's a card I can use to buy things when I don't have cash in my pocket. That's close enough. He thinks debt is the work of the devil."

"Wow," was the only word the startled woman was able to get out.

Over lunch Ryan asked rather absently, "How will we manage our checking account if we're both making withdrawals?"

"What do you mean?" Jamie asked, swallowing a bite of her sandwich.

Ryan furrowed her brow at Jamie's lack of understanding of the basic tenets of finance. "I want to make sure we don't get overdrawn."

Jamie blinked slowly. "How much are you planning on taking out?"

"I don't know, but we'll need groceries and gas for the car and all sorts of things. Da's right, you know. It costs a pretty pence to keep me fed."

"Honey, you can write as many checks as you want. My accountant balances the checkbook at the end of the month."

"But, Jamie—"

Her partner cut her off. "Ryan, my last statement showed I had over a hundred thousand dollars in that account. Chill."

"A hundred thousand dollars! Are you crazy? That money should be earning interest!"

"I know it's a lot," Jamie soothed, "and it is earning interest. We earn a little bit on that account. Two percent, I think."

Ryan took a very deep breath and let it out slowly. "How much do you know about your financial picture?"

"Not much, other than that it's rosy," Jamie kidded gently.

"I don't think you're being advised very well if they let you earn a measly 2 percent on that much money. With the market the way it is, you should have most of that in a mutual fund."

Jamie was surprised to hear Ryan speak so knowledgeably, having gotten the impression that she was a financial Luddite. "Do you know much about investments?"

"Not a lot, but I understand math, and finance is really an offshoot of that. Would you like to understand your finances better?"

"I really would. Maybe you can help me."

"I'd be happy to," Ryan said as she collected their plates. "But for now, it's off to work for me and practice for you, little one."

"Okay, big one. Want a ride?"

"Nah, I think I'll take my bike. Gotta keep those spark plugs clean."

On Wednesday evening Jim called Jamie just as they were clearing the dinner dishes. "Did I catch you at a good time?" he asked.

"Sure, Daddy, we just finished dinner. What's up?"

"A couple of things. But primarily I'd like you to come down for the weekend. I have a few things to discuss with you, and I'd prefer to do it in person."

"I suppose we could come down," she considered, furrowing her brow at Ryan. They exchanged glances and Jamie gave a slight nod as Ryan mouthed, "Your father?"

"I'd like to see you alone," he said with a hitch in his normally assured voice. "Is that possible?"

Since she was on her cell, she stepped onto the front porch so Ryan couldn't hear. She'd tell her anything that happened, but she knew that hearing one side of this type of discussion was a little unsettling. "Daddy," she said, "I know this is hard for you, and I promise I'll try to give you time to adjust, but Ryan's my partner. I share everything with her. I understand that you don't know her well and you probably feel a little uncomfortable around her. I'm willing to spend time with you alone, like I did when I was with Jack, but I won't stay overnight without her."

She could hear the heavy sigh he let out as he took this information in. It took him a second, but he silently acknowledged her position by changing his request. "How about golf on Sunday?"

"Sure. Eight o'clock?"

"That's fine," he said. "See you then. Oh, and Jamie?"

"Yes, Daddy?"

"This really isn't that hard for me. I want you to be happy, and if this relationship is what you want, I don't have any serious objections."

Wishing desperately that she had her father on a speakerphone so that Ryan could hear what he'd just said, she managed to stutter, "Th...thank you. That means a great deal to me."

"You mean a great deal to me, Jamie. Always remember that."

The course was crowded, but Jim managed to convince the starter to let them go off as a twosome. They chatted about their respective weeks for the first few holes, both managing to get over their slight discomfort with each other in a short time. Jamie was playing so well, Jim spent another five holes just marveling at her increased skills.

On the sixteenth tee he finally got to his agenda. "I was upset this week when I was notified that you'd converted your checking account to joint status."

"Why were you notified?" she asked, a bit perturbed that Mr. Merriman would notify her father.

"I *am* your trustee. Your monthly allowance goes into that account, so I receive confirmation of all changes."

"Daddy, you know I would have gotten a complete distribution if I'd married Jack. The funds Ryan and I are sharing are truly a drop in the bucket. Even if you don't trust her, I hope you trust me," she said with a note of hurt. "I want her to have some spending money and this is how I choose to do it. Please don't second-guess me."

He strode to the tee and hit his drive, remaining silent until she was finished with her shot. "I certainly don't mean to second-guess you, Jamie. I'm just concerned."

"There's absolutely nothing to be concerned about. Ryan is the most trustworthy person I've ever met."

Jim looked at his daughter carefully as they got into the cart and drove to the fairway. "She might be, and I truly hope that she is, but *I* don't know her. You have to understand my position here."

Trying her best to soften her attitude, Jamie patted him lightly on the knee. "I can see that you don't have a good feeling for her yet. I guarantee that over time you'll come to agree with me, but I can see that it'll take a while."

"I just have one question," he said slowly, making sure that he had her attention. "Did Ryan, in any way, try to talk you into this?"

Jamie tossed her head back and laughed heartily at the question, causing her father to react with a very puzzled look. "I'm sorry, Daddy," she gasped. "The thought of Ryan doing that is just too funny. I practically had to drag her into that bank to make the change." Giving her father a confident smile she said, "I think money *is* going to be an issue in our relationship, but only because she wishes I didn't have so much of it."

He nodded slowly, looking like a man who was sincerely trying to understand a concept that was completely beyond his grasp.

After the round, they decided to have brunch together in the grill. Jamie wished she didn't need to bring up the topic, but since her father had made it clear to Ryan that he wanted her to pay rent, she knew she had to approach it sometime. "Daddy," she began, fidgeting a little in her seat. "I, uhm, Ryan told me that you want her to begin to pay rent to live with me."

He paused mid-bite and gave her a serious look. With a sigh, he replaced his fork and pursed his lips. "I think it's best. Having her pay her own way will show me that her intentions are honest."

Jamie cocked her head a little and asked the question that had been lingering in the back of her mind. "Would you have done the same for Jack? If he'd been attending Boalt," naming the law school at Cal, "would you have expected him to pay to live with me?"

Jim gave the question a moment's thought, looking to Jamie like he was trying to find a way to wiggle out of having to answer. "No, I wouldn't."

"I didn't think so," she said, looking directly into his eyes. "Daddy, the bond I have with Ryan is deeper than what I had with Jack. If she were a man, we'd already be married. It's important to me that you eventually come to realize that."

He nodded briefly, acknowledging her wish. "I understand that's how you feel, and I promise to try. That's all that I can do." Running his hand through his hair, he nodded once more. "I'd feel better if she continued to support herself the same way she has, but since this means so much to you, I agree to withdraw my request. She doesn't have to pay rent."

She graced him with a sunny smile, terribly pleased that he was so willing to listen to reason. "She lived with her family before and had no living expenses to speak of. So, in essence, she is supporting herself in the same way she was before."

He laughed a bit at this and said, "Not really what I had in mind, but again, I defer to your judgment on this. You've always been very level-headed, and I assume you'll stay the same."

Jamie reached across the table and squeezed his hand, beaming a smile at him. "I'm very glad that you're my father."

When Jamie pulled into the tiny driveway of the O'Flaherty home, she heard many sets of feet scampering down the stairs to greet her. "You look like you could use a hand," Ryan said, grasping Jamie's huge golf bag with both hands and yanking it out of the passenger seat.

Duffy decided to run around to the more interesting side of the car, and as Jamie pushed the door open, his sturdy body shuffled backwards just enough to give her the bare minimum for clearance. "I've gotta say, you two always make me feel welcome," she sputtered as Duffy put his paws on her thighs and struggled to reach her face. Looking over at Ryan's amused smile, she playfully demanded, "Did you ever give any thought to teaching your boy not to jump on people?"

Her tone was light, and she was obviously teasing, but Ryan's brow furrowed and she commanded in a sharp voice, "Duffy! Off!" Giving her a puzzled glance, he immediately rested all four feet on the ground, his curly black tail thumping loudly against the concrete. The dog's big black eyes darted from Jamie to Ryan, who still looked a little cross. "I didn't know that bothered you." Her voice was quiet, and there was a definite shadow in her normally open gaze.

Walking around the car, Jamie placed her hand on Ryan's back, giving it a little rub. "Everything okay?"

Ryan looked embarrassed and nodded. "Yeah, fine. I just wish you'd told me that Duffy's jumping bothered you." A hint of a pout played around her lips, and even though Jamie's fervent wish was to grab her and kiss the adorable little face, she knew that wasn't the wise choice since Ryan was obviously in a snit over something.

Ryan had shifted the golf bag onto her shoulder, and the three of them made their way onto the deck. "Let's sit outside for a bit," Jamie suggested, noticing a glass of lemonade and a book lying on a table.

The two of them sat on the cushioned loveseat, Duffy looking around for a way to be as close as possible to Jamie while being as comfortable as he could manage. He chose to lie at her feet, hoping for a head rub if the opportunity presented itself. To his complete pleasure, Jamie's hand was almost at the perfect spot to do just that, and she tangled her fingers in his jet-black hair, making him happy. "I'll deny it in public," Jamie said, "but I have to admit that Duffy is my second favorite O'Flaherty."

The tone of her voice was very gentle, and Ryan's reluctant smile brightened her face. "I think everyone knows that already. Although Duffy thinks he's your absolute favorite."

"Nope. He's a distant second. But he is very dear to me, and I think you know that I love having him jump on me to welcome me home." Her free hand was trailing up and down Ryan's khaki-clad thigh, and she smiled when she realized that both O'Flahertys were leaning in for more pressure on their respective parts.

"I thought so," Ryan said, a confused look on her face, "but your tone was really sharp, and I thought you meant it."

Jamie knew that her tone had not been the least bit sharp, and she suspected that she knew the source of the problem, but didn't want to bring it up. One of the things that she had absolutely hated about Jack was his irritating habit of attributing every show of bad temper to her period, and she had decided that she would never do that to Ryan. Deciding that it would serve no purpose to disagree, she gave a little scratch to Ryan's thigh and soothed, "I'm sorry if I sounded sharp. I certainly didn't mean to. I love Duffy, and I love you, and I want both of you to jump on me and wag your tails when I come home."

Her tone, combined with her sincerity, did the trick, and Ryan snaked an arm around her, leaning over to nuzzle her neck. A few gentle kisses followed, with Ryan finally lifting her head to murmur, "Someone was in the sand today."

"Just once." Jamie laughed softly, rubbing her head against Ryan's chin. "But I got a faceful when the wind shifted."

"It goes well with the salt on your skin," Ryan teased, allowing her tongue to swipe across her partner's neck. She shifted a bit on the seat and leaned in heavily, pinning Jamie to the seat back. When her leg moved between Jamie's, the smirking blonde knew how they would spend the rest of the afternoon. Ryan was practically straddling her, but Jamie didn't have any intention of complaining. Their lips met softly, but the softness quickly progressed to firm and then rough kisses, Ryan's desire clearly in overdrive. Her kisses were nearly consuming, and Jamie managed to wedge her hands between their bodies and push her back just an inch or two.

"Slow down, Tiger," she urged, smiling as Ryan continued to kiss and nibble on her lips. "We've got all day. We don't have to rush."

"I like to rush." Ryan's deep voice rumbled as she pushed back against her lover, trapping her hands between them. "First I wanna rush," she murmured, capturing Jamie's lips in a flurry of hungry kisses. "Then I wanna go slow." Another round of kisses followed, this time slow and soft and delicate—so different from the first, but just as heavy with the promise of an afternoon of lovemaking.

Ryan's determined hand slipped between Jamie's thighs, and as she felt the damp skin beneath the thin cotton shorts, the look in her eyes said their first round of passion might be "al fresco". No one was home, and even though they were facing the street, their position atop the garage made it impossible for pedestrians to see them. The people in the house directly across the street could see the entire deck, but she didn't know the current occupants very well since they'd only lived in the house a short time. They were a young couple with a new baby, and Ryan guessed they had better things to do on a Saturday than sit in their bedroom looking at her. *Still, Jamie wouldn't like it if we could be seen...*

All of these thoughts flitted through Ryan's mind as Jamie lay quietly beneath her. Her need for satisfaction warred with her knowledge of Jamie's need for privacy. To Ryan's relief, Jamie shifted and wedged her leg tightly between Ryan's thighs, smiling when Ryan groaned and twitched her hips to intensify the contact. "Ooh, you read my mind."

"You couldn't be more transparent if you tried, Tiger," Jamie murmured as Ryan started to push against her. She was almost at a good rhythm when Duffy let out a low growl and scrambled to his feet. He was standing at the top of the stairs, tail wagging hesitantly, ears up, head cocked, by the time Ryan heard the first footstep on the stairs.

"Shit," she growled, rolling off Jamie to compose herself as much as possible. "Duffy, sit!" she ordered, and without hesitation he did so, now looking very happy at the prospect of greeting their guest.

"Hello," called out a hesitant voice, seconds before Mary Elizabeth Andrews peeked up from the staircase.

"Mrs. Andrews," Ryan gasped, hopping up as though she'd been pinched. "H...hello." Ryan strode across the deck, her hand extended.

The older woman grasped it as she reached the deck, giving Ryan a firm handshake. "I'm sorry I didn't call first or let you know I was coming up..." she trailed off, and Ryan mentally cursed Conor for failing to put a doorbell at the bottom of the stairs as he had often promised.

"No problem," Ryan said with a cordial smile affixed to her face. "You remember my partner, Jamie, don't you?"

Jamie got up and shook the older woman's hand, adding a practiced smile. "Good to see you again," Jamie said, all of her normal warmth absent.

"Yes, yes, it's good to see you too, Jamie," she said, looking as if she would rather be almost anywhere else. Returning her gaze to Ryan, she asked, "Do you have a few minutes?"

"Sure," she said graciously. "Have a seat." The hesitant woman did so, casting a quick glance at Jamie to determine if she would join them. Ryan grasped her partner's hand, pulling her down next to her on the loveseat, settling that question rather decisively. "I was planning on calling you sometime this weekend," Ryan said. "I suppose your visit is for the same purpose."

The older woman nodded briefly. Her brow was knit, her expression contrite and earnest. "Sara told me what you two had discussed, and even though I have so much to regret, I wanted to tell you that I didn't tell anyone about what happened, Ryan. I would never do that to you."

Ryan's expression grew chilly, and she fixed the woman with an ice-blue gaze. "Haven't you caused me enough harm? I'd think that after all of this time you could admit what you did and be done with it."

Their visitor looked completely taken aback. She sat up a little taller in her chair and leaned forward, returning Ryan's gaze. "Ryan, I've known you since you were a small child. I knew your mother, and I'm proud to say she was my friend. I wouldn't tarnish the relationship she and I had by hurting you intentionally. I know that my actions hurt you, and I'm terribly sorry for them. But I did not—I swear—tell anyone about you."

Ryan gazed deeply into her warm brown eyes and let the memories of their long relationship flow through her mind. She remembered how close she had been to the woman who now faced her, and she acknowledged that it wasn't in her character to do what she had suspected her of. In fact, one of the reasons that she had been so stunned by her betrayal was because it was so completely unexpected. "So who did?" Ryan whispered, a stab of pain lodging in her chest when she hit upon the only other possibility. Her eyes filled with tears as she considered that Sara must be the one lying to her. Jamie's arm came to circle her waist, providing much-needed support, and Ryan leaned against her heavily.

"I don't know," the older woman said, her own eyes now filled with tears. "I know I didn't, and I know Sara didn't. Please, please believe me, Ryan."

"How can I?" Ryan said in a loud voice as she jumped to her feet, causing Duffy to scramble behind the loveseat in alarm. "*I* certainly didn't tell anyone! It wasn't written on my forehead. Either I told, you told, or Sara told."

Mrs. Andrews closed her eyes tightly, her lips pressed together as she tried to come up with a possible explanation for the rumor. "I've been thinking about this constantly since Sara told me, and I think that it might have been written on your forehead." At Ryan's stunned look, she hastened to explain. "I don't mean that literally, of course, but when I think back to that time, I'm amazed that I didn't put a label on the way you behaved around Sara."

Ryan flopped down onto the loveseat, her legs feeling too weak to hold her any longer. She dropped her head into her hands and rubbed her face briskly, an unconscious habit indicating complete frustration that Jamie had seen far too often lately. "What do you mean, Mrs. Andrews?" Jamie asked.

The woman looked a little uncomfortable to be discussing this in front of a near stranger, but Ryan obviously wanted Jamie by her side, so she gathered her thoughts and said, "When I think about it now, Ryan had begun to act more like a...a boyfriend toward Sara than a girlfriend. She hung on her every word, laughed uproariously at the slightest joke..." She looked at the embarrassed blush that was on Ryan's face and assured her, "I don't mean to embarrass you, Ryan, and I swear it didn't register at the time, but looking back, it was fairly obvious. You treated Sara like you treat Jamie now."

The younger women were holding hands, and Jamie unconsciously tightened her grip around Ryan's waist.

"I wish to God that I'd spoken to you about it then, to save you both so much pain," Mrs. Andrews added. "Maybe you wouldn't have..." she left the statement unfinished, seeming at a loss for how to characterize Ryan's physical overtures toward her daughter.

Ryan wasn't sure how to respond to the comment. Since she was sure that Sara hadn't come out to her mother, she obviously couldn't state her wish that the woman had brought it up—so that she and Sara could have admitted their love and worked through the problems associated with it. Instead, she just nodded briefly, deciding that saying nothing was the best option at this point.

"So," Jamie led, "you think what—that other people just guessed?" The skepticism in her voice was blatant, and Mrs. Andrews wished she'd been able to speak to Ryan alone.

She nodded quickly, saying, "Something like that. Sara and Ryan were much more than friends, Jamie, you have to remember that. They were absolutely inseparable. They never had the usual fights that most girls do. I can only imagine that when they stopped seeing each other so abruptly, some of the other girls might have guessed what tore them apart." She looked at Jamie rather helplessly and said, "It's the only thing that I can think of."

Ryan let out a massive sigh, causing both women to turn their attention to her. Jamie was just on the verge of telling Mrs. Andrews that her idea was ridiculous, when her partner surprised her by saying, "It's a long shot, but I guess it's within the realm of possibility." She looked at Mrs. Andrews intensely; the older woman's gaze never wavered. "I wish I could let this rest, but I can't. I'm going to find out what happened—if I have to track down every girl in that school."

A small smile formed at the corners of Mrs. Andrews's mouth, and she nodded her head slightly. "I've never seen you back down from a challenge. I'll help you in any way that I can. I let you down once. I promise I won't do it again."

Jamie couldn't help but ask the obvious question. "If you didn't spread the rumors about Ryan, what *do* you feel so guilty about?"

Her brown eyes fluttered closed, and a look of genuine pain crossed her face. "I can still see the look on Ryan's face when I sent her away." She stared at her folded hands, tears rolling down her cheeks. "I regret that more than anything I've ever done. Ryan needed somebody to help her get through that troubling time, and I abandoned her." She lifted her head, stared directly into Ryan's red-rimmed eyes and whispered, "I'm so very sorry, Ryan. Just because Sara didn't feel that way toward you was no reason to turn my back on you. I just didn't know what to do, and I let my fear take over. Can you ever forgive me?"

Ryan got to her feet and closed the short distance, squatting down in front of the sobbing woman who threw her arms around Ryan's neck. "I forgive you," she whispered, just loud enough for Jamie to hear.

Jamie was moved by Ryan's enormous capacity to forgive, but she was still not convinced of their visitor's honesty. She held her tongue while the two women embraced and cried a bit, finally going into the house to get a box of tissues. When she returned, Ryan was standing, wiping at her eyes with the back of her hand. She gratefully accepted the box, and she and her guest spent a few minutes composing themselves. When it seemed appropriate, Jamie asked the question that had been lingering in the back of her mind. "Why have you avoided Martin, Brendan and even Maeve all of these years?"

Ryan rolled her eyes, wishing her little district attorney would give this one a rest, but the older woman didn't seem offended in the least. "At first, I didn't know if Ryan had told her family about what had happened," she said. "I certainly wasn't going to say anything if she hadn't. I guess I just started going out of my way to avoid them, and after a while, they started avoiding me. I felt guilty enough to know that I deserved their anger, and I suppose I took the coward's way out. I just hate to cause a scene," she murmured self-consciously, and Ryan had to acknowledge that, while Mrs. Andrews had many good qualities, she was never one to stand up for herself. Ryan also knew that incurring the O'Flaherty wrath wasn't something that most people would seek out and that her father had been very, very angry about what had transpired.

"That makes sense," Ryan said, sparing a small smile for the obviously relieved woman. "What's done is done," she said. "Let's try to start over. Jamie and I are going to start attending Mass regularly, and I'd really like to feel like we can all be friends once again."

A warm smile lit up Mrs. Andrews's face, and she said, "I can't tell you how much I'd like that. As a matter of fact, I think I'll stroll down the street and try to make amends with your aunt right now."

"She's the easy one," Ryan laughed gently, not bothering to add that her father would be a tougher sell.

"Practice makes perfect," Mrs. Andrews said, smiling. "By the time I work up to your father, I should be pretty good at this."

"Don't worry," Ryan assured her. "I'll put Jamie on the job. She has him wrapped around her little finger."

The woman smiled at Jamie. "You're going to run out of little fingers, with Martin around one and Ryan around the other."

"Is it that obvious?" Ryan asked, dropping her face into her hands. "I'm older, I'm taller, I'm bigger. It just doesn't make any sense."

Mrs. Andrews rose and placed her hand on Ryan's shoulder. "Love doesn't make sense," she said softly. "I'm just very glad that you've found it."

Chapter Three

A half hour later, they were curled up around each other in bed, Ryan's ardor completely forgotten. She was lying on her back, and Jamie rested against her chest, listening to the strong, slow heartbeat.

"Whatcha thinkin' 'bout?"

"I'm thinking about what in the hell I'm gonna tell Da," Ryan grumped.

Jamie struggled to sit up, facing her partner. "Are you worried about that?"

Ryan shook her head. "No, not worried. But it's gonna be tough to get him over his anger. I don't want to tell him that Sara's a lesbian, and I certainly don't have any intention of telling him what happened when she came to the house." Here she shivered involuntarily, reminding Jamie of her repentance. "I just hate to hide things from him. He can always tell when I'm holding something back."

"Let me do it," Jamie offered unexpectedly.

"Huh?" Ryan sat up and faced her with a puzzled look. "You'd tell him?"

"Sure. I don't mean to brag, but he is very compliant around me."

Ryan laughed heartily at that understatement. "He's worse than I am, if that's possible."

"I wouldn't go that far," Jamie teased, earning a pinch. "No, really, let's take a nap, and when he comes home from work, I'll go have a talk with him."

Ryan pursed her lips for a moment before gratefully accepting the offer. "I should do it myself, but if you're willing, have at it." With that she dropped onto the bed and placed her pillow over her face, muttering through the fabric, "Lock the door when you leave. I'm hiding until it's all over."

When Jamie came downstairs a little after 6:00, Ryan was sitting in front of her computer, typing furiously. She was obviously very intent since she didn't hear her partner approach. A sharp gasp flew from her lips when Jamie lightly touched her shoulder, and she complained, "Jeez! Don't sneak up on me like that." There was a touch of irritation in her voice, but Jamie didn't mention it.

"Sorry, love," she whispered, bending to place a gentle kiss on the top of her head.

To Jamie's pleasure, Ryan turned her chair around and gazed at her with contrite blue eyes. "I'm sorry I'm being so bitchy today. Forgive me?"

"You've done nothing that requires forgiveness." She climbed onto her lap, draping an arm around her shoulders so that she could hold on tight. "You're just an itsy, bitsy, teeny, tiny bit grouchy today." She held her index finger about a millimeter from her thumb. "It's barely noticeable."

Ryan laughed a little at her partner's description, knowing it was deliberately inaccurate. "I think I'm extra grouchy because of all of the stuff going on in my head," she said. "I was just trying to remember everything that happened when I went back to school for my senior year." She twitched her head toward her desk, indicating the yearbook lying open. "I'm making a list of all of the girls who could possibly have any info."

"Well, I can take one worry off your mind," Jamie said. "I spoke with your father, and after a bit I called Maeve, and she came over, too. We all talked it out, and I think he's willing to play nice."

"Really?" Ryan's face lit up, and Jamie was once again struck by how easy it was to bring a smile to her lovely face. "Do you think he understood?"

"It took a little while," Jamie admitted. "You must have gotten your capacity to forgive from your mother." She rolled her eyes a little, and Ryan nodded emphatically.

"Da's natural impulse is to tell people off in no uncertain terms and never speak to them again. He has a really tough time letting things go."

"I think, in this case, he can see how Mrs. Andrews was caught up in trying to protect Sara. Once I convinced him that neither of them had spread the rumors, he seemed much more willing to forgive them both."

"Aunt Maeve believes her story, doesn't she?" A shadow of doubt passed over Ryan's eyes, but Jamie was able to reassure her completely.

"Maeve says that she's certain of it. She says that Mary Elizabeth has her share of faults, but lying isn't one of them."

Ryan nodded, then rested her head against Jamie's chest. "Thank you for talking to him. I just didn't relish the thought of a whole emotional scene today. I feel too unstable."

"Feel better now?" Jamie asked, running her hand lightly across the soft cotton of Ryan's T-shirt.

"Yeah. I feel good. Is Aunt Maeve still here?"

"Yes. She's staying for dinner. She brought a little visitor, too."

Ryan patted her partner's butt, shooing her off her lap. "My favorite girl! Why didn't you say so?" she demanded, heading for the stairs. When she reached them, she turned and smiled at her partner, amending her statement. "You'll always be my favorite girl; she's just easier to carry." And with that she crossed the distance between them in two large strides and tossed Jamie over her shoulder like a sack of spuds.

"Ryan! Put me down!"

"You have to say the magic words," Ryan teased, climbing the stairs quickly despite Jamie's weight.

"I will not."

Ryan's right arm was locked around Jamie's thighs, holding her securely, but her left was free to wander, and it trailed over the taut cotton covering Jamie's ass. "Caitlin might be easier to carry, but the view is a lot better with you."

Deciding to give up the struggle, Jamie relaxed and enjoyed the short trip. Seeing her partner act playful was always one of her favorite things, and when she was honest with herself, she had to admit that she loved to feel the powerful body moving under her. *We've got to get to bed early tonight*, she thought, watching the muscles in Ryan's back flex. *I'm still simmering from our session on the deck.*

Jamie emerged from the kitchen an hour later to check out the shrieks coming from the living room. "What in the heck are you two doing?"

Ryan was on her hands and knees, one end of a heavy rope toy clutched in her teeth. The other end of the toy was firmly held in Duffy's. Caitlin was sitting on the floor, shrieking with laughter as she excitedly slapped at Ryan, spurring her on. Ryan was growling audibly, Duffy slightly less so, but they were clearly enjoying the game. They were both tugging on the toy with as much power as they could generate, and Ryan was giving him a run for his money, even though his body was built for the contest. It was clear that

Duffy was trying to be gentle with his owner, and just as clear that Ryan wasn't cutting him a bit of slack.

Jamie stood with her hands on her hips, surveying the scene for a moment, before turning to ask Martin, "Has Ryan had all of her shots?"

"Pardon, dear?" he asked, stepping out of the kitchen to join her. His amused expression mirrored that of his daughter-in-law, and he shook his head. "Don't worry, Duffy's up-to-date on all of his vaccinations."

"I wasn't worried about Ryan," she said, casting another fond glance at her partner. "I was worried about Duffy."

"I'll go get the baby for you, Maeve," Jamie offered at a little past 9:00. Caitlin's mood had turned sour, and Ryan had decided to take her downstairs to feed and change her. That had been nearly a half hour ago, and Maeve was now ready to leave.

When she reached the bottom of the stairs, Jamie saw that the diaper change had led to a nap—for both of the cousins. *Such a sweet pair*, she thought, gazing at them cuddled together on the bed. She hated to wake her partner, but Ryan's long arm was wrapped firmly around Caitlin's body, and she knew that Ryan would awaken the instant she moved the little one.

Much to her surprise, however, Ryan barely budged as she extricated the baby. Caitlin was limp in her arms as she carried her up the stairs, handing her over to Maeve with a kiss on the baby's blonde head. "My baby's as sound asleep as this one is. I think I'll just let her sleep in her clothes tonight."

"That's what I always did," Martin said. "She'd get so grumpy when I woke her to put on her pajamas that I gave up the fight after a while."

"You're a wise man," Jamie said, kissing both Martin and Maeve good night.

"Not so much wise as practical," he said. "Once she was prone and quiet, I didn't want to risk riling her up again."

As Jamie descended the stairs again, she grumbled to herself, *I was looking forward to riling her up tonight. Oh, well, we'll have other nights.*

After brushing her teeth, she quickly stripped and climbed into bed. *This is going to be tough. She's on top of the covers, but it's way too cold for me to be outside of them, too.* The fog had rolled in, giving a definite chill to the air, and she knew she wouldn't have the benefit of Ryan's bare skin to help keep her warm. *If I've got to get her under the covers, I might as well undress her*, she thought logically. *I'll just start taking her clothes off, and she'll wake up enough to help me.*

She started at the bottom, figuring that was the easy part. The shoes and socks came off without complaint, Ryan never stirring. *God, she's out like a light.* Jamie had never seen her partner so totally zonked, and she considered that this might be a part of her premenstrual symptoms. *Of course, keeping up with Caitlin for hours at a time might have done it, also.* It took a little more wrangling, but she managed to remove her T-shirt quite efficiently. As she pulled it from her body, Ryan rolled onto her side with a weak groan, then flopped onto her belly, once again sound asleep. *Thank you very much.* Jamie smiled, now able to unhook her bra. Seeing all that smooth skin stretched out before her made Jamie's pulse beat a little more strongly, but she tried to quiet her insistent libido. *Even though she's told me she'd like to be awakened that way, it feels kinda funny. I mean, I know she wouldn't mind, but I don't think I have the nerve.*

Looking down at the firm muscles hidden under all that tempting skin caused Jamie to waver in her determination to keep her hands to herself. *I could kiss her just a little bit. Kissing her in her sleep isn't any big deal.* Her fingers itched to touch the lovely woman lying before her so exposed and enticing. Almost of its own accord, her left hand traveled to her partner's back and delicately passed over the muscles in her shoulders. Her fingers glided over the subtle dips and curves, touching the skin as lightly and as softly as a whisper. *Oh, this is not a good idea*, she groaned, already feeling a heaviness low in her belly.

Ryan moaned in her sleep, sounding almost as if she was trying to speak. Abruptly, she rolled over onto her back once again, nearly trapping Jamie with her weight. *Oh, that helps*, the smaller woman grumbled. *It's bad enough I want to take you in your sleep. Now I have to look at those perfect breasts with that lacy white bra half-covering them.*

Since her original idea had been to undress her partner, Jamie slowly slipped the bra off, resisting the insistent urge to touch the pale skin. The lamplight cast a warm glow upon Ryan's bare chest, and Jamie spent a few long minutes watching the steady rise and fall of her breathing. Unconsciously, she found her head drawing closer and closer to her favorite body part, and before she knew it, she was hovering over one soft pink nipple, her mouth watering at the mere prospect of drawing the nub inside.

A deep sigh escaped from Ryan's slightly open mouth, the intake of breath causing her nipple to rise a little higher than normal, and suddenly, the object of Jamie's desire was enveloped by her warm, wet lips. *Oh, yes. It's mine now.*

Her tongue gently swirled around the firming nipple, feeling its shape and contour magically transform under her touch. With a soft, wet kiss she relinquished her prize, lifting her head to gaze at her partner.

Ryan was obviously still asleep, her body's response to Jamie autonomic rather than volitional. Her left breast was firm, riding high on her chest, the nipple stiff and deep pink, while the right remained somnolent, the flesh soft and pliant, the nipple relaxed.

Oh, I want that one, too, she thought, staring at the oblivious breast. But she didn't know how to get at it without waking Ryan. With a start, she realized just how much fun it was to play with her partner while she slept, and she immediately felt a little guilty. She reminded herself, *She's asked you to do this. She was as horny as a mink this afternoon, and she was completely frustrated. Don't be such a prude. It's not like she'll sleep through it, for goodness sake! As soon as you really start to touch her, she'll wake up and you'll both be happy.*

Unable to resist a challenge, even when it was self-imposed, she pondered the situation for a moment. Hitting upon an idea, she reached down and lightly tickled Ryan's exposed left side. She uttered a sound that was close to, but not quite, a word, and swatted weakly at the hand. Another tickle—another ineffectual swat. Finally, on the third try, Ryan turned onto her left side, presenting her right breast to her partner. *Come to mama!* Jamie crowed, dipping her head to lave the lazy nipple into action. It didn't take long before the right vied with the left for rigidity, but before she was finished, Ryan flopped onto her back once again. Surprisingly, her arms lifted over her head, hands lightly touching near the headboard, presenting her breasts to Jamie's gaze in a most attractive fashion. *That's odd*, Jamie mused, *I've never seen her sleep that way before.*

She didn't spend too much time on her musings, since Ryan's grandeur was so beautifully displayed. Jamie bent her head once again, helping the left nipple to regain supremacy over the right, when she noticed the slightest of hip movements from her sleeping partner. *Hip thrusts? In her sleep? Hmm, I don't think so.* Pulling away just a few inches, Jamie detected clear signs of Ryan's wakefulness. Her chest wasn't rising and falling with the same slow cadence as before. Now it was moving quickly, although it looked as though

Ryan was consciously trying to smooth out her breathing to resemble the previous pattern. Both breasts were firm, both nipples equally taut. *I think someone's playing 'possum, and I think I like it. I knew she'd like this, I guess I just didn't know she'd like it enough to continue with it when she was actually awake. Ah, well, I like to please my baby, so I'll play as long as she wants to.*

Running her hand down the center of Ryan's body, she smiled to herself as she detected the beginnings of goose bumps chasing down Ryan's torso. *Umm-hmm.* She stifled a giggle. *Somebody's wide awake but doesn't want me to know it. Your wish is my command.*

Slowly, steadily, she unbuttoned the fly on Ryan's khakis, sneaking her hand inside when she had them fully open. *Where are your boxers, Buffy?* A thorough inspection revealed nothing but smooth, warm flesh as her hand dipped lower and lower. *Going commando, sweetie?* But just as she became certain Ryan had omitted underwear, her hand touched a bit of lace. Her very interested fingertips traced the outline, determining that Ryan wore some very, very low-cut lace panties. *Oh, this is better than I'd hoped for.* She moaned, unable to stop the sound from springing from her lips. Her happy fingers found that the panties rode very low over Ryan's mound, but came up a bit on the sides to reach the tops of her hipbones. *Very, very nice. Why haven't I seen these before? You know I'm a sucker for sexy undies.* With a shake of her head, Jamie reminded herself that Ryan couldn't hear her thoughts. *This is so weird. I know she's awake, and she probably knows that I know, but it still feels kinda kinky to do this.* Another smile settled on her face as she acknowledged, *That's definitely why Ryan wants to do it, and if I'm honest, I have to admit that it feels hot because it's just a tiny bit taboo.*

Her hand slipped completely into Ryan's pants, fingers inching along the length of her partner's belly, settling on her warm mound. As her hand slid down another inch or two, she snuck a quick glance up at Ryan's face and nearly barked out a laugh when she saw her partner pull her lower lip in and bite down firmly. *Oh, I'm torturing the poor thing.* A mental chuckle accompanied her thought, and she harkened back to Mia's observation that she was a dom in disguise. *God, I do really enjoy this. I'd never want to cause her pain, well, maybe a good kinda pain*, she amended with a sly smile, catching another glimpse of her partner's tension-filled face, *but teasing her like this is absolutely delicious.*

Focusing on the warmth that enveloped her hand, Jamie snuggled it deeper inside the loose-fitting slacks. *Thank you for not wearing your jeans today, or this would be mission impossible.* Adding an extra bit of pressure with her middle finger, she trailed her hand slowly up and down the center of Ryan's warmth, a shiver chasing down her spine when her hand touched the moist lace fabric between the spread legs. *Those legs weren't spread that far apart a minute ago.* Focusing on Ryan's feet, she saw one heel inching across the mattress, trying to provide a wider target for questing fingers.

The khakis Ryan had on were very well-worn, and the fabric had grown thin through repeated washings. Since Jamie had conquered as much territory as possible within the confines of the slacks, she withdrew her hand, smiling as Ryan gave a tiny hip thrust as she pulled out. Placing her hand between the spread legs, she focused on Ryan's placid face while raking her fingernails up the center seam of the slacks. As expected, the prone woman had a terribly difficult time keeping her composure, but Jamie had to acknowledge that Ryan did a much better job of it than she would have in her position.

Trying a slightly different tactic, she moved the seam aside a few inches, and lightly scratched up and down the soft, thin fabric with her short nails, ignoring the strangled gasp that sprang from her lover. She could easily feel the slight protuberance of Ryan's sex under her fingers, her mouth going dry as she flicked her fingers lightly against the cloth-covered flesh.

Ryan was unable to stop the shiver that started at the top of her head and raced down her body. Jamie watched her flesh twitch, mesmerized by the bare flesh and the rock-hard nipples that were reaching for the sky.

Jamie's fingers played and teased the aching flesh, using a bit more pressure than normal because of the fabric barriers. She could see the pulse throbbing in Ryan's neck, could hear her respiration speed up and grow shallow, could discern a fine sheen of perspiration across her full breasts. It was clear that her partner was nearly ready to climax, but Jamie didn't want to bring her off while she was still clothed. She thought that Ryan would have a better orgasm with direct stimulation, but she wasn't certain that she could get her pants off while keeping up the game. Deciding to give it a try, she grasped the material near Ryan's ass and gave it a good tug, nearly laughing when the hips rose a couple of inches to allow the slacks to slide down easily. Jamie pulled on the hems and tossed them aside, already focused on the next barrier.

The deliciously sexy white lace panties had become nearly transparent where they rested against Ryan's pulsing need. They were obviously soaked with the evidence of her arousal, and Jamie's heart raced when she detected the heady, humid scent of desire. Her mouth watered, and the throbbing between her own legs became so intense that she had to slip her hand between her thighs and stroke herself for a few moments to take the edge off. Her sadistic streak returned when she pulled her hand away and slowly waved her wet fingers over Ryan's twitching nose—only to gasp aloud as a dark head shot forward and sucked two fingers deeply into a warm mouth.

"Ryan!" she cried, unable to hold in her laugh. "Have you been awake the whole time?"

The bright blue eyes were still closed, but a smile played at the corners of her mouth as she slowly shook her head, continuing to suck on Jamie's fingers.

"Give me back my hand, Buffy," Jamie demanded, as she tried to break the suction. "I'm not done playing with you."

Ryan's lids popped open, and she released Jamie's fingers, simultaneously tossing the smaller woman onto her back. "That's what you think, hot stuff," she growled. "Playtime's over. It's time to get down to business." She climbed onto her partner's body, intent on claiming what she needed.

To Ryan's utter surprise, Jamie entwined her legs with those of her taller and stronger partner, shifted her hips abruptly, and tossed the astonished woman onto her back once more. She climbed aboard Ryan's body, moving up until they were nose to nose. Adopting a fiercely determined look, she growled, "My game. My rules."

Ryan blinked slowly, almost unable to comprehend exactly what her partner meant. She was so slow on the uptake that Jamie finally asked softly, "Has no one ever taught you patience?"

Ryan shook her head slowly, unsure of what she was even responding to, but sensing that she was supposed to answer.

"Then now's as good a time as any for your first lesson." With that Jamie grasped Ryan's hands and placed them level with her head, making her look as if she were being robbed. "Lie still and nobody gets hurt," she commanded, smiling down at her partner.

It took just a few moments for Ryan's arousal to be ratcheted back to its previous level, and a few moments longer for it to be cranked higher still. Jamie started at her breasts, her enjoyment of the firm, supple flesh so contagious that Ryan's arousal came as much from watching the pleasure on her partner's face as it did from the sensation itself. Jamie attacked the mounds with gusto, leaving Ryan breathless after just a few minutes of her ravenous feeding.

Ryan had been compliant, but there was a tension to her body that reminded Jamie of a large animal that was humoring its trainer. Both the animal and the trainer knew the animal could do as it liked, but the trainer hoped the treats and praise she doled out would allow the game to continue. But after a few minutes the tension faded. Jamie sensed the shift in Ryan's attitude, and she slowed down a bit, now not as worried that Ryan would take charge. She was hovering over the white panties, trying to decide her next move, when Ryan's hands slid down and started to remove them.

"Did I ask for your help? I distinctly remember instructing you to keep your hands flat on the bed."

Ryan gave her an amused look and relaxed again, docilely placing her hands back where Jamie had originally indicated. "A thousand pardons, mistress," she murmured, averting her eyes acquiescently.

Jamie couldn't resist a playful pinch to her exposed ribs. "I'll mistress you," she growled. "Now behave, or you're going solo."

Ryan's mouth closed immediately, but she had to get in a playful dig by dramatically zipping her lips closed.

Jamie crawled up to Ryan's level and lay down so they were face to face. "Is this really okay with you?"

Ryan smiled and teasingly asked for clarification. "Can I move my hands for a minute?"

"Yes, Ryan, you may move your hands." A smirk involuntarily appeared on Jamie's face while she waited for her partner to answer her question.

"C'mere," Ryan instructed, holding her arm out in invitation. Jamie cuddled up to her warm body, instantly reassured by the safety of her partner's embrace. "I've been with lots of women," she said softly, "but I've only allowed one or two others to run the show."

"I don't have to—" Jamie began, but Ryan silenced her with a gentle kiss.

"I didn't allow other women to top me because I didn't trust them. I didn't like to let other women make me feel vulnerable or needy. But it's not like that with you. You know how much I need you, and you know how much I trust you. I'm really, really happy that you feel confident enough to play like this."

"So it's really okay?" Jamie asked, her voice betraying her lingering concern. "I mean, just because I like something doesn't mean that…"

Ryan faced her fully, a devastatingly sexy smile affixed to her handsome face. "I'm throbbing so much, I'm starting to cramp," she said. "My body likes this very, very much. And my mind has generously agreed to stay on the sidelines and let my body have her way." She stretched out fully on the bed, her arms flat in the manner Jamie had requested, her legs slightly spread. "Little Ryan thinks this is one of the best ideas you've ever had." Her hips thrust in Jamie's direction a few times, making Little Ryan's presence known.

The luminescent smile that lit Jamie's entire face made Ryan's heart swell with pleasure. "Have I told you how much I love you?" Jamie asked, leaning down to plant soft, sweet kisses all over Ryan's face. "Have I told you how much I love making love with you?"

Her questions received a softly murmured, "Yes," uttered in a languidly sexy voice that sent chills down Jamie's spine. "You tell me, you show me, every single day." Ryan had not moved a muscle, and her body was beautifully displayed by her submissive pose. "My body is yours. Touch me, love me, in any way that pleases you. I'm yours completely." Her eyes fluttered closed, and Jamie felt her breath catch as she marveled at the heartfelt offer her lover had made.

"Thank you," she whispered, bending to kiss Ryan's warm, moist lips. One kiss became many, and moments later, she was lying fully atop the long body, grasping Ryan's head with both hands, holding her steady as the kisses rained down. True to her word, the taller woman did not move an inch, and Jamie thrilled to the sensation of being totally in control. Her arousal reached another peak when she heard a soft, sexy groan rumble through Ryan's chest and felt her muscles twitch and throb as she tried to control her response. "Easy, Tiger," she soothed, running her hands lightly over Ryan's flushed face. "I'll take care of you."

Ryan nodded briefly, and her desire-darkened eyes fixed Jamie with a pleading look. She spoke not a word, but her body revealed every wish, and Jamie decided that her patience and acceptance had to be rewarded. Sliding down her slick body, Jamie maneuvered Ryan's legs over her shoulders and settled down comfortably between her thighs.

The thoroughly soaked panties remained in place, providing a very pleasing visual for Jamie's appreciative eyes. She leaned in and rubbed her pursed lips up and down the center of Ryan's sex, smiling gently as she felt the coiled body twitch roughly, but remain remarkably passive. Ryan nearly always tangled her fingers in Jamie's hair or guided her head as she loved her, and the smaller woman briefly hoped that the enforced passivity wouldn't hamper her partner's pleasure. But as that thought was running through her head, a low, throaty growl rumbled up from Ryan's chest, assuring her that she was thoroughly enjoying the experience.

The stretchy lace tickled Jamie's soft lips, and she wondered how Ryan experienced the sensation on her even more sensitive lips. She let her teeth rake gently along the swollen flesh visible beneath the skintight panties, her own growl surprising her as it escaped her lips. Her hands rested on Ryan's belly, feeling the muscles twitch and contract as she struggled valiantly to remain still. Jamie's soft nuzzling grew a little firmer, a little faster, as she felt her own desire begin to spiral out of control. Her fingers dug into the hard muscle lurking just under the soft layer of flesh, reveling in the feel of the rock-hard bands of sinew.

Their voices joined together, groaning, whimpering, and gasping with pleasure as Jamie's head began to move more quickly against the lace-covered warmth. She couldn't stand the torture another moment, and her hand dropped and roughly pushed the fabric aside as she dove in, finally touching the burning flesh with her wet, hot tongue.

"Ah!" Ryan cried, her entire body twitching and spasming wildly. "Please, Jamie. Please."

One small hand shot up and rested upon Ryan's belly, silently assuring her that she would soon be satisfied. When the tightly coiled body relaxed just a bit, Jamie brought her hand down and smoothly slid her index finger into Ryan's wetness.

"Oh, yeah!" she groaned. "That's it. Come on, let me feel you!"

As she continued to lave the tender, smooth skin, Jamie satisfied her partner's request and slipped another digit inside, causing Ryan's hips to thrust up to meet her. She'd never felt her partner so receptive to penetration, and after a moment, she added a third finger, knowing her choice was right when a satisfied hiss whistled through Ryan's teeth as her ass hit the bed.

As Jamie's fingers pumped firmly, she slowly became aware of an insistent thumping that matched her rhythm. Prying her eyes open, she glanced up and saw that Ryan's hands had slipped under the headboard, and that she was banging it against the wall with each thrust. *Oh, Lord. If Conor hears that, we'll be teased to death.*

Ignoring her worry to focus again on her prize, Jamie used her fingers to seek out every surface of the slick channel they rested in, wresting different sounds from Ryan as she moved about. When she focused on a spot that always drove her partner wild, Ryan's body abruptly stilled, even her raspy breathing came to a halt. Even though her movement stopped, Jamie could feel the energy coiling in her, like the deathly silence right before a tornado. She sucked Ryan's entire clit into her mouth at that moment, pulling gently on the bundle of pulsing nerves.

"Oh, God!" Ryan's hands flew from the headboard and latched onto Jamie's head, grinding it into herself, legs locking behind her neck. As her climax slammed through her body, she writhed upon the bed, taking her partner with her as she panted and gasped for air. Jamie held on tightly, every sense on overload as she tried to avoid hurting Ryan or herself. They rolled around on the bed, thrashing about wildly as the spasms seemed to flow from Ryan's body right through Jamie's.

The storm finally passed, and after a few more strangled cries, Ryan collapsed, her body completely spent. Jamie started to withdraw her fingers, but Ryan's weak moan stopped her immediately. So Jamie eased her cramping muscles by stretching her body out while resting her head on Ryan's thigh, content to feel the wild pulse still beating against her cheek.

It took quite a while, but eventually Ryan's fingers tangled in her lover's hair, and she spoke in a rough, low voice. "I think I might just have to keep those fingers, babe. You don't mind, do you?"

"Not a bit," she said. "You'll have to start wearing skirts though."

"Hmm, unacceptable. I guess you can try to reclaim them." She brought her legs up so that her feet were resting on the mattress, and Jamie slipped out easily, despite Ryan's prediction.

"All clear," she grinned, climbing up to rest in Ryan's arms.

"I feel like I've run the marathon, chopped a cord of wood, and spent a night in a Turkish prison."

Jamie sat up to gaze into her eyes, seeing the teasing twinkle. "You complaining?"

"Nope. I was just wondering why I wanted to do it all over again." She laughed, gathering her partner into her arms to roll around the bed. She wound up on her back, with Jamie fully on top of her. "Now I have to decide how to repay you for the experience." She had a very thoughtful look on her face, but Jamie settled the matter immediately.

"Just kiss me," she demanded, her voice rough with need. "I want to feel your body under mine and taste your sweet mouth."

Ryan met her partner's needs, managing to satisfy each of her desires as their lovemaking continued deep into the night.

A pair of panting, sweating, sticky, entwined bodies slowly tried to disentangle themselves from each other several hours later. "This is not good," Ryan muttered as she tossed her feet off the bed and sat up.

Jamie stuck a hand out and placed it on her slick back, giving it a small pat. "Dizzy?" she asked solicitously, considering how much fluid her partner lost during their extended bout of lovemaking. "It's no wonder."

A very small chuckle accompanied Ryan's reply. "Yeah, I am a little dizzy, now that you mention it, but I was referring to the fact that my last orgasm didn't ease my cramping any. I guess it wasn't just unquenched desire I was feeling."

"Oh, you think you got your period?"

"Yeah. Feels like it." Ryan got up and stretched, popping her shoulders as she grasped her hands and stuck them straight up over her head.

Jamie spent a moment watching her, reminding her overstimulated libido that they'd had enough for one evening. "Gonna take some Motrin?"

"Yeah. I'll get 'em when I rinse off in the shower."

Ryan emerged a few minutes later, pleased to find Jamie changing the sheets.

"One more good thing about never bringing women home before I met you. I saved a lot of mileage on the mattress and the linens."

Jamie tucked in the thin top sheet and wondered how much worse the lumpy mattress and well-worn sheets could get, but she made no comment, realizing that Ryan was not the type to waste money on something as frivolous as expensive sheets. "Come lie down and let me rub your tummy," Jamie offered.

"Mmm, it's my back today," Ryan said, lying facedown on the clean sheets. "Lower back, right side." Looking idly at the clock as Jamie sat astride her thighs, Ryan commented, "Do you know it's three in the morning?"

"Time flies when you're having fun," Jamie said, trying to hide the yawn that struggled to reveal itself.

"Oh, that's the spot," Ryan murmured, her chin resting on her crossed arms. "That feels fabulous."

"You've been saying that for hours," Jamie said, laughing.

"It was true then, and it's true now." Ryan let out a heavy sigh, and Jamie could feel some of the tension leave her back. Her breathing started to even out, and after a few more minutes of the gentle massage, Ryan was sound asleep.

"Pleasant dreams." Placing a very soft kiss on Ryan's back, Jamie climbed off her body and drew the sheet over both of them. A moment later, lulled by the soft pattern of her lover's breathing, Jamie joined her in sleep.

Chapter Four

"**M**rmmff."

"Oh, you're up," Jamie said quietly as she walked over to the bed and sat on the edge. "How do you feel? Is your back any better?"

"Mrmmff," Ryan grunted again as the pillow went back over her head.

"Are you a grouchy little bear today?" Jamie ran her hand over Ryan's stomach, tickling the soft, smooth skin.

"Don't want to get up," she growled, turning onto her side to halt the rubbing.

"Okay. You obviously don't feel well, so you can go back to sleep. I'm going upstairs to have a little breakfast. You come up later." Jamie bent and placed a kiss on her tummy.

"Don't leave me," Ryan whined, in full pout.

"Oh, you are grouchy, aren't you?" Jamie climbed back into bed and wrapped her lover in her arms. "Do you want to be cuddled?"

"Mmm-hmm," came the mumbled reply as Ryan contentedly nestled back against her body.

"Okay, we'll cuddle until you want to get up." Jamie felt her grouchy bear relax and drift off to sleep again.

It was nearly 9:00 when Ryan's eyes opened again. She sat up with a start and looked around wildly to find the clock. "My God! Do you know what time it is?"

Jamie got up from the loveseat and came to sit by the bed. "I tried to wake you up, but you were very determined to stay in bed. I figured you wouldn't be that way if you really didn't need your rest. It's okay; we haven't missed anything."

"But I never sleep this late."

"Well, you did today. It's no big deal. Really."

"The boys will make fun of me," she said, pouting.

"I bet they don't. I bet they're concerned about you."

"No, they'll make fun of me," she said as she stuck her lower lip out.

"Let's go upstairs and see, okay?"

"Okay," Ryan glumly agreed as she got up and looked through her drawers to find some pajamas, mumbling under her breath, "They're gonna make fun of me."

Jamie had taken her shower hours earlier and was fully dressed in khaki shorts and a yellow polo shirt, her preppy look further enhanced by well-worn Topsiders without socks. As they reached the living room, she took her partner's hand and guided her into the dining room. Conor was still at the table, and he looked up quickly when he saw them.

"We've been worried about you guys. Are you okay?"

"Fine," Ryan murmured, sitting down heavily in a chair.

Conor looked at Jamie, but she didn't want to make a big deal out of Ryan's mood, so she just went into the kitchen to give Martin a kiss. As she greeted him, she picked up the bottle of Motrin and shook a couple of tablets into her hand. "Very, very bad mood," she whispered.

He handed her a glass and whispered back, "Did she get her period?"

Jamie found the question surprising. She was certain that her father had no idea that she even had a cycle, much less when it fell. But when she gave it a moment's thought, she realized that Martin was probably the one who explained the whole thing to his young daughter, so he would logically be more aware of her physical issues.

Jamie nodded while she filled the glass with water. "She didn't get much sleep, either. That makes her grouchy anyway."

"I should warn you that this happens nearly every month. Her mother was the same." He smiled at Jamie with a little twinkle in his eyes. "I suppose that's another reason for me to be thankful that Siobhán has you. Now *you* have to deal with her."

Jamie beamed up at him. "It's my pleasure to deal with her. I'm just glad no one teased her about getting up late. She actually might bite today."

He gave her a big wink. "I know how to cheer her up."

Jamie went back into the dining room and sat next to her grumpy lover. "What were you talking about in the kitchen?" Ryan asked suspiciously.

"Nothing. Martin just wondered how you were feeling."

"He should ask me. I can speak for myself." She rested her head on the table.

Conor gave Jamie a puzzled look, and she rolled her eyes and mouthed, "Be nice."

Martin came in moments later and gave Ryan a rather gross-looking dish of thickly sliced bread covered in warm milk. She glanced up at him with a childlike smile and eagerly proceeded to add at least two tablespoons of sugar onto the bread. "You eat your goody while I get you something more substantial," he said, giving her a little head rub.

"Goody?" Jamie asked, privately thinking that the dish didn't look very good at all.

"It's the breakfast of Irish children, or at least it was in the bad old days," Martin said. "When you couldn't afford a rasher of bacon or a dozen eggs, this was a handy substitute."

"Mama made this for me when I was sick," a small voice volunteered.

Jamie turned and saw the most adorable, wide-open blue eyes that she had ever seen, gazing at her with all of the maturity of a five-year-old. It was all she could do not to wrestle the fragile woman onto her lap and spoon-feed her, but she sensed that Ryan's mood could go either way, so she just smiled and squeezed her hand as she continued to eat.

Ten minutes later, Martin returned and placed a bowl of oatmeal in front of his daughter. It had been smoothed out flat, and he had used a long slice of banana to make a mouth, two slices for eyes, a strawberry for a nose and a mass of blueberries for a curly hairdo.

Ryan looked up at him and gave him her first full smile of the day. He leaned over and gave her a long hug, which she gratefully accepted. He asked softly, "Is my baby feeling sick today?"

She merely nodded with her lip stuck out again.

"My poor little Siobhán," he soothed as he rubbed her shoulders. Soon she began to relax completely into the massage, her head bobbing up and down weakly. After a while, he smoothed her hair back and leaned over again. "Is that better, precious one?" She gave him yet another smile and nodded her head. "You let me take care of you today, okay?"

"Okay," she said as she began to eat her oatmeal. As the contents of the bowl disappeared, so did her grumpy mood, and by the time the bowl was clean, she was her normal, happy self, much to Jamie's amazement.

After she had eaten a second bowl of oatmeal and a bagel, she went downstairs to take a shower while Jamie stayed at the table and chatted with Martin and Conor. When Ryan was out of earshot, she asked, "This happens every month?"

"You get used to it," Conor said blithely. "I'm just glad we only had one girl in the family."

Martin shot him a look as he explained. "Siobhán was just a tiny thing when her mother first fell ill. From that time on, most of the energies of the house had to revolve around Fionnuala. I'm afraid my little one lost out on a lot of the pampering that a young child needs to feel special. It doesn't happen very often, but when she wakes up in a very grumpy mood, my advice is to treat her like she's about three years old. That's a winner every time."

Jamie got up and stood behind his chair. She wrapped her arms around his neck and gave him a hug. "I swear you are the best father on earth."

"Ha. I only wish that were so." He shook his head, and his eyes glazed over in an expression that Jamie had come to learn meant he was thinking of the past. "It was all trial and error. I made far more than my share of errors. Especially with Siobhán." He grew pensive, gazing into his coffee mug for a few moments. "Coming from a family of brothers and having only boys didn't prepare me very well for my little one," he admitted. "I know I let her down a number of times, but I tried to learn from my mistakes. I don't know how it happened, but she certainly has grown into a fine young woman."

"Hey, how about the rest of us?" Conor asked. "Aren't we fine young men?"

Martin gave him an appraising glance, unable to hide his impish smile. "You have your moments, lad. But your sister has a leg up on all of you for bringing this one into the family." Getting to his feet, he stood behind Jamie and gave her a kiss on the head. "You're a gift to us all," he said, squeezing her shoulder.

"That she is, Da," Ryan announced from the doorway, causing a blush to suffuse Jamie's cheeks immediately. "She brings joy to my life each and every day."

"So, what do you want to do today?" Ryan asked once they were back in their room.

Jamie had a feeling that several hours of sex was not on Ryan's agenda, so she tried to think of a vertical activity that they could do together. "We could go get Caitlin and take her to the park."

Ryan mulled that over for a bit, but reminded her, "We'd have to take her to the local one. No wheels."

"Hmm," Jamie mused. "Can't we borrow a truck?" They had the Boxster with them, but the little two-seater could accommodate either Caitlin or Ryan, not both.

"Just Da's," Ryan said. "And that doesn't help a bit." Martin had a small truck with bucket seats, also one seat short for their purposes.

"Wanna play golf?"

"Okay. Where do you want to go?"

Jamie considered which public course might be least busy on a beautiful, clear day in July and decided that the answer was none. She was only able to take Ryan to Olympic once a month and she hated to use her guest privilege so early in the month. "Maybe we should just go to the driving range. We can do that at Olympic without it counting as a visit for you."

"Okay," Ryan agreed, getting up to change into suitable attire. "Give me a second to look wealthy enough to slip under the radar screen."

"Funny. Very funny," Jamie smiled, slapping her sharply on the butt.

"Daddy was right," Jamie mused, as they tried to figure out some way to get both golf bags into the Boxster.

"About what?" Ryan's analytical mind calculated all of the angles, and she finally decided that there was absolutely no way to get more than one bag in the trunk, and it had to be hers. Jamie's bag was a full-sized touring bag, just like the pros used. It allowed her to carry everything from a rain suit to oversized Polartec mittens for cold, foggy mornings, but it wouldn't fit in the trunk. If the bag was going in the car, Ryan had to go in the trunk, and she was adamantly opposed to that idea.

"He thinks I should get a bigger car."

"Really? I thought you liked the Boxster?"

"Oh, I do. It's just that it's such a hassle to take my clubs home after I play."

Ryan considered that for a moment. "Why don't you buy another set of clubs? It wouldn't solve the whole problem, but at least you wouldn't have to lug them home every time you played Olympic."

Jamie glanced at her to see if she was kidding, but when it became apparent that she wasn't, she gently informed her, "I've been building that set of clubs since I was sixteen. They're impossible to recreate."

"Really?" she asked ingenuously. "Don't they still make Ping clubs?"

"Of course they do, but they don't make this particular model. I've got a little extra weight built into the club heads on my short irons, and custom shafts on them, so they're just not replicable. I've been using this putter since I was twelve, and the metal woods—"

Ryan held up a hand, thoroughly convinced that another set of clubs was not an option. "Just a thought," she said, trying to decide how to merge their clubs to make the trip worthwhile. "We've gotta take my bag, so why don't you pick out a few clubs you want, and we'll get going."

"We could borrow a truck for this," Jamie mused.

"Yes, but the clubs would just fly around in the bed of the truck."

"Hmm, that's not really how I'd like to make an entrance at Olympic. My parents are being pretty darned good about our relationship, but that would change immediately if I started driving around in a pickup truck with my clubs banging around in the back. Some sins are not forgivable."

Ryan laughed at her hyperbole, at the same time recognizing that it was really not much of an exaggeration.

They looked a little out of place sharing a bag of clubs on the driving range, but it allowed them to work together, which pleased them both.

Ryan had exhausted her interest after hitting one bucket's worth of balls, so she sat on the springy ground behind her partner and watched her work her way through her available clubs, hitting one crisp shot after another. The day was warm, but a nice breeze flowed across her skin as the sun lulled her into near torpor. A soft voice behind her caused her to jump noticeably, and a gentle hand lightly squeezed her shoulder. "I'm sorry I startled you, Ryan."

She turned to gaze up at Catherine, the sun glowing behind her head, making her look a little like the icon of a medieval saint. "Hi," Ryan said, scrambling to her feet.

Surprisingly, Catherine leaned in and placed a soft kiss on her cheek. Ryan stood rather awkwardly, waiting for Jamie to see her mother. Thankfully she did, rescuing Ryan from her indecision about how to return the greeting. "Mother! What a nice surprise. Playing tennis?"

"Yes, I just finished, but Miriam mentioned that you were here," she said, referring to the locker room attendant.

While the Evans women spoke, Ryan spent a moment taking in her mother-in-law. Even though Catherine said that she had already played tennis, Ryan mused that she must either have been significantly superior to her opponent, or they both played a very relaxed game.

The woman looked as though she had done nothing more strenuous than take a slow walk in a shady park. She wore a very pale blue tennis dress, the cut and the fit showing off her slim body. A white cotton sweater was draped loosely around her shoulders, a fashion choice that Ryan recognized as a favorite affectation of her partner, too. Even looking closely, Ryan was unable to decide if the older woman wore makeup. It seemed anathema to her to play a sport while wearing it, but Catherine's skin looked so flawless—with just the slightest blush on her cheeks—that Ryan thought it had to be cosmetically achieved. *Whatever she does, it looks great on her.* "Pardon?" she asked, seeing two pairs of questioning eyes gazing at her.

"Would you like to have lunch with me?" Catherine was directing a hopeful look at her, and Ryan realized that here was yet another Evans woman she was powerless to refuse.

"I'd love to." Ryan gave her a dazzling smile, causing Catherine to respond in kind.

Ryan felt a bit uncomfortable when their server delivered their lunch and tried to arrange most of the plates in front of her. Catherine had ordered a garden salad without dressing to go along with the Bloody Mary she was working on. Jamie echoed her mother's choice of entrée, but she had some vinaigrette on hers. The cheeseburger, fries, coleslaw, and chocolate malted that Ryan had chosen fit, barely, on the remainder of the small table, and she gave her partner a sheepish look as she dug in.

"She's a growing girl," Jamie said, sharing a smile with her mother.

"It's very refreshing to share a meal with someone who obviously enjoys eating." Catherine smiled at Ryan, appearing to be relaxed and comfortable in her presence.

"Oh, I enjoy it enough for a family of four."

They spent the better part of an hour exchanging small talk about their respective weeks, with Jamie again bringing up the issue of buying a larger car. "Why don't you do that?" Catherine asked. "It seems silly to try to carry things around in your tiny car. I could fill up that little trunk with one trip to Union Square."

Ryan observed the casual way the Evans women talked about a decision to spend a substantial amount of money on something that Jamie didn't really need. "You haven't really expressed an opinion about this," Jamie said, addressing her partner.

Ryan looked up from her plate. "Mrrf frem," she said, indicating that she was too busy eating to render her opinion at the moment.

"For what it's worth, I think you should get that nice little Mercedes SUV," Catherine said. "Andrea Whiting has one, and it's very handy. Then you'd have your little convertible and a nice, big car to carry things."

Oh boy, this is going to be a struggle, Ryan thought, picturing a stable of cars parked in front of her Noe Valley home.

Jamie excused herself to use the facilities, and Catherine turned to Ryan. "You don't appear to be very comfortable with the idea of Jamie buying another car. Is that so?"

Ryan looked up, a little startled that Catherine could read her thoughts without her having said a word. "I uhm, I guess it just seems like something we don't need, so it seems pretty frivolous to me."

Catherine looked slightly confused. "Oh. I thought Jamie said it was difficult to carry her clubs and take your little cousin in her car."

"Well, it is."

"Isn't that reason enough, dear?" she asked, her head cocked in question.

"I've gone without a car up to this point, Catherine. It's never really bothered me, so I guess my perspective is a little different from Jamie's."

Catherine gave her a long, appraising glance, holding Ryan's gaze for a moment. "I like your perspective. I hope you're able to keep it."

It dawned on Ryan that Catherine was referring to the enormous power of money to change people. "I think I'm pretty well grounded. I know it's going to be hard for me to adjust to Jamie's money, but I think we'll do fine as long as we're both willing to give a little."

"Are you willing to give on this issue?" she asked, quirking a grin.

"I suppose I will," Ryan admitted. "I start out with such resolve, but she starts working on me, and before I know it I find my head nodding up and down. I still don't know how she does it."

"She's her father's daughter," Catherine said, smiling. "I don't think Jim's lost five arguments in his whole life. He just wears you down."

Ryan smiled, thinking that that wasn't exactly the tactic her partner used, but Jamie's was equally effective.

Several hours later, after a long afternoon nap, Ryan woke feeling refreshed and happy. Her cramps were gone, she had enjoyed a nice sleep, they'd had a pleasant lunch with Catherine, and they were having company for dinner, which always meant something special on the menu.

"You awake, love?" Jamie's quiet voice tickled the sensitive skin on Ryan's neck, and she giggled a little in response. "Mmm, you're not only awake, you must feel better, too."

"I feel fine," Ryan said. "If I can knock my cramps out right at first they're never a problem."

"I'm glad." Jamie snuggled up a little tighter and placed a few soft kisses on Ryan's neck. "When do we have to get ready for dinner?"

"Same time as usual," Ryan said. "We'll probably eat around 6:00."

"Should I wear a dress?" Jamie asked, unsure of the level of formality required to dine with the parish priest.

"This is just Father Pender," Ryan reminded her. "He's like a member of the family."

"You sure?"

Ryan hopped up and slipped back into her navy blue poplin slacks, adding the blue and white checked polo she had worn to play golf. "I'm done," she said, grinning.

"You're incorrigible." Jamie smiled at her partner and wrapped her in a hug. "And that's just how I like you."

By 9:00 that evening they were snuggled together in bed, trying to make up for the late night of the previous evening. Jamie was gently rubbing the small of Ryan's back, making sure that no residual tension remained. "Father Pender looked a little surprised when you introduced me as your spouse," she said.

Ryan chuckled a little, recalling the startled look they had received from the priest. "I thought it was kinda funny. I'm sure he knows I'm firmly committed to the lesbian lifestyle. Jeez, he knows every other bit of gossip in San Francisco."

"Did you ever tell him that you were a lesbian?"

"Yeah, he was actually the first person I told. I knew he would keep my confidence, so I talked to him right after the whole thing with Sara. He was less than helpful," she said, frowning.

"What happened?"

"He wasn't obnoxious or anything," Ryan said quickly. "He just wasn't helpful. I wanted advice on how to get on with my life, as a lesbian, but he wanted to get me to go to this Catholic group called Courage."

"Courage?"

"Yeah, Courage," Ryan grumbled, shaking her head at the memory. "It's a support group to help gay people have the courage to resist the urge to be sexual."

Jamie's hand stilled, and she lay close to her partner, asking in a soft voice, "Did you want that?"

Ryan's dark head shook, her hair trailing across her pillow. "Not in the least," she said. "I'll admit that I felt pretty shitty about myself, but I never considered trying to be someone I wasn't. I thanked Father Pender and threw the phone number in the trash can outside of the rectory."

"Did he ever talk to you about it again?"

"Nope. As I said, I'm sure he knows that I've dated a lot of women. Maybe that's why he was surprised that I've settled down."

"Oh, you're settled all right," Jamie giggled, wrapping her arms tightly around her partner.

"Settled makes me happy." Ryan snuggled even closer against Jamie's warm body, secure in her love and her unwavering support.

Chapter Five

As they flew across the Bay Bridge on Monday morning, Jamie commented, "There sure isn't much traffic this morning."

Glancing at her, Ryan said, "It's 5:45. Most people aren't stupid enough to be out at this hour."

"Good point. I guess I'm even stupider than you are, since I'm going with you voluntarily, and I don't even like to run."

"Nah. You're just crazy about me, and you can't stand to let me out of your sight for two hours."

"You're right on the money, as usual."

"Morning, girls." Jordan Ericsson tossed her long blonde hair and leveled a cool gaze at Jamie. They were standing in front of the Recreational Sports Facility, stretching lightly before the morning run. Ryan was bent over, getting the kinks out of her back, but she managed to grunt out a hello.

"Wanna stretch it out a little today?" Jordan's tone was casual, almost bored, but Jamie could detect a note of challenge that she assumed wouldn't go unanswered by her mate.

"I suppose I could take the clamps off," Ryan agreed, matching Jordan's tone exactly. "You don't mind if we take off for a little bit, do you, Jamie?"

Oh boy, I'm not gonna see either of them for the next hour. "No, that's fine. I'll be waiting for you in my usual place." Jamie smiled at the pair, knowing that little tests like these were the types of challenges that Ryan thrived on.

Before Coach Placer even gave them the signal, Jordan flashed a taunting smile at Ryan and called, "Normal route—twice." Before Ryan could even blink, the laughing woman took off, leaving Ryan in her wake.

Grumbling, she bent to place a kiss on Jamie's cheek and unnecessarily advised, "You might want to go at your own pace."

Jamie gave her a you've-got-to-be-kidding-to-even-say-that look, and nodded somberly. "Right. I'd hate to kick your butt in front of your teammates."

Oblivious to the joke, her blue eyes locked on Jordan's departing form, Ryan absently said, "Good. See ya."

Jamie watched Ryan chase after Jordan. *Of all the things she needs in the world, the very last one is another person in her life to bring out her competitive side.*

Jamie finished her single lap of the normal route with the more moderate members of the team, then spent a few minutes lying on the grass, stretching. She was just about finished when Jordan came loping up, looking far cooler than she should have after a ten-mile run. Barely breathing hard, she approached Jamie and flopped down on the ground next to her. "Ryan must have stopped for coffee," she commented blithely.

"Uh-huh," Jamie said, deciding it was best to remain neutral in what she assumed would become a chronic contest.

A few seconds later, Ryan came barreling over to them, face flushed, chest heaving. "Holy shit!" she cried, dropping like a rock to land next to Jamie. "Why are you wasting your time in school when you could be with the Olympic track team, training for Sydney?"

Jordan gave her a very confident smile, getting to her feet to stretch her hamstrings. "Oh, I'll be in Sydney," she said, "but I'll be on the volleyball team." With that, she stood and gave Ryan a wink, adding a little wave as she jogged back to the facility to shower.

Ryan didn't say another word, focusing on her post-run stretching. After a little while she extended her legs and bent from the waist, asking Jamie, "Sit on my back, will you?"

"That's an innovative change," she quipped, trying to wrest a smile from her partner. "You normally like me coming at you from the other direction."

"Uh-huh," Ryan grunted, obviously still mulling over her defeat. Jamie dutifully sat on her back, helping Ryan reach the very deep stretch that she liked to get out of her hamstrings. "Maybe I wasn't warmed up enough," she said, more to herself than Jamie.

"Does it really matter if Jordan's faster than you are?" Jamie wasn't trying to be insensitive, but she thought it best to have a little perspective. Ryan and Jordan were not competing for spots on the track team, they were teammates in a sport that didn't require blinding speed, so the entire issue seemed silly to her.

Ryan obviously did not see the issue in the same light. She focused her ice blue eyes on her partner and said slowly, "She's *not* faster than I am. Ten miles is a little long for me. Let me get that little greyhound on the track, and I'd kick her ass so bad she couldn't sit for a week." Ryan's eyes were nearly burning in their intensity, and Jamie immediately decided that this was not the time to try to inject a dose of reality.

"I'm sure you're right. I've seen how fast you are at the shorter distances..."

"I'm plenty fast at the longer distances, too," Ryan said sharply. "I just have to spend a little time working on my stamina."

Jamie smiled rather than rolling her eyes, since she knew that wouldn't be appreciated. *Great. Just great. It's bad enough she has to compete with her brothers and all of her cousins. Now she has to beat Jordan, too. It's gonna be a* long *summer.*

On Tuesday morning, Jamie proposed a plan that she hoped would satisfy both of their morning needs. "I'd like to go with you to work out in the gym this morning, but I really need my wake-up routine. Can you keep yourself occupied until 9:00?"

Ryan mulled over the request, agreeing to an accommodation. "I think I'll go over to the track. If I'm gonna be in top shape, I need to work on my speed. I'll meet you in the weight room at 9:30. That okay?"

"It's great." She took her latté and her newspaper and headed for the backyard, musing, *Did they change the rules of volleyball since I last watched it? I was certain that you didn't have to sprint from one end of the court to the other before you were allowed to hit the ball. Thanks, Jordan, thanks a lot.*

The day was cool and brisk, so Jamie decided to sit on the steps of the Recreational Sports Facility to wait for her partner. As expected, a very soggy-looking Ryan came bounding up, right on time. "You don't look like you're going *to* a workout." Jamie rose to place a small kiss on Ryan's flushed cheek.

"I'm good to go," she said. "I got some good work in this morning, working on my form. I've been clenching my fists a little, and a flaw like that can really slow ya down."

She looked completely serious, and Jamie didn't have the heart to tell her that her hand position could not possibly have accounted for her second-place showing the day before. *Jordan had just plain dusted her—by a lot.* Instead, she offered an encouraging smile, grasping Ryan's hand as she did so. "You're dangerously fast, Buffy. And I should know." As they walked through the quiet halls of the RSF, Jamie continually bumped her partner with her hip, turning it into a little game that quickly got out of hand. By the time they reached the door of the weight room, Jamie was shrieking and laughing hysterically. She flew into the room and grasped the horizontal bar with both hands, bracing her body against the other half of the double door which had luckily been bolted shut.

Ryan yanked on the door with all her might, managing to pull it forward a few inches. "You know I'll get in there eventually, Jamie," she bellowed, "and when I do…" She left the threat incomplete, trying to let Jamie's imagination conjure up what the punishment would be.

"You'll never break me," the smaller woman yelled through the heavy steel door. "I can hold you off for hours."

Ryan laughed evilly, deciding to let go of the door handle completely for a few moments, knowing that her partner would tire quickly. She shoved her face against the small, oblong window, smashing her normally attractive features into a gruesome-looking mask. Her laugh rang out again, and she thanked the gods that every office they had passed was empty.

"You don't scare me," Jamie called out. "Hit me with your best shot."

"Winner gives the loser a massage."

"Deal."

"Limber up your fingers, babe, you're gonna need 'em." Ryan braced her foot on the locked portion of the door and grabbed the handle with both hands. She depressed the lever to unlock the latch, then yanked with every bit of her considerable strength, only to have the door move less than an inch. Time and again she yanked, letting out a frustrated groan as she did. On her last try she barked out a loud growl and slid to the floor in defeat when the door again failed to budge.

"Give up?"

"Yes," Ryan grumbled before she slumped against the locked half of the door.

Jamie opened the door tentatively, expecting her partner to leap at her, looking for vengeance. Instead, she was still sitting on the floor looking totally defeated. "Maybe I'm too old for this," she said when Jamie squatted down next to her.

"Why do you say that?" Jamie immediately felt bad about her little game, realizing too late that Ryan needed an ego boost.

"I'm not as fast as I thought, I'm not as strong as I thought..." She trailed off weakly, looking more discouraged than Jamie had ever seen her.

"You're as strong as three women."

Ryan replied with a bitter laugh, grumbling, "I think I'm just fooling myself. I can't even beat one. Any one," she muttered, recalling Jordan's trouncing of the day before.

"Honey, you can beat three. Believe me." She ruffled Ryan's hair as she stood and yanked the door open, revealing Jordan and a freshman teammate named Heather who were both trying, and failing, to look innocent. "I had a little help," Jamie said, hoping Ryan wasn't angry with her.

Very amused blue eyes looked up at her, a pleased grin replacing her frown. "Three, huh?" She barked out a little chuckle as she got to her feet. "Not bad," Jamie heard her mutter under her breath. "Not bad at all."

The foursome worked out together for about half an hour. Technically, "together" wasn't the correct word, but they were in the same space for that amount of time. Heather was the first to fall by the wayside, mumbling a quiet "See ya" as she made her escape.

Jamie held out a good while longer, matching the jocks exercise for exercise. She was quite proud of herself, even though she was pumping half the weight of the other two. But when they dropped to the floor to start banging out one-armed push-ups, she allowed her good sense to take over and pulled out a mat to start stretching.

"Box jumps?" Ryan asked, raising an eyebrow.

"Uhm, sure," Jordan said, "I've got a little juice left in my tank. I was here for quite a while before you two showed up," she said, revealing a tiny chink in her self-confidence as she snuck a surreptitious glance at Ryan's pumped thighs.

Jamie wasn't familiar with the term "box jumps," but she got the idea when Ryan pulled out three sizes of sturdy wooden boxes and placed them a couple of feet apart. Jordan followed suit, placing her boxes well away from Ryan's to avoid their running into each other. "Wanna make a game of it?" Ryan asked casually.

"If you must," Jordan said with a much more studied aloofness. "Whatever gets your juices flowing."

Ryan refrained from making the graphic joke she would have made before Jamie, or BJ, as she privately referred to the time prior to their pairing. She was content to save her naughty sense of humor for her partner, but she did have to police herself a bit. She had been teasing and playing with other women for six years, and it had become second nature to her, but she didn't want anyone to get the wrong idea, especially anyone as fabulous-looking as Jordan.

"Follow the leader." Ryan called the challenge, waiting for Jordan to complain. When she didn't, Ryan started on the smallest step. She jumped onto the step and back to the floor, her feet close together, arms flexed slightly at the elbow. Several repeats of this motion led her to the next box, and she ran off an even dozen crisp repetitions. Jordan was keeping up with her, but Jamie could see the signs of fatigue on the thinner woman's face. Her mouth was slightly open, and her chest was moving more quickly than Ryan's. *Who wouldn't want to trade places with me?* Jamie smirked to herself. *I get to watch two fantastic-looking women work out, and nobody notices when I stare at their bouncing breasts.*

Ryan picked up the pace, going to the tallest of the boxes and launching into a blistering set of reps. Jamie stared at the pair, amazed that they were both able to continue with the grueling test of stamina. Jordan's skin was now a deep pink, and beads of sweat flew off her face as she leapt in concert with Ryan.

For her part, Ryan still looked good, given how long they'd been jumping. Her face was darker than normal, and she also perspired freely, but she wasn't gasping for air like Jordan was.

"Shit!" Jordan cried, withdrawing from the competition. Both hands flew to her waist, massaging what looked to be a painful stitch in her side.

Jamie approached her and placed a hand on her bent back. "You okay?"

"Fine. Fine." Her voice was muffled and strained, and she seemed more annoyed than in pain. "Just have to work this cramp out."

The rhythmic "thump, thump, thump" that continued in the background finally attracted Jamie's attention, and she turned her head to gaze at her partner. "Honey," she called, "you can stop now."

"I've…got…a…little…left," she huffed, her sweat-drenched bangs flopping into her eyes with each jump.

Jordan was finally able to stand, and she wiped her body down with a towel while she watched Ryan bang away. "I'm guessing she sleeps on a bed of nails," she groused.

"Nah," Jamie laughed, "she's actually kind of a hedonist." They spent a moment staring at the straining woman, both impressed, though only Jamie would admit to it. "She does have a lot of determination, though."

Jordan mumbled something indecipherable and sat down to stretch. Jamie joined her, and after another minute Ryan finally gave out. She flopped down with a wet "plop," stretching out fully on the mat next to Jamie. The smaller woman could feel the moist heat radiating off her body, smell her rich, earthy scent, see the sweat rolling down her skin in tiny rivulets. She wanted nothing more than to strip off her clothes and rub her body all over Ryan's, but she thought that might be considered slightly rude, so she controlled herself.

After an amazingly short time, Ryan said, "I was gonna do a little ab work. Anybody wanna join me?"

Jordan mumbled an epithet that caused Jamie to gape and Ryan to giggle. "A 'no' would be sufficient," Ryan said, laughing.

Looking at her, Jordan mumbled, "You're not human," before dropping back onto her mat.

"Just what I thought about you when you were kicking my butt yesterday morning," Ryan said, as she hooked her feet onto a slant board to do some sit-ups.

Jamie was very pleased that her partner and Jordan were starting to acknowledge that each had some unique talents, for she knew that Ryan would loosen up considerably if her interactions with Jordan became more playful.

Soon Ryan was lost in her own little world, and Jordan continued to sneak quick looks at her as she worked. "So, what's the story with her? She's obviously a gifted athlete, she certainly doesn't seem to have a problem with training, why is she a walk-on as a senior?"

"Long story," Jamie said, shaking her head to indicate that she was not going to share the story at the moment. "Ask her sometime when you have an hour."

Jordan didn't pursue the issue, continuing to cast surreptitious glances at her new teammate. "She's gonna help us a lot this year. I'm really glad she decided to join."

"Why don't you tell her that?"

Jordan laughed softly. "Yeah, I'll do that sometime."

"So, did you mean it when you said you expect to make the Olympic team?"

Now the cool blue eyes took on a definite fire. "Oh, I'll make it, all right. I've dedicated my life to this, and if Ryan can help us nail a few more wins, I should be a lock."

"I hope you make it," Jamie said. "I've never known an Olympian."

"Maybe you and the masochist can come to Sydney to watch us." She gave Jamie a big smile that chased away every shred of reserve from her face. "Well, I've gotta get going," she said, struggling to her feet. "I've got a shoot this afternoon."

"Shoot?" Jamie asked, and as the very tall woman looked down at her, a light bulb went off in Jamie's head. "That's where I've seen you before! You're in a Gap ad."

Jordan gave her a devastatingly sexy smile, along with a rather demure nod. "It's a living," she tossed over her shoulder as she grabbed her gym bag and left the room.

"Ryan," Jamie said as soon as the blonde departed, "Jordan did one of those Gap ads that are up and down Market Street. That's why she looked so familiar to me."

"Huh," Ryan mumbled, grunting out a few more sit-ups. "Makes sense. She's got the body and the looks for it."

"You're right about the body," Jamie mused, thinking back to the leggy blonde. "She's fine."

"Oh, are we discovering an affinity for blondes? I thought you were a fan of brunettes?" It was clear that Ryan was teasing, so Jamie felt free to be honest.

"Does it bother you that I, uhm, notice other women?"

"Nope. Not a bit," Ryan said, throwing her legs to the ground and leaning in to place a sweaty kiss on Jamie's head. "As long as I get to take you home at night, you can look all you want."

"Not a worry, Tiger," Jamie laughed. "You're stuck with me."

"I'm not stuck *with* you," Ryan said, playfully tweaking her partner's nose, "but I'm definitely stuck *on* you."

"I prefer to think that we're stuck on each other." Jamie wrapped her arms around the steaming body and took a deep breath, inhaling her comforting scent. She looked up and crooked a grin at her partner, "You're so hot and wet, we might be stuck permanently."

"I've really gotta stretch after this workout," Ryan said. "You can help me finish quicker, though."

For the next fifteen minutes, they worked together, pushing, pulling, stretching, and bending Ryan's flexible body into a series of contortions. The larger woman finally finished by going to the wall and lying down with her head about a foot from the wooden dowels that were used to hook a slant board onto. She tossed her legs in the air and let them fall to the floor above her head, her now-loose hamstrings allowing her to achieve the position that would normally be difficult for her. "Hook my heels under the fourth bar," she grunted, her voice constricted by the pressure of her body. The bar she indicated was about two feet high, and Jamie managed to get Ryan's heels under the bar. After letting her lats and hamstrings get used to the increased stretch, she asked Jamie to lower her feet down another two rungs. To Jamie's amazement, the straining woman continued to grunt out, "Down," until her toes touched the ground.

Jamie shook her head, staring at her partner in amused wonder. Ryan's head was poking up from between her own thighs, her face red from the strain, but otherwise looking perfectly relaxed. "You can do this, and you still felt the need to have a girlfriend?"

Releasing her legs, Ryan stretched out and smiled up at her lover. "No interest. Besides," she said, placing a tender kiss on her own hand, "Lefty would get jealous."

Jamie spent the afternoon working with the pro at Olympic that her father had so enthusiastically recommended. Mark was a good teacher, and she was quite pleased with his very positive comments about her chances of making the team. She was humming a little tune when she entered the house, and she looked around for a moment before venturing outside to find Ryan in what was obviously becoming one of her favorite spots.

Her long body was curled up on the wooden arbor bench, her left foot resting on the seat. A notebook was open, resting on her raised leg, and her face bore a studious expression as she made notes.

"Hi," Jamie said as she approached, not wanting to startle her.

Ryan let out a sigh and placed the notebook and her pencil on the seat, rising to greet her partner. "Have a good day?"

"I did. I worked with Mark for a long time at the range, and then we played a round. It's really starting to click for me. My confidence is getting better every day."

"That's very good to hear," Ryan said, giving her a squeeze.

Jamie picked up the notebook and took a seat, motioning Ryan down beside her. "You seem a little flat today. What's on your mind?"

Ryan was absolutely silent for a minute, trying to gather her thoughts. "I talked to Sara today."

Jamie flinched visibly, her whole body recoiling reflexively from the mental image of Sara kissing her partner—an image she had not been able to remove from her memory even though she had only seen the kiss in her imagination. "Talked?" she managed, her voice thin with tension.

Ryan snaked an arm around her partner, pulling her close against her body. "Yeah. We talked on the phone. I wouldn't think of seeing her again if you weren't with me."

Surprisingly, Jamie sat up and placed a hand flat against Ryan's chest, her eyes flashing. "No. That's not necessary. I trust you. You can see Sara, or any other person that you want to see. I don't ever want you to feel that you have to get my permission to live your life."

With a slow, gentle smile curling her mouth, Ryan gave her partner a grateful hug. "I appreciate that. But I don't have a need to see Sara again. I just called her to try to get a little more info out of her. The good news is that I'm pretty confident that she was telling the truth, and that she wasn't the one who told the girls at school."

"That must be a relief," Jamie said, leaning her head against Ryan's shoulder. Just sitting together and listening to her partner's strong, slow heartbeat calmed her, and she felt her equilibrium returning.

"Yeah, though I was already pretty sure I believed her. We just talked about the other girls on the team and tried to figure out who could have started the rumors."

"What did you come up with?"

"Nada. I'm beginning to think that Mrs. Andrews was right. Maybe the other girls just guessed."

"So are you gonna give up?"

Ryan laughed softly, shaking her head. "Hardly. My mind's made up. I'm gonna get to the bottom of this. It might take me a while, but somebody knows what happened, and I'm gonna find out. I think my next move is to talk to my old coach."

Jamie tried to recall what she knew about this woman, finding that she didn't even recall her name. "Have you kept up with her?"

"Nope. The day she told me that it was best if I quit was the last time we spoke privately. She'd say hello when I saw her in the halls, but our relationship was basically over at that point."

"Are you just gonna show up and try to talk to her?"

"No. I don't want to waste a trip. I called the school after I spoke with Sara, and the person I spoke with said that Coach Ratzinger was running a clinic for high school girls on Friday. I thought I'd go over when it was finishing up. Then she won't be able to duck me."

"Do you want me to go with you?" Jamie was certain that this was going to be a tough visit for her lover, and she fervently hoped that Ryan would allow her to go along for moral support.

"Sure. I'm a little nervous about having you see me if I act stupid, but you might also be able to help me stay calm."

"Uhm, who's gonna keep me calm?" the smaller woman queried, just the hint of a smile playing at her mouth. "You're always more in control than I am."

"Good point," Ryan said, a matching smile beginning to bloom. "Oh well, if I'm gonna be in jail for assault, there's nobody I'd rather share a cell with than you."

As soon as Ryan finished with her last client on Friday afternoon, they took off for the city, managing to get home quickly. The soccer clinic was scheduled from 1:00 until 6:00, and Ryan wanted to arrive a little after that in hopes of catching the coach alone. Regrettably, it wasn't even 4:00, and Ryan was already antsy. "I need to blow off some energy, but I don't want to run again."

"I can help you expend some energy," Jamie offered, quirking an eyebrow in her improving mimicry of Ryan's habit. Ryan was wearing a blue and white checked cotton camp shirt, and Jamie teasingly slipped her hand between the top two buttons, scratching the smooth fabric of Ryan's sports bra.

The larger hand grasped the interloper and gently removed it. "I don't say this often, in fact, I don't remember the last time I said it, but I'm not in the mood. Do you mind?"

"Of course not. I'm not really in the mood either. I just thought it might relax you a little."

Ryan laced her hands behind Jamie's neck, gazing at her fondly as she did so. "Have I told you what a wonderful partner you are?"

"You have. You tell me and show me all the time. But speaking of show and tell, I'd really like to get a feel for the person you were when this was all going down. Do you have some pictures from your senior year?"

"I can do much better than that," Ryan said. Minutes later they were in Martin's room, the home of the only television in the house. No one else was home, so they had the place to themselves. Ryan ran her finger across the neatly labeled videotapes that rested on a shelf under the TV. "Here we go," she said as she pulled a tape out. She removed it from the sleeve and handed the cardboard to Jamie. "State Championship-Soccer 1992," read the legend.

Ryan popped the tape in and jumped onto the bed with the remote. Jamie climbed up next to her and cuddled up against her warm body. "We didn't have a video camera, but every time Da thought the occasion merited it, he would borrow one from one of the guys at work. I think the fellow regretted ever making the offer because Da had the darn thing every other week. This tape is from our final game of my junior year." Jamie noticed that her face had taken on a certain sadness, so she cuddled up a little tighter to offer some comfort. "Now you've got to remember," Ryan said, "that the videographer has a certain prejudice."

As the tape began to roll, Jamie had to laugh at Ryan's assessment. She imagined that most videos of a soccer game would show the whole field, or at least try to follow the ball. But this one was of nothing but Ryan. It was impossible to tell what was going on until the ball came near the goal, since Martin had filled the frame with nothing but his daughter. But in Jamie's view, he had made exactly the correct choice.

Needing to see every detail, Jamie climbed off the bed to stand near the TV. Time and again she turned to look at her smirking lover, going back and forth between the image on the screen and the reality lying on the bed.

In a way, Ryan looked just like she had in 1992. The hair was in the same style it had been up until her recent haircut and her face was clearly recognizable. But in other ways, the young woman pacing around in the goal looked like a completely different person.

Even though her face was similar, the young Ryan had a softness to her features that the adult version lacked. It was as if her current strong features were hidden under a layer of baby fat, and after a few more glances, Jamie decided that was exactly what the difference was. There was a roundness to her cheeks that was completely adorable, and Jamie decided immediately that if they had met when Ryan was seventeen and she fourteen, she would have skipped the heterosexual interlude that had kept her occupied for so many years.

She guessed that Ryan had weighed no more than 150 pounds, a good 40 to 50 pounds less than her ideal weight now. She also looked several inches shorter, so the lower weight was expected. The young Ryan was very slim through the hips and thighs, with none of the definition that she now had. Her shoulders were so remarkably broad that she looked a bit like she had left the hanger in her shirt, but there was no visible musculature there, either. Jamie had never considered this term for her partner, but she had to admit that she looked almost willowy at this young age. It was quite a surprise to her, and so different from the current image that Jamie was almost nonplussed. *Thank God she's not just a math nerd*, Jamie silently mused. *I'm sure I'd still love her, but I would* so *miss those muscles.*

As she stared at the screen, she recognized that the thing that both impressed and saddened her was the guileless enthusiasm that the young Ryan radiated as she ran around in her goal. Even though her lover was often childlike and joyous, there was a purity of spirit that she'd had at seventeen that was likely lost forever. The young woman looked as if she expected nothing but good things to happen to her, while today Ryan had a certain reserved cynicism that clouded her features from time to time. This young woman had no idea how tumultuous her life would become in a few short months, and Jamie doubted that she would have believed anyone who had tried to tell her.

She was full of energy and optimism and enthusiasm for life, and Jamie immediately felt her anger focus on the adults who had taken that from her.

As the game wound down, the video captured the joyous celebration as the team emerged victorious. But the most touching moment was when the camera focused on Ryan and Sara hugging each other with unbridled elation. When their hug ended, they each kept an arm around the other's shoulder as they grinned into the camera for a full minute. Eventually their heads tilted until they rested against each other in a playful fashion. The video ended with the image of their joyous faces etched into Jamie's mind. When she turned to look at her lover again, she caught a heartbreakingly sad look on Ryan's handsome features, and she leapt onto the bed and cuddled her furiously for a long while, finally lifting Ryan's tear-streaked face to promise, "We'll find out what happened. I swear."

An hour later they were sitting on the ground watching a group of hopeful young girls work out on a small field in Alta Plaza Park. Jamie'd had no idea that Ryan's school was in such an elegant neighborhood, but she was afraid to ask the obvious question of how the O'Flahertys could have afforded to send Ryan there.

The school was located in the middle of Pacific Heights, arguably the most prestigious neighborhood in San Francisco, just a few blocks from the park they were currently in. The school itself was housed in a massive old mansion built for the Flood family in 1916; Ryan explained that since the school had no athletic facilities they had reached agreements with the public and private parks and schools in the area to use various facilities for different sports.

As if she could read Jamie's mind, Ryan volunteered, "I could only go to Sacred Heart because of scholarships. When I was in grade school, I assumed I'd go to the local Catholic high school that my brothers had attended. But Sara's mom convinced her to go to Sacred Heart, and I spent all of eighth grade badgering Da to see if we could afford it, too. Of course we couldn't, and my heart just about broke. I can honestly say that was the only time it bothered me that we didn't have money."

Jamie gazed at her pensively, trying to imagine what it would be like to want something so desperately but be unable to attain it because of a lack of money. She realized that there would always be a chasm between their experiences and that at some level she could never really understand what it would feel like to have money limit your dreams. She was just happy that it would never be an issue for Ryan or any of the O'Flahertys again.

Ryan continued her tale. "Sara made the soccer team when she was a freshman, and I hopped on the bus every time I was free to come watch her play. She introduced me to the coach, and before I knew it, one of the admissions counselors called Da and said they wanted to offer me a scholarship. I think that was one of the happiest days of my life," she said winsomely.

Ryan leaned back on her braced arms and looked up at the sky while she reflected on those days. "You know," she said as she pulled a long blade of grass and stuck it between her teeth, "I don't think I've ever considered why it meant so much to me to get that scholarship. But I think it's the same reason that the scholarship to Cal meant so much."

Jamie sat up a little straighter and stared at Ryan, but the taller woman seemed to need to focus on the sky to concentrate. "School had always been easy for me. I don't think you know this, but I was treated like I was really special because of my abilities in math." Jamie did in fact know just how special Ryan was, but she decided not to reveal what Martin and Conor had told her. Instead she nodded when Ryan turned to catch her eye. "But Da had always stressed that gifts like that shouldn't make us feel good about ourselves. He said that we should be happy with whatever we got from God. So it bothered me to have people make such a fuss over my math abilities. It just seemed wrong, you know?" she asked as she tilted her head and gazed at her partner. Jamie gripped her shoulder and nodded her head in understanding.

"But even though I had a lot of God-given talent in sports, the biggest reason for my success was because of hard work. I don't think I've ever made it clear just how hard I worked to be good at soccer. I'd honestly say that I spent three to four hours a day working on my footwork and my passing. I was there for an hour before practice, and I stayed for at least an hour afterward. Since I was a midfielder when I was young, those skills were really important to my game. No matter what season it was, I worked on my soccer skills for at least an hour a day, even when I was actively playing softball or field hockey."

Jamie brushed the hair from her face and said softly, "I don't think I realized how hard you worked. I thought it came naturally for you."

"It did," Ryan agreed. "I had talent, and that's not something you can learn. I also had the body to be good at the sports I played. But the people who succeed are the ones who take their talent and work their asses off. And that's the part I'm proud of. The scholarship to Cal was based on my efforts, not on my gifts, and to have my coach turn on me and take that away was a hurt that I don't think I'll ever get over." She turned onto her stomach and gazed at Jamie with a cold fire of determination in her sapphire eyes. "I'm going to find out what happened if I have to skin her alive to get her to talk."

Jamie felt her body jerk backwards as Ryan uttered those words. She had never seen her lover truly angry, but she was seeing it today. She knew that they wouldn't leave this field without some degree of satisfaction. She just hoped that it came peacefully.

Chapter Six

T he clinic was winding down, and Coach Ratzinger spent quite a few minutes talking to individual girls and their parents. As the last of the kids drifted away, Ryan got to her feet and pulled Jamie up. Jamie grasped her hand and gazed into her still-fiery eyes, saying, "Do whatever you need to do. I'm behind you."

The gentleness couldn't stay hidden for long as Ryan's mouth curled into a sweet smile. "Thank you. That means a lot."

She strode across the field with a mature, determined gait. Jamie held back a bit to let her get comfortable with the situation and found herself stopping about twenty-five feet from Ryan to watch her approach the woman.

Ryan was nearly on top of the coach when she stopped and crossed her arms over her broad chest. The coach had been gathering up her supplies and was bent over at the waist when Ryan approached. She looked up and gasped when she saw the imposing woman looming over her. Everything she had been holding dropped to the ground, and Jamie could detect her fear from twenty feet away.

"H…H…Hello Ryan," she squeaked out as she stood at her full height and gazed up. Even viewed from a distance, Ryan looked imposing to Jamie; she could only imagine how the coach felt. Ryan was at least six inches taller than the coach and a good fifty pounds heavier, but her size wasn't where the menace came from. That was clearly from her cold, steel blue eyes.

"I'm on a quest," she said, her eyes locked onto the older woman.

"A quest?"

"Yes, a quest," Ryan said. "Some things happened during my senior year that almost ruined my life. I believe that you either know who orchestrated those events or that you personally participated in them."

"Me?" she asked, wide-eyed. "Why would I do that?"

"Good question," Ryan said somberly. "I want to know what you know, Coach. And I want to know now."

"Now?" the coach asked slowly as she looked around, obviously hoping that someone could help her if Ryan attempted to break her in half.

Ryan didn't reply. Instead, she stood up even taller and narrowed her eyes until they were like blue lasers.

The coach obviously decided that playing dumb wasn't going to carry the day, so she lowered her eyes to the ground and whispered, "I was afraid."

Jamie had been advancing on the pair slowly, and as she drew near she could see a glimmer of Ryan's gentleness begin to reappear. Ryan's arms dropped to her sides, and she leaned in toward the coach with a less imposing look on her face. "Afraid of what?"

As Jamie came closer still, she noted with amazement that Coach Ratzinger was at least sixty years old. From a distance, her trim body and obviously dyed hair made her appear thirty years younger, but her actual age was apparent from her sun-lined face. "I was afraid of losing my job," she said as her face colored in shame. She looked to be on the verge of tears, and it was obvious that Ryan couldn't keep the pressure on.

"Let's go over to the school and talk," Ryan said, bending to help pick up the dropped gear.

The older woman looked up at Ryan as she stood and said, "Thank you. I could use a chair."

Jamie covered the short distance that separated them, and Ryan slid her arm around her shoulders. "This is my partner, Jamie."

Jamie's manners took over, and she extended her hand cordially. The coach's weak grasp made even Jamie feel some sympathy for her, but it would take a lot more than a sob story to cause her to forgive the woman's actions if they had been the cause of her partner's pain.

They walked the two blocks together, the stilted silence putting everyone's nerves on edge. Trying to ease the tension, Ryan gave the coach a brief update on her life and informed her that she was finally playing for Cal. She also revealed that she had been offered a spot on the soccer team but had turned it down, not going into her reasons for doing so.

When they reached the building, the coach opened the stately doors with her key and led them to a cramped office in the basement. As Ryan and Jamie entered, the coach stood outside and scanned the hall, as if she wanted to make sure no one had seen her enter. After she locked the door she spoke in a voice so quiet that both women had to lean in to hear her. "I'm sure this doesn't help, but I want you to know that I didn't have a good night's sleep for over three years because of what I did to you, Ryan. I know there's no way to make it up to you, so I won't even offer. I just want you to know that I thought you were a fine young woman. I hope you're happy now in your...uhm...relationship."

"I am," Ryan said in a louder, but still circumspect voice. "I'm very happy with my life. But I want to know why you ruined my chances to go to Cal."

Her eyes grew wide and she tried to explain: "That wasn't my intent. I know you would have been a great addition to the program at Cal..."

"Coach," Ryan said softly, her gaze intent and unwavering, "the volleyball coach was led to believe that I was emotionally unstable. *You* told him that. I assume you told the other coaches roughly the same story."

The older woman dropped her head into her hands, rubbing them briskly against her face. "I had to tell them *something*," she said. "Every coach at Cal called me to ask why you had dropped off the team. I tried to protect you; I thought I was doing the right thing."

"You thought you were protecting me by telling them that I was emotionally unstable?" Her voice was rising in pitch, and the volume was increasing proportionately.

"I didn't want to tell them that you were...gay." She whispered the last word, saying it so quietly that the women had to read her lips. "I didn't want to ruin your life." She looked so absolutely pathetic that Jamie felt a little sorry for her, but not sorry enough to forgive her.

"You thought," Ryan said carefully, "that revealing that I was gay was worse than telling them that I was emotionally unstable?" Her breath was coming faster, and she looked as if she was about to lose it. Jamie placed a hand on the small of Ryan's back, gently stroking her.

"Once that gets out you can never—ever—get past it," Coach Ratzinger said, clearly trying to make the young woman see how damaging it could be to have her sexual orientation revealed.

"Coach," Ryan said, her eyes wide in amazement, "I'm out to everyone, and I do mean everyone. I tell everyone in my life, and I have since I was eighteen. It's never been a problem for me."

"You do?" the obviously stunned woman mouthed, the words too quiet to be heard.

"Yes. I do. I always have, and I always will." Ryan was silent for a moment, gazing at the older woman with a strangely compassionate look. "You haven't ever been able to tell anyone, have you?"

Her tone was so gentle, so accepting, that the shaken woman found her head shaking despite her fear. "No, no one knows," she whispered. As the words left her lips she seemed to almost collapse into herself, and seconds later she was curled into a ball, sobbing roughly.

Before Jamie knew what had happened, Ryan was on her knees in front of the older woman, folding her into her arms. The coach struggled for a moment, then locked her arms around Ryan's neck and cried like a child.

I will never understand her capacity for forgiveness, Jamie thought, trying to control her own tears, *but it's one of the most wonderful things about her.*

Ryan comforted the older woman as best she could, but it was obvious that her tears had been building for many years and were not going to be whisked away easily. Ryan patted her back gently for a few minutes, then uttered a deep sigh as she slumped back into her chair. Ryan looked very tired, exhausted, really, and Jamie realized how very hard this was for her. She made eye contact with her partner and raised an eyebrow, cocking her head toward the door. But Ryan wasn't finished. She had come to learn the entire story, and she wasn't going to leave until she did.

She sat in her chair, looking tired but calm, waiting for the coach to be able to speak again.

After a long while, the older woman looked up through her red-rimmed eyes, almost surprised that there were two women in her office. She cocked her head slightly, silently asking Ryan what else she wanted of her.

"I think I understand what happened with the coaches at Cal," she began, "but I still don't understand why you didn't support me when the other girls came to you. That was such a betrayal," she said softly, her eyes filling with tears. "Why did you do that to me?"

"I tried, Ryan," she mumbled, shaking her head slowly. "I swear I tried." She looked up, hoping that weak explanation would suffice, but Ryan's unblinking eyes never left her face. After a long, tense moment, she sighed heavily and tried to offer an explanation. "Tammy Anderson came to me and told me that she and the other girls wanted you off the team. She said that they knew you 'did something' to Sara, and they were afraid that you would try something with one of them."

"And...? This is where you tried to help?" Ryan was not giving an inch.

"Yes," she insisted. "I told Tammy that she was being ridiculous, and that even if what she heard about you and Sara was true, it didn't have any bearing on the team."

"Uh-huh," Ryan said, crossing her arms over her chest, a very skeptical look settling on her face. "Then what?"

"Tammy wouldn't let it drop," she said, looking down at the floor. "She and Cathy Bennett went to see Mother Superior, still demanding that you be thrown off the team."

"Sister Mary Magdalene was behind this?" Ryan's brow furrowed, finding it hard to believe that the sister who was always so supportive would betray her.

"Not behind it," she said. "But she had the entire school to think about. Even though she was very fond of you…"

Ryan jumped to her feet, startling both the coach and Jamie. The blood was rushing to her face, and Jamie could see a vein in her temple throbbing angrily. "It didn't matter that she was fond of me. It didn't matter that you knew I wasn't a threat to anyone. It didn't matter that I didn't do *one fucking thing* that I'm ashamed of! All, I repeat, *all* that mattered was keeping the peace, placating the little assholes who caused a stink. *Tell me I'm wrong!*" she thundered, her voice so loud that Jamie's ears hurt. She flopped back down into the padded metal chair, all of the fire extinguished. "Tell me I'm wrong," she murmured weakly, a fragile, wounded look on her face.

As Ryan collapsed, Jamie's immediate instinct was to continue to rail at the coach, but she knew that this was Ryan's issue, so she tried to control her raging emotions.

Coach Ratzinger locked eyes with the defeated woman, holding her gaze for a moment. "You're right. It sickens me to admit it, but you're right." Jamie felt her anger start to swell, but still she held her tongue. The coach muttered, "It's hard to keep everyone happy, but I did the best I could."

That ridiculous excuse finally pushed Jamie over the edge. "*How could you?*" She jumped to her feet, looking like she was going to grab the older woman and shake her senseless. "You nearly destroyed her life just to avoid a little gossip…a little controversy? *How can you live with yourself?*" Jamie was shaking with anger, heat radiating off her body so profusely that the small room became uncomfortably warm almost immediately.

Ryan slipped her fingers into the back pocket of Jamie's jeans, gently pulling her back toward her chair. Jamie struggled against her hold, and it looked as though Ryan would have to sit on her to keep her from assaulting the older woman. Seeing Jamie so upset calmed Ryan down a little and she broke the tension by asking, "Did the fact that you were a lesbian have anything to do with this?"

Another heavy sigh preceded the coach's answer. "Yes, I guess I have to say it did. No one here knows about me, Ryan. No one. But Sister is a perceptive woman, and I think she's always suspected. She came to me and asked if I could stand having a bright light fall on the program if these girls continued their protest." She shook her head slowly, unable to face either woman. "I was fifty-eight years old. I'd never made more than $38,000 a year, and my whole future depended on the pension that I'd receive. I know what I did was wrong, but I didn't know what else to do. If the parents of those girls got involved, there was no way I could stand up to the scrutiny."

"So you traded Ryan's future for your own," Jamie snarled, still so angry she was nauseated.

"I didn't think it would hurt her that badly," the older woman said. "Ryan had so much going for her, I just assumed she'd go on to college and put this behind her. I'm still amazed that none of the other schools offered you a scholarship. I was sure that Duke wasn't fazed—"

"I had other offers," Ryan admitted. "I was just too depressed to even think about going anywhere else."

"I had no idea," Coach Ratzinger muttered. "You always seemed so self-confident."

"I was *seventeen*," Ryan reminded her. "No one has unshakable confidence at seventeen."

"I was selfish and afraid," the coach said. "I hope that I'd have more guts if this were to happen today." She looked down at the ground and added, "But I doubt that I would."

Ryan stood and regarded the woman for a few moments. She nodded to Jamie to indicate she was ready to leave. "It's over now," she said. "I appreciate that you were honest with me."

"As ashamed as I am, I'm really glad you came to see me, Ryan. It's more reassuring than you'll ever know for me to see what a fine young woman you've become. I...I'm proud to have known you," she said as she broke into sobs again.

Ryan didn't try to comfort the coach this time. She gave her one final look, grasped her shaking shoulder and gave it a gentle squeeze as she said, "Good luck this season."

On the way out of the building, Jamie had to stop to gather herself before she could even think of driving. She found that they were standing in front of a gleaming trophy case. There were loving cups and medallions and plaques of all shapes and sizes, a few of them with her lover's name prominently featured. A large plaque read "Student-Athlete of the Year" and she noticed that Ryan's name was listed as the winner in 1990, 1991, and 1992. Another large trophy in the shape of a gold soccer ball was engraved with "California State Champions 1992." A faded photograph lying next to the trophy showed the entire squad from the winning team. It featured a grinning Ryan sitting on the ground with a ball nestled in her lap. An equally happy Sara was standing directly behind her, the tips of her fingers resting lightly on Ryan's shoulders.

Jamie fought to keep the tears from her eyes, but she was completely unsuccessful. She heard the choked voice behind her whisper, "I went out the back door all during senior year just so I didn't have to look at this picture."

"I'm so sorry," Jamie cried as she flung her arms around Ryan's shaking body.

They hugged tightly for many minutes until Ryan finally lifted her head and said, "You can't have everything. If every single bit of this hadn't happened, I wouldn't have been at Cal last year. No matter what else has happened, not being with you would have been the real tragedy."

"Thanks," Jamie whispered as she kissed her softly.

Ryan looked down on her with a shy smile on her tear-streaked face. "Will you indulge one girlish fantasy for me?"

"Anything," Jamie said, knowing there was no request from her partner that she would refuse.

Ryan took her by the hand and led her to the grand entrance of the school. She pushed open the door and left Jamie on the first polished marble step while she stood on the next one down. She wrapped her arms around her lover and gave her a melancholy smile. "Kiss me like you don't believe it's a sin," she asked softly.

Looking at her partner with every ounce of love she possessed, Jamie voiced her true belief. "It's not a sin—it's a sacrament." She dipped her head and kissed her partner with every tender emotion she could muster.

No one was home for dinner, so they stopped to get carryout from one of Ryan's favorite Mexican restaurants. Jamie wasn't as enthusiastic as Ryan was about the merits of the neighborhood restaurants, but her lover got such pleasure from eating ethnic junk food that she willingly went along with her choice. As they cleaned up their mess, Jamie asked, "Can I see some more videos?"

"Sure. What are you interested in?"

"I want to see you close up. Do you have any of you just talking?"

"Yeah, I think I can find one," she said as she walked back into Martin's room.

Moments later, Ryan popped in a tape labeled, "Conor's graduation. 1989." "I like this one because my Aunt Moira is in it." As the tape began to roll, Jamie sat on the bed and watched a large number of black-robed people receive their high school diplomas. It was hard to tell who was who, but when it was time for Conor to receive his diploma Martin had obviously gone to the front of the stage, because a grinning Conor came into focus. He looked so young and innocent Jamie almost got tears in her eyes, seeing his callow features. Ryan fast-forwarded the tape, passing up the speakers and the procession of graduates. She started it again when the party began at the O'Flaherty home. The camera panned to a very young Ryan, the gangly fourteen-year-old coming into focus. She was holding a small baby. "That's my cousin Brenna," she said. "Isn't she a doll?"

Jamie had to admit that she was a doll, but she was referring to the baby-sitter more than the baby, even though both were adorable. Seconds later a small-boned, auburn-haired woman came into the picture, sitting next to Ryan and posing for the camera for a few moments. Jamie looked at the framed picture of Ryan's mother on the dresser and marveled at the similarities. "Wow, she looks just like your mom."

"Yeah," Ryan said with a trace of sadness in her voice. "I was always crazy for my Aunt Moira. I wonder if it's because she reminds me so much of Mama." The woman in the tape seemed equally fond of young Ryan. She wrapped her arm around her and kissed her cheek as they grinned together into the camera.

"She looks like she's pretty crazy for you, too," Jamie said.

"Yeah, she loves me a lot. I really want you to meet her. I know you'd love her, and she'd be over the moon for you."

"Then let's go," she said.

"Just like that?"

"Yeah, just like that. We can go before school starts if you want. We've got enough miles to go first-class."

"Oh, I'd have to think about it," she said warily. "I...I...let's talk about it later."

"Okay. But if you want to go, we'll go."

They turned their attention back to the screen. Moira took Brenna back, but the camera stayed focused on Ryan for a few minutes. She looked into the camera and said, in a voice that was a good octave higher than her adult tone, "Happy graduation, Conor. You're my favorite second oldest brother." She collapsed in a fit of giggles at her lame joke, and it was all Jamie could do not to go up to the TV and kiss that sweet, childlike face. Young Ryan got to her feet and stood and stretched for a moment, the camera still focused on her, but no longer aware that she was the object of attention. She shifted her weight onto one leg and put her arm around Conor, who now stood right next to her. The camera captured her burgeoning womanhood as she batted her bright blue eyes at her big brother. She was obviously not trying to look sexy, but there was something so appealing about this girl on the verge of womanhood that Jamie found herself totally aroused.

"Ryan, I swear I've never said these words before, and I swear I'll never say them again, but I'm getting hot looking at a fourteen-year-old girl!"

Ryan was behind her like a shot. She wrapped her arms around her and murmured into her ear, "What makes you hot?"

"I don't know," she said as the camera continued to focus on the young Ryan. "You're just so pure and virginal-looking. Like a statue of a young Greek goddess. There's something so completely sexy-looking about you at this age. It just boggles my mind."

"This is about when Conor's friends started treating me nicer," Ryan said with a smirk. "I thought they'd finally realized that I was cool, but in retrospect I think they wanted more than just to hang out with me."

"Conor would've killed them if they'd made a move on you."

"He wouldn't have been able to. After Da got done with them, there wouldn't have been enough left to make a stain on the carpet."

"Well, lucky for me, I get to have the adult version of that hot little girl," Jamie said as she leaned back against her lover.

Ryan flipped her over onto her back and was kissing her senseless when Conor started to enter the room a few moments later, unnoticed by the passionate partners. His voice nearly sent Jamie to the ceiling when he said, "Oh, darn, I thought maybe you had porn on."

He came into the room, and saw the image of his young sister on the TV. He gave Jamie a smirk and said, "You have no idea how many of my friends wanted to do just what you're doing to her."

They went to bed very early that night, the emotion of the day hitting both of them as soon as they lay down.

Both were well rested on Saturday morning, and Ryan actually felt better than she had in quite a while. Even though her talk with her former coach had been upsetting, it was just so satisfying to finally get some answers that she was quite upbeat.

Deciding to play a round of golf, they struggled for a good fifteen minutes to figure out a way to get Jamie's golf clubs into the Boxster. "This is ridiculous," Ryan muttered as Jamie finally had to hold the bag between her legs. The top had to be lowered to accommodate the height of the bag, and the cool, foggy morning was not ideal weather to go topless.

"I think we need to bite the bullet," Jamie said over the sound of the wind whistling through the clubs.

"What bullet is that?" Ryan shouted.

"We need a real car, and we need it now."

"Oh God," Ryan moaned, knowing that the determined look on her partner's face meant that the decision had already been made.

Ryan came up with so many suggestions for ways to avoid buying a new car that Jamie could hardly concentrate on her golf game. "Honey, why does this bother you so much?" she finally asked after she had shot down every one of Ryan's concerns.

"It's so much money!" she cried. "And it just seems ridiculous to have a big car in Berkeley."

"I doubt that we'll use it that much in Berkeley. I think we'll take it to San Francisco on the weekends and when we play golf."

Ryan stopped dead in her tracks and stared at her partner for a moment. "You're keeping the Boxster?"

"Well, yeah. I like the Boxster, and it was a gift from Daddy. I'd like to keep it for a long time. Maybe forever. It can be the first of my collection."

"Two cars? Two cars in Berkeley? Oh, Jamie, that's just ridiculous." She was shaking her head, looking like Jamie had asked if she could have a pony.

"Because...?"

"It's a waste. Most people our age don't have one car, we certainly don't need two."

Jamie climbed into the golf cart, composing her thoughts before she presented her case. "Okay," she finally said. "If you're certain that you don't feel comfortable with more than one car, I'll sell or trade in the Boxster."

Ryan smiled, amazed at winning the argument so easily. "I'm glad you're willing to see my point," she said as the cart lurched forward.

"So, when should we put the ads in the paper?"

"Ads?"

"Yeah. I'm sure we'll have to sell your Harley ourselves. Car dealers won't take it in trade."

The cart stopped so violently that it skidded a bit on the gravel path. "Sell my Harley? You've got to be kidding." Her blue eyes were so wide it was comical.

"You want one vehicle; isn't the bike a vehicle?" Her green eyes gave the appearance of total innocence, but Ryan knew that was a lie.

"But my bike is important to me. It's like a member of the family." Her voice took on a pathetic, pleading tone.

"The Boxster's important to me, too. It's not very practical, but it can be driven in the rain..." Her implication was clear, and Ryan wondered once again why her partner wasn't interested in going to law school, since she was obviously gifted as an advocate for her own position.

"Have I ever told you that I absolutely hate how your mind works?" Her smile extended to her eyes, but Jamie knew there wasn't a shred of honesty in her words.

"I really don't want to bulldoze you, but I'd buy another car if we weren't together, so why can't I do it now? It makes me uncomfortable to feel like I have to ask your permission to spend money. I've never liked to have anyone supervise my spending habits, and I don't think that's gonna change in the near future."

Ryan nodded, realizing that Jamie had probably never had to justify her spending to anyone. "I don't want you to feel like that. It's your money, and you can do whatever you want with it."

Jamie took her hand and gave it a small kiss, blowing the fine coating of sand from it as she smiled up at her partner. "One correction. It's our money, and I want to work together so we both feel comfortable spending it."

Ryan tossed an arm over her shoulders and gave her a squeeze. "If you truly want me to be comfortable, we'll work together to *not* spend it."

Jamie gave her a playful bump with her hip, deciding, "I guess it won't kill me if you're not comfortable."

When they returned home, Conor joined in the car debate, which raged on for quite a while. Conor had very strong opinions on SUVs, being strongly in favor of big, muscular V-8s powerful enough to pull a ton of passengers and cargo. Jamie wanted the smallest vehicle that would serve their needs, but she wanted a nice, comfortable ride. Ryan wanted the least expensive, sturdiest SUV available so long as it had four-wheel-drive. After ruling out most of the cars in the class, they were left with four: Jamie's choices, the Lexus RX 300 and the Mercedes ML 320, and Ryan's favorites, the Ford Explorer and the Nissan Xterra. Conor was still pulling for the Chevy Suburban, but when he realized that neither woman favored his choice, he sided with Jamie's pick of the Lexus. He argued that the Lexus was much more comfortable than the Explorer and that it had a good-sized engine that would be able to power them up the Sierra Nevada for skiing in the winter.

"How about I pick which of yours I want, and you pick which of mine you want?" Ryan proposed.

"Okay," Jamie said. "I pick the Explorer. The Xterra is cute, but it doesn't look very sturdy."

"I pick the Lexus," Ryan decided.

"How come?"

"No good reason," Ryan said. "I just don't feel old enough to buy a Mercedes."

Jamie laughed at her reasoning, reminding her, "There's no age requirement. I checked."

"That's my choice, and I'm sticking with it," Ryan said, dashing downstairs to her computer to do a little research on the two remaining choices. She logged onto the Internet and did a few searches, obtaining the list price for each basic vehicle and the price of every possible option. She also found out that Ford was offering a rebate on the base model Explorer which brightened her day significantly.

When her research didn't sway Jamie's vote, they decided to go test-drive both cars. But just as they were getting ready to leave, Tommy called and asked if they could watch the baby. They conferred and decided that she wouldn't be too much trouble, so they piled into Conor's truck and went to pick her up.

Since Ryan called dibs, they went to the Ford dealer first. Their feet had barely hit the ground before an eager salesman descended upon them. "Hi, folks," he beamed. "Lovely day to buy a new car, isn't it?"

Jamie took the lead, telling him that she and her friend, pointing to Ryan, wanted to look at an Explorer. He seemed to hear her, since he led them over to the huge selection of Explorers in every color and with every option. Ryan said she was only interested in the four-wheel-drive base model, and that's when she lost the salesman's interest. She was bouncing Caitlin on her hip and the salesman kept telling her how cute the little darling was, but she noticed that they didn't make their way toward the cars that she had indicated.

The salesman, Jay, kept chatting with Conor about the Explorer, trying to get Conor to declare his preferences. After allowing him to rattle on for a few minutes, Jamie pleasantly interrupted him. "Ah, Jay, my friend said she wanted to see the four-wheel-drive base model. Can you show us that?"

"Sure, sure," he said expansively. "I just was telling your husband that the next step up is well worth the price."

"He's not my husband," she said, "and he's not buying the car. We are," she said as she pointed again at Ryan.

"Oh, well, that's fine. No problem." He led them to a car that seemed to fit Ryan's description, but he once again directed his comments to Conor, completely ignoring Ryan.

Jamie had finally had enough. "Jay," she said sweetly, "Ryan here is the one who's interested in this car. Why don't you answer her questions?"

He turned to Conor and laughed a bit. Looking back at Jamie he said, "Your boyfriend and your baby would be a lot more comfortable in the Limited Edition. Why don't we look at that first?"

Jamie stared at her shoes for a moment, then looked up at Jay with a deadly smile. "He's not my boyfriend. He's not my husband. That's not my baby. But *she's* my girlfriend and *she's* the one who wants to look at this stupid car. If she wants it, I'm buying it for her. So the only two people that you should be addressing are her and me."

"Oh," he said, the light starting to come on. "Oh! Okay, so this is just for you two. Jeez," he laughed, finding the situation quite humorous. "Honest mistake. You can just never tell in San Francisco, can you?" he asked with a weak chuckle. "You girls just don't look like…"

"*Like what?*" Jamie asked, with fire in her green eyes.

"Uhm, like…uhm…like you're old enough to buy a car like this," he said with a strained smile on his sweating face.

Conor walked over to Ryan, picked up the baby, turned on his heel and began to walk away, calling over his shoulder, "I still say the Lexus is the better car, but I'll leave you kids to your fun."

Jay was stuck with the now steaming Jamie and the less perturbed, but still miffed Ryan. "Heh, heh," he chuckled nervously. "So, who wants to drive?"

Ryan decided to conduct the test drive. But she was thwarted once again by having to follow a prescribed route around the block—once. This tiny track didn't allow her to take it over potholes or railroad tracks or any of the other normal hazards of city driving. The heavy traffic didn't allow her to go over thirty miles an hour, so she had no idea how the car accelerated. All in all, it was a frustrating experience that was exacerbated by Jay's constant rambling from the backseat. Ryan's head was throbbing by the time they returned to the lot. She tossed the keys over her shoulder, nearly hitting Jay in the head as she muttered, "We'll let you know." Jamie trotted behind her, catching up as they reached Conor and the baby who were waiting by the truck. Jamie heard her partner mutter "fuck-head" as she got into the passenger seat, meeting Conor's wide-eyed expression with a warning shake of her head. For a change, he didn't try to make the situation worse, and they rode in silence to the Lexus dealer.

When they arrived, Jamie launched into her business mode immediately, striding into the dealership and asking to speak to the floor manager. An attractive woman came out and Jamie introduced herself. "Hi, I'm Jamie Evans. This is my lover, Ryan O'Flaherty. We're interested in buying an RX 300. We'd like to speak to someone who doesn't mind working with women and who isn't shocked by lesbianism. Do you have anyone who can help us?"

The woman laughed and extended her hand. "I'm Sandra Fletcher. I rather like working with women, and I've known a few lesbians in my life.

I've yet to be shocked by them, unless they were purposely going for that reaction, so I can probably help you."

"Great," Jamie said. "We haven't seen the car yet, so we want to see what you have, what options are available, and then we want to take a test drive. Ryan is quite the car buff, and she's only interested in buying if we can go on a real test drive with a route of our own choosing. Can you arrange that too?"

"Sure," she said easily. "We trust our customers to take the cars wherever they wish. No problem at all."

Conor poked his head out from around the corner and asked, "Is it safe?"

Jamie laughed and motioned him over. "Sandra, this is Ryan's brother and their cousin, Caitlin. Conor's a little nervous about being treated like the brains in this organization, so feel free to ignore him."

"I bet you're not ignored very often," Sandra said with a wink.

"I like this place lots better than the last," Conor said, as they walked toward the lot.

The cars were remarkably similar, with very few options available. Every car on the lot came with leather seating and all had CD players installed, so the only choice to be made was color. "Which one do you want to drive?" Sandra asked.

"I like burgundy," Jamie said. Ryan had no objection, so Sandra went into the office and came back with the keys. She handed them to Jamie and said, "Have a nice ride."

"You're not coming with us?" Ryan asked.

"Nope. I just needed to copy your driver's licenses for our insurance. We trust you."

"I'll stay as your security deposit," Conor offered, giving Sandra a grin.

She smiled back at him and said, "If they don't come back, can I keep you?"

"You can keep me even if they do come back."

"Let's go," Ryan said as she rolled her eyes. "This is getting painful."

Much to her regret, Ryan thoroughly enjoyed driving the vehicle. It rode very much like a car, but it had all the beneficial attributes of an SUV. Jamie loved the ride and the numerous appointments that came standard, and she played with the moon roof and the CD player until she nearly drove Ryan to distraction.

"Honey, can you leave the little buttons alone for just a minute?" Ryan asked patiently.

"I like the buttons," Jamie replied. "That's the best part of car shopping."

"You really like this car, don't you?"

"Yeah, I do. Don't you?"

"Yeah, it's really nice, but I just feel funny spending this much for a car. We could get by so much cheaper."

"That's true, but why not get what we want if we can afford it?"

"I don't know. It just seems so extravagant."

"Is this you talking or something else?" Jamie asked, her suspicions awakened.

Ryan thought about the question for a few moments, her face scrunched up in a frown. "It's partly me and partly my upbringing," she finally said. "It's frowned upon to show how much money you have. The 'poor mouth' was invented in Ireland, you know," she added with a small chuckle. "If you win the Sweepstakes and someone asks how you're doing you should say, 'Oh, just barely making the ends meet. It's a struggle every day.'"

Jamie laughed at her adorable brogue, but showed her understanding by saying, "If you really feel uncomfortable, we can buy something much less expensive. But your family's gonna know that I've got money, so I don't think it'll be a shock for them if we have a nice car."

"Okay, let me think about it. You're leaving the decision up to me?"

"Yeah. I choose this, but I don't want to do anything that you don't feel good about. You're the one who'll be driving it most of the time, so you need to get what you want."

When they got back to the dealership they went into Sandra's office. Conor was already there, entertaining his captive audience. He was a hit, as usual, with Caitlin, but Sandra seemed to be enjoying herself also. "So, how did you enjoy the test drive?" Sandra asked as Ryan set the keys on the desk.

"We both liked it," Ryan said, "but I need to think about it for a few minutes. Conor, can I talk to you?"

"Sure," he said as he hopped up and handed Jamie the baby. "Hang on to this for me, will you?" he joked as he followed Ryan out. When they'd moved away from Sandra's office, he asked, "What's up?"

"Jamie really likes this one, and I do, too, but I'm uncomfortable spending this much money on a car. What do you think the rest of the family will think if we start buying things like this?"

"Are you really worried about that?"

"Yeah, I am," she said. "I don't want to look like we're lording it over everyone else."

"Everybody likes Jamie, and I think they know she's got bucks. I mean it's kind of obvious after you've been around her for a while. She just looks rich," he said with a smile. "I don't think they'd want you to live like everyone else if you've really got it. That's almost insulting. It's like you're saying, 'We've got money, but we act like we're poor because we know you'll be jealous.' I don't think that would go over well, sis."

She slid her arms around his waist and gave him a firm hug. "Thanks, Conor. That helped a lot."

As they entered the office Jamie piped up, "Did you know this and the Mercedes are the only two SUVs that have side-impact protection systems? Caitlin would be much safer..."

Ryan sighed, still feeling a little sick to her stomach. "You don't have to sell me on the car," she said. "I like it, I really do. It's just so much money."

Now Sandra jumped into the discussion. "Jamie tells me that you're also interested in the Explorer. Would you feel more comfortable if I could sell you a Lexus for around the same price?"

"Uhm, that'd be nice," Ryan drawled. "Would we get a title with it, or is it hot?"

"It's not hot," she assured her. "And it's already been broken in."

An hour later, the twosome was cruising home in their gently used, one-year-old, sand-colored Lexus, both happy with the outcome of the negotiations. "Don't you love this?" Jamie asked excitedly as she once again punched every available button.

Ryan gave her an indulgent smile and admitted, "It's absolutely marvelous. I'm as excited as I was when I bought my Harley."

"Remind me to call my trust officer and ask him to make an income distribution to cover this, will you?"

"How'd you pay for it?" Ryan asked with a frown, unaware of the financial negotiations since she'd been changing Caitlin's diaper during much of them.

"I charged it, of course."

"You charged it?"

"Yep. I charge everything for the airline miles. This little baby," she said fondly as she patted the dash, "just added enough points for a free trip to Europe."

The rest of Saturday was spent giving Ryan's uncles rides in the car, and much to Jamie's amazement, each cousin was allowed to take it for a test drive. She had assumed that Ryan would be protective of her first car, and wouldn't let another driver within ten feet of it, but she was pleased to see that her partner was more concerned with her cousins' feelings than she was for her car. When the last of the test drives was completed it was a little after 9:00, and minutes after getting horizontal, Ryan was sound asleep, the owner's manual for the Lexus spread open on her chest like a tiny blanket.

This is so cute, Jamie giggled softly upon emerging from the bath. *She's just like a kid with a cherished new toy. I bet that manual is memorized by tomorrow night.* She gently removed the book, turning off the bedside lamp as she did so. Ryan murmured something unintelligible, and made an uncoordinated attempt to hold on to the manual, but Jamie tenderly patted her and assured her, "Don't worry, love, your little book will be right here in the morning, just waiting to be devoured."

Chapter Seven

"**W**anna go for a little run with me, punkin?"

The warm, moist breath that caressed Jamie's ear made her think of nothing but snuggling a little tighter against the speaker, and she decided to do just that. During the night Ryan had chased her to the very edge of the bed, where she now lay on her left side, dangerously close to being pushed off. Her partner's heavy arm was draped around her waist, and as a sign of acknowledgment of the question Jamie grasped it and tugged until Ryan's large hand rested comfortably on her breast. Letting out a very heavy sigh, she twitched her butt against Ryan's lap and dozed off immediately.

Hmm, what to do? What to do? Ryan thought, trying to resist the lure of Jamie's warm embrace so she could think clearly. *Two more seconds of being wrapped around her like this, and I'm gonna be out like a light. And the problem with that is what?* She smirked at her compulsive nature and cuddled up as tightly as she could, her own sigh rivaling Jamie's as she joined her beloved in slumber.

"You're very bad for my discipline, you know," Ryan teased an hour later, while they were running up the first big hill on Noe.

"It's Sunday, we don't have to be anywhere until Mass, and we can easily go to the eleven o'clock if we miss the nine-thirty. What's the problem?"

"No problem at all, Jamers. It's just odd for me to be tempted to stay in bed. It's something I'm *so* not used to."

Jamie cast a sidelong glance at her and asked, "You don't mind, do you? I mean…"

Ryan saw the tentative look she was getting and reached out with a long arm to grasp the hem of her partner's T-shirt. Pulling Jamie to a halt and immediately wrapping her in a hug, she promised, "Not only don't I mind, it's one of the most decadently delicious feelings in the world. Lying in bed with you in the morning is honestly the highlight of my day." She bent a little and tilted her head to offer a gentle kiss, which Jamie gladly accepted.

"I love it too," the smaller woman agreed, adding a tiny kiss of her own. "It makes me feel so warm, and safe, and loved. I feel like a little bear cub all curled up in her mother's embrace."

Taking off again, Ryan mulled over her partner's comments for a moment. "Bear cub, huh? Strangely enough, that feels apt. When I'm wrapped around you I feel kinda like a big brown bear protecting my precious cub."

"And when I'm cuddling you, I feel protective, too," Jamie mused. "We're a pair, aren't we?" She laughed gently, her eyes crinkling up in the grin that Ryan so loved.

"We are indeed," Ryan conceded, a devilish look coming over her as she grasped Jamie's hand firmly and hung a hard right, careening down 21st Street, one of the steepest in the city. Once they started down the hill, their momentum propelled them all the way to the bottom, both women laughing riotously.

"Are you trying to kill me?" Jamie panted as they slowed to a jog when they reached the foot of the steep incline. "You know I can't keep up with you."

"It wasn't up," Ryan innocently insisted, "it was down. Why should that be a problem?"

"You big goof!" Her outrage was mostly faked, and the hard swat she gave to Ryan's butt was entirely playful, but Ryan was clearly in an even more playful mood, and she began to chase Jamie back up the hill, trying to grab her for a pinch.

Halfway up, they passed a couple saying their good-nights, even though it was after 8:00 a.m. The woman was mostly sitting in the driver's seat of a shiny, new, jade green BMW 325i convertible, with a man trying to resist being pulled into the driver's seat—headfirst. His long frame was bent completely over, one bare foot off the ground as he struggled, and Ryan wondered how his equipment was going to avoid injury if the obviously determined woman had her way. They were kissing passionately, but it was apparent that this was a bit of a game, too, and Ryan gave a nod of approval to the woman. *Go for it, sister*, she smirked as they passed. Jamie had slowed noticeably, no longer able to maintain their chase, and as Ryan turned to check on her progress she took another look at the poor fellow who was being manhandled so effectively, nearly screaming when she realized that it was Brendan. *Oh my God. I guess he's not thinking of joining the priesthood.*

With regret, Brendan wrenched himself away from his date's clutches just as Jamie drew near. He gaped when he saw her, and she gasped aloud when he stood and she realized that he was wearing only a pair of boxer shorts. Her startled eyes went to his groin and then to his face, as his equally startled eyes went from her face to his groin, and he slapped his knees together audibly as he crossed his large hands over the main feature he didn't share with his sister. As his eyes lifted again, Jamie saw the near-pleading look in their blue depths, and she mercifully looked away, trying her best to appear to be a casual jogger.

Ryan did the same, turning and running up the hill, leaving Brendan what little dignity he had left at the moment.

By the time both women reached the crest of the hill, Jamie was slapping Ryan forcefully while accusing, "I thought he didn't have a girlfriend!"

Fending off her blows, Ryan defended herself. "I didn't know he did! Believe me, that was the last thing I wanted to see."

"Jesus. I'll never be able to look him in the eye again."

Ryan rolled her own blue orbs dramatically, getting to the real problem. "If you'd been looking in his eyes, neither one of you would be embarrassed right now."

"Well, God, Ryan. A man in boxer shorts that would wake the dead stands up right in front of me. It was kinda like a car accident. I knew I should avert my eyes, but I just couldn't help myself."

Ryan grimaced as she recalled, "Those shorts were wild. The last time I did his laundry, he was still wearing tighty-whities."

An impish look covered Jamie's face as she observed, "I thought they were kinda cute, and Lord knows he didn't look like he had a thing to be ashamed of."

Ryan jabbed her fingers into her ears, and she began to hum some nonsense song loudly, not stopping until Jamie signaled that she would behave. "I prefer to think of my brothers as life-sized Ken dolls," she said. "In my mind they're perfectly smooth 'down there,' thank you very much, and you can just keep any evidence to the contrary to yourself." It took a second for Jamie to realize that Ryan was being totally serious.

"I'm sorry. That was really insensitive of me. God, I can only imagine how I'd feel if you saw my father's...uhm...assets." She shivered all over, and Ryan joined her as the image of seeing Jim's bare ass at his city apartment once again lodged in her mind.

"New topic," Ryan begged, knowing this was dangerous ground. "How 'bout this weather we've been having, huh? Think it's gonna rain?"

"Okay," Jamie agreed. "Let's just go home, take a shower, and go to church. Maybe if we pray hard enough we can be blessed with selective amnesia."

Before Jamie could blink, Ryan was running down the street, obviously intent on trying the suggestion.

After Mass, they sat at the dining room table with Conor and Martin, keeping their own counsel about the incident, when Martin commented, "I wonder why Brendan wasn't at Mass this morning? I hope he's not under the weather."

Having seen her brother lurking in the last pew when she returned from communion, Ryan only said, "I'll run over and check on him. You don't mind doing my share of the cleanup, do you?"

"Of course not," Jamie agreed immediately. "You go visit with your brother."

Martin gave her a slightly puzzled glance, probably thinking that the telephone was an easier means of finding out the information, but he just patted her on the shoulder and said, "If he's not well, I'll bring him some lunch later."

"I'm sure he's fine, Da. Maybe he's just taking it easy this morning." *Or maybe he's gonna hide until Jamie and I forget that we saw him in his skivvies.*

Her hesitant knock was answered quickly, as if Brendan was expecting a visit. He opened the door and turned without a word, crossing the room to sink listlessly onto the sofa. "Go ahead," he muttered, sounding thoroughly defeated.

"Go ahead with what?" She followed him across the room to grab a straight-backed chair and straddle it.

"Grill me about her," he grumbled.

She leaned forward in the chair, balancing on two of the sturdy legs. This activity was expressly prohibited in her own house, and she indulged in the forbidden pleasure every chance she got. Her hand reached out to pat him lightly on the leg and she said, "I'd never do that to you, Bren. I wanted to apologize for catching you at a bad moment."

His black hair had fallen over one eye, and he glanced over at her warily as he pushed it back in place. "Really? You're not gonna bust my chops?"

"Why would I do that?" She was actually quite insulted that he would assume she would be so crass. "I never treat you like that."

His elbows were resting on his knees, and he dropped his head into his hands and shook it roughly. "I'm sorry. I honestly don't know whether I'm coming or going. I just, I just don't know what I'm doing." He looked so forlorn that she couldn't stay angry with him.

"That's okay, Bren. Tell me what's up." She had a very good idea of what was going on, since she'd been in the same situation just a few months before, but she wanted him to tell her, if he felt comfortable doing so.

"I'm really confused about this." He ran his hands through his hair, causing a shock of the thick black locks to fall forward again. "I just don't know what to do."

Rocking slowly on the chair, Ryan nodded her encouragement, staying quiet to let him think.

"Have I ever told you about Maggie Reardon?"

Ryan shook her head, reminding her brother, "You've never talked about any girl, Brendan. For all I know, you're gay."

"*Gay?* You think I'm gay?"

His look was a cross between shock and outrage, and Ryan immediately grew defensive. "Hey! It's not like that's a bad thing, ya know."

He blushed deeply as he shook his head again, looking frustrated and embarrassed. "Of course it's not. I just had no idea that you'd think that."

"I don't really," she said, "but that's one viable explanation for why you keep your life so private."

He got up and paced across the floor, looking very serious. "I just fell into the habit when I was young. It's really nice not to be the focus of teasing about my personal life, and I've gotten used to it. I mean, if you could have privacy, wouldn't you want it?"

She thought about that for a moment, acknowledging that she had weathered an awful lot of teasing from her entire family throughout the years. Most of it, she had to admit, came from her almost pathological need to share her life with her family, and she had to concede that she would have gotten off a lot easier if she had been less forthcoming about things. "I see your point," she said. "So, now that you've been outed as a straight guy, tell me about her."

He gave her his first smile of the day and began, "We met when we were in law school. End of fall term, first year." His pacing stilled, and his face took on a faraway look as he recalled, "I was totally gone, sis. I was certain that she was the one, and as things went on, I gave serious thought to asking her to marry me when we graduated."

Ryan's eyes went wide at this disclosure. She'd always assumed that Brendan had dates and that he probably enjoyed the intimate company of women, but she'd never seriously considered that he might have fallen in love at one point. "What happened?" she asked.

"We started interviewing for jobs at the beginning of our third year," he said. "After I saw her list of choices, it became clear that she was focused on returning to Chicago. That's her home, you know."

Ryan nodded, even though she obviously had not known.

"Luckily, I hadn't broached the topic of marriage, so at least I didn't look like a total fool." He chuckled mirthlessly as he kicked at an imaginary object on the rug. "She got an offer from a big firm in Chicago and accepted it before she even told me about it."

"So she didn't feel the way you did?" she asked gently.

"Oh, she said she did," he said. "She seemed to think that I'd follow her to Chicago. But that's not my home," he said. "I loved her, but I'd been gone long enough. I couldn't wait to get back home again." Ryan nodded, knowing that it would be virtually impossible for her to leave San Francisco permanently. "She felt the same way about her family and Chicago," he said. "We must not have loved each other enough, because neither of us was willing to give up our needs for the other."

Thank you, God, for making Jamie be from the Bay Area. I know I'd follow her anywhere, but I'd be miserable living a thousand miles from my home. "So have you kept in touch?"

"No. It was too painful," he said, "but I've never met anyone I was more attracted to. And now that she's here…" He trailed off, clearly at a loss.

"What's the problem, Bren? Does she live here now?"

"Yeah, she moved here a few months ago. Her firm needed a second chair for some high-profile trials they're involved in." He shook his head slowly, looking at his sister with sad blue eyes. "She's not the same, Ryan. I mean, I'm still really attracted to her, as you could probably tell. But she's not the same girl I fell in love with."

"She's not a girl any longer, Bren. She's almost thirty years old, if she's your age. People change a lot in their twenties."

"I know, I know," he conceded. "I just, she's not shy and quiet and innocent like she was then." Looking like he was on the verge of tears, he said, "She's a shark."

"A shark? How do you mean that?"

"A high-powered attorney shark," he grumbled disdainfully. "She's…aggressive now."

"Oh," she nodded. "She's a top now, huh?"

"Top?" His confused mind considered the question and a slow flush crept up his cheeks, and he squeaked, "You mean uhm…sexually?"

A broad smile settled on Ryan's face as she regarded his blushing countenance. "No, Bren, I actually meant her attitude. It sounds like her job has toughened her up and made her more dominant."

Now his blush grew even fiercer, and he nodded his head quickly. "She's dominant all right. Jesus, Ryan, I'm complaining about her, but I hardly recognize myself. She's got me wearing these ridiculous boxer shorts, I'm running around the neighborhood almost naked just to get another kiss. I'm losing my mind!"

The voice of experience waggled an eyebrow as she asked in a conspiratorial tone, "That's not a bad thing, is it? It's kinda nice to be with someone who brings out your wild side."

He gulped noticeably and agreed completely. "No, it's ahh…kinda nice. But it's so weird. I don't know if she was always like this and I didn't notice it, or if she's really changed that much."

"Probably a little of both," she guessed. "People don't generally have major personality changes in just a few years. She probably just chose a line of work that helped bring out her natural aggression."

He flopped down on the sofa again and moaned, "Don't remind me. We always talked about doing something meaningful. But now she's a…she's a…" his mouth curled into a grimace as he spat out, "litigator."

"Oh, you poor baby." She got up from her chair and sat on the arm of the sofa, draping her arm around his slumped shoulders and giving him a hug. Ryan had always considered Brendan one of the most anti-lawyer lawyers in the world. He loved his job and was very proud of the work he did, but he had an intense dislike that bordered on hatred for large corporate law firms and their legions of highly paid hired guns. "What kind of law does she practice?"

"Corporate," he grumbled. "The fattest of the fat cats."

"So she what…? Forecloses on widows and orphans?" She was clearly teasing him now, but he wasn't in the mood to play the game, and he answered seriously.

"No, although I'm sure she would if they told her to. She does a lot of work with the dot coms. Right now she's working on a very big suit brought by recording artists against one of those music download sites." Ryan knew that the Bay Area had been the birthplace of the Internet start-up phenomenon, and many of the tiny companies had been catapulted into multimillion-dollar firms at their first offering of stock to the public. She was also very familiar with the MP3 music-sharing sites and knew that the record companies were doing whatever they could to shut them down.

"Well, that's not so bad, Bren. It's not like she's stealing from the poor to give to the rich."

Her words provided little solace to her brother, and he continued to slump against the couch. "It doesn't mean anything. That's my point. It's just a very, very large paycheck to do nothing of importance. She's so bright and has such a good heart. It sickens me that she's using her brain to make a bunch of nineteen-year-old computer geeks into multimillionaires. She could make such a difference if she would use her skills to help people."

Ryan hated to burst Brendan's bubble, but she felt that she needed to be honest. "She can't help people if that isn't where her heart lies. Maybe that's not who she is."

He got up so abruptly that he almost knocked her off the arm of the couch. Once again he started to pace around his small apartment, his arms crossed against his chest, hands shoved into his armpits. "That's my problem. I don't know who she is anymore. I can't figure it out."

"What does she say when you talk about this stuff? Does she want to continue doing this kind of work? Is she happy with her job?"

He blushed again, looking over at Ryan through a lock of black hair hanging over his eyes. "We uhm, don't really talk all that much," he admitted. "She works ungodly hours, and, well, you know how it is," he added, looking to her for understanding.

"I do indeed," she nodded. "But you need to stay vertical a little while and discuss these things. If you let yourself fall in love with her again and then find out you can't make a go of it, it's gonna be brutal."

"It's too late for that, Ryan," he said softly, looking like he was confessing to a homicide. "I'm already gone."

She rose from her perch and came over to give him a firm hug. "I'm happy for you, Bren. I'd love to meet her." Pulling back, but leaving her arms around his waist, she warned, "You'd better bring her over for dinner soon, or you'll never hear the end of it. Da would be devastated to know you're this serious about someone he's never met."

"I will, I will," he mumbled. "I've just been waiting until I felt more settled about the whole thing. I've never felt this out-of-control."

"Bad news, bro," she regretfully informed him, a wry smirk firmly settled on her face. "That feeling lasts for a very, very long time."

After their discussion, Ryan convinced Brendan to play a round of golf with them in the afternoon. They chose a public course, and the interminable wait for nearly every shot gave them plenty of time to chat.

Brendan was very forthcoming with Jamie about his dilemma, and she provided, as usual, a very sympathetic ear. Watching them interact, Ryan mused once again about how lucky she was to have chosen such an empathetic, loving partner. All of the boys acted like Jamie was as close as kin, and Ryan spent a moment hoping that she would eventually feel that way toward Brendan's love.

"So, if I bring her to dinner, you guys will both back me up?" he asked while they were knocking the heads off some tall weeds and waiting to tee up on the sixth hole.

"Absolutely," Jamie said. "Do you think she'll have a hard time with the teasing?"

He laughed at that and assured her, "She comes from a big family, too. I think she's used to our type of humor."

"Why did she leave Chicago? Was she forced to transfer?"

He shook his head quickly, a slight furrow settled on his forehead. "No, she was...I guess she had her heart broken. She was dating this guy for almost five years and finally realized that he was never going to be willing to get married, so she broke up with him. She wants to have a family, and she wouldn't give that up for the guy."

Ryan did the math and computed that Maggie must have gone directly from Brendan to the unnamed boyfriend, since not quite six years had passed since he graduated from law school. "Is she really over him?" she asked, trying not to sound suspicious.

He pursed his lips and nodded thoughtfully. "Yeah, I think so. She says she spent the last year trying to give him a chance to change his mind, but he didn't want kids, and he wasn't even sure he wanted to marry." He looked down at his sister and commented, "I don't get that."

"I don't either, Bren," she said, smiling at her partner. "I don't either. They don't call it marital bliss for nothing."

Weeks earlier, they had tried to arrange a date for Reverend Evans to finally come for Sunday dinner, but due to scheduling conflicts, this was the first day he'd been available. Jamie had been relaxed about the meeting, but as the day wore on she began to get more and more agitated. He was due to arrive at 5:30, and as the time grew near, her discomfort grew. "You're nervous, aren't you?" Ryan asked with a chuckle as Jamie checked her watch for the fifth time.

She agreed, holding her thumb and index finger an inch apart. "A tiny bit."

"What makes you nervous?" Ryan asked as she got up and wrapped her arms around Jamie from behind.

Jamie clasped her hands over Ryan's arms and turned her head just enough to kiss her cheek. "I'm not sure. He's crazy about you, and I'm sure everyone will be nice to him. I guess it just means a lot to me to have everyone like him."

"He's one of the most likeable men I've ever met," Ryan assured her. "Everyone likes your grandfather."

"I know," she said as she nodded. "It's just important to me."

"Don't worry. We love anyone you love. It comes with the package. Now let's go pick him up and stop worrying about it, okay?"

"Okay," she agreed, accepting a kiss and a gentle hug that, as usual, helped calm her anxiety.

Two hours later, Charlie and Martin were regaling each other with their favorite stories while Brendan, Conor, Ryan, and Jamie worked away in the kitchen, cleaning up the huge mess that was the result of Martin's elaborate meal. "Your grandfather is a great guy," Brendan said.

"Yeah," Conor agreed. "He hardly seems like a priest at all. He's like a real guy."

"Well, he is a real guy," Jamie said with a laugh.

"You know what I mean," he said. "Father Pender's a guy, but he doesn't seem like a real guy. Maybe it's because Episcopal priests can marry," he mused. "I have a hard time trusting anyone who takes a vow of celibacy. Makes me doubt his sanity," he said in a completely serious tone.

"Conor's spiritual leanings run very deep," Ryan joked as she snapped him on the butt with a dish towel.

"I just can't understand believing in a God who gives you all these fun parts and then tells you not to use them," he said. "You Episcopalians have the right idea."

"No confession either, Conor," Jamie said.

"Jeez, why didn't we go that way? I think I'm gonna switch."

"You don't belong to anything," Ryan scoffed. "How can you switch?"

"Good point as usual, sis."

"I'm a little surprised that you two don't go to Charlie's church," Brendan said.

"We're still not locked in with the Catholics," Ryan said, "but St. Phil's is convenient, and it's nice to help out with Caitlin. We probably should formally join a church one of these days. We might well wind up Episcopalians. I'm about on my last nerve with Rome."

"Most of us are," Brendan said. "Luckily the Vatican doesn't have all that much influence at the parish level."

"Well, I'd sure like to keep them out of my bedroom," Ryan grumbled.

The phone rang, and since dinner was over, Ryan was free to answer. "Hello?"

"Hey, Ryan. Niall. The boys are going to come over and play cards. You guys up for it?"

"Tonight?" she asked, her brow furrowing a bit.

"Yeah. Right now. You're done with dinner, aren't ya?"

"Yeah. We're finished eating, but I can't play. Jamie's grandfather's here for dinner. Let me see if the boys want to. Hold on a sec."

Holding the phone against her blouse she asked in her usual familial shorthand, "Cards?"

"Where?" Brendan asked.

"Niall's."

Brendan smiled. "Cool."

"I'm in," Conor agreed.

Before Ryan could pick the phone back up, Jamie placed a hand over hers and asked, "Would you like to play?"

Her response was immediate. "Yeah. I love to play with the guys, but there will be plenty of games. No big deal."

"Honey, if you want to play, go right ahead. To tell you the truth, I'd like a little alone time with Poppa. Get a ride with the boys, and after I spend some time at Poppa's, I'll come join you."

"Cool." Ryan's eyes lit up and she informed her cousin, "Count us in, Niall. Beer, chips, and chairs?"

"Right-o," he replied. "See ya."

"Beer, chips, and chairs?" Jamie asked, unsure of what that code meant.

"Yeah. Niall has no furniture, so we all have to bring our own chairs. This group eats chips like there's no tomorrow, so we always bring extra. The beer is self-evident," she added with a grin.

Jamie leaned against her, pinning her to the kitchen counter. "You be careful trying to keep up with the boys, slugger."

"You're going to bring me home, so I don't have to be careful," Ryan reminded her with a kiss to the tip of her nose. "I can drink myself into a stupor."

"That is an image I cannot conceive of," Jamie said, laughing.

"Why can't I find a girl that encourages me to play cards and doesn't mind when I drink?" Conor said. "Ryan gets all the breaks."

"Keep one around long enough to learn her last name, and maybe you can get a break too," Ryan replied, tilting her head to give Jamie a chaste kiss. Neither woman moved, each staring lovingly into the eyes of the other, until Brendan finally had to break the mood.

"We gonna go, or make eyes at each other all night?"

"We're going," Ryan said, waving him on. "Give me a minute to say good-bye to my girl."

"We won't start the car," Conor said, "I've only got a half tank of gas."

"Go to the Necessaries and buy the beer and chips," she said, naming the tiny store located at the end of their block. The proper name of the place was the Resident Store, but for some reason the O'Flahertys had always called it the Necessaries. "I'll be waiting for you when you get back."

"Sure you will," Conor scoffed, bending to kiss Jamie on the top of her head. "See you later, short stuff."

She swatted him on the seat as he walked by, sticking out her tongue for good measure. "I'm not considered short when I'm among normal-sized people, Conor."

"Ooh, are you gonna let her talk like that about us, Ryan?"

"I've got no control over her mouth, Conor," Ryan said, smiling down at her impish partner.

"Sure you do," Jamie purred, lacing her hands through Ryan's hair as she pulled her down for a scorcher. They smiled through the kiss as they heard two sets of feet beat a hasty retreat. They had quickly learned that nothing cleared a room like a serious kiss, but they used the trick judiciously, to make sure they didn't wear it out.

"You sure you don't mind if I go?"

Jamie shook her head, her fine blonde tresses swaying with the movement. "Not at all. I really need to devote some quality time to Poppa, and this gives me a good opportunity. Have fun, and don't let them take all of your money."

Ryan smiled and kissed all around her face, delighting in the giggles she could always elicit. Her lips moved to Jamie's ear, and she whispered, "How do you know we play for money?"

"Because you're O'Flahertys," Jamie whispered back, the answer obvious to even the most casual observer.

At 10:00 Liam let Jamie in the door of the small house in Sunset. Peering through the smoke, she saw her lover sitting at a redwood table that had obviously been brought in from the backyard, the only furnished part of Niall's home. Ryan sat on a stackable metal chair, rocking back and forth on the two back legs, her own legs splayed wide apart for balance. Several tightly fanned cards were tucked into her left hand, a long, lit cigar in her right. "Oh goody," Jamie muttered, causing Liam to chuckle, "cigars!"

Only Donal and Ryan were playing the current hand, and neither dark head so much as twitched in her direction, even though Jamie was certain Ryan knew she had entered the room. Her face was completely impassive, as was Donal's, and every set of eyes in the room flicked from one to the other, waiting for the next move. A sizeable sum of money was lying on the table, most of it singles, but Jamie spotted a few tens and twenties in the pile. *My God, I can't imagine her throwing away money like this. And smoking! What else don't I know about her?*

In front of Ryan lay a four, a six, a seven, an eight, and a nine, all hearts. Jamie was quite familiar with poker and played seven-card stud frequently, so she assumed Ryan held a five and either a three or a ten in her hand. Donal was displaying a mess on the table, showing aces of clubs and diamonds and not much else. Jamie assumed he had the other two aces in his hand, but if her guess about Ryan's hand was correct, she would beat his four of a kind. Donal leveled his gaze at Ryan and spoke, "Show 'em."

She smirked slightly and placed two cards on the table, now displaying her complete hand: a deuce, a four, a six, a seven, an eight, a nine, and an ace—all of hearts.

With a vicious slap of his hand on the solid table, Donal jumped to his feet and cried, "God damn it! God damn it all to hell. She got me again."

Ryan didn't even look up, smiling serenely as she pulled the cash toward herself and started to organize it. "H'lo, Jamie," she said blithely, her words a little mumbled since she was forced to stick the rather large cigar into her mouth to gather up her loot.

Donal had stalked off to the backyard to cool off, and Jamie snuck around to his side of the table to pick up his cards. She nearly dropped them when she saw that he carried one ace and a seven of diamonds in his hand. "You lunatics were betting this kind of pot with three of a kind and a flush?"

Ryan's lone raised eyebrow and her nodding head were her only answer. The pot was now neatly arranged, and she withdrew the cigar and exhaled a series of smoke rings into the air. "Cards is more about guts than luck," she said, obviously pleased with herself.

The remaining family members all laughed at that, with Brendan correcting her. "No, Ryan, cards is all about playing with the one member of the family that doesn't believe you can count 'em. The rest of us have learned our lesson."

Jamie cast a suspicious glance in her partner's direction and went down her list. "I didn't know you smoked, I didn't know you bet this kind of money, and I certainly didn't know you could count cards. Anything else you'd like to reveal tonight?"

"I could be convinced," she said with a saucy grin. "Let's go home and I'll show you." The men all laughed at the nonplussed look on Jamie's face, and Ryan immediately apologized. "Sorry, babe, I've been with the unwashed masses too long. They're rubbing off on me."

Jamie crossed over to her, grasping her chin to tilt her head toward the light. "You're looking a little glassy, love. I think your tongue has been loosened by too much beer."

"Ohh…" Conor began, but both women glared at him, and he kept his ribald comment to himself.

"Let's go," Jamie urged, pulling Ryan to her feet.

Donal stormed back into the house just as they started for the door, demanding, "Hey, no fair. You've gotta give me a chance to get even."

Ryan shook her head, knowing that would never happen. "What did you start with?"

"Fifty," he muttered, slightly embarrassed.

She extracted the wad from her pocket and peeled off two twenties. "Don't bring so much money next time." Jamie was amazed when the lanky young man accepted the refund and shoved it into his pocket.

"Thanks," he said, pulling her into a hug.

"Hey, I lost money too," Conor complained.

"You were out of that last hand before I had my cards in order," she scoffed, ruffling his hair affectionately.

"I didn't say I lost it to you," he said. "I just lost it."

"Let's go, babe," Ryan said, turning to Jamie. "I have a feeling the game's gonna start up again, and I'd rather quit while I'm ahead."

Jamie took the cigar from Ryan's hand and extinguished it. Once it was cool, she placed it in the pocket of Ryan's blouse, patting it gently as she said, "No smoking in my car, love. Especially not cigars." They said their good-nights and walked the three blocks to the Boxster. "Can you really count cards?" Jamie asked as she hit the automatic lock release.

"Yeah. It's not that hard," Ryan said, sliding her long body into the small car.

"Maybe not on your planet," Jamie said, "but we earthlings can't do that."

Ryan sighed, resting her head against the headrest. "The boys all think it's a math thing…but it's not."

Jamie looked at her and noticed an adorable childlike expression on Ryan's face. She looked like she had a secret that she wanted to share, but she also wanted to hang onto it for a while. "What is it then?"

"It's just concentration and memory. I had a two, a four, a six, a seven, an eight, a nine, and an ace, right?"

"Right," she said, even though she'd already forgotten Ryan's cards.

"I had a pretty good suspicion that Donal had three aces, and that's what he had."

"But how—" Jamie began, but Ryan launched into her analysis immediately.

"There were two kings, three queens, two jacks and a ten in the up cards. Given the suits, he couldn't have had a royal flush. There was a break in every suit, meaning he couldn't have had a straight flush either. I knew he didn't have four of a kind, since at least one card of every denomination was showing. That left a full house." She let out another sigh and said, "A full house was a definite possibility, but I had a feeling he was working on aces. Donal's very undisciplined, but even he doesn't usually go that deep with only a pair. So I figured he had three of a kind. Given how much he bet, I assumed he had high cards, and the only high cards that hadn't been accounted for were aces."

Jamie's head was reeling trying to keep up with Ryan's exposition, and she was stone cold sober. "So, how did you know he didn't have a full house?"

"Oh, I didn't," Ryan said. "Not until he raised me big at the end of the hand. Donal only bets like that if he's unsure or has a sure winner. A full house isn't a sure winner, so I figured he had the aces." She grinned at her partner and added a wink. "They think I win because of math, but it's at least half because they're so darned predictable."

Chapter Eight

When they walked into their room at the O'Flaherty home, Ryan turned her back to the bed, flexed her knees, and jumped neatly right into the center of it. Linking her hands behind her head, she crossed her booted feet at the ankle and smiled serenely at Jamie. "Sleepy?"

Jamie shook her head slowly, trying to determine if she was being flirted with. She allowed a seductive smile to show, just in case, and said, "Be right back. I had one too many glasses of tea tonight."

When she returned, still dressed in her outfit from dinner, Ryan looked even more relaxed, but her eyes were flashing playfully. "Wanna play?" Her voice took on its usual stunningly sexy timbre, and Jamie immediately felt the first stirrings of arousal tug at her. Even though Ryan's tone and look were familiar, she didn't usually ask for sex quite this way, and Jamie thought she'd better seek clarification.

"Wanna play what?" she asked slowly, tilting her head as she approached the bed.

"Stay there," Ryan cautioned, taking the cigar from her pocket and pointing at Jamie with it, her eyes narrowing dangerously. "Stay right there."

Following orders, Jamie did just as her partner asked, and she waited patiently to receive the next request.

"I wanna play a game," Ryan murmured, her honey-toned voice causing Jamie's knees to grow weak. "Do you wanna play with me?"

"There isn't a game in the world I'd ever refuse to play with you. Name it."

Ryan rolled over and turned on her bedside CD player, flipping through the discs until she found the one that she wanted. The soft, slow strains of a sensual jazz beat filled the air, and as Ryan rolled onto her back, she once again linked her hands behind her head. Blinking slowly, she stated her request. "I want you to dance."

"Dance?" Jamie asked, extending her hand in invitation. "Okay, but you're gonna have to get up to dance with me."

"I didn't ask you to dance *with* me," Ryan averred. Her deep blue eyes grew even darker as they bore into Jamie's. "I asked you to dance *for* me."

"For you...like...*for* you?" she asked. Her stomach did a little flip.

"Exactly," Ryan murmured, sticking the cigar in her mouth and nodding her head slowly, a sexy grin tugging at her lips. "*For* me."

Indecision combined with increasing arousal to render Jamie absolutely speechless. She stood in the middle of the room, arms folded over her waist as though she were chilled. Sensing her unease, Ryan looked her in the eye and said, "If you're not into it, it's no big deal. I just thought it would be...interesting." Ryan's eyes still emitted an overpoweringly sensual allure, even though her words were giving Jamie an out if she didn't want to play.

Given that, before Ryan, she'd only been fully intimate with Jack, and they'd never played sexy games, Jamie had never done the type of thing that Ryan was suggesting, and a part of her wanted to dismiss the idea and stick with their norm. But another, more insistent part told her to go for it. One of the things she most enjoyed about their lovemaking was that Ryan was apparently hell-bent on keeping it fresh and exciting, and she wanted to encourage that as much as possible, even when it meant doing something that was outside her comfort zone. Dancing in a sexually suggestive manner was, in fact, way outside her comfort zone, but Ryan had yet to have a bad idea when it came to sex, and Jamie doubted that she was going to break that streak tonight. Summoning her courage and chasing her doubts to the back of her mind, Jamie smiled at her lover and nodded her head decisively. "I think it would be very...interesting," she agreed, mimicking Ryan's tone as well as her choice of words. "Just remember, I've never done this before, so don't expect a professional-caliber performance."

A self-satisfied grin met her disclaimer, and Ryan assured her, "I have a sneaking suspicion that you have hidden talents in this area, babe. Give it a whirl."

Taking a moment to decide how to approach the matter, Jamie assessed her outfit and found it perfect for the plan she was conjuring up. Keeping her gaze fixed on Ryan's face, she began to sway with the music, letting the beat be her guide. Her hips started to move in a gentle rhythm, and within a few measures she was moving gracefully, slowly losing herself in the music.

As her body took over, she recalled one of the sayings that Ryan had written in the training journal that she had given her for Christmas. The motto had stuck with her ever since, because it perfectly described Ryan's outlook on life and was the type of behavior that Jamie wanted to emulate. "Sing as if no one can hear you. Dance as if no one can see you. Love as if today is your last day on earth." Taking the aphorism to heart, Jamie let her body express her desire, closing her eyes as the slow, steady beat became her world. She moved gracefully about the room, not even considering Ryan's reaction to her display. She was truly dancing as if no one could see her, that simple motto allowing her much more freedom to express herself than she would have had if she had been doing this only for Ryan.

As the song drew to a close, Jamie opened her eyes to see her lover sitting up on the bed, looking very...alert. Her eyes were wide and flashing with desire as she stared, mouth slightly open, at the spectacle that was being presented before her. "That was absolutely fantastic," she murmured.

"Another?" Jamie needlessly asked as the next song began.

Unable to form complex sentences, Ryan just nodded, licking her lips in anticipation. Jamie walked over to the bedside table and grabbed the small box of wooden matches they kept for lighting candles. Moving around the room, she lit every candle in the place, and there were quite a few scattered about. She flicked off the overhead light, crossed back to the bed, and extended her hand to Ryan. Pulling her to her feet, she moved her backwards until she was in front of her desk chair, then gave her a little push, smiling when Ryan sank into it. Lighting another match, she put the cigar to Ryan's lips and instructed, "Suck." Wide eyes greeted her order, but the tanned cheeks pulled inward as Ryan complied, puffing on the cigar to light it fully.

Leaning over from the waist, Jamie gave her partner a seductive smile while her hand slipped into the pocket of Ryan's chinos, pulling out the substantial wad of bills. "Don't be stingy," she warned, slapping both Ryan's cheeks with the bundle. She laughed at the absolutely stunned expression on her partner's face, reveling in her ability to continually surprise the vastly more experienced woman.

Gathering her courage, Jamie began to put on a show for her partner, dancing much more suggestively this time. Her unstructured print dress closely followed her curves. Tiny covered buttons, running from the neckline to the hem, held the dress closed, and as her body began to move once more, she leaned over right in front of Ryan, her cleavage presented in a most inviting fashion. Her hand dropped to the hem of her short dress, where she began to unfasten the buttons, one by one. Ryan's hand lifted to examine the treasures being displayed right in front of her face, but Jamie shook her head decisively. "Uh-uh-uh," she teased. "House rules. You can look, but not touch."

She had to stifle a laugh at the flummoxed look on Ryan's face. *I don't know why I get nervous about playing with her*, she thought wryly. *She's so easy.*

Ryan's hands dutifully fell to her thighs, the still-massive cigar drooping dangerously from her lips. Jamie playfully pushed it into a horizontal position, leaning over to whisper, "You're getting limp."

Ryan grinned up at her, some of her usual bravado returning now that Jamie was clearly showing that this was still a game. She removed the cigar and rocked back in the chair, smiling up at her partner. "There's not one part of me that's limp. Everything's alert and ready for action."

Jamie had not stopped dancing throughout this interchange, still moving gently to the beat. She turned around and wiggled her hips, her short dress swaying seductively. "I'll be the judge of that, if you're lucky." With that threat, she turned and began to undo a few more buttons, stopping at mid-thigh this time.

Lifting her foot, she insinuated it between Ryan's spread legs, the heel of her delicate sandals catching on the edge of the chair. The motion exposed her leg nearly to her panties, and Ryan looked up the expanse of toned thigh, a very pleased smile gracing her face. "Like 'em?" Jamie asked, referring to her stockings. Since they had been together, she had only worn a dress a couple of times. On the last occasion, Ryan had made a teasing comment about the unattractive red line that normal pantyhose made on her stomach, and Jamie had privately sworn that the offending hose would never again touch her body. True to her vow, she had discarded every pair she owned, replacing them with thigh-high stockings, a lacy band of elasticized material holding them tight.

The dark head nodded slowly as Ryan struggled to obey Jamie's orders that she was not allowed to touch her. Having the muscular thighs displayed in such an arousing manner was almost too much for Ryan. Having to do something with her hands, as well as needing a little oral stimulation, she popped the cigar back into her mouth and took a few puffs, blowing the smoke well away from her partner. "I like them very, very much," she finally said, once she had calmed down a bit.

Satisfied with her answer, Jamie proceeded to undo another dozen of the tiny buttons, moving her body tauntingly the entire time. Now the dress hung open from her waist to her thighs, her lacy white panties peeking out occasionally as she twirled.

Ryan was beside herself with desire, the pulsing between her legs nearly painful. She reached down to adjust a bit, but once again, Jamie interrupted her. "Can't touch yourself, sport. House rules. And speaking of rules, this isn't a charity, ya know. How about prying some of those bills out of your fist?"

Ryan blinked slowly, gazing vacantly from her hand to Jamie's lips, trying to ascertain if this was really her lover speaking, or some remarkable look-alike.

"Maybe you need a little more incentive," Jamie purred, once again bending at the waist as she opened all of the remaining buttons, her lace-clad breasts just an inch from Ryan's face.

Ryan knew she was expected to participate in this game, but she was having a very tough time getting that message to her extremities. She finally managed to grasp a few bills from her wad and tuck them into the top of Jamie's stocking, pausing just a moment to caress the unbelievably soft skin of her upper thigh with the back of her fingers.

Standing up quickly, Jamie dropped the now loose dress from her shoulders, shaking her shoulders quickly to aid in the process. Of course, that action caused her breasts to jiggle, creating heightened interest from her partner. Ryan immediately nestled two twenties right into the heart of her cleavage, earning a grateful smile from her dancer. "Good girl," she praised. "That just earned you another dance."

Luckily for Ryan, the next number had a decidedly sexy beat, and Jamie used the song to excellent advantage, bending, squatting, shimmying her hips and shoulders, all in a fiendishly contrived plot to drive Ryan absolutely stark raving mad. The plan was working perfectly, judging by the vacant look in her eyes and the fidgeting she was doing. Turning up the heat, Jamie shoved her foot right between Ryan's thighs, using the rounded toe of her sandal to scrape up and down the seam of Ryan's cotton pants.

The reaction was a little more than Jamie had anticipated, with Ryan bending over at the waist, trying to close her legs to avoid any more contact. "Don't you like that?" Jamie hummed into her ear.

Her head nodded furiously, and she gasped, "I can't let you do that and not touch you. I'm trying to behave." She looked up at Jamie with a pathetic expression on her face and reminded her, "I'm only human."

"You're a fine human, too," Jamie insisted, and as a reward, she grasped the back of Ryan's head and rubbed Ryan's face into her cleavage, letting her breathe in her scent while the lace tickled her face. When she released her, Ryan flopped back against the back of her chair, gasping for breath, eyes comically wide.

"Like that?" At Ryan's slow nod, she reminded her, "Then pay for it." She smiled when another packet of folded bills was gently tucked between her full breasts. Turning around, she removed all the money and tossed it on the bed, not wanting its scent or appearance to get in the way of Ryan's enjoyment.

Even though it was obvious that Ryan didn't need, and couldn't stand, much more teasing, Jamie had to give her the full treatment, so she asked, "Would you like a private dance?"

Smacking her lips together, Ryan croaked out, "Yeah. That'd be great."

Slowly, seductively, Jamie lifted her leg, holding Ryan's shoulders for support. Straddling her lap, she began to gyrate to the music, continually shaking her shoulders as she thrust her hips into the incredibly aroused woman. She took the now cool cigar from Ryan's mouth and tossed it onto her desk. Then she tauntingly rubbed her breasts into Ryan's nearly drooling face and whispered, "Twenty dollars for each minute." She nearly burst out laughing when Ryan took her entire bankroll and offered it up to Jamie, her face never leaving the milky white cleavage that she was so happily nuzzling.

"Just for that, you can take off my bra," she whispered, amazed when the lacy garment was hanging from her shoulders just a nanosecond later. *Boy, she's good*, she mused, considering that practice really did make perfect. Now Ryan's entire face got into the act, ably aided by her warm, soft hands. The tables began to turn once she got her mouth and hands on those perfect mounds, and within seconds Jamie was grinding herself against her lover, the pretext of the game completely forgotten.

In an impressive show of strength, Ryan rose from the chair, Jamie still attached to her lap. They fell to the bed as one, and Ryan began tearing at her own clothes to free herself from their confines. However, once her mouth left Jamie's breasts, the smaller woman was able to think once again, and she grasped her hands firmly, instructing, "Let me."

Even though it was clear her torture would be prolonged, Ryan willingly let her hands drop. The sky blue cotton broadcloth blouse was fairly easy to remove, and the white cotton bra went quickly, too. But Jamie got a little sidetracked when she saw her favorite parts of Ryan's anatomy revealed, and she had to pause to greet them lavishly.

When Jamie realized that she was on her back, with Ryan humping her leg, she decided that it was time to at least get her partner's pants off her. She wrestled her onto her back and unbuckled the black leather belt, getting the button and zipper undone with little difficulty. Ryan lifted her hips to aid in the removal of the wrinkled, generously cut slacks. Jamie pulled them off over her boots and then laughed aloud when she saw what she was wearing underneath. "Where did you get those?"

Ryan had on a pair of cotton boxer shorts, in a blindingly bright mélange of Hawaiian patterns. Rolling her over, Jamie saw that five separate patterns covered her—bright blue, navy blue, red, green, and gold, all with different designs stenciled upon the backgrounds.

"Brendan gave them to me," she said, laughing.

The mere thought of that was slightly troubling to Jamie. "You wear your brother's underwear?" *Smoking, betting, wearing Brendan's clothes. This is a little too much information.*

"No, silly. His girlfriend gave him a bunch of these. He hadn't worn these. They were still in the package."

"But why...?"

"'Cause you said they were cute when you saw him in them this morning. I thought you'd like 'em on me, too."

Jamie surveyed the look and found that she liked them even better on Ryan. They somehow fit her personality, a wild, untamed side lurking just beneath the surface, that only an intimate few got to experience. "I love 'em," she said. "I'm buying you more immediately."

"They're called Uglies," Ryan said with a smirk. "Their slogan is 'So ugly she'll beg you to take them off.'" Her rapidly waggling eyebrows were a clear invitation, and Jamie was only too happy to accommodate her.

She moved down Ryan's body, kissing a seductive path from her breastbone to her navel, stopping to tease around the sensitive skin with the tip of her tongue. Then, just to keep the game going, she bent and unfastened each of the five buttons of the shorts with her teeth. Ryan was groaning continually as Jamie's soft hair tickled her belly while she worked away, and the slow, wet kisses that the smaller woman continued to bestow on her stomach were not helping matters in the least.

Finally finishing her task, Jamie grasped the now-open fabric and teasingly commented, "I'm a little afraid to take these off you. Playing poker, smoking cigars, wearing men's underwear…I'm afraid of what I'm going to find down there."

"You can find anything down there your little heart desires if you let me get my toy chest," Ryan said, throwing the gauntlet at her lover's feet.

Jamie shook her head almost immediately. "I think I'd like the girl that I married back. I'm not ready to have you *that* much like your brothers."

Grasping her around the waist, Ryan rolled her partner onto her back, twitching her hips to help the fabric slip down her body. "I'm back, and I'm all yours."

The watch alarm chirped at 5:15 on the button, and with practiced hands, Ryan turned it off before the third chirp, managing, as usual, to avoid waking her partner. *Oh, Lord, why did I drink all that beer and smoke that damned cigar? I feel like I haven't had a sip of water in days.* She rolled to the edge of the bed, disentangling her arms from around Jamie's body as she moved. Tossing her leg over the bed, she abruptly flew off its surface, landing hard—face first. Luckily, her hands shot out before her head hit the floor and she was spared injury. The very loud noise and the ensuing string of curses woke Jamie, who scrambled to see what had happened. "Honey?" The room was still dark, and when Jamie flicked on the bedside lamp she erupted in giggles. Ryan was lying facedown on the floor, her print boxers down around her ankles, her smooth black leather motorcycle boots still firmly laced on her feet.

"We've got to start going to bed barefoot," she grumbled, rolling over to extricate herself from her predicament.

Reaching down beneath the covers, Jamie realized that she still wore not only her stockings, but her sandals as well. "Let's make it a rule," she agreed, leaning over the bed to offer an early morning kiss to her partner. Pulling back quickly she amended, "One more rule. No smoking unless both of us do it. It was sexy last night, now it's just vile."

Ryan smiled ruefully. "You had me so out of my mind that I smoked the damn thing in the house."

"You didn't take two puffs off it. You were too busy drooling to keep it lit."

"Just the same, we'd better wash the sheets and keep the windows open. Da will tan my hide if he smells even a whiff of smoke down here."

Ryan was tired and a little dehydrated, but that didn't excuse her from running with the volleyball team. Jamie was under no such edict, so she stayed in bed, waving goodbye to Ryan with only a touch of guilt.

Pleased to encounter a cool, fog-shrouded Berkeley, Ryan took off with a small group of her teammates and struggled through their required five miles. Just as she was cruising to a stop, Jordan sidled up beside her and said, "I'm gonna do another five. Wanna come?"

"No way," she demurred. "I had a tough night last night. I need some breakfast."

"I can go that way too," Jordan said. "Let's hit the showers."

As they walked toward the locker room, Ryan commented, "I think I've figured out why you're such a good runner. You're part cheetah, aren't you?"

"I was the state champion in the fifteen hundred in high school," she said a little smugly. "I've run cross-country for years, too. Running's what I do best."

"I don't come up against many people who can beat me that easily," Ryan said. "You really put me in my place. Again."

"Let me buy you breakfast to make up for humiliating you," Jordan offered with a teasing gleam in her eyes.

"Okay," Ryan said. "I just need to find a phone to tell Jamie."

"Short leash, huh?" Jordan smirked at Ryan's scowl and reached into her gym bag to hand her a cell phone.

"I wouldn't call it a leash, but there's no one I'd rather spend my time with," Ryan said, being very clear about where her allegiances lay.

Jordan didn't seem offended by her statement. Instead she laughed softly and challenged Ryan's sincerity. "So, why accept my invitation? Shouldn't you be running home?"

Ryan concentrated on dialing the phone for a second, looking back at Jordan as the phone began to ring. "If traffic weren't so bad getting across the Bay Bridge, I'd be gone already." She smiled at her teammate and gave her a playful wink, smiling even more broadly when Jamie picked up the phone. "Hi, love," she said. Jordan made a face and went into the locker room to avoid the mush.

Jordan was just stepping out of the shower as Ryan started stripping. "Did your mistress grant permission for you to have a meal without her?" the lanky blonde asked.

Ryan was kicking off her shorts, as she turned to look at Jordan. *Whoa*, she thought. *Find somewhere else to look!* Even though they had run together several times, they had never been in the showers at the same time, and Ryan was astounded by the vision that greeted her. Jordan was a very good-looking woman in clothes, but much to Ryan's chagrin, she was nearly flawless naked. Just a tiny bit taller than Ryan, she was as fair as Ryan was dark. Her long blonde hair hung straight down her back, and her fair skin was kissed by the sun everywhere except the area covered by the very sexy white thong she was shimmying into. Jordan was of Swedish extraction, and she possessed the dichotomy of lovely blonde hair contrasted with skin that tanned to a beautiful light golden bronze. She had the long, lean look of an elite runner, but she also had a sleekly powerful upper body. Her breasts looked natural, but they were so perfect that they could have been silicone enhanced. Even though Ryan had told Jamie that she thought she would always look at women, this one was way too attractive and way too naked for her to feel comfortable with.

"Uhm, not really," she said as she looked deep into her gym bag for nothing at all. Jordan came over to stand right next to her, completely unconcerned with her near nudity.

"So we're not having breakfast together?" she asked, puzzled by Ryan's odd response.

"What? Oh, yeah, we're having breakfast. Sure. No problem."

"Do you need something?" Jordan asked. "I've got everything you might need in my locker."

"Oh, that's what I need. I need to talk to the equipment manager about getting a locker."

"And you were looking in your gym bag for that?"

"Uhm, I forgot what I was looking for," Ryan said as her face flushed. "I'll be right out. You can meet me outside if you want." She stripped off the rest of her clothes so quickly that she could have created a friction spark, and scampered toward the shower area.

"Hey," Jordan said, "before you get in the shower, would you put some moisture lotion on my back?"

Ryan knew she had to acquiesce since there was no logical or believable reason to refuse. *Gee, Jordan, I'd love to, but I'll go into anaphylactic shock if I touch lanolin.* She took a breath, walked back to the bench, and started to rub a big glob of the aloe-scented lotion into the toned back. She had rarely dated a woman as tall as she, and as she rubbed her fingers over the long expanse, she briefly considered that it would be nice to have a big girlfriend. There was something nice about having all that smooth real estate sliding under her fingers, but as soon as the thought came into her mind she shoved it out. *Your shopping days are over. Very good things come in small packages. Count your blessings.*

She finished her task as quickly as she could and took a longer-than-normal shower to make sure Jordan would be dressed when she finished. *What's up with you? It's impossible to be more satisfied than you are. Why on earth do you let a beautiful woman get you all flustered?* She didn't really have an answer for that question, reasoning that years of conditioning were going to take a while to overcome.

When she came out of the shower a few minutes later, Jordan was sitting right where she had left her, although, thankfully, clothed this time. Feeling Jordan's calm, appraising gaze linger on her body, Ryan got dressed quickly, so quickly that she didn't even tie her shoes properly. As they started to leave the locker room, she tripped on a lace and nearly fell flat on her face. Jordan caught her as she fell, grabbing her firmly around the waist and holding on tight as Ryan regained her feet. They were facing each other, only inches apart, and Ryan felt a stirring of desire shoot through her groin as those perfect breasts pressed against her. *Oh, for God's sake,* she chastised her body. *Don't do this to me. I'm very happily married.* But her body insistently reminded her that an extremely attractive woman was holding her very close, and it was only doing the job that she had rigorously trained it to do.

She stood under her own power and thanked Jordan for catching her. "You must be pretty strong," she grinned nervously. "I'm a handful."

"I've handled bigger than you," she said, with a little more innuendo than Ryan was comfortable with. As they left the building Jordan asked, "Hey, would you mind driving? I'd like to go to North Berkeley. There's a good place there that I never get to go to."

"No problem," Ryan said and led her friend to the Lexus.

"Nice wheels," whistled Jordan, admiring the car.

"Uhm, it's actually Jamie's car. I own a motorcycle," she said, finding herself embarrassed to admit that her partner had, in fact, bought the car for her.

"Ooh, I *love* bikes," the lanky blonde enthused. "Will you give me a ride someday?"

"Sure," Ryan said, privately thinking, *As long as Jamie sits right between us. I don't want those breasts anywhere near me again.*

Thankfully, Ryan overcame her nervousness and they had a very pleasant breakfast together. As they talked about school and their athletic careers, Ryan learned that Jordan's resumé was just as impressive as her own, more so, actually, when one considered that she was only twenty-one and very much in the running to make the women's Olympic volleyball team.

They were working on another cup of coffee when Jordan casually asked, "So, are you exclusively lesbian?"

Barely avoiding spitting all over her teammate, Ryan swallowed while nodding furiously. "Absolutely!"

"Chill, babe," Jordan laughed. "I'm just trying to get to know you better."

Once again Ryan flushed, thinking that she spent a lot of time doing so around Jordan. "Always have been. Always will be. How about you?"

"God, no!" Jordan was shaking her head slowly, a small frown drawing her dark blonde eyebrows slightly together. "I'm...open-minded."

"So am I," Ryan said. "As long as the person has breasts and a vagina." Her slightly goofy smile caused Jordan to laugh heartily, and Ryan was struck by how much more attractive she was when she was relaxed. *Great, just what I need is for her to be* more *attractive.*

Thankfully, Jordan's increased attractiveness was accompanied by an increased level of comfort for both women, and by the end of breakfast Ryan was pretty confident that Jordan was just being friendly, not flirty. Jordan seemed very comfortable with herself, and she also seemed quite frank, even blunt, in her questioning. But Ryan didn't get any sexual vibes from her, and she was pleased that her new friend seemed very interested in hearing about Jamie and how they had become a couple.

"So, what about you? Are you seeing any 'people' now?" Ryan asked.

"No one in particular," Jordan said. "I don't allow myself to get too involved. My focus is volleyball, and it's hard to meet anyone who wants to come second to my passion."

"So, you've never been in love?"

Jordan's icy mask slid into place, and her hooded eyes concealed every emotion. "I didn't say that," she said rather brusquely. "But I'm not in love now, and I don't expect that to change for quite some time. Nothing is going to prevent me from reaching my goals. Nothing."

When Jamie returned home that evening, Ryan was sitting on the front porch, a beer in her hand and a contemplative look on her face. "Hey, babe," Jamie called in greeting, getting out of the car.

"One question," Ryan demanded, getting right down to business. "Where in the holy hell did you learn how to give a lap dance like that?"

Jamie nearly collapsed in laughter, the look on Ryan's face so completely puzzled that she was tempted to extend the torture and milk it for all it was worth. Taking pity on her partner, she sat down next to her. "On Mia's birthday, the only thing she wanted for a present was for a group of her friends to go to a strip club." Jamie laughed, remembering how adamant her friend had been about her party. "I assumed we'd go to some place where guys dance for women, but since half of Mia's friends are guys, and they're the ones who picked the place..." she trailed off.

"Where was I when this happened?"

"Her birthday's around Christmas," Jamie said. "We were on break at the time."

"Did ya have fun?" Ryan asked, eyebrows twitching.

Jamie pursed her lips as she recalled, "It was okay. I mean, Mia had a great time, of course, and we all got so drunk that I could hardly see straight. Thank God we had the foresight to rent a limo."

"So, the women didn't do anything for you?"

"No," Jamie said. "I mean, if it were just me and one of the women I might have been more interested, but watching a group of women try to sexually excite people for money didn't do a thing for me." She cocked her head, trying to remember exactly how she had felt. "It seemed kinda sad, you know?"

"Sad? I've never heard that term used for a strip club."

"Yeah. Sad that the women had to do that for money, and sad for the men that had to pay someone to dance for them. I thought it was just sad that they couldn't do that with their own partners."

"Like I can," Ryan said, nuzzling her head into Jamie's sweet-smelling neck. "Being married to you is a very good thing. A very good thing, indeed."

Now that her therapist was back from vacation, Jamie arrived home a little later than usual that Wednesday evening. She poked her head into the refrigerator, staring at the contents for a moment, wishing some of them would transform themselves into immediately edible food. "I'm starving. What do you want to do for dinner tonight?"

"I'm happy to cook," Ryan said. "I didn't start anything because I didn't have any idea of when you'd be home."

Jamie opened the door again, her nose twitching while her brow furrowed slightly. "The refrigerator doesn't smell right," she said, poking her head all the way inside.

"It will by tomorrow," Ryan said. "I spent an hour cleaning every darned surface in there after I got rid of that stinky cheese you forgot about."

"My cheese!" Jamie dashed to the trash can and pulled out two very fragrant loosely wrapped bundles. Luckily, they were the only items in the fresh plastic bag, since Maria Los had cleaned the kitchen and thrown out the trash earlier in the day.

Ryan shoved her hands into the pockets of her khakis and rocked back and forth on her heels. "Uh-oh. Now I think I understand what in the heck Maria Los was trying to say." She looked a little embarrassed, but it was obvious that she found the situation rather funny. "I took the cheese out, she put it back. I took it out again, and she put it right back in. She got about two inches from my face and actually wagged her finger at me. I had to wait until she left to throw it away again."

Jamie burst out in laughter, grabbing a chair to support her weak legs. "I had a long discussion with her about this right after she started to work for me," she said. "She thinks I'm absolutely nuts, I'm sure, but she's protected my cheese ever since."

Ryan looked very skeptical as she approached and took the packets from Jamie's hands. Lifting them to her nose, she sniffed, making a face as she did so. "Do you really plan on eating these? They smell like…jeez, I don't even know what they smell like."

Jamie gave her a knowing smile and said, "Our dinner plans have been made, babe. Let's hop on your bike and go pick up a few things. We're gonna have a little cheese tasting tonight."

It took over an hour to go to the correct bakery for French baguettes, the correct cheese store for a few wedges of hard cheese and three types of olives and a wine shop for two bottles of red wine.

Once they arrived home, Ryan was put in charge of slicing some peaches and making melon balls, while Jamie prepared the cheese and sliced the bread. When everything was ready they repaired to the backyard to begin the lesson/meal.

"Okay," Jamie began, assuming her best professorial demeanor. "I love soft cheese, but it's impossible to find it properly ripened. So I practice affinage in my home." She laughed at her statement, but Ryan gave her a very blank look. "Affinage is the practice of ripening cheese," she said. "I'm trying to teach myself to be a fromager-affineur."

"Uhm, how do you know if you're doing it right?" Ryan asked, thinking that this sounded suspiciously like the all-too-common news items recounting dozens of people at a church picnic dying from spoiled potato salad.

"I know what I like," she said. "It's mostly a matter of taste."

"Uh-huh," Ryan nodded, not looking even a little bit convinced. "I think I'll stick with the nice yellow stuff in the safe, hermetically sealed plastic wrapper."

"Oh, come on. When have you been afraid of a new sensual experience?"

That did the trick. Blue eyes brightened, a sly smile creeping onto Ryan's face. "Did you say sensual?"

"Yep. Trust me on this one, babe. We're gonna have fun tonight."

Ahh, what's a little botulism between friends? "Let's boogie."

"I like the Pont l'Evêque, slathered across the small of your back, with a little Châteauneuf-du-Pape to wash it down." Ryan was sitting cross-legged on the ground, using her discarded jeans to keep the grass from tickling her sensitive skin. Her head was resting against Jamie's back, the soft rise of her partner's buttocks filling her vision.

"I knew that you'd like properly aged cheese."

"Oh, I liked it all right," Ryan said. "Of course, the delicious serving platter affected my enjoyment a little bit. I was very, very glad that it didn't taste as strong as it smelled, though."

"That's funny, isn't it? You smell it when it's aged and it nearly overwhelms you, but the flavor is much more subtle and complex."

"I swear, if I told Da you have me eating fruit and cheese for dinner, he'd think I'd lost my mind. At my house, that would be a very small appetizer."

"You're not still hungry, are you?"

"Nope. All of my senses and appetites have been completely satisfied."

"All of them?"

"Yep. How about yours?"

"Oh, yeah." She rolled over, dislodging Ryan's head for a moment. "I was just thinking about that, as a matter of fact."

"Tell me," Ryan said, placing her chin on Jamie's hipbone.

"I've always been focused on taste and texture when I eat something I really like, but you've helped expand my focus. It's like the world is opening up for me. Do you know what I mean?"

"Kinda…"

"It's like this," Jamie said. "I love the Morbier that we had tonight. Those two glossy, pale yellow layers of cheese have always reminded me of fruit and nuts. I've had it dozens of times, but I'd never noticed how delightful the aroma was. Tonight it hit me—it smells just like you do when you work out."

"I smell like cheese?"

"No, you don't generally smell like cheese. But this cheese and you both smell a little like new-mown hay."

Ryan grinned up at her. "Hay, huh? I guess that makes sense since I eat like a horse."

"That you do," she said. "But there was more than that. I spread some of that creamy yellow cheese on your breasts, and I was hit by how absolutely wonderful the color and the texture were. It was just so glossy, almost luminescent. And then when I licked it off you. Wow. I mean, it just amazed me how an experience I've had so many times seems brand-new when I share it with you."

"Or *on* me," Ryan said.

"Especially on you. I guess my point is that you've made me so much more aware of my senses. I feel like I'm just starting to experience everything that life has to offer."

"'Just starting' is the operative phrase, babe," Ryan said. "We've got a lot of years ahead of us to fully exploit all of our senses."

Jamie leaned over and tugged on her partner, urging her to lie atop her body. She looked deeply into Ryan's eyes and said, "For that journey, I couldn't have picked a better traveling companion."

Chapter Nine

T he next night, Ryan impulsively decided that she wanted to go out to
dinner. "I want to talk to you about something, and I don't wanna be
distracted."

A look of concern flashed across Jamie's face. "Is everything all right?"

"Yes," Ryan smiled, knowing it would be a while before Jamie wasn't a
little skittish about having an unplanned talk of any kind. "I want to talk
about our future careers."

"Okay. I'll be down in fifteen minutes, and we can walk over to
Telegraph and get something. Unless you have something else in mind."

"Nope. A walk would be good. Gives me a chance to hold your hand,"
she said, grasping Jamie's hand and kissing it.

Jamie stood on her tiptoes and puckered up. "You are such a romantic."

As they walked along in the warm evening, Ryan reflected, "I really
meant what I said about loving to hold your hand. My hand fits so perfectly
around yours, like they were made for each other."

"I think they were," Jamie said, squeezing Ryan's larger hand. "Oh,
Mother called earlier. Would you like to have brunch with her on Sunday?"

"Sure. Just her?"

"Yeah. Daddy's out of the country for another week."

"That'd be fun," Ryan said. "I've enjoyed the time we've spent together
so far." *And if Jim's not there, all the better.*

"I'll try to set it up around noon. I don't want to miss Sunday dinner with
your family."

"You really do like that, don't you?" Ryan asked with a gentle smile.

"Yeah. It makes me feel all warm inside to be a part of the family."

"You're the first person I've dated who understood that," Ryan said. "But I'm glad no one else did. If Tracy had loved my family, I'd probably be with her right now, and I know I wouldn't be nearly as happy."

"And I'd be so jealous I'd probably have had to stop seeing you as just a friend." A look of deep pain flashed across Jamie's face.

Ryan saw the look and felt a similar pang in her gut. "I don't think I could have let you go. I'd have snapped out of my denial."

"Denial? You were in denial?"

"Oh, yeah. I didn't know it then, but I was falling in love with you even when I was with Tracy." She stopped and looked contemplative for a second before starting to walk again. "It's funny. Just the other day I was thinking about how, from the first time we were together, I began to depend on seeing you. Wanna know a secret?"

"Sure."

"Remember how we used to stop and get juice after our psych class?"

"Yeah, that's when I started to really get to know you."

"The first day we did that I suggested we go right next door because I knew that's where the closest vending machines were. But my next class was clear across campus. I cherished every moment that we spent together, so I'd wait until I literally had to run the whole way to make it. People used to give me some very strange looks when I came barreling in, gasping for breath."

Jamie stopped and stared up at her with a delighted grin on her face. "Why didn't you tell me that? We could have gone somewhere else."

"Don't know. Didn't even occur to me. I just liked being with you and that was what we did. I didn't mind, and it gave me a nice little boost. I'd have some juice and then do some sprints to keep the blood flowing."

Over two big bowls of sizzling rice soup, Ryan brought up her dilemma. "I need to talk about grad school. I've gotta get my apps in."

"I thought you were going to apply to a bunch of them and pick the best one after you get your acceptance letters."

Ryan stirred her soup absently, starting to speak several times, but stopping herself immediately.

"Tell me what's bothering you. It's obvious that something is."

She sighed heavily and placed her spoon next to her bowl, folding her hands in front of her. "I'm having a tough time letting go of my dream."

"Your dream? Letting go…? Ryan, I have no idea what you're talking about."

She blinked slowly, staring at Jamie as she said, "I wanna be a fire fighter."

The blood drained from Jamie's face, and her nerveless hand dropped the spoon into the soup, splashing warm liquid all over the tablecloth. "You what?"

"I knew you'd react this way," Ryan muttered, folding her arms over her chest. "That's why I haven't talked about it before."

"I'm sorry," Jamie said, regaining her composure. "But I had no idea. You've never even given a hint that you wanted to do that."

"That's one of the reasons I started working out so intensely. I've wanted this since I was a little kid, and if we weren't together I'd already be applying for admission to the academy."

Jamie's brow furrowed, and she looked at her partner carefully. "Why is our being together stopping you?"

Ryan sighed and said, "Because I know it'd make you crazy. Doing this would make me happy. It'd satisfy a desire I've had since I was little. But I know it'd be awful for you."

"What does your father think? I'm sure you've talked to him about it."

"He's always told me that it's not a good job for a married person. It's a hard life for the fire fighter, but it's much harder on her spouse. I used to think that the way I lived my life was just perfect for the career I wanted. I had brief flings with women and then moved on. Nobody was ever that attached to me, so they wouldn't be that invested in what I did for a living. But it's not like that now. I just don't think I can have you, and our children, worrying if I'm going to come home at the end of my shift."

Jamie's heart was still racing, and her concerns started flowing out. "My God, Ryan. Knowing how focused you get, you'd be killed inside of a week. You'd go in after some poor soul even if there was no chance of getting him out. I just don't think you could distance yourself enough to be able to accept the loss of human life."

Ryan gave her a wry smile and said, "I never thought of it that way, but you're probably right. They spend a lot of time training to make sure they don't take unnecessary risks, but it'd be incredibly hard for me to let someone die if I thought there was a chance I could save him."

"So are you willing to give up the dream?"

Ryan's dark hair cascaded around her shoulders as she nodded her head slowly. "I think I have to, but it's incredibly hard. I've always known that this is what I'd do. I love the physical side of it, I love the adrenaline that runs through your body when you hear the alarm. And I love that the entrance requirements are so tough. They're basically the same for men and women, and that really stokes me."

"Wouldn't the thought of actually going into a burning building freak you out?" Jamie asked, shivering.

"Yeah, I think I'd be less than honest if I couldn't admit that. But I was actually more interested in aquatic rescue. They have a swift water rescue team that I've been focused on."

"Jeez, like that would be much safer? You'd drown rather than burn?"

"Good point," Ryan agreed, smirking. "I'm sure I'd be imprudent in the water, too."

"Aren't you interested in anything besides being a fire fighter?"

"Yeah, sure I am. But none of the other possibilities have the visceral pull that fire fighting does. Maybe it's in my genes, but it just fits my personality."

"I can see that," Jamie said. "But it would make me crazy, and it'd be hard for our kids. If this is something that you really need to do, I hope you know that I'll support you. But it clearly wouldn't be my choice for you. It wouldn't be in my top one hundred choices for you."

"I knew that you'd feel that way, and I don't blame you. I just want you to know that fire fighting is where my heart lies, so it might be hard for me to muster up much enthusiasm for any of my tamer interests."

"The most tame profession could get a little wild with you around. How about med school? Wouldn't some of your interests be satisfied if you did something like be a trauma surgeon or something wild like that?"

"I guess that would suit me."

"Would you let me pay for medical school if you decided to go?"

"I'd let you lend me the money. Maybe we could come up with a deal where I work off the debt," she said with a wiggling eyebrow.

"Hey, why buy the cow when you're already getting the milk for free?"

"Good point. Besides, you're about to suck me dry as it is," Ryan said as she slumped down in her chair.

Jamie laughed at her antics and then asked, "Would you be happy being a doctor?"

"Well, the idea is kind of new for me, so I haven't given it a lot of thought. The positive side is that I'd love to help people one on one. I'm sure I'd love being a pediatrician, even though it would be hard to see kids who were truly sick or dying. And I think I'd like being a gynecologist or an obstetrician."

"Go with what you love," Jamie said. "You could probably opt out of some of the classes based on life experience."

"Very funny," Ryan said, sneaking her hand under the table to pinch her thigh.

"Well, why not apply and see what happens?"

"I guess I will. I took the MCAT just for fun, but now I guess I'm glad I did. Getting in and paying for the degree isn't what has me concerned right now. I'm more interested in talking this out to see if that's the kind of life we want."

"Being a doctor is a big time commitment," Jamie said. "But we might as well see what happens with your applications. No use in worrying if it's not gonna happen."

"Yeah, you're right, as usual."

"So what programs will you apply to?"

"I guess math, bio, chem, and med school."

"Where?"

"Berkeley and UCSF," she said as though this was obvious, naming the two most selective state schools in the Bay Area.

"Shouldn't you apply to some safe schools?"

"No, if I can't get in where I want to go, I'd rather wait and apply again."

"What are your grades like? You've never mentioned them."

"They're pretty good," she said, avoiding Jamie's eyes. "My grade report came today."

"Did mine come too?"

"No. Just mine."

"How'd you do?"

She fished into her pocket and pulled out the little white slip, holding it tightly in her hands looking at Jamie with a shy, childlike expression. "I've never shown my grades to another person. I don't even tell Da." She slid it across the table and let Jamie unfold it. The blonde's jaw dropped as she stared at the paper for a few long seconds.

"Ryan," she said with a disgusted look, sliding the report back across the table, "that isn't human."

Broad shoulders shrugged helplessly.

"I guess people like you don't need a *safe school*," Jamie muttered.

"Hey, don't make a big deal about this. I sure as hell don't."

"Why not? You work hard to get the grades. Why aren't you proud of 'em?"

"They don't mean anything," Ryan said dismissively. "When I had that terrible senior semester, I was the same person that I was the semester before and the semester after. But people treated me differently when my average fell. That was small minded and stupid, and since then grades don't mean much to me. I take the classes that interest me, and I try to learn as much from them as I can. As long as I stay interested, the grades follow."

"You're so mature sometimes that it's scary," Jamie said as she shook her head.

Ryan spent the next few minutes trying to hit sugar cubes with her chopstick, using the little wooden stick as a bat. She got a few good licks in, and Jamie had to dive for one so it didn't hit the waitress. The woman gave Ryan a stern look as she placed their entrées on the table. Jamie shook her head as she laughed at her chastised partner. "And the opposite is true, too."

As they walked home hand in hand, Ryan said, "We spent all of dinner talking about me. It's your turn now. Have you given much thought to grad school?"

"Yeah, I have. I know I could do English lit and get a Ph.D. studying something that I really love. But I don't want to teach, so I don't know if it makes sense to spend the time. I used to think that I wanted to write, but I've been less interested in that since we've been together."

"Why do you think that is?" Ryan inquired, just then realizing that Jamie didn't even seem to be writing in her journal.

"I'm not sure. I just don't spend much time reflecting anymore. I've been spending too much time actually *living* my life," she said with a laugh.

"Maybe you needed your writing to help you work some things out before."

"You might say that. I think every short story I've ever written has at least one really strong, sexually ambiguous woman in it. Could I *be* any more clueless?"

Ryan laughed at her characterization, but asked again, "So what else interests you? You don't have to stay in school if you don't want to, you know. You could start figuring out how to give money away."

"Yeah, that's true. But there is something else I'm interested in."

"What?" Ryan asked as she turned to her.

"Psychology."

"Really?" A delighted grin lit up Ryan's face. "Did Lesbianism 101 put that idea in your head?"

"No," she laughed. "But being in therapy has. I've really learned a lot about myself in the months that I've been working with Anna, and I think I'd like to help other people do the same."

"Wow," Ryan said. "That would really be cool. And since you don't have to worry about money, you could work with people who couldn't normally afford it."

"Yeah, that would be the cool thing," she agreed. "So I think I'll apply to Berkeley and at least one other. *I* need a safe school," she said as she stuck out her tongue.

"Hey," Ryan warned. "Don't stick that out if you're not gonna use it."

"Who's gonna stop me?" she asked with an impish grin as she began to run down the street.

"Winner gets to go first!" Ryan declared as she loudly stomped for a few steps behind her racing lover. As soon as Jamie had a good head start, she slowed down to a saunter. *I like going last,* she thought smugly as she watched her lover fly down the street.

On Thursday morning, Jordan and Ryan were shuffling down the halls of the Recreational Sports Facility, their legs so sore neither woman could lift them to walk normally. "The season's gonna be a breeze compared with the workouts we've been doing," Jordan said.

"Mmm, this isn't all that much different from what I normally do," Ryan said nonchalantly, stretching the truth a few miles.

"Uh-huh," Jordan said, poking her sharply in the gut. "And that's why you can barely pick your feet up." It was clear that Jordan had Ryan's number, but their boasting and teasing had become an important element in the way they connected, with both women enjoying the playful dynamic.

"I always walk like this," Ryan said, stifling a laugh. "You're just so self-involved that you barely notice me."

"The third element of your statement is the truth," Jordan chuckled. "The first two—total lies."

Rounding the corner, they continued their banter until a woman's voice called out, "Ryan, Jordan, hold on a minute."

They stopped and waited as a middle-aged woman jogged down the hall to greet them both. As she got closer, Ryan recognized Mary Hayes, the women's basketball coach. "A word with you both?"

"Sure," Jordan said, giving Ryan a quick glance.

"Any chance I could convince either of you to consider being two-sport athletes this year? We're just two players away from being a force in the PAC-10."

More like five players, Ryan thought, considering the dismal showing of the basketball team for the last thirty years.

"Not me, Coach," Jordan said quickly. "With any luck I'll be in Colorado Springs before the year's out. I'm sure you could talk Ryan into joining you, though. She's got energy to burn. Our little workouts hardly affect her at all." Jordan shot Ryan a demonic grin, patted her cheek, and announced, "I've got to run. Catch you in the morning, Ryan." Extending her hand, she shook the coach's and shuffled down the hall, leaving Ryan to continue the conversation.

"Bye, Jordan," both women called after her. The coach made no move to repeat her question, and Ryan reminded herself that Mary Hayes was a woman of few words. The older woman just tilted her head slightly, waiting for Ryan to answer her query.

"I uhm…" she hesitated, considering the proposal. "I might be interested," she finally said. "This is my last year—"

Before she could even finish her sentence, Coach Hayes slapped her on her very wet back and said, "Four o'clock today good for you?"

Looking slightly confused, Ryan nodded.

"Good. Meet me at the court. I want to see if your skills have eroded since I last saw you play."

Ryan recalled the trouncing that USF had delivered to Cal two years before when she buried them with a season high of twenty-seven points. At the time, she'd been decidedly miffed by the double and triple team that the Bears had tried to smother her with, and she remembered feeling that the game was more of a mugging than a fair contest. "I'll be there," she said, unable to resist the challenge.

Walking home from the gym, she came to her senses and thought, *I'd better think of a way to spin this with Jamie, or that last mugging I got will seem like a day at the beach.*

"Jamie?" she called when she entered the house.

Receiving no answer, she went into the backyard, smiling to herself when she saw her partner stretched out on a chaise, sections of the newspaper spread around her and a large coffee mug resting on a table at her elbow. Her Walkman was also lying on the table, and Ryan checked her watch to confirm that "Morning Edition" was now over.

"Hi, love," she said, walking to the foot of the chaise.

Jamie shot her a suspicious look. "What did you do?"

"Do?" she asked. "Why do you assume I've done something?" Her pure, innocent face was testament to her virtuousness.

"Dendrobium orchids are my favorite flower, and the bunch you have in your hand must have cost you thirty bucks. For you to part with thirty bucks means that you think you have something very big to apologize for. So let's cut to the chase and get it over with. Now, what did you do?" Her voice was serious, but the twinkling green eyes gave a clearer indication of her mental state.

"I didn't *do* anything," Ryan insisted, sitting down on the end of the chaise. "I'm thinking of doing something…but I haven't done it yet."

Accepting the flowers from her partner, Jamie traced the delicate blossoms with the tip of her finger, seemingly intent only on their form. "So these represent a peremptory apology?" she asked coyly.

"No, I wouldn't say they're an apology," Ryan said. "I just wanted to show you that I was thinking about you and to tell you how important you are to me. I want you to know that I value our relationship more than anything and that our having time together means a great deal to me."

Jamie's head cocked, and she stared deeply into Ryan's eyes. "Are you moving out or something? This sounds bad."

"Of course not," she said, laughing. "We're together for life, you goof, and don't you forget it. I just got an offer today that I'm considering—"

"This better not be the type of offer you used to get." Now Jamie's fierce gaze matched her tone of voice, and Ryan realized she'd better get to the point.

"Actually, this *was* the type of offer I used to get, but it wasn't sexual. The basketball coach approached me and asked if I might like to play this year."

"Play?" Jamie asked slowly. "This year?"

"Yeah. This year."

"But how would you…I mean you've already committed to Coach Placer, and…"

"Basketball is a winter sport, babe. I'd finish the volleyball season and then start playing basketball. I did this at USF, too. It's not that hard."

Shaking her flowers right in Ryan's face, Jamie mused, "Thirty bucks says something about this is hard. Now spill it."

Ryan laughed gently, both pleased and chagrined that her partner knew her so well. "It'd take a lot of my time," she said. "I might like playing, but I don't want you to feel neglected. Basketball has a longer season than volleyball does, and there's a lot more travel involved."

Jamie mulled that over for a few moments, finally asking, "Do you really believe that we'll be together for the rest of our lives?"

Eyebrows shooting up dramatically, Ryan declared, "Of course I do. I made a vow to you."

Tickling her nose with the orchid blossoms, Jamie nodded. "I do, too. And given that we both believe that, there's no reason to avoid things you want to do, even if they keep us apart more than either of us likes. I don't want our relationship to keep you from doing anything, Ryan." Leaning forward to kiss her partner's salty lips, she added, "Well, other than that one thing, that is."

"No interest in doing that with anyone else," Ryan insisted. "You're all that I can handle…and I'm still not sure I can handle you."

"Come on, big talker," Jamie said, getting to her feet and extending a hand. "Let's get you showered so you don't stiffen up."

"Oh, I'm way past stiff," Ryan said. "And it's gonna get worse. I told Coach Hayes I'd meet her this afternoon to demonstrate that I can still play."

"This afternoon?" Jamie was none too happy with the scheduling of this little demonstration, but she knew that complaining wouldn't convince her hardheaded lover to put it off. "Grab a change of clothes, hot stuff. We're going to the spa."

Two hours later, Ryan was simmering in the deep, herbal-scented spa, while Jamie lay on a chaise near the bubbling pool. The smaller woman had just had her nails done, so she couldn't go into the spa until the polish dried. "I always thought you did your own nails," Ryan murmured, the deep relaxation of her sports massage combining with the 103-degree water to render her nearly unconscious.

"Not likely," Jamie said, laughing. "I haven't done my own nails since I was twelve."

"Hmm, I've never had a manicure. I don't think I'd like it."

"I like the manicure," Jamie said. "But I *love* the pedicure."

"Hmm, I'd love that too, but I don't want a stranger to do it."

"You're on, Tiger. I'll be your own personal pedicurist. I think I'll paint your nails hot pink."

"No way, babe. I want the nice, clear stuff you use on yours."

"You're no fun," Jamie pouted.

"Let's see if you think that after you play with my feet for a while," Ryan purred, suddenly shaking off her lethargy.

At four o'clock they were back at the Recreational Sports Facility. Jamie thought Ryan looked simply adorable in a black nylon sleeveless v-neck T-shirt and a pair of black nylon running shorts. She also wore thick white socks under black high-top basketball shoes, and to Jamie's studied gaze she looked long and sleek and slightly dangerous, just the way she liked her.

As they entered the court, a woman of medium height and below-average weight strode over and extended her hand. "Good to see you again, Ryan," she said with a cool, intelligent-looking gaze.

"You too, Coach Hayes." Turning to her lover she made the introductions. "Coach, this is my partner, Jamie Evans."

The coach offered her hand and gave Jamie a smile that did not extend to her eyes. "Jamie, this is Mary Hayes." They shook hands but Jamie just nodded after getting no positive vibes from the woman. She didn't look antagonistic, just very serious and businesslike.

"Well, Ryan," she said as she placed her hands on her hips and gazed at the younger woman's long body, "whether or not you play for us, it's nice not to have you kicking our asses for USF." She made this statement with such a blank expression that Ryan was unable to tell if it was a compliment or a complaint.

"Yeah, I had a couple of good games when I played there," she said, looking a little uncomfortable.

"Well, let's get to work," the coach said, clearly tired of what she must have considered excessive small talk.

Three assistant coaches took the floor as Ryan tightened her laces. Two were considerably younger than Coach Hayes, possibly as young as or younger than Ryan. They had all obviously been players at one time, given their height and their dexterity with the ball as they warmed up a little, but the third woman was a tall, middle-aged, stocky black woman who looked like her playing days were long behind her. She walked up to Ryan and extended a hand. "Lynette Dix," she said with a big, friendly smile. "When I heard you'd transferred to Cal, I thanked the Lord that we wouldn't automatically have an 'L' on our schedule whenever we played USF."

"I think you're being a little generous," Ryan chuckled, but her cheeks reddened just a bit at the compliment.

"No, not at all," the woman said. "I was after Mary all last year to call you and see if you wanted to try out this year. Once we heard you were going to play volleyball, we decided to see if you'd consider two sports."

"Thanks," Ryan said, beaming a happy smile at the warm welcome. "I hope you still feel that way after I've worked out."

"No worries on my part," she said, smiling. "You can hoop!"

Coach Hayes was clearly running the show, and she decided to have Ryan show her defensive skills first. The head coach stood in the center of the floor and watched closely as the two young assistants played two on one with Ryan. They spent almost fifteen minutes banging against her as they tried to score, with Jamie marveling as she watched her lover move fluidly around the court. Ryan seemed to know how to move her feet to keep her position between the shooter and the basket, moving easily when she chose, but absolutely refusing to be moved involuntarily. No matter how often or how hard the assistants slammed into her, she maintained her poise and her position.

On three separate occasions Ryan easily stole the ball from the other players. She would give them a half smile and gently toss it back to them, daring them to come at her again. Her hands were very quick slapping at the ball as they tried to dribble past her, but her quick feet were what really distinguished her. She just seemed to know which way her opponents would turn, even when they were in the air. She was never truly burned by a head fake, because once she started to fall for one she had the ability to correct her mistake and regroup. After one such play, the taller of the two assistants slammed the ball down hard, letting it bounce the length of the floor in slowly descending arcs. At this subtle signal of termination, all three bent over at the waist, gasping for breath. *She must be dying if she's showing this much*, Jamie thought with alarm, knowing that Ryan hated to show others that she was physically stressed.

To Jamie's displeasure, the coach only allowed Ryan a few moments to catch her breath before she told her to run fifty full-court drives. With nary a word of protest, Ryan jogged to the end of the court, accepted the in-bounds pass from Lynette, and began to dribble it the length of the court while being guarded by both defenders. The point of the game was to stop and shoot over both women while making as many baskets as possible. She missed as many as she made, but Jamie was terribly impressed by her ball-handling skills as well as by her shooting style. The assistants were clearly giving this exercise everything they had, and they were very aggressive in defending against Ryan. Jamie thought it was fantastic that she made any baskets at all given the relentless pressure she faced.

After another fifteen minutes of this torture, the assistants flopped down on the bench to rest. Ryan grabbed a bottle of Gatorade and chugged it, looking over at Jamie and giving her a cocky wink. As soon as she was hydrated, she was told to stay in the key and take jump shots. This was normally not a problem, but she had to get her own rebounds. Jamie's eyes grew wide as she watched her set, shoot, and run all in one fluid motion. She made at least 75 percent of her shots, but when she missed, she went after the rebound with a vengeance, showing nothing but a blur of motion for another fifteen minutes. After a while, it hurt just to watch as her straining body ran continuously. Ryan's bangs hung limply in her eyes, and even though her hair was pulled back in a ponytail, it stuck to her neck and shoulders. She wiped the sweat from her eyes every time she had the chance, but it was clear from her red-rimmed eyes that they were burning from the salt. Finally, the coach told her to stop, but rather than give her a rest, she immediately asked her to shoot free throws.

Wordlessly, Ryan stood on the free throw line and took a few deep breaths. She wiped the sweat from her eyes again and bent a bit at the knees as she dribbled the ball three times. She shot so many free throws that Jamie lost count. She did, however, have Ryan's free throw routine completely memorized. Each shot was a carbon copy of the previous one. She grabbed the ball from Coach Dix, who was snagging rebounds, and held it with both hands close to her waist. She wiped her eyes with the back of her left hand, and then dribbled three times with that same hand. She held the ball in both hands again, this time higher on her chest. One deep breath, a slight bend at the knee, and the ball was launched with the same fluid push, again and again. As the ball slid through the net her shooting hand would bend at the wrist with her fingers pointing toward the floor. Jamie was fascinated to see that on the rare shot that failed to hit its mark, the hand did not drop. It was obvious that Ryan knew whether the shot was good or not immediately upon release, and the little hand motion was her own unconscious way of signaling that the shot was good.

After a very long time Coach Hayes asked Ryan to come out to the three-point line. The fatigued woman actually asked for a moment to grab another bottle of Gatorade, which once again surprised Jamie. The coach nodded and Ryan slugged down a whole bottle, not even stopping to breathe between gulps. There was no confident little wink this time, as Ryan didn't even turn in Jamie's direction. She did, however, grab a towel that one of the assistants tossed to her and wipe her face and arms thoroughly to remove the sweat before trotting back onto the court.

When she took her position again, Jamie noticed that Coach Hayes had positioned five rolling ball racks spaced a few feet apart along the three-point line. Each rack held six balls, and as Ryan looked up at her, the coach said, "This is a little drill we do in practice. Start at either end you choose, but you need to go through the racks in order. You get one point for each one you make. It pays to work on your three-pointers," she said with a chuckle. "The winner doesn't have to run sprints after practice," she said with her first genuine smile of the day.

Ryan returned her smile a bit cautiously and walked over to the rack on the right side of the basket. "Oh, did I mention that you only get three minutes?" Coach Hayes said.

One graceful eyebrow rose one half of an inch, but it was enough for Jamie to realize that her lover was being challenged. *Look out*, she thought to herself. *She's gonna kick ass on this one.*

And kick ass she did. As Ryan picked up the first ball, Jamie looked at the big clock on the wall with the sweep second hand. Ryan flew through the first rack, trying to get comfortable. She only made two, but as she ran to the next rack her eyes were fiercely focused on the basket. This time she made six of six and Jamie almost jumped in the air and shouted her approval. Three of six fell from the top of the key, four of six from the next rack, and as Ryan got to the last rack, she paused for the first time and set herself fully. Even though Jamie was sure she couldn't see the clock, Ryan seemed to know that she had time to do this set carefully. Swoosh! The first ball slid in so easily that it looked like it didn't even touch the net on the way through. Five more swooshes followed, giving the smiling woman twenty-one points.

The coach was obviously satisfied as she broke into her second smile of the day and slapped Ryan on the back. Jamie could hear the wet "plop" all the way over where she was sitting, a good thirty feet away. The other coaches all came up and slapped her in a similar fashion. *What's with all the slapping? That skin is sensitive…and it belongs to me.*

She was too far away to hear exactly what they were saying, but it was clear that they were pleased and impressed with Ryan's performance. Ryan smiled and chatted for a few more minutes before she jogged over to Jamie. "How'd I do?" she asked with a wan grin.

Regarding Ryan's wet hair, the nylon clothes literally stuck to her body, and the sweat dripping from the tips of her fingers, Jamie said, "Hold on a sec," and trotted over to the departing coaches.

She caught up with them just as they were exiting the court, speaking for just a few moments and pointing at Ryan, who rolled her eyes in embarrassment. She nodded and ran back, grinning at her with a shy little smile. "They're going to let you use the whirlpool and the showers. They said to meet them in the locker room. I'm going to the bookstore to buy you some dry shorts and a shirt."

"But—" Ryan started to say, but was cut off.

"Go on. The coaches are going to shower too. If they had any doubts about the shape you're in, you can dispel them as soon as you strip." She pushed Ryan in their direction as she gave her a hard slap on the butt. When her lover whirled to glare at her, she innocently remarked, "I'm just trying to be one of the girls."

It was seven o'clock by the time Ryan was loose enough to climb out of the Jacuzzi and put on the dry clothes that Jamie had left for her. She emerged from the locker room and was surprised to find a note on the door that said "Come to room 115 at Haas" in her lover's handwriting. Walking through the labyrinth of offices in the brand-new complex, she finally found the correct suite. Several offices ran along the back wall of the large space and room 115 was clearly marked as the office of "Lynette Dix, Assistant Head Basketball Coach."

Ryan poked her dark head into the office to find Jamie chatting with the coach in an animated, friendly fashion. "Hi," Jamie called out when she caught sight of her lover.

"Hi, yourself," Ryan grinned as she grabbed a chair.

"I believe I'm being cross-examined," the older woman said to Ryan, a good-natured smile on her face.

"She does that to everyone, Coach, don't let her intimidate you."

"I'd prefer it if you'd call me Lynette."

"No problem," Ryan said. "So, what's going on here?"

"I didn't like the vibes I was getting from Coach Hayes, and Lynette here seemed really approachable," Jamie said. "I thought I'd see if she'd give me the straight story, since I knew you wouldn't ask." She made this last statement with a pair of rolling eyes in the direction of her lover.

"I see," Ryan said thoughtfully. "And what did you find out, my little detective?"

"I think Jamie has some legitimate concerns," Lynette said. "Mary does come across as being rather gruff and unyielding. I wish I could tell you that was an act, but it really isn't. Mary's a true perfectionist, and she most definitely likes things done her way."

"Well, she is the coach," Ryan reasoned.

"She certainly is, and she likes her players to remember that," she said. "If you're looking for a place to play 'playground style,' this isn't it. She likes a very formal, set offense, and she wants defense to be the most important part of the game. I honestly think she'd be happy if we won a game by a score of two to nothing."

"That doesn't bother me," Ryan said. "I like to score, but I love to play defense, and I can play on the playground any time I want with my family. I'd like to play on a nice, organized team."

"One other big thing," Lynette said slowly. "Coach Hayes doesn't like to spend much time with the players on a personal level. If you need a lot of handholding, or a lot of feedback, you will not get it from her. She's more like the general of a small army going into battle. She wants to come up with the game plan, and then she wants the assistants to implement it and get the troops ready to fight. When we go into battle she leads us, but it's all according to the game plan. She'd rather lose and stick to the plan than win by having the players be creative."

Ryan leaned back in her chair and considered the coach's words. "Are you this honest with all of your recruits?" she asked with a small smile. "'Cause if you are, I don't see how you get five women to sign up."

Lynette laughed at Ryan's observation and said, "No, I'm not usually this honest. But you're an adult, Ryan, and you're not doing this for the same reason most of the girls are. I know you want to play to have fun and compete. That's obviously the kind of woman you are. I just hate to see you devote a lot of time to this if it's not going to satisfy your needs."

"I'm betting you have more personnel problems than you know what to do with, don't you?" Ryan asked perceptively.

"*Well*," she drawled with a big grin, "I wouldn't say it's the happiest place on earth right now."

"You didn't lose many players to graduation," Ryan reasoned. "I'd think things would be on the upswing, assuming your freshmen turn out to be as talented as I'm reading about."

Lynette smiled at this and said, "The *Daily Californian* only knows what we tell them about our freshmen. As you know, everybody who plays at the Division One level was a very good player in high school. But this is a big leap in class, and we never know how a player will adjust."

"So what do you think your chances are of being competitive?"

Lynette thought for a minute and decided to be completely honest. "We'd be much improved with you. We don't have a consistent scorer at forward, and our defense was pretty poor last year. That's usually the last thing a freshman learns, so without you, I think we'll be near the cellar again."

"Winning is always important to me," Ryan admitted, "but it's not my primary motivation for playing. I like to challenge myself, and helping a poor team become better would be exciting for me." She leveled a gaze at Lynette and asked the question that would have a very large impact on her decision. "One big question. Will I have a problem being open about my relationship with Jamie?"

Lynette sat for a moment, clearly trying to think of the ramifications of the question. "You wouldn't be the only lesbian on the team," she said thoughtfully. "Coach doesn't seem to have a problem with that, but I'm not sure I can give you an easy answer. The other lesbian isn't very popular, but I don't think it's because of her sexual orientation." Her brow was knotted in concentration as Ryan waited patiently. "I just can't answer you definitively, Ryan. All I know is that I'm a lesbian too, and Coach knows it. I've never gotten any flak from her, or the administration, but I'm not out to the other players, so I can't say for sure how they would react."

Ryan nodded thoughtfully and stood, extending her hand to the coach. "You've been tremendously helpful, Lynette," she said. "Jamie and I will discuss it, and I'll let you know if I want to try out for one of your walk-on spots."

"Ryan," she said as she stood and clasped the strong hand with both of hers, "you won't have to try out. You'd be the best player on our team if you'd agree to play." Ryan looked a little shocked, but she continued. "The best score on that three-point drill all last year was a fifteen."

Ryan's open-mouthed look caused Lynette to laugh long and hard. "We'd love to have you, and I truly believe that you could help make us competitive in the PAC-10. I hope you'll join us."

Chapter Ten

"**W**ow," Jamie said softly as they exited the building. "Good thing she's not selling cars. She'd go broke in a week."

"Yeah, that was a bit of brutal honesty," Ryan agreed. She turned to her partner and said, "I want to talk about this some more, but if I don't get some food, I'm afraid I'm gonna cause a scene."

Jamie's gentle laugh was accompanied by a playful swat on the seat. "Let's walk down Telegraph and stop at the first place that gets your attention."

They settled on the first place they hit that didn't have a long line. When the server arrived, Ryan abandoned all pretense of propriety and said, "I've gotta have something in my stomach fast. Bring us whatever appetizer is fastest."

"Let me tell you the specials for the day," the young man replied, ignoring Ryan's clear request.

"You must not have understood me," she said. "Please go into the kitchen and grab the quickest thing in there. We can chat when you come back."

Jamie stared at her as the irritated server sniffed but proceeded to follow her lover's orders. "I've never seen you act so..." she struggled for a term that wasn't too offensive, but found that she couldn't think of one.

"I wasn't kidding," Ryan said softly. As Jamie looked at her carefully, she noticed that under her lover's tanned face a tinge of gray had replaced the pink hue of good health that she normally exhibited.

"Honey, what's wrong?"

"I didn't get enough to eat today," she muttered, seemingly angry with herself. "After we were done at the spa I was afraid to eat much, since I knew I'd be working my butt off this afternoon. I feel sick."

The server returned to unceremoniously drop a platter of antipasto onto the table, with Ryan digging into it so quickly that she nearly made sparks fly. He watched her, a bit in awe, as he described the specials to Jamie. When he finished speaking, Ryan looked up at him with one of her most charming smiles and said, "I apologize for being so rude. But I was about to pass out, and I guarantee you wouldn't want me falling on you."

"That's okay," he said, apparently placated. "You were obviously serious." He watched her continue to plow through the platter. "Did you want an entrée too?"

"At least!" she cried, laughing around a mouthful of marinated red peppers.

"Sweetheart," Jamie chided after the server left, "you've got to make sure you get a decent meal, especially when you're working out like this."

"I know, I know. I didn't take very good care of myself today. It's hard to find high-quality snacks that can fuel me when I get into a bind like that."

"Do you have a space at the gym where you can keep things?"

"Yeah, there's a small locker in the office for each of us."

"Let's fill it with some things for situations like this. No matter what you do this fall, you're gonna be stressing your body, and you need to keep your weight up."

"I know. That's a good idea."

Their entrées were delivered quickly, and conversation came to a standstill while Ryan polished off her linguini with clam sauce. "Can't hold a candle to yours," she said dismissively as she eyed Jamie's veal piccata.

"Go on." Jamie pushed the plate across the table. "I should know better than to ever expect to finish an entrée."

Ryan gave her a guilty look, but nonetheless downed the remainder of the veal dish in moments. While she ate, she commented, "Do you think I should consider the basketball team?"

Jamie knew the question was coming and she had already prepared her answer. "If it were me, I wouldn't have any interest in being in that hornet's nest. But I don't think most of the things Lynette said would really bother you. So it all comes down to enjoyment. Do you enjoy playing basketball enough to ignore the bullshit?"

"I think so," Ryan said rather thoughtfully. "I know you don't think this way, but the fact that it sounds like it'll be difficult makes it more appealing to me."

Jamie smiled at her and nodded her head. "I might have been wrong about Lynette," she mused. "A good car salesperson tailors her pitch to her audience. I think she knew that the truth would appeal to you."

"Could be," Ryan agreed with a self-effacing chuckle. "I just hope I'm not buying a lemon with this team."

Later that night, Ryan was just getting down to some serious neck nibbling when Jamie's cell phone rang, causing the little phone to dance on the dresser. "Uhm, mind if I get that?" Jamie was lying prone on the bed, Ryan's powerful body hovering over her, most of her weight resting on her braced arms.

"Go ahead." Ryan smiled sweetly, not moving a muscle.

A quick tickle to the armpit caused Ryan to rethink her reluctance to move, and she rolled into a not-so-little ball to escape her partner's twitching fingers. Jamie swatted her on the butt as she scampered off the bed to retrieve the phone. Grabbing it on the sixth ring she panted, "Hello?"

"Jamie? Did I catch you at a bad time?"

"No, Daddy," she said, a little uncomfortable to be talking to her father while she was naked and on the verge of making love. She slipped into her robe, rolling her eyes at Ryan, who was trying to suppress a giggle. "I was just getting ready for bed."

"You *have* been working hard," he said. "It's only 8:30." There was a moment of silence, giving him time to think of what his daughter was doing in bed at 8:30 at night. "Uhm, I called to speak to you about a call I received from Tuck today."

"Yes?" Jamie had assumed that her trust officer, Tuck Gray, would mention her request for an income distribution to her father, but she didn't think it would be so soon. "Is there a problem?"

He hesitated for a moment, his irritation showing when he said, "Other than the fact that you didn't ask my permission, no."

She blinked slowly, completely unaccustomed to being required to account for her purchases. "Ask for permission?" she said slowly, meeting eyes with Ryan, who looked pained. "Since when do I have to ask *your* permission to spend *my* money?"

"Since you started spending $25,000 on a car," he said, his temper still flaring. "I should think that requesting a $25,000 distribution might warrant a mention."

"We talked about this when we played golf, Daddy. If I recall, it was your idea that I buy a car."

His voice was softer now, and she could hear the hurt as he said, "I thought we'd do this together."

Oh-oh, he's jealous. She mentally kicked herself for failing to realize this might happen. "I'm sorry. I didn't mean to make you feel left out."

"That's hardly the issue, Jamie," he huffed, and now she kicked herself for wounding his pride. "I'm your trustee, and it's my duty to make sure your money is handled properly."

"Daddy," she said evenly, "I didn't buy a Ferrari Testarossa. I bought the small Lexus SUV."

"You can't buy that car for $25,000 dollars."

"You can if it's used," she countered. "Ryan was uncomfortable spending so much money, so she convinced me to buy a demo."

"A demo? You bought a demo?"

"Yeah, you know, a car that the dealer uses for test drives and for the salespeople to drive."

"I know what a demo is, Jamie," he sniffed. "I just want you to ask me next time."

"We're not going to be in the market for another car for a very long while. If Ryan's in charge, we'll drive this one until the wheels fall off."

"I don't just mean about cars. I'd like to know before you request any type of funds transfer."

She counted to ten, hoping the little pause would allow her temper to calm. Regrettably, it didn't, and she snapped, "I've never had to do that before. I'd like to know why you're trying to exert more control over me as I grow older. Shouldn't it be the reverse?"

"Spending this amount of money makes me doubt your maturity."

She took in a deep breath, trying valiantly to stop herself from saying something she would regret. "That's very disappointing to hear. I don't think I've done anything to make you feel that way, but of course, you're in charge, so I'm forced to abide by your orders." She knew she was being bitchy, but he had really hurt her feelings, and she wanted him to know it.

"That's not fair, Jamie," he insisted. "I'm not giving you orders. I'm making a reasonable request."

"A request that I have to follow." She let that sink in and then said, "Ryan's waiting for me. I have to go. Good night." As she switched off the phone, she dropped it onto her desk and flopped down onto the bed next to Ryan. "That went well."

"Is he mad that you bought a car, or mad that you didn't ask for permission?" Ryan asked, surmising the gist of the conversation.

"Neither, if my guess is correct. I think he's hurt that I didn't take him with me, but he's embarrassed to admit that."

"Bummer," Ryan muttered solicitously. "Doesn't sound like it ended well."

Jamie rubbed her eyes with her fists, irritated with herself for having lost her temper. "No, it didn't, but I should have behaved better. I just can't stand to be dictated to about money."

I can vouch for that, Ryan silently agreed. "What're the rules about getting money from your trust?"

"I don't think I know what all of the rules are," she said. "I don't even have a copy of the trust agreement. I wanted to show it to you, so I looked for it before we went to Pebble Beach, but I didn't have one. I called Daddy to ask for a copy, and, as usual, he assured me that I have enough money for a dozen lifetimes, and that I had nothing to worry about." She made a sour face.

"I'm sorry he hurt your feelings, babe," Ryan soothed, rubbing Jamie's back gently.

"I'll get over it," she grumbled. "It's happened before and it'll happen again." She let out a breath and smiled. "He needs to feel like he's in charge, even though he's not."

On Friday morning, Jamie woke to the pleasant sensation of soft fingers lightly running over her stomach and thighs. Without a word, she reached down and guided the hand so the touch came up a little higher. Ryan's chuckle rumbled into her ear, "Sorry I wasn't covering all of the favorite terrain."

"You were covering all of yours," she corrected sleepily, "just not all of mine."

Ryan's wide-awake voice purred into her ear. "I'm ready to rock."

"I can tell," Jamie drawled as she rubbed her backside into Ryan's lap. "Do you want to do something about it?"

"Yeah, but we really should get up. We've gotta meet the team in a half hour, and I don't want a quickie."

"Okay," Jamie agreed as she rolled onto her back and stretched sensually for several minutes. Ryan watched with a gleam in her eye that would not quit. Jamie caught the look and teased, "That leer makes me think your baser instincts might win out this morning."

Ryan shook her head and hopped out of bed. "Nope. I'm staying on the straight and narrow. But I want to hit the sack by 8:00 tonight. I've got big plans for you."

"Can we do that at home?"

"What? Have sex?" Ryan replied with wide eyes. "Fine time to ask now."

"No, silly. Can we go to bed that early? Won't you feel a little funny if everyone's at home?"

"Nope. If we're going to live there, we have to treat it like it's ours. If we think that we have to be with the family all the time, it just won't work. We need to keep our own schedule and let them adapt. They've already been very respectful of our closed door, and we didn't even have to mention it."

"That's true. I guess we have to establish a pattern they can get used to."

"Right. I think we should decide if we want to eat with the family and tell them in advance. Kind of like I used to do. I don't want to feel like I'm in high school again."

"Let's talk to your father and see what we can work out."

"Okay, we'll give it a try."

Late that afternoon, Jamie sat in the kitchen "helping" Martin prepare dinner. Marta had given her more challenging tasks when she was four years old, but she acknowledged that every cook had his own routine, and she didn't want to press the issue.

"Where's herself?" Martin asked after a few minutes. "I've never seen this much space between the two of you."

Jamie gave him a puzzled look, and he explained, "That's a term used for the man or woman of the house. It's sort of a joke, but we sometimes refer to Siobhán as 'herself,' you know, kind of like the queen bee?"

"I get it," she said, acknowledging that Ryan had been the woman of the house for many years. "And you'd be 'himself?'"

"Well," he laughed, "I should be, but we usually refer to Conor that way. It fits, doesn't it?"

She laughed. "Now that you mention it... Oh, in answer to your question, Ryan's on her computer answering her e-mail."

"Thank goodness we don't have to pay the long-distance charges for that service. It's bad enough having to call Ireland to talk to her grandparents."

Jamie smiled at his exaggerated complaint, knowing that he wouldn't complain if there were a charge for e-mail. They worked companionably for a few more minutes before he asked, "How do you think things are going for you staying here on the weekends, darlin'? I know it's important for you two to have your privacy."

"Funny you should mention that, Martin. We were talking about that this morning," she said. "I think it's going really well, but we wanted to make sure of a few things."

"Like what things, for example?"

Jamie mentally scowled at her partner for leaving her to handle this discussion, but she decided to continue on. "Like if we want to go to our room as soon as we come home at night," she said, hoping she wasn't blushing from the embarrassment she felt.

"You're going to have to get over your shyness about wanting to be alone. I know what it's like, darlin'. And once Maeve and I are together, I plan on spending a great deal of time with her—completely alone."

She smiled at the delighted look in his eyes and said, "I swear I don't know how you've managed being without a mate all these years, Martin. You just don't seem like the kind of fellow who would choose to be alone."

He laughed wryly, acknowledging the truth of her statement. "I do best when I'm well loved," he admitted. "But for the first seven or so years after Fi died, I wouldn't have noticed if I was surrounded by beautiful women. It's been difficult for the last few years, I'll confess. I knew that I wanted Maeve to be mine, but I couldn't say anything while she was still a married woman."

"I really admire your restraint," she said. "It shows how much you respect her."

"Oh, I do," he said. "But I'm ready to move forward now. I'm counting the days until we can be together."

"So you aren't..." she hinted.

"Oh, no," he said as his own cheeks flushed. "I wouldn't dream of asking for that before I made a public commitment to her. You don't treat a woman like Maeve that way."

She gave him a beaming smile as she patted his hand. "She's a very lucky woman, Martin."

"Are you talking about me?" Ryan asked from the doorway.

"That we were," Martin teased. "You've one in a million here, Siobhán."

"You don't have to tell me, Da. But I think she's more precious than that. If she were only one in a million there'd be two thousand women just like her in China alone. And that can't be true."

"That's a perfectly valid point. Would you like a snack before dinner?"

"When have I ever refused?"

He whipped up a little treat for her and handed her the plate, which she took into the dining room. Both Jamie and Martin joined her, and after a second Martin said, "Jamie tells me that we need to work out some new rules for how we communicate."

Ryan cocked her head at her partner, silently asking to be filled in on the conversation.

"I told your father what we talked about this morning," Jamie said.

Ryan nodded. "Well, I think everything has gone well so far, but we just want to make sure we don't offend any of you if we want some time alone."

"I really do understand, Siobhán. What would make you feel comfortable?"

"I guess my main concern is dinnertime. Let's assume that we all won't eat dinner together. But if we plan on being home, and we want to be social, we'll let you know by 3:00, so you can plan the meal. How would that work?"

"That would work for me," he said. "It could be our old system, but reversed."

"We want to feel comfortable that you and the boys don't mind if we come home and go straight to our room."

"I don't mind at all, darlin'. I want you girls to enjoy each other. The first year of your relationship should be a time where you're together almost constantly. I'd feel uncomfortable if you wanted to spend all your time with us. I'd think things weren't going that well in the bedroom."

"Things are going just fine in the bedroom," Ryan said with a big grin at her blushing partner. "At least they are for me. Jamie?" Blue eyes blinked innocently, waiting for Jamie to collect herself enough to reply.

"Don't think I don't know that you do that only to make me blush, Ryan," she said as she walked over to her grinning partner. "But two can play that game." She climbed onto Ryan's lap and grabbed her face with both hands, planting a searing kiss on her lips and holding on until she could feel the heat begin to suffuse her face.

"Does this happen every afternoon?" Conor asked as he walked into the room. "I'm gonna have to start coming home earlier. I didn't know there was lap dancing during happy hour."

Ryan burst out laughing, unable to stop even though she hated to encourage her often obnoxious brother. Jamie buried her face in Ryan's shaking neck and moaned, "Kill me now, and put me out of my misery."

After dinner, they cleaned the kitchen while Martin read the newspaper. The Giants were playing the Dodgers, and the men were getting ready to retire to Martin's room to watch the game when Ryan extended her hand toward her partner. "Time for bed," she said.

"Bed?" asked Conor. "Isn't it a little early?"

Martin gave him a glance and narrowed his eyes. Ryan just laughed and said, "We're tired, Conor."

"You don't look tired," he said rather densely.

"For God's sake, Conor," Martin interceded. "They're newlyweds, boy. Have you no discretion?"

"Well, why didn't you say so?"

"Jaysus!" Martin cried, completely exasperated at his son's thick-headedness. "The girls don't want to have to make a general announcement when they want to have sex, boy."

Jamie's eyes were firmly closed, and she shook her head slowly. "I may never have it again at this rate," she muttered.

"Oh, yes you will," Ryan said with a gleeful laugh as she picked her up and tossed her over her shoulder. "We're going to have sex, boys, amuse yourselves!"

They dashed down the stairs, and Ryan kicked the door closed. Crossing to the bed in a few strides, she tossed Jamie onto it, then immediately fell onto her. Ryan began to cover her face and neck with a multitude of kisses. "Two days is too long," she breathed as she rubbed against her.

"And you're too dressed," Jamie chided from beneath the barrage of kisses.

Ryan gave her a sexy grin and stood up to undress. Jamie did the same, and in minutes they were both naked. Ryan trotted over to lock the door. "In case they're tempted to respond to your screams," she said with a gleam in her eyes.

As Jamie ran into the bathroom she called out, "I'm getting ready for bed now. I have a feeling I won't be ambulatory later." Ryan followed suit, taking a quick shower just to make sure she was ready for anything.

Emerging from the bath, she leapt onto the bed and wrestled Jamie down until she was pinned. Then she braced her body slightly on her hands and knees so that her weight was not too much for her partner to bear. Her head dipped and she began kissing her again, but much more sensually this time. The kissing went on and on, getting deeper and deeper, until they were both breathless. Ryan was flushed with desire as she lifted her head slightly and shivered from head to toe. Her eyes were slightly unfocused, and she was obviously struggling to control her breathing.

"Mmm, you're wound up like a top," Jamie breathed as she ran her hands up and down Ryan's shaking back.

Ryan dropped her head again and whispered right into Jamie's ear, warm breath tickling her sensitive skin. "I've been dreaming about this all day. I thought about you when I was running, when I took my shower, when I was working out, and especially when we were upstairs tonight. It took every bit of self-control to spend a few minutes being sociable. I knew I was only moments from holding you like this, and it made me so wet," she said as she enunciated each syllable carefully.

Jamie loved nothing more than to have her lover put words to her desire. She rubbed her belly against Ryan's in a slow, sensual dance, silently urging her on.

"If no one had been home, we'd be in the front hallway right now," Ryan breathed. "You wouldn't have gotten two steps into the house before I'd have had you on the floor. I want you like I've been fantasizing all day—naked, wet and ready. Are you ready for me?"

"Mmm-hmm," Jamie moaned. "I'm ready. I'm so ready." Her hips continued to undulate under her lover. She slowly tilted her pelvis as she spread her legs so that her hot center rubbed against Ryan's dark curls. "Feel how hot I am for you. Feel me, baby," she moaned as she began to slowly thrust against her.

Ryan slid her hand between their wet bodies. She slipped her fingers between Jamie's lips and gasped in delight at the wetness. Jamie's head began to roll from side to side as Ryan's soft fingers lightly stroked her. Her hips continued to thrust as her legs spread even farther apart. "Come inside me. Let me feel you."

Ryan squeezed her legs together tightly to ease some of the tension building up inside her vulva. She took a deep breath and slipped two fingers smoothly inside her lover, hissing out a sigh of pleasure as she felt herself enveloped by the warmth. Jamie gasped and backed up a little as she struggled to accept the fullness. As soon as she acclimated to the penetration, she began to move against Ryan's hand. She grabbed Ryan by both shoulders and squeezed hard as she continued to thrust.

In a burst of strength that surprised them both, she jerked her hips and flipped her larger lover onto her back. Then she raised herself slightly so that she was sitting on her heels, straddling Ryan. Jamie grasped her lover's arm and moved it until she could control her hand. Slowly, but forcefully, she began to thrust Ryan's hand into herself. Her breathing quickened and became a rough rasp as she gasped with each strong push. Soon she had both hands wrapped around Ryan's forearm, driving in hard. When she felt that she was getting all the force she could manage from Ryan's hand, she began to thrust her hips forward with the same intensity. She grunted and gasped with each rough thrust until her mouth opened as her head fell back. "*Oh, God!*" she panted. "Fuck me! Fuck me! *Fuck me!*" she screamed as her body flew into spasms. She fell onto Ryan's chest with a whump, her muscles unable to support her body for another second. Ryan's arm was trapped between them, her hand still embedded deep inside.

Jamie's tender flesh pulsed and throbbed around Ryan's fingers as she sucked in gulps of air, trying to satisfy her burning lungs. Finally she blew out a very deep breath and rolled onto her side, sliding off easily because of their sweat-soaked bodies. She grimaced and twitched as she slowly pulled Ryan's fingers from her still spasming body and then lay motionless, completely spent, for several minutes.

Meanwhile, Ryan was rather frantically trying to return some feeling to her numb hand. She shook it repeatedly as she rubbed her forearm with her other hand. The pins-and-needles sensation began, and she grimaced as she waited for the blood to return. Finally, it began to feel somewhat normal, and she rolled onto her side to wrap her recovering arm around her lover's waist. "I thought you didn't like that word," Ryan's deep voice rumbled.

"What word?" Jamie asked weakly.

In a conversational tone, Ryan pronounced the word crisply. "Fuck."

"Fuck what?" she asked, totally confused.

"I believe the term was 'Fuck me. Fuck me. *Fuck me!*'" Ryan said as she imitated her tone, but not her volume.

Jamie looked at her with wide-open eyes. "I said that?"

Ryan slowly nodded with a wide grin firmly in place.

"Just like that?"

Another nod. "Only louder," she added with an even wider grin.

"Oh my God. Your family heard me!"

"No, they didn't. You know how loud the boys are, and we can't hear them. I'm sure they're watching baseball, and we could never be heard over that. Don't worry, they didn't hear a thing."

"Jeez," Jamie said as she expelled a deep breath. "I don't know what you did to me, but I'll be amazed if I can walk tomorrow."

"Ice is the best thing for an injury. I think we have some Popsicles upstairs…"

"Oh, sure, that'd be…" Jamie started to scoff, but paused a second and added with a sultry grin, "interesting."

"Be right back," Ryan said excitedly as she tried to hop off the bed.

"Hold on, Tiger," she said as she grabbed her arm. "We need rubber sheets before we do that on the bed."

"Hmm, rubber sheets, huh?"

Slapping her firmly on the butt, Jamie smiled and said, "You think everything is hot, don't you?"

"In the right context, everything is."

Jamie wrapped her arms around Ryan's waist and squeezed her tightly. "You are such a hot little love machine."

Ryan spent the next hour showing her just how hot she was. For a change, Ryan was actually able to have two orgasms, although that was mostly because the first one came less than a minute after Jamie first touched her. As she closed her eyes to sleep, Ryan spent a moment reflecting on the new nickname Jamie had bestowed on her, hoping that "Quickdraw" did not stick. She did, after all, still have a reputation to uphold.

Early the next morning Ryan climbed the stairs, dressed in her running clothes. As she entered the kitchen, she met Conor on his way out the back door. Jamie was not in sight, and he leaned over conspiratorially and asked, "Are you sure you're a girl?"

"Yeah, I'm pretty sure. Why?"

"Well, what Jamie was begging for last night didn't seem like something you could do if you were a girl."

Ryan advanced on him, backing him up against the door with a darkly menacing look in her eyes. "If you tell her that you can hear us…" she threatened.

"Hey, it's not my fault," he said. "You know you can hear through the open ductwork."

"*I* know that, Conor," she spat. "But Jamie doesn't know it. It's hard enough for her to be comfortable having sex with you lunks in the house. If she knew you could hear us, she'd never let me touch her again. I've spent years doing it in cars and bars and on sofas, with parents and ex-girlfriends barging in on me. I'm not going back to that. Ever!" she barked as she punched her finger into his chest.

"It's only in Da's room that you can hear anything," he reminded her. "It was pretty funny. As soon as you started howling, Da got up and went into the living room. About two minutes later Brendan said he had to go home. They were dropping like flies."

"What about you?"

"Hey, I'm just trying to get some pointers. I've never had a woman beg me like that."

"You'll never *be* with another woman if you let Jamie hear one word of this," she said in her most ominous tone. "And later today you and I are going to seal that ductwork. I don't care if we freeze to death this winter. Your little peep show is over," she hissed as she stormed out of the house.

Conor glumly watched his sister through the open door. *Damn! Now I'll never learn how she gets her to squeal like that.*

Chapter Eleven

"**W**ould you like to ingratiate yourself with the extended family today?" Ryan asked after they had showered later that morning.

"You mean I haven't ingratiated myself yet? Is this a constant quest?" Jamie's eyes were twinkling, and Ryan recognized her teasing tone.

"Regrettably, it is constant," she said, speaking the truth. Jamie cocked her head and gave Ryan a puzzled look. "I'm teasing about having to ingratiate yourself, of course. The bottom line is that no matter what you do they all love you and always will. But everybody expects everyone else to help out when they need it, and right now Niall needs help."

"With…?"

"Everything." Ryan sat down heavily on the bed, shaking her head slowly. "As you saw the other night, he's a long way from being able to move in. He said he was going to try to get by with doing as little as possible, but he keeps adding projects. Now he's completely redoing the kitchen, and he needs everybody he can get to help. I feel like I need to go. Do you mind?"

"Of course not. What can we do?"

"Uhm, I know what I can do, but I don't know what you can do. Have you ever done any remodeling?"

Jamie thought for a moment and said, "Well, I've helped out at a few barn raisings down in Hillsborough, and my mother and I added on a spare bedroom…"

Ryan laughed at her partner's obvious teasing. "I didn't think you had, but you get mad sometimes when I assume you haven't done stuff. I'm trying to be sensitive."

Jamie sat next to her on the bed and slung an arm around her waist. "You're very sensitive. But feel free to assume I've not remodeled any homes. I've watched people remodel both of our houses, but all I learned was how to pick out appliances and fixtures. I don't think that's what you have in mind."

"No, this project is a little more hands-on than that. I don't mind going alone if you'd like to play golf or something today."

"Nope." She shook her head firmly, her still-wet hair sending droplets of moisture all over Ryan. "We're a package deal, babe. If nothing else, I'll make lunch."

"So what do we wear to this little event?" Jamie asked as she finished drying her hair.

"Oh, loose jeans, overalls, carpenter's pants. Whatever you have that'll protect your legs from splinters, but let you scramble around easily. Oh, and you need to wear your work boots." With that, Ryan ran upstairs to make them a quick breakfast.

Who does she think she's married to? One of those people on PBS on Saturday mornings? I mean, I have boots, but I can't imagine my new Ferragamos are what she has in mind.

When Jamie came upstairs, Ryan spent a moment gazing at her outfit with approval. She was wearing overalls, as requested, but these were not typical overalls, which made sense to Ryan, since Jamie was not a typical construction worker. They were made of a sturdy twill, which was good, but they were a bright, sunshine yellow, which would obviously show every bit of dust and dirt they encountered. They didn't fit like normal overalls either—these hugged her curves in a most flattering fashion, a detail that Ryan greatly appreciated.

"Are you gonna leer at me all day?" Jamie asked, placing her hands on her hips and adopting a tough look.

"I would expect so," Ryan nodded. "I've never been more attracted to a member of the crew. Love your outfit."

"You said overalls—this is all I have." She stood in front of the mirror in the living room and fussed a bit with her grass-green-and-white checked shirt. "Are long sleeves a good idea?"

"Yeah," Ryan said, snuggling up behind her. "Long sleeves are a good idea. It's nice and cool today, so they'll protect your arms, and you shouldn't be too hot." She looked down at Jamie's feet to see her normal running shoes. "No boots?"

"None that I want to scuff up."

"What about your Doc Martens?"

Jamie looked down at her outfit and stuck her foot out speculatively. Her brow was furrowed as she considered the question. Finally, her head shook decisively. "No, black would look a little severe with my outfit. I want ones like you have," she said, looking at Ryan's tan pigskin boots.

"Okey dokey," Ryan agreed slowly, having never heard a member of the crew worry about whether his shoes clashed with his outfit, "but you probably won't wear them often. Maybe you should just wear what you have. I hate to see you waste a hundred bucks on new ones."

Better to waste $100,000 than $500, she thought, knowing that her fawn-colored Ferragamos would be her selection if she were forced to choose from her current wardrobe. "No problem. I'd like to have some like yours. I have a feeling this won't be a one-shot deal, anyway."

"You're right on that one. Niall's got enough work to keep us occupied all year long."

Much to Ryan's dismay, Jamie put as much thought into buying boots as Niall had into buying the house. The salesman eventually left her to her own devices after he had shown her every style that they carried in her size. Ryan insisted that as long as she was going to spend the money on work boots, she should buy a steel-toed model, and she eventually chose ones identical to Ryan's.

With one momentous decision out of the way, Ryan took her lover to the work glove display and cooled her heels while she debated over those. When she had made her selection, Ryan took her by the arm to head to the parking lot. "I want to get some carpenter's pants like you have," Jamie protested, but Ryan was firm in her resolve.

"I'd like to get to Niall's while there's still a bit of daylight," she said, checking her watch.

"Very funny," Jamie scoffed, elbowing her in the ribs.

"Look, babe, I know that you care more about your pants than your shoes. If I extrapolate the amount of time you spent on your shoes…"

"I get the point, Buffy. I'll buy the pants on my own time." She stuck her tongue out playfully, mentally reminding herself that the teasing had just begun. A houseful of O'Flaherty men meant she had better prepare herself to be the butt of jokes all day long.

The guys were surprised but pleased to see them and after teasing Jamie about her new shoes they made some suggestions about how they could help. Only Niall, Padraig, and Conor were on the job this morning, since they were the carpenters of the family and the main task was hanging cabinets. Ryan was assigned chalk line duty since she was the most agile of the group, and Jamie was given the task of using the level to make sure everything was square before the cabinets were attached. The work went quickly, since all of the boys were actually pros. Jamie realized that they could easily handle the task without her, but she enjoyed helping out and soon expanded her duties to include sweeping up and fetching screws and bolts. She got a lot of pleasure out of watching her partner fit right into the team and was quite amazed to see that the little crew communicated almost without words. They chatted about a number of things, but most of the construction talk was "left," "right," "good," "mark," and "nail it." Since the boys were stronger, they held the cabinets in place after Jamie's leveling task, while Ryan drove the screws into the studs with a big cordless drill. She scampered around on a ladder, or straddled one of the base cabinets, as if she had been doing the job all her life. *Of course*, Jamie thought, *knowing the O'Flahertys, she might have been doing jobs like this throughout her life.*

Jamie was even more impressed with how the boys treated Ryan. They all recognized her competency, and her strength, and they had no problem with integrating her completely. Jamie was just a tiny bit jealous that they all still treated her like a girl, but she realized that they had never seen her show any skills, and in fact, she had to acknowledge that she didn't have any in this area.

By 11:30 the men were getting hungry, so Jamie offered to go fetch lunch. Ryan automatically grabbed the keys to accompany her as Conor warned that they should buy enough for eight since more cousins were sure to come. "They can smell free food all the way back to Noe, you know."

They walked to the Lexus hand in hand. "I could have gone alone," Jamie said.

Frowning, Ryan asked, "Did you want to?"

"Of course not. I'd always rather be with you."

Ryan chuckled, hitting the remote door locks and listening for the reassuring click. "And just what makes you think I don't feel the same about you?"

"Good point," Jamie said. "I guess I just feel more expendable today. It's obvious that my little jobs are pretty much just to keep me occupied."

"Hey, I started out the same way," Ryan said. "It took a long time until I was trusted to contribute more."

Batting her bright green eyes, Jamie ingenuously asked, "And that was when?"

"Uhm, I guess I was around ten when my uncles let me start helping out with the big stuff. But I had to sweep up for years."

"Uh-huh," Jamie nodded, patting Ryan's thigh. "It's okay, babe. I don't mind that they treat me like a girl. I'm used to it."

Ryan saw the resigned look on her partner's face. "Give 'em some time. It's hard to work a new person in, but when they see how competent you are, they'll start trusting you."

"Okay," Jamie agreed, not believing her for one instant, but deciding it wasn't something to get upset about.

After an expensive trip to the local deli, Jamie asked, "When do you think the house will be finished? Niall must be anxious to move in."

"Not likely," Ryan said, laughing. "Conor and I have a bet that he never will."

"Huh?"

"I don't think he really wants to leave home. He had a fight with Uncle Patrick about something or other and bought the house out of spite, in my humble opinion. He's had it for over a year, and he keeps coming up with something major that has to be done before he can even consider moving in."

"Conor thinks he wants to leave?"

"No, Conor thinks Niall's too hardheaded to admit that he doesn't want to move away from his ma. It all comes down to whether he's gonna let his pride take over." She shook her head and muttered, "Hardheaded and proud. I don't know where he gets it from."

"Must be from your Aunt Deirdre's side of the family," Jamie assured her, working hard to keep from laughing aloud.

They weren't back in the house for five minutes before Colm and Kieran showed up—both ravenous. Jamie took care of getting everyone set up with a plate, also noticing that Ryan had forgotten to take a root beer. She went out to the small backyard, carrying a bottle for her lover and presented it to her with a flourish. "You take such good care of me," Ryan said as Jamie bent for a kiss.

"Hey, we're trying to eat here," Niall complained. "No mushy stuff."

Just for spite, Ryan yanked Jamie from her feet, pulling her across her lap and planting a very big kiss on her lovely mouth. The blonde twined her hands behind Ryan's neck and leaned back in her embrace with a cute smile on her face. "What was that for?" she asked as all the boys groaned.

"I can't let these lugs dictate my level of mush!" she declared defiantly. "You'll note that I'm the only one with a girl. If I listened to them, I'd be single too."

The cabinets were all in, so Colm prepared to set the ceramic tile. The brothers spent a few minutes debating what pattern to use, using no words at all. Niall took a few tiles and set them on the floor in a straightforward square set. Colm scratched his head and moved them into a more complex pattern, folding his arms across his chest as they both stared at the proposal for a minute. Niall knelt and moved them back into the plain set, grunted once, and went outside to have a beer. Jamie had been watching this interchange and she noticed that Colm didn't look very happy about the decision, but he started assembling his materials.

The carpenters, save for Ryan, considered their work finished, so they stayed outside to relax in the warm sun and have a beer. Kieran, the brother between Niall and Colm in age, was the plasterer in the family, and his task was next since there were a few holes in the wall made during the new placement of the cabinets. He waited around for a bit, but Colm finally told him he could go join the boys, and he'd call him when he needed him.

Jamie was particularly fond of Colm, really appreciating his quiet, thoughtful approach to things. He was a bit of an artist and spent as much time designing his tile creations as he did installing them. He wasn't very happy to be called on to perform such a straightforward task, since he knew he could create something more eye-catching, but he didn't like to push his opinions too forcefully. Jamie watched him survey the wall and counter areas. He crossed his muscular arms over his chest once again and shook his head as he walked over to start mixing his thin-set.

"You're not happy with the design, are you?" Jamie asked.

He laughed softly, looking a little embarrassed. "It's that obvious?"

"What would you rather do?"

Ryan could smell trouble, so she patted Colm on the back and said, "Good luck," as she went to the refrigerator to grab a beer and join the boys in the backyard. She caught the impudent tongue stuck out in her direction and answered it with a blown kiss.

"I'll show you my idea if you're really interested," Colm said. "None of the boyos care about design."

"I'm really interested. I want to learn how to do something so I can contribute more, and this interests me the most. Do you think I could be your assistant?"

"I'd love to have a willing apprentice," he said. "Let me get some Kraft paper and show you what I'd like to do." Colm cut a piece of Kraft paper slightly larger than the wall surface and taped it to the floor. He knelt down and used his straightedge to quickly draw the accurate borders of the surface he would cover. "Okay, here's what Niall wants," he explained as he expertly spaced the four-inch squares straight across and down the paper. They looked very neat, but Jamie agreed that there was no imagination involved.

"And here's what I want to do," he said as he went to the corner to pull out two boxes of tile. He produced a tile with a small curve on the bottom edge and showed Jamie how it would frame the bottom of the wall where the wall met the counter. "Niall wants a jack on jack bond," he explained as he laid out a small square, with each tile sitting directly above the other. "But I want to do a running bond." He then laid out a pyramid shape, where each tile corner sat on the middle of the tile underneath it. "I hate jack on jack because you see every imperfection in the wall. A running bond hides a multitude of sins."

"Let's lay this out the way you want and let him decide if he likes it," she suggested. "Once he sees how nice it looks, I'm sure he'll appreciate it."

"Well, I don't know about that," he laughed. "But he won't want me to waste the time to redo it."

"That was my second thought," she conceded as she realized she had found a kindred soul.

"Wanna see what else I want to try?" he asked with an eyebrow wiggle to rival Ryan's.

"Absolutely."

He opened his other box and took out a beautiful emerald green four-inch tile. He showed Jamie how he wanted to set the green tiles on the diagonal in a horizontal line right across the center of the wall. He said he planned to do the same on the counter and then he produced a box of matching green bullnose tiles that would frame the corners of the counter. She agreed that his ideas would make the kitchen look clean and sharp and very well thought out. "Let's do it," she said as she gave her co-conspirator a handshake.

Before they started, she delivered fresh beers to everyone to keep them out of the kitchen for a while. Of course, Ryan merited another kiss just for looking cute, and the boys had to razz her a bit for that.

Colm worked incredibly fast as he expertly laid out the tile. He nipped the edges of the surrounding tiles to accommodate the diagonal tiles and when he was finished, Jamie was very enthusiastic. "That looks absolutely superb. I'll go get Niall."

The entire group came trooping in and looked at the design for a minute. Finally Niall pursed his lips and said, "Hmm, green looks good. Go for it."

Jamie chided them for their non-artistic ways and sent them back to the yard to stay out of trouble. She patted Colm on the back and reminded him, "An artist is never appreciated in his own time."

By four o'clock Jamie had more information about tile in her head than she would have ever thought possible. Her clothes were covered with thin-set mortar, and she had so much grit under her nails she knew she'd have to take a nail brush to them to make them decent again. The walls were finished, and Ryan providentially entered the kitchen just as the pair was setting the last row on the counter. Ryan spent a few minutes pulling dried bits of quick-set from Jamie's dusty hair, bending to kiss her gently. "I've got to take your assistant home and soak her for a few hours, Colm," she said. "Have you ever been this dirty?"

Jamie thought for a few seconds and shook her head. "I'd have to say no to that. But I kinda like it." Her eyes were twinkling, and she looked very childlike and playful.

"It's fun to be filthy," Ryan agreed wholeheartedly.

"You've been a tremendous help, Jamie," Colm said as he gave her a kiss on the cheek. "I think I can have you pretty well trained with a few more projects. Are you up for the shower in the master bathroom?"

"Yep. I can help either Saturday or Sunday."

"Fine," he said. "I'm going to come over on Wednesday evening to grout. Any interest?"

"I wouldn't miss it for the world." Looking up at Ryan she said proudly, "I'm an apprentice."

"Did you have fun?" Ryan asked as they approached the car.

"Yep. Looks like you did too," she gently chided her as she got a whiff of her breath, then quickly snuck her hand into Ryan's pocket to remove the keys. "How many beers did you have?"

"Just two," she said. "I should have stopped at one, but you know how it is when you're with the boyos."

"No, I can't say that I do know," she said. "I don't even know why you call them boyos."

"Oh, that's a term for kind of a wild, sexually adventuresome guy. Kind of like a playboy, but the term is more affectionate than that."

"What's the equivalent for a girl?"

"There isn't a cute one. Terms for sexually active women are universally derogatory, like slag."

"Well, I thought it was cute to see all of you boyos sitting in the yard drinking beer. You're just like them, you know," she insisted as she slid into the leather seating of the Lexus and adjusted the electric seat from its full extension to accommodate her shorter legs.

"Yeah, I am when we're together, but I like to think I have a more feminine side when I'm with you," Ryan said as she slid her hand up Jamie's thigh.

"Watch it, boyo, you bruised the merchandise last night. That's a 'no-fly zone' today."

Ryan cast a glance down at her own fully functioning equipment and patted herself as she said, "All systems are go down here." Jamie turned to see bright eyes, a waggling eyebrow, and a delightfully crooked grin.

"As usual, I can't resist your romantic offer," she laughed. "Let me soak in the tub to get some of this mortar off, and I'll take you for a little spin."

"Make you a deal," Ryan said. "I'll clean your overalls while you clean yourself. Then we can meet in bed for a quickie and a nap."

"As usual, your ideas are simply brilliant." Jamie smiled broadly, looking forward to both parts of Ryan's suggestion.

The physical labor of the day caused both women to fall asleep early, which made getting up for eight o'clock Mass a breeze. They needed to get an early start to be on time for their brunch date with Catherine, and at 10:30 on the dot Ryan pulled the Boxster into the valet parking lot of the Claremont Hotel and hopped out, surveying the property now that it was summer and the roses were in bloom. "They're keeping our little study sanctuary up nicely," she said to Jamie as the smaller woman took her hand and led her into the dining room.

Jamie was looking around the big, old hotel with a very fond expression, recalling the closeness she had felt being able to cuddle with her partner every night during their short stay. "I guess we won't have to come back here to study for finals this term, huh?"

"No, we don't have to," Ryan said, "but I'd be more than willing to come back for a night just for old times' sake. I'd like to get you in that big bathtub with me." Her bright eyes and leering grin nearly caused Jamie to detour to the front desk to make a reservation for that very night, but since her mother was waiting she soldiered on.

Catherine was sitting by the pool and sipping what Ryan guessed was a Bloody Mary. As she stood to greet them, Ryan was again taken by what a lovely woman she was. She wore a pale blue summery dress that somehow managed to make her look cool, youthful, and sophisticated. An attractive straw hat framed her pale blonde hair, adding to her summery image. She extended her hand to Ryan, shaking it firmly, then leaning in for a kiss to both cheeks. Jamie received roughly the same greeting, minus the handshake.

The waiter dashed over, and the younger women chose their usual beverage, drawing a smile from Catherine when Jamie placed the order without even looking at Ryan. They passed a few minutes in small talk, and Jamie recounted her indoctrination into the O'Flaherty Laborers Guild. They were nearly finished with their lattés when Catherine looked at Jamie and got to the real reason she had requested the meeting. "Your father told me that you had words over the car you bought and thought you might be upset about it. I just want to assure you that he doesn't speak for me about the issue. I hope you know that I want you to feel free to spend your money in any way that you wish, Jamie."

"I don't see how that's possible, Mother," she protested. "Daddy is a trustee…"

"As am I," Catherine firmly said. "I generally don't get involved in financial discussions with your father. I've learned that it's rarely beneficial to our marriage to do so. But I'll not have him second-guessing how you spend such a negligible amount of money."

The pained look on Jamie's face grew more constricted as her mother spoke. "I don't want to cause friction between the two of you."

"I appreciate that," Catherine said, covering Jamie's hand with her own. "I fail to see any other option at this point, though."

Jamie was quiet as the waiter delivered their meals, mulling over her response. "There is another option," she said. "I want to handle this myself. I'd really prefer that you didn't get involved right now. I appreciate the offer more than I can say, but I don't want to see this issue hurt us as a family."

Ryan's already high regard for Jamie grew markedly as her partner made this statement. She knew that the argument with Jim had hurt her, and she knew that Catherine could make it go away by handling it for her. The fact that Jamie put family harmony ahead of her own comfort was admirable, and Ryan's smile conveyed her approval.

Catherine nodded and took a contemplative sip of her drink. "All right," she agreed. "I'll not mention anything unless you ask me to get involved."

"Thanks, Mother," Jamie said. "Let's hope this blows over quickly, and he realizes that I'm capable of making my own financial decisions."

"I certainly hope so." Catherine looked a little worried, but she moved on. "How do you feel things are going between us in general?" she asked. "Are we being supportive?"

Jamie smiled at her mother. "*You're* being absolutely marvelous, Mother, but Daddy has a long way to go."

Catherine knew this was true from her private discussions with Jim, but she was uncertain how much of this had been transmitted to Jamie. "Tell me how you mean that."

Jamie sighed, shook her head slightly and said, "He's been okay about the lesbian angle, which surprised the heck out of me. But he seems focused on the money. I'm not sure exactly what he said when we were over for dinner, since my beloved won't give me any details." She cast a smirk in Ryan's direction. "But I have the impression that he thinks Ryan is interested in my bank account as much as she is in me."

Catherine shook her head and muttered, "This reminds me of fraternity hazing."

"You're going to have to explain that one," Jamie chuckled.

Catherine smiled and said, "My point is that pledges are treated abysmally by their older frat brothers, but the next year they do the same thing to the incoming class. Instead of having empathy for the situation these boys are in, they treat them as poorly, if not worse, than they themselves were treated."

"And this relates to us how?"

"Jamie, do you know much about the welcome my family extended to your father?" Ryan smiled at Catherine's quick intelligence that reminded her so much of her partner.

"No, neither of you talks about your youth much."

"Oh, it's such ancient history," Catherine said blithely, "I suppose I didn't think you'd be interested. But I want to give you a little insight into how things went for your father."

Both young women nodded their interest, and Catherine began. "I don't know how much you know about my family, Ryan, but when I was young we were one of the wealthiest families in the Bay Area. Now this is before all of these new high-tech billionaires hit the scene. This was back in the days when a hundred million dollars was a lot of money. And in contrast to the computer people who run the world now, my family earned our money the old-fashioned way," she said, "by exploiting immigrants and the poor."

She laughed at her wry joke, and both young women did the same. *She does have a sense of humor when she's away from Jim*, Ryan mused. *Kinda self-deprecating, but that's pretty appealing.*

"Anyway, I was just a sophomore at Stanford when a sorority sister of mine coerced me into going on a blind date with a much older man." She laughed gently at the memory. "I was impressed with Jim from the first time I met him," she said. "He just seemed so determined and sure of himself. And I really liked the fact that he wasn't afraid of hard work." Turning to Ryan she said, "Having a job is considered a sign of feeblemindedness in my family." Her mouth was smiling, but her eyes were deadly serious, and Ryan understood that she actually meant what she said.

"I didn't take Jim home to meet my family, mainly because I knew they wouldn't approve, and I hated to be told what to do." Ryan looked up to the sky and rolled her eyes a bit until Jamie pinched her on the side.

"I saw that," she muttered.

"Just thinking that the apple doesn't fall far from the tree," Ryan said with a grin.

"We do share some personality traits," Catherine said as she cast a fond look at her smirking daughter. "Anyway, at the end of the school year we decided to get married. My parents were justifiably shocked that the first time they met Jim was when we went to tell them the news. But just as I expected, they were rather violently opposed to the idea."

"What happened?" Jamie asked, having never met her grandmother and having few clear memories of her grandfather, who had died when she was five.

"My father acted like it was Field Marshall Cinque showing up at the door!" she laughed. When two blank faces stared at her, she explained. "More ancient history, I'm afraid. A few years before this, a radical terrorist group kidnapped the daughter of William Randolph Hearst—one of my father's good friends, by the way."

"Was that Patty Hearst?" Ryan asked, vaguely familiar with the incident.

"Exactly," Catherine agreed. "Patty was a few years older than I, and she was a lovely young woman, very traditional and a seemingly happy girl. We actually went to the same prep school, so I knew her fairly well. Anyway, she was kidnapped from her Berkeley apartment, which was not far from your home, young lady," she said to Jamie. "This group set about brainwashing poor Patty and before long she was a 'willing' participant in their bank robberies and other such acts."

"Was she really a willing participant?" Jamie asked in amazement.

"Not in my opinion," Catherine said. "But the jury believed she was, and she was sent to prison. Oh, I could talk about this for days," she laughed, "but the point is that times were very turbulent, and though my parents were terribly upset that I was going to marry, I think they were more upset about my 'rebellion.'"

"Getting married doesn't sound very rebellious to me," Jamie mused.

"Especially back then. A traditional marriage with a church service was almost unheard of for people my age. There were so many weddings in Golden Gate Park that you could hardly move through there on a Saturday," she said, chuckling. "But I had always been a very compliant child, and this was the first, and only, decision of mine that they didn't agree with."

"So when did they come around?" Jamie asked, thinking her mother's story sounded remarkably similar to her own.

"Mother never did," Catherine said, with a sharp pang of loss streaking across her face. "She died just a few months after the wedding, and I'm pained to say that we didn't reconcile. She was terribly unhappy that I wasn't going to have a life on my own. I don't know why it was so important to her, but she was very invested in my finishing school and having some sort of professional life before I settled down."

"She wanted you to get a job?" Jamie asked, trying to understand the logic behind this.

"Well, not a real job," Catherine laughed. "I was an art history major, and she wanted me to work at a European museum. She was very upset by the changes in the States, and she wanted me to spend more time in a 'civilized society,' as she referred to the continent."

"Do you regret your decision?" Jamie asked tentatively, hoping that her mother was happy with the choices she had made.

"Regret? Look at what I got in the bargain," she said fondly as she patted her daughter's cheek. "I've never regretted my decision to have you, dear."

Warning bells went off in Ryan's head when she realized that Catherine had completely avoided the question. Jamie, however, didn't seem to notice. "But what if you could have had me later? Would you have liked to have gone to Europe and worked for a while?"

Catherine took in a deep, contemplative breath. "If I could have orchestrated my future, I *would* have gone to Europe after graduation and worked for a few years. I think I would have found the work very fulfilling, but the biggest reason I would have enjoyed it is that it would have made my mother so happy. I'll regret every day of my life that she died when there was so much distance between us." Turning to Jamie with tears in her eyes, she begged, "Please, please don't ever drift away from me like I did with my mother."

Jamie was stunned by this information; it was clear that she didn't quite know how to react. She finally stuck her hand out and grasped her mother's small hand in hers. "I won't, Mother," she promised. "I won't drift away from you."

Ryan was struggling with her own emotions at this tender scene, but they were interrupted by the arrival of their server, asking if they needed anything else. Catherine excused herself to dry her eyes, and Jamie stared at her partner with an amazed look on her face. "I had no idea," she murmured, shaking her head.

"It explains that little visit to your house in April," Ryan commented, referring to the time Catherine had dropped in on Jamie to try to enhance their tenuous connection.

"Yeah, I guess it does," she conceded, staring at her omelet for long minutes.

When Catherine came back, her pleasant smile was back in place, along with her normally placid attitude. She sipped at her fresh drink and asked, "You don't remember your grandfather much, do you, Jamie?"

Jamie shook her head slightly, not wanting to reveal that nearly all she recalled was a short, slight man with a cigar in one hand and a drink in the other. "I do remember being on his boat," she offered, trying to put a good spin on her memories.

"He did love to sail," Catherine agreed. "That's what finally proved to be the bridge between him and your father."

"Really? How so?"

"My father was less than impressed with Jim," Catherine said. "He thought I should marry one of the young men from our social circle, someone who came from money, too. Jim had no social connections at all," Catherine laughed, "and my father thought he was primarily after my money."

"A common theme," Jamie mused.

"Yes, it is," Catherine said. "It's funny. We had so much money that we couldn't have spent it all if we'd tried. It seems that the more you have, the more you worry about someone trying to take it from you."

"You don't seem like that," Ryan observed, feeling a little embarrassed that she had spoken this thought aloud.

Catherine smiled at her and said, "Far be it from me to disclaim my wealth, but I've come to see that money does not buy happiness. A good, loving, supportive relationship is hard to come by, Ryan. Making the other person's financial status of prime importance is just ridiculous, in my opinion."

"When did Grandfather change his opinion?" Jamie wondered.

"It took a while," Catherine said. "But once we had you I think he realized that he was stuck with your father, and he tried to find something in common with him. That turned out to be sailing," she said with a fond smile, thinking back to that time. "Your father grew to love the water nearly as much as my father did, and they bonded during their long hours of working together on Father's boat." Her expression grew sad as she continued. "My father was ill for much of your childhood," she recalled. "It became a comfort to him to believe that Jim would take over for him, and keep an eye on the family fortune. Obviously he grew to trust him, or he wouldn't have named your father as a co-trustee of his estate." A flash of anger darted across Catherine's features so quickly that Ryan almost thought she had imagined it. However, it became clear that she felt some residual anger over the arrangement when she said, "Your grandfather was the type of man who believed that a woman couldn't be trusted to handle complex financial issues."

"That seems like a common theme, also," Jamie muttered. "Are you sure you and Daddy weren't switched at birth? You seem more like Poppa's daughter."

"That's about the nicest compliment I've ever heard," Catherine smiled. "I only wish I were like Charles."

"I'm confused about one thing," Jamie said as they ate their meal. "I thought you graduated from Stanford."

"Oh, I did," she said. "When you were six months old, I went back full time. It was hard on all of us since your father was a first-year associate at Morris & Foster at the time, but I was determined to finish. It seemed like a very small thing I could do to make my mother proud of me…even though it was too late," she mused quietly.

"I'm sure she was proud of you," Jamie insisted.

Ryan turned to Catherine and fixed her with empathetic blue eyes. "My mother died when I was very young, but I truly believe that she shares in all of my accomplishments. I'm sure yours does too, Catherine."

"I hope so, Ryan," she said softly. "I hope so."

After brunch, Jamie and Ryan spent a little time walking around the grounds of the stately old hotel, finally sitting down on a bench to watch a tennis match. "That was pretty revealing," Jamie mused.

"It was," Ryan agreed, slipping Jamie's hand into her own. "I like your mom more every time we're together."

Jamie turned and gazed into Ryan's eyes for a moment. "You know, I do, too. I do, too."

Chapter Twelve

O n Monday morning, the volleyball team made their way through the obligatory five-mile run, with even Ryan and Jordan sticking to the bare minimum. Their grueling workouts were driving them both to the brink of exhaustion, but neither could admit that to the other.

"Do you want to get breakfast afterwards?" Ryan asked as they neared the end of the loop.

"Sure. I don't have anything scheduled for the rest of the day."

"Great. Meet me in the locker room."

After a quick shower, she and Jordan went out for a real breakfast. Normally when they grabbed a bite it was just coffee and muffins, but Ryan was feeling generous, so she offered to take her new friend to a nice little cafe on a quiet street in Berkeley.

"I've never asked you, Ryan, how long have you and Jamie been together?"

"Officially, since June the fifteenth."

"That's all?" she gaped. "The way you talk, I thought you'd been joined at the hip for a year or so, at least. Do you think this is permanent?"

"I'm certain of it. I dated a lot, and I do mean a lot," she said emphatically. "I never even really had a girlfriend. But once I got to know Jamie, I was hooked. I couldn't even enjoy casual sex anymore. She ruined me!" she said with a hearty laugh.

Jordan gave her a shy smile and said, "I guess I shouldn't wait around then, huh?"

Ryan sat up very straight in her seat and looked at her slowly. "Uhm, if you mean…"

"It's okay," she replied as she patted her thigh. "I'd never make a move on someone who was attached. I've heard of your reputation, and I thought we might have a little fling someday. I'm not interested in anything long-term, but I thought we could have a lot of fun together. Too bad, though; you look like your reputation's well deserved."

"Uhm, thanks," Ryan said weakly.

"Hey, did that upset you? I didn't mean to make you uncomfortable. I just like for things to be clear."

"It's okay, really," she said as they pulled up in front of the restaurant. When they were seated, they quickly perused the menus, and both ordered omelets and bagels. When the server left, Ryan said, "I need some practice with how to say no and not feel awkward. I've spent a lot of years saying yes, and this is much harder."

"So you're monogamous?"

"Yes!" she said with some alarm. "I mean, I'm not sure that we've ever said that word, but we're together for life. This isn't something I'm doing until someone better comes along." She chuckled softly, adding, "I'd have to wait several lifetimes for that to happen, and even then it would only be because of evolutionary improvements."

"Calm down, Ryan," Jordan laughed. "I'm not coming on to you. I just didn't know how you'd structured your relationship. I know a lot of people in committed relationships who still have sex outside."

"That's not for us. I want to expend my energies on both of us getting what we need from each other."

Jordan nodded as she took in this information. After a minute, she smiled slyly. "So you really were a player, huh?"

Ryan sighed, deciding to reveal the truth. "Yeah, I really was."

"Hasn't it been hard to give up the excitement of meeting someone new and having that first flush of excitement the first time you kiss?"

"I don't really admit this to Jamie, but it's gonna be a challenge for me. And I'm sure there'll be some low times in our relationship, where other women will look particularly good. But I'm gonna be twenty-four this year. I've been sleeping with everyone who caught my eye since I was seventeen. I think that's enough excitement for one lifetime."

"I don't know," Jordan said. "I think I get off on the thrill of the chase a lot more than the capture. I get bored with people pretty quickly."

"Hey, no one loved the chase more than I did. But I'm discovering that really opening yourself up to love has rewards much greater than the thrill of the chase. Knowing that someone loves you for more than your body or your face is a very powerful feeling. Knowing that they'll stick by you when things are hard is really meaningful for me. I wouldn't trade Jamie for the chance to be with every gorgeous woman in the world. She means everything to me."

Jordan just shook her head. "Boy, are you ever in deep. I think we need to pay a visit to Telegraph after breakfast. I want to buy you a little something to commemorate your enslavement."

Jamie fumbled for her phone, finally getting it open on the fourth ring. "Hi," came the low voice on the other end, the melodic tone so familiar, but still possessing the ability to make her smile every time she heard it.

"Hi, I'm almost there. Don't start without me." They had planned on going to the gym for a workout, and Jamie was on her way to meet Ryan there.

"Oh, I won't," Ryan said. "You're an integral ingredient."

"Ryan," she said suspiciously, "what's going on?"

"I want to change our plans a little."

"Really? What do you want to do?"

"You," she replied huskily.

Jamie quickly pulled over to the curb to make sure that her cell phone wasn't distorting the message. "What did you say?"

"I said," she enunciated precisely, "that I…want…to…do…you. I want to do you several times, as a matter of fact. I want to do you right this very minute. And I want to keep on doing you until you beg for mercy."

The startled, yet aroused woman tried to create enough moisture in her mouth to be able to respond, finally getting out, "Where are you?"

"Our house."

"Give me five."

It actually only took four, but that was because she ran from the car to the house and took the porch stairs two at a time. The door opened before she could knock, and a hand reached out and grabbed her wrist, pulling her in forcefully. Her feet left the floor as her lover whisked her into her arms and carried her up the stairs, her determination as obvious as her desire. Jamie was kicking off her shoes as they ascended, and when Ryan tossed her down onto the bed she immediately started to unbutton her jeans.

"Unh-uh," Ryan said, her dark head shaking slowly. She placed her hands on Jamie's and gently lifted them from her waistband, placing them onto the bed. "Let me."

A gentle, knowing smile settled on Jamie's face as she locked eyes with her partner. Ryan seemed to truly love undressing her, and the smaller woman knew that a significant portion of Ryan's arousal came from performing this act. *If I'd known we were going to do this, I'd have worn something sexier than a sports bra*, she mused, thinking of Ryan's strong preference for her sexiest lingerie.

Ryan knelt down on the floor and began to tease the clothes off her very willing partner. It took nearly ten minutes to render her completely nude, but none of the time was wasted. The loosening of every button was followed by gentle kisses upon each inch of newly exposed skin. Kisses rained down on her belly as her shirt was opened in an excruciatingly slow manner. Once the buttons had been opened, the kisses followed the sliding fabric down each arm until Jamie's squirming became too intense for Ryan to concentrate. She placed her hands very firmly upon wriggling hips and held her completely still. Very serious blue eyes gazed at Jamie, fully capturing her attention. Ryan's voice was low, and slow, and terrifically sexy, and her eyes glittered with the promise of how she planned to love her partner. "I don't want you to move another inch. If you do, I won't do this," she said as she abruptly bent and kissed a wet path from the base of Jamie's belly, up her torso, around a shoulder and down to her fingertips.

Following instructions to perfection, nary a muscle twitched as the path of kisses was created. But Ryan had not forbidden moaning, groaning, or panting, and these were done with abandon. Ryan smiled at Jamie and placed a very gentle kiss upon her hungry lips. "You're doing very, very well." But when Jamie tried to intensify the kiss, Ryan pulled back, clearly needing to be in complete control. "Unh-unh-unh," she chided, tapping the tip of Jamie's nose with her finger. "Your only task is to lie back and let me love you. I'm in charge today."

A silent nod gave Ryan permission to lead the dance, and the glittering highlights in the moss green eyes indicated that Jamie was very happy with the turn of events.

Ryan was still fully clothed in blue jeans and a red tank top, but she didn't waste the time to undress. "Now remember not to move...at all. I'm going to keep my hands on your hips. If you so much as flinch, I'm going to stop. Do you understand?"

Jamie nodded her head only enough to signal her complete acceptance.

Climbing onto the bed again, Ryan started at the very tip of Jamie's ear, nibbling, kissing, and sucking a blazing path across her cheek and onto her moist, parted lips. The gasp of pleasure accompanied by the low, sexy moan seemed to be too much for Ryan to take, and her hands started to shake. Ryan leaned in again, this time lingering on Jamie's lips until it became too hard to breathe. She sat up, panting slightly, and took a deep breath. Jamie was staring at her with hooded eyes, her face a study in desire—her lips slightly swollen from the intense kissing mixed with her arousal and her nostrils flaring with each breath. She struggled to keep her eyes open, batting them seductively at Ryan.

Still firmly holding her hips, Ryan bent her head to touch Jamie's aching breasts for the first time. She loved each tender mound with equal intensity and dedication, lavishing soft kisses upon both, as she felt her partner's struggle to avoid moving against her. Focusing again, she interspersed light bites with soft, wet swipes of her tongue; forceful sucks with tender mouthings; delicate suckling with firm nuzzling, each met with a different cry or gasp. Jamie faithfully followed her admonishment and did not move, not even twitching her burning muscles. She did, however, give Ryan every instruction that she needed without using her body. The more forceful the touch, the more forceful the moan. The nibbles were rewarded with grunts. The sharp little bites received gasps of appreciation. The slow, loving suckling received low, deep sighs.

Since Jamie had proven herself to be so compliant, Ryan finally let go of her hips. She raised both hands to hold a breast firmly at the base, forcing the flesh upwards and stretching the skin taut. When she lowered her head, she began to suck the entire mound into her mouth as deeply as she could. After just a few powerful pulls Jamie cried out loudly, simultaneously breaking every rule. Her hands flew to Ryan's head, pulling her roughly against her tortured flesh. Her hips lifted off the bed and began to futilely thrust into the air. Her breathing became louder and more ragged, as a growl began low in her chest. Seconds later she screamed out her release as she held onto Ryan's head, rolling frantically from side to side, taking Ryan's attached head right with her. Her hold did not loosen in the least as she ground her breast against her lover in decreasingly desperate thrusts, her breathing slowing down with her increasingly weak motions. Finally spent, she released her grip and let her arms fall to the bed.

Her legs were splayed open limply beneath Ryan, and her breathing was quick and shallow. A few anemic moans barely had enough force to be heard, but Ryan smiled at each, knowing a sincere, albeit weak, ovation when she heard one.

Laughing a little as she rolled off Jamie's sweat-drenched body, she shook her head regretfully and said, "You moved. I'm gonna have to stop now. I hate to do it, but a promise is a promise."

"Have I ever told you how much I love your ideas?" Jamie asked weakly, a faint laugh joining her partner's.

"You've mentioned something along those lines," Ryan acknowledged, slipping an arm under Jamie's shoulders to pull her into a warm embrace. "I have to give you some credit with inspiring my ideas, though. They're not as much fun when I act on them alone."

"You just keep talking; I'm having too much trouble getting my mouth to work."

"Ohh," Ryan pouted teasingly, "I had big plans for that mouth. Will it work again later?"

Jamie sighed heavily and affected a long-suffering sigh. "Oh, all right. I suppose you deserve some small reward for your brilliant idea."

As Jamie began to unbutton Ryan's jeans, she noticed a large wet spot on the front of her thigh. "How did that get there?"

"You don't remember locking your legs around my thigh and humping me?"

"Unh-uh," she said blankly, having no memory whatsoever of said act. "Are you sure you didn't come that way?"

"Oh, I almost came that way," she said with a sexy grin. "And speaking of coming, may I compliment you on having your first breast orgasm?"

"You've always known they were my favorite erogenous zone. Now you know just how much I like them."

"I like them an awful lot too," she said fondly, tapping each pink nipple with her fingertip.

"Well, I like yours too, and I want to see them." Jamie began to tug at Ryan's tank top. "Umm, I love it when you don't wear a bra. Your breasts just look so scrumptious jiggling around under here," she said as she slid her hands under the snug top to cup the flesh.

"I really shouldn't go out in public without a bra," Ryan said, smiling at the view she had of Jamie's eager hands roaming around under her top, "but I forgot to take an extra with me this morning."

"You didn't forget," Jamie murmured, leaning close to mouth a firming nipple through the cotton material.

"Pardon?"

"You didn't forget. I took it out of your gym bag when you were putting on your shoes."

"You did what?"

"I swiped it," she said, propping her chin gently on Ryan's breast to look into her eyes. "I saw that you had packed this sexy tank top, and I love to see you moving around in it." Both eyebrows waggled impishly, with Ryan only able to shake her head in amusement.

"You are something else, Ms. Evans. You never cease to amaze me."

"That's the plan," she said, getting back to work. After she pulled the tank top from Ryan's body, she began to work on her jeans again. As the last button opened, she pulled the fabric apart and looked down into the fly suspiciously. "No panties? I didn't take those out."

Ryan feigned a casual attitude. "No. I started out with my boxers but Jordan convinced me to take them off."

"Pardon?" she asked slowly, drawing the word out until it sounded like it had three syllables.

"Jordan convinced me to take off my underwear. And once it was off, I figured I might as well leave it off."

"If you want to have a butt left to put underwear on, you'll explain that comment posthaste."

"Nope," she said, rolling on top of her lover. "You can figure it out for yourself. I'm not telling."

"Ryan," she said in a menacing growl.

"Nope, not telling."

Diving for her taunting partner, she began to tickle her in earnest. She got her fingers up under her ribs on her right side, clearly her most sensitive spot. She dug in deeply and was rewarded with near hysterical laughter, but Ryan would not give in. Since a counterattack was in progress, Jamie tried to cover her own ribs while continuing the assault on her lover, but they ended up grappling with each other and rolling around wildly on the bed, shrieking with laughter.

One mighty hip check found Jamie rolling off the rather high bed and onto the floor. Ryan leaned over to help her up and was roughly pulled down herself. She tumbled over slowly, her jeans sliding from her hips, and wound up sprawled across Jamie's lap, facedown.

"Ryan!" she shrieked as she took in the sight before her. "What have you done to yourself?"

Emblazoned across her lover's right cheek was the word "Jamie" tattooed in a pretty script with a little red heart dotting the "i."

"Do you like it?"

"You got a tattoo?" the blonde asked once again, stunned beyond belief.

"Do you like it?"

"Uhm, I didn't know you were the tattoo kind of girl," Jamie said haltingly, trying to remember if laser tattoo removal worked better on a fresh one.

"I'm not," she laughed. "I'd faint with every needle prick. This is just temporary. It should last about two weeks."

"You big goof, I believed I had to go through life looking at my name on your ass." Since she had the pseudo-tattooed butt so attractively arranged on her lap, she had to spend a few moments spanking the cute round cheeks with both hands. She was pounding out a fierce bass beat when she abruptly stopped. "What did Jordan have to do with this?"

Ryan sucked in a breath, trying to control her laughter. "She was asking me about our relationship. After I went on and on about how much I loved you and how wonderful being in love was, she decided I needed to give you some tangible proof of my undying devotion."

"So you had to take off your underwear?"

"Yeah. They use this permanent type of dye. I didn't want to get it on my white underwear, so I just left them off."

"Was Jordan with you the whole time?" she asked with a hint of jealousy infusing her words.

"Yeah. Why, does that bother you?"

Jamie closed her eyes for a moment, trying to get a handle on her feelings. "It's kind of odd to think of you with your pants off in front of her, so, yeah, I guess it does."

"She sees me in the shower almost every day. We all get dressed in front of each other. It's a jock thing. We don't look at each other sexually."

"Oh, so you didn't use to sleep with the people on your teams," she said, already knowing the answer.

"Uhm, I guess that wasn't a very good argument, huh?"

"Not very."

"You get naked in front of Mia."

"That's true, but we aren't gay. Or at least we weren't. Or I wasn't. Oh, you know what I mean," she finally said in frustration.

"Jamie, I can't control the reaction people have to me, but I can control how I feel about other women and their bodies. And I'm not interested in any other naked body. Yours is the only one that holds my attention."

"So now I have to think of you in that locker room with a dozen other women lusting after your body."

"I don't know of any other lesbians on the team, if Jordan's even a lesbian. And if anyone's body was going to be lusted after, it'd be Jordan's. She's nearly perfect."

Jamie cocked her head and stared at Ryan for a long minute. "I thought you didn't notice other women in the locker room?"

One eyebrow lifted slowly, as Ryan gave her a very suspicious look. "If you can honestly tell me that you haven't surreptitiously checked out other women, even when you were 'straight,' you can have that point."

"Okay, okay, so I have. This just feels weird to me."

"It doesn't to me. I don't want to feel uncomfortable around my teammates. I've been in athletics for a long time, and I'm really used to being naked around people. I don't want to change the way that I behave. So please try to understand and to trust me."

"I do trust you. But I've got the feeling that Jordan is used to getting what she wants, and I got some vibes that she might want you," she said, looking carefully at Ryan to gauge her reaction.

"If she were in the locker room stark naked with her legs spread wide open begging me to do her, I wouldn't give her a second thought. You are my only love. Emphasis on the 'only.' So please try to accept this. Okay?"

"I'll try," she agreed. "But don't take anyone with you if you go to get your clitoris pierced. That's over the line."

They spent the next hour playing and making love. At noon Jamie awakened from her stupor and looked over at her partner. "We should get up so we can get some lunch."

Ryan rolled over with a moan. "I'm too tired," she whined. "You did me good. Too good."

"Come on." Jamie tried to pull her to a sitting position, astounded, as usual, by how tremendously heavy Ryan was. She got no assistance whatsoever, finally giving up and getting out of bed alone.

Starting the shower, she stood in the bath, waiting for the water to warm up. "Oh, I wish I had someone to shower with me," she said aloud. "I have some spots that are particularly hard to clean…"

"Need a hand?" a sexy, low voice purred in her ear, while warm hands grasped her around the waist.

"You are sooooo easy," Jamie laughed.

"Only for you, babe," Ryan insisted. "Only for you."

Ryan returned home from work a little after 3:00, and just as she got in the door her pager went off. "Oh, great," she muttered as she looked at the familiar area code. She flopped down on the loveseat in the living room, portable phone nestled against her ear. "Sara? Ryan. What's up?"

"Hi, Ryan," Sara's soft voice replied. "Nothing much is up, but the bar exam starts tomorrow, and after that I'm taking off for a long-delayed vacation. I just wanted to let you know in case you needed to get in touch about your search."

"Hey, that's really nice of you," Ryan said. "I sure wish you good luck. I remember when Brendan was taking the bar. He was a basket case."

"I'm not much better. I'm calling everyone I know who isn't taking it, just to keep my mind off it."

"You can rest assured that I'll never take it," Ryan laughed. "And thanks for being interested in my search. I'm at the point now of having to contact all of the girls from the team, and that's going to be a real bitch."

"Look, Ryan," she said. "I know we've been over this before, and I'm sure you've thought about it a million times, but is there anyone else you could have told? Even inadvertently?"

Ryan took in a deep breath and shook her head. "It wouldn't have been too hard to figure out I was a lesbian, Sara. I was draped around some woman every chance I got. But I didn't tell anyone about what happened between us." Ryan had been idly rubbing Duffy's head during the entire conversation. Her hand stilled as she was hit by a thought. "I take that back. I told one person—Father Pender—but that was during confession, and I'm sure he'd never breach his vows."

"No, I agree, he wouldn't do that." She paused thoughtfully and said, "It surprises me that your father hustled you off to Father Pender, too."

"Too?" Ryan asked, slightly puzzled. "You talked to Father Pender?"

"Talk is a little strong," she said. "My father marched me over there and stood guard while I went to confession."

Ryan sat in stunned silence, listening to her own heartbeat pounding in her chest. "He wouldn't! He couldn't!"

Understanding the implication, Sara said, "Ryan, Father Pender takes his vows very, very seriously. I know he's a gossip, but he would never do something so horrible."

"I find it impossible to believe too. But it sure as hell adds up."

Sara was quiet for a moment, letting her analytically trained mind consider all the facts. "When did you tell him?"

"Uhm, right before school started. Probably August sometime. I was in Ireland all summer, and I know it was after that. How about you?"

"Around the same," she recalled.

Ryan paused for a moment and thought about the timing. "Why so late? I would think your parents would have gotten over it by then."

Sara's sigh was audible, nearly louder than her voice, which said, "They would have, if I had. When I was getting ready to go to Cal, I told my mother that I couldn't stop thinking about you. I told her that I had to call you…" her voice trailed off, and Ryan thought she could detect some tears.

"What happened?" Ryan asked gently.

"She told my father. Apparently she hadn't said anything before. He really flipped out and scared the living daylights out of me. He's normally so quiet and calm, but he was just wild."

"What did you say to Father Pender?"

"I was so scared I don't have any idea what I said. All I know is that he gave me a long lecture about avoiding temptation and told me that I had to resist my 'urges.'"

"Damn. He didn't say anything like that to me," Ryan said. "He tried to get me to join that group that urges abstinence, but I think he could tell I thought it was bullshit."

"I doubt he would have tried to talk you out of anything, Ryan," Sara said. "You were never the type who could be coerced."

Ryan thought about that for a moment, and realized that at eighteen, Sara would have appeared quite malleable. It wasn't that she didn't have a strong character, but she was always very focused on pleasing the authority figures in her life, something Ryan had yet to get the hang of.

"Well, it looks like old Father Pender is going to have a very pissed-off visitor in about an hour, and he'd better be in a talkative mood."

"Are you sure you want me to go with you?" Jamie was nearly jogging to keep up with her long-legged lover. They were cruising up the hill between Ryan's home and the church, and Jamie was nearly out of breath.

Ryan slowed, doing her best to calm her racing heart. "I'm just so pissed off I want to throttle him. He's like family to us. I swear, Jamie, if he admits this, I'm going to the Archbishop! I won't have him betray another person if I can help it."

"Honey," Jamie said with as much calm as she could muster, "this isn't the way to approach him if you want him to admit to something. I really think you need to calm down."

Ryan slowed even more, acknowledging that her partner was correct, but feeling very out of control. She nodded once, shoving her hands in her pockets roughly, a decided slump to her normally proud shoulders. They walked the rest of the way in silence, but instead of going to the rectory where the priest lived, Ryan detoured to the church and sat down in a pew to gather her jumbled thoughts. Jamie sat right next to her, a hand on her back, providing as much solace as she could. It took about fifteen minutes, but Ryan finally stood and stretched, getting some of the accumulated tension out of her back.

She extended a hand to Jamie and slid her arms around her. "I really think I need to talk to him alone," she whispered. "I think he'll be unwilling to reveal much if we're both there. Will you wait for me?"

"Of course I will. You take as long as you need. I'll be waiting right here."

The minutes ticked by, with Jamie becoming more anxious with the passing of each one. Almost thirty minutes had passed and Jamie was on the verge of going to find her partner when a long frame cast a massive shadow down the center aisle. Jamie was on her feet in a flash. "Are you okay?" she asked, her eyes darting to Ryan's pale face. Her hands automatically went to Ryan's arms, running up and down them slowly.

"Yeah. I'm all right. Sick to my stomach, and a massive headache, but I'm fine."

"Wanna talk about it?"

"Later," she mumbled, needing some time to sort out the jumble of emotions causing her head to pound.

Ryan didn't want to go to her family's home, even though they were in the neighborhood. She knew that she couldn't help but show how upset she was, and she wasn't in the mood for another scene. Instead, they grabbed a quick bite and headed back to Berkeley. Jamie drove, since Ryan was too scattered to focus. Placing one hand on the steering wheel and the other on Ryan's leg, Jamie gave it a gentle rub. "Anytime you want to talk about it, just let me know, love. No rush."

Ryan smiled over at her, once again pleased that her partner respected her boundaries. "I hate growing up," she muttered, lowering her seat as far back as she could and staring at the roof of the car.

"Pardon?" Jamie couldn't figure out how this was on point, but she knew Ryan would explain herself.

"It was nice being a kid and believing that adults knew what the hell they were doing. I trusted everyone when I was young, and even though I know you can't survive like that, I really miss those days sometimes."

Patting her thigh, Jamie reminded her of one important benefit of adulthood. "Yeah, but you didn't get to have sex with the girls on your sleepovers," she teased, deciding that a little levity was a good thing.

As usual, a delighted grin settled on Ryan's face at the thought of sex. "I guess I'll trade being jaded for sex, but I'm still mighty pissed off."

"Wanna tell me about it?"

"I'll spare you the rationalizing and get to the bottom line," Ryan said. "Mrs. Andrews talked to him a day after everything went down. But she didn't talk to him in the confessional. They just had a chat. Because she didn't tell him to keep it confidential, he didn't feel he was under any obligation to."

Jamie's mouth dropped open, and she cast so many glances at her partner that Ryan finally said, "I don't want to fall into the Bay. Keep your eyes on the road."

"Ryan, that's…that's…that's criminal. My grandfather isn't bound by any vow to keep confidences, but he sure as hell does. You don't skate by on a technicality!"

"I agree, but he certainly did."

Jamie was still too flabbergasted to think clearly, but she managed to pull herself together enough to ask, "Did he at least apologize?"

"Nope. He truly doesn't think he did anything wrong. Because he talked to Sister Mary Magdalene before Sara or I confessed, he doesn't think he violated our trust. As a matter of fact, he seems to think he was protecting me."

"Get out!"

Blazing green eyes locked on Ryan. "Focus, babe," Ryan said, pointing at the roadway.

"How on earth does he justify that?" Jamie was dutifully staring at the road, but her hands were gripping the wheel furiously, her knuckles whitening under the pressure.

A deep sigh came from Ryan's lungs, and she ran both hands through her hair, settling it against her shoulders. "He said that he knew word would get out, and he wanted someone in authority to know the truth about what had happened. He claims he went to Mother Superior and told her that he knew both Sara and me and that we were good kids who were just having a tough time with this. I don't have any reason to doubt him on this, since he was so forthcoming about everything else, but he swears that she's the only one he told."

"And she told the other students?"

"Don't know. Gonna find out," Ryan declared with a fierce glower on her normally placid features.

Chapter Thirteen

A s soon as Ryan returned from her team run on Wednesday morning, she was on the phone with her high school, trying to schedule an appointment with the principal.

"Any luck?" Jamie asked when Ryan placed the receiver back into the cradle.

"Yeah, but not until tomorrow. I hate to drive back across the bridge in morning traffic, but I need to talk to her as soon as possible."

Jamie pursed her lips, obviously thinking. "I've got an idea."

"What's that?"

"I'm going over to help Colm this afternoon, and I figured that as long as I was on that side of the Bay, I might ask Mother to dinner. She's leaving for Rhode Island on Friday, you know."

"Nope. Had no idea." Ryan tossed her feet onto the floor and stood to do some stretching.

Jamie watched Ryan's bare body contort for a few minutes, finding that her train of thought had abruptly left the tracks.

"You were saying?" Ryan prompted, knowing that her partner was a sucker for her stretching routine.

"Oh, right. Uhm…" she fumbled, trying to recall what she'd been talking about. "Oh, I got it!" she said proudly. "Mother goes to Rhode Island for the entire month of August to see her extended family. I'm sure I've told you that."

"Honey, your mother is always going somewhere. I haven't learned her schedule yet."

"Well, this trip is a given," Jamie said. "I just thought that it'd be nice to have a little send-off for her. She's been so nice to us."

Ryan sat on the bed next to her partner. "I'm happy to go. Just tell me where and when."

"I'm meeting Colm at 2:00, so why don't you come over to Niall's when you're finished with work. Then we can stay overnight at your house and be close to your appointment."

"Sounds like a plan," Ryan said. "I'll look forward to escorting the lovely Evans women tonight."

They decided on Zuni Café, since it was close to the freeway and not too far from Ryan's. After they were settled with a nice bottle of wine and a large bottle of mineral water, Catherine thanked them for inviting her and spent a few minutes expounding on how lovely each young woman looked.

Catherine seemed to know a lot about food, and she made several comments on the menu while they perused it. Calling the server over, she asked some pointed questions about the origin of the oysters, what type of parmigiano cheese was used on the Caesar salad, and other details that were far over Ryan's head. When all her questions had been answered, Catherine asked if they minded if she ordered for them. Ryan was glad for any help, so she readily accepted the offer. Jamie smiled and also assented.

The menu was not overly large, and Ryan noted with surprise that Catherine ordered every appetizer on the menu. "That's one way to avoid having to make the tough decisions," Ryan laughed.

Catherine smiled in return. "I've noticed that you seem to have a very healthy appetite. I want to make sure that you don't leave hungry."

"That rarely happens, Mother," Jamie said. "She invariably steals at least a quarter of my entrée."

"It's my duty," Ryan said. "I'm a charter member of the 'Clean Plate Club.'"

While the younger women devoured their large entrées, Catherine nibbled on a small caviar appetizer that couldn't have satisfied even Caitlin's tiny stomach. "Ryan," she said when the entrées had been cleared from the table, "are you aware of my annual pilgrimage to Newport to visit my family?"

She nodded briefly. "Jamie's told me that you go for a month every year. Is this your mother's or father's family?"

"Mother's," she said. "My father's family has been in California since the Gold Rush. The eastern roots are long forgotten."

Mine's been here since the Summer of Love, Ryan thought, but she wasn't sure how Catherine would take her joke, so she kept it to herself.

"I know this is sudden," Catherine said, showing a little hesitation, "but this year I wanted to see if Jamie would accompany me for part of the time."

Jamie had never felt quite as trapped as she did at that moment. Her mother was being more connected and more understanding about her situation than she could ever have dreamed possible and she was being extremely cordial to Ryan. To say no would be callous and disloyal, but she would rather have gone over Niagara Falls in a barrel than spend a month with her tedious relatives. Her face must have reflected her feelings because Catherine said, "If you're opposed, don't give it another moment's thought, dear." But even in this short exchange, Jamie could see the disappointment register in the deep brown eyes.

"No, no, it's not that," she hastened to explain, even though it was. "I just don't know if we can work it out. School starts early this year and I have my golf tryouts…"

Ryan, always helpful, interjected, "We've got most of August free. School doesn't start until August the twenty-third, remember?"

"Thanks, hon," she said with a rigid smile. "Well, I guess that settles it. When would you like me?"

"Any time you can spare would be wonderful. Why don't you two discuss it and call me in Rhode Island?"

"Okay," Jamie said. "But I can only spare a week. Even at that I don't know if it'll be bearable to be around me." At her mother's questioning glance she explained, "It's hard for me to go play golf without her."

As she reached over and grasped her lover's hand, they shared a tender smile that caused Catherine to say, "It didn't dawn on me that a short separation would be hard for you both. I don't want to cause any discomfort, girls. We can do this another time."

"No," Ryan said. "I think it would be good for you two to have some time together. And Jamie and I can see if absence truly does make the heart grow fonder."

Jamie smiled gently at her partner and said, "There are limits to everything; I couldn't possibly be any fonder of you."

Ryan didn't reply verbally, but her love-filled eyes spoke volumes. It was actually a little too intimate for Catherine to witness, so she called the waiter over and asked for the dessert cart. Just as she suspected, once Ryan had a dazzling array of sweets in front of her, she broke the tender exchange and got down to the business of eating.

"Did you realize that your father was home, Jamie?" Catherine asked casually as they sipped their after-dinner coffee.

"Yes, I assumed he was," she said quietly, her eyes fixed on her folded hands.

Catherine placed her hand atop Jamie's and gazed at her daughter until the green eyes lifted to meet hers. "I understand this is hard for you, and I'm not asking you to do anything you aren't ready to do. I just want to remind you that your father has far too much pride for his own good. You might have to make the first step to reestablish contact."

Jamie nodded, acknowledging the truth of her mother's statement. "I don't mind that so much, Mother. I mean, it's what I'm used to."

Catherine felt a great deal of empathy for her daughter, knowing that the young girl had always had to go the extra step to stay in her father's good graces. It wasn't that Jim was irrational; in fact, it usually took quite a lot to anger him. But he had a very difficult time saying that he was sorry, and Jamie usually gave in before he did. "I know that's true," she said. "I wish it weren't so, but I don't think he'll change at this point."

"It's not that I won't apologize," Jamie said. "I was very touchy when we spoke, and I did react badly. I just worry that this will happen again and again. I wish I knew how to get past the entire issue."

She looked very frustrated, and Catherine was considering what to say when Ryan's hand went to her daughter's face and softly stroked her cheek. The gesture was small, almost insignificant, but when Jamie looked up into Ryan's eyes, Catherine watched in amazement as her frown disappeared, immediately replaced by a small grin filled with affection.

"I'll get involved if you wish, Jamie. I hope you know that," Catherine said to her.

"I know, Mother," she said, "and I appreciate it. But I think I have to work this out on my own." She shook her head in frustration and ran her hand through her hair. "I know I have my work cut out for me to convince him that I'm an adult, but it annoys me that he insists on keeping me in the dark."

"Tell me how you mean that."

"He won't even give me a copy of my trust agreement. He seems to think that I should be satisfied with him making my decisions for me."

"Jamie," Catherine soothed, "haven't you learned that confronting your father directly never works? Go around him, dear."

"How?"

"You haven't been to the bank in years. Why not drop by to say hello to Tuck and get a copy of the agreement you've misplaced?"

"But I didn't mis—" Jamie started to say, but stopped short when she caught the twinkle in her mother's eyes. "That's very devious."

"Devious, perhaps," Catherine said, "but also efficient. Why go through the wall when you can go around it?"

I like this woman more and more, Ryan mused, watching mother and daughter as they shared a laugh.

It wasn't very late when their server cleared all the plates from the table, and it quickly became clear that Catherine didn't want to go home. She'd already offered after-dinner drinks, but neither Jamie nor Ryan was in the mood for any more alcohol. Signaling the server, Catherine said, "I'd like another espresso; can I convince either of you to join me?"

Ryan realized that she was merely trying to extend the evening, so she agreed. "I'd love to, but I need a decaf if I'm going to get to sleep."

She nodded and gave the order to the server. Since they were going to be there for a while, Jamie figured it was a good time to bring up the topic that had been in the back of her mind for several weeks. "You know, Mother, one of the reasons that I want the trust agreement is so that I can decide what to do with the trust distribution that I was entitled to at my last birthday."

Catherine paused, her body language revealing nothing of her feelings about this declaration. The server was on his way with the coffee, and she waited until he departed to ask, "Why now, Jamie? I thought you were happy to leave the money in place until you had some definite plan for it."

"I did," she said. "But Ryan's shown me how to look at my statements more carefully, and I'm unhappy with the performance of the fund. I could do as well in a savings account, Mother, and that's just ridiculous in this market."

"Do you need more money? I'm sure we could raise your monthly allowance now that Ryan..."

"No, no," Jamie interrupted. "I have plenty of money. But eventually Ryan and I want to use our money to start a charitable foundation of some sort. The more I can earn, the more we'll be able to give away."

Catherine smiled at her daughter and said, "I wish I could say that your great-great-grandfather would be proud of you for that, but in truth he'd turn over in his grave to think that you were planning on giving his hard-earned money away."

Looking at her mother with careful regard, Jamie asked, "What about you? Your opinion means more to me than that of a long-dead relative."

Giving her daughter an identical look, Catherine smiled and replied, "I'm always proud of you. I think it's a fabulous idea if you can distribute some of this money during your life. I guarantee that you won't get any support from the extended family, but you'll have my complete approval."

Jamie laughed, her eyes crinkling up in their usual fashion. "You and the rest of the family give scads of money away."

"Oh, we give money to our favorite charities and to all of the major cultural institutions, but that's just to keep our way of life intact. As much as I love the opera and the symphony, I never delude myself into thinking that I'm significantly changing anyone's life by supporting them." She sounded so bitter and self-deprecating that Ryan nearly asked her why she continued to behave this way if she had so little regard for it. But she didn't yet know Catherine well enough to question her choices, so she held her tongue.

"I think your support of the arts is very important," Jamie said. "Music and dance and art have a very meaningful impact on people. Don't diminish that."

Fixing her daughter with her velvety brown eyes, Catherine asked, "Is that how you want to distribute *your* money?"

Jamie was silent for a moment, staring at her folded hands while she tried to think of a graceful way to answer that question. "No, it's not, but not because it's not important. I'd like to do something to help individuals with quality-of-life issues, things like housing and even medical care for people who don't qualify for other programs."

Catherine nodded, took a sip of her espresso, and murmured, "That's what I expected. I don't think you'll ever spend your days going from one charity luncheon to the next, talking to a group of people who care far more about who's wearing what than actually helping others."

Giving her mother a very compassionate look, Jamie said, "You don't have to do that, either. You could really make a difference in people's lives."

"I'm not unhappy with my life," Catherine insisted, a touch too enthusiastically to be believed. "I've found my place in this world, and it suits me perfectly. I just don't think it would suit you." She smiled and said,

"Now, back to your request. If you truly feel that you're ready to start managing your own money, I have no problem with your taking your distribution. Would you like me to talk to your father before I leave for Rhode Island?"

"No, I think I should do that myself," Jamie said. "I'll try to patch things up with Daddy, and then talk to him about the distribution later. I'm not in a big rush."

"That's good," Catherine said. "Feel free to tell him that we've already spoken if that helps your cause."

What odd ways these people have of communicating, Ryan thought. *It's like they form little alliances. I hope to God we never fall into this, it would kill me to think our kids couldn't talk to both of us together.*

Both Jamie and Ryan looked like they were about to fall asleep by this time, and Catherine signaled the server for their bill. "I'm tired myself," she said. "I think I'll go stay at the apartment."

Warning bells went off in Ryan's head, and she tried to think of a way to prevent Catherine from getting a very unwelcome surprise. "Is Jim staying in the city tonight?"

"Yes, dear, he is. He said he had a conference call at 3:00 a.m. He often stays here when he has that type of thing to attend to."

"Does he know you're coming?" Ryan asked, her mouth moving faster than her brain.

Catherine gave her a puzzled look, but answered anyway, "No, he doesn't."

"You'd better call first," Ryan said, trying to think of a reasonable reason why Catherine should call first. Finally, it came to her, and she blurted out, "Jamie says he entertains clients there. You wouldn't want to interrupt a business meeting."

Catherine's puzzled look remained, but she nodded and fished in her purse for her small cell phone. "That's a good idea. Thank you for suggesting it." She speed dialed the number, waiting patiently for an answer. "Hello, Jim," she said, obviously to an answering machine. "I thought I'd come stay at the apartment with you tonight. I'll be over in a few—oh, hello," she said, after Jim must have picked up. "No, no special reason. I was in the city having dinner with Jamie and Ryan, and I just thought…no, I understand. Don't give it another thought. Will I see you tomorrow? Oh, I see," she said, her eyes betraying her disappointment.

"Well, I suppose I'll see you when I return from Rhode Island, then. Take care. Good night."

Giving Ryan a half smile, she placed the phone back into her purse. "Thanks for the suggestion, Ryan. He was involved in a meeting at his apartment. I'll just head home."

"Are you sure, Mother? You could stay at the Palace." Jamie knew that the luxurious old hotel was one of her mother's favorites, and she thought she might like to spend the evening there to avoid the long drive to Hillsborough.

"No, no, it's no bother. I just thought it would be fun to stay in the city and see your father. He's been gone so much lately, and with me leaving for Rhode Island…" She trailed off, looking sadder than Ryan could stand to see. "Oh well, we've had longer separations than a month," she said, trying to sound blithe. "It's nothing in the greater scheme of things."

Please, oh please, never, ever let me say that about Jamie.

The next morning, Ryan was too anxious to eat breakfast immediately, so they decided to head down to Union Street for a cup of coffee. Sitting outside on the warm summer day, Jamie couldn't help but notice the lines of stress on Ryan's face. She had her darkest sunglasses on, concealing her eyes, but small lines of tension were etched into her forehead, and an unusual tautness around her mouth revealed just how anxious she was.

Ryan's hand was resting on the small metal café table, and Jamie covered it with her own. "This is really tough for you, isn't it?"

"Yeah." Her head nodded slightly, a stoic mask covering her usually expressive features. "I've been upset about Sister's role ever since Coach Ratzinger told me that she allowed me to be the sacrificial lamb, but what Father Pender told me is just too much."

"Were you close to her?"

Jamie's question was simple, and it merited a simple answer, but Ryan knew that she couldn't give her one. "I'm not sure how to answer that," she said quietly. "I really thought that I could rely on her, and I believed in her…it's…it's really hard to think she spread the rumors about me."

"Did you spend much time with her?" Jamie had spent a grand total of ten minutes with the headmaster of her prep school, and it puzzled her to think that Ryan would have had much of a relationship with this woman.

A small, wry laugh preceded Ryan's reply. "Yeah, I'd say we spent more time together than she wished." At Jamie's confused look, she continued. "You have to stop and think of who I was, and what my school was," she reminded her. "I wasn't from the poorest family, but I was definitely in the bottom five. Most of the girls were from very wealthy, very socially connected families, and in many ways I stuck out like a sore thumb. I mean, I wasn't only working-class, I was basically an immigrant."

Jamie laughed at this description, disputing its accuracy. "That's a little strong."

"No, it's not," Ryan said. "I wasn't who I am now. I was raised in a very isolated, protected environment. All of my relatives are from Ireland, and in some ways we really keep to ourselves. My world was my family, my neighborhood, and my parish. I wasn't exposed to much diversity. I was in Sister's office every third day, asking her about one thing or another." Ryan's face took on a sad look as she added, "Or crying about some bit of teasing or an unkind remark."

"You were teased because you didn't have money?"

Ryan nodded. "Partly that, and partly because I didn't seem like the other kids. I mean, you've got to remember that I spoke with an Irish accent, I didn't watch MTV, I didn't know any of the current songs…I really was like an immigrant."

Jamie shook her head, thinking of a young Ryan, struggling to fit in amongst her new classmates. "I don't think I realized you spoke with an accent. When did you lose it?"

"It came and went," Ryan said. "I spent every summer with my family in Ireland and I wanted to fit in, so I spoke like them when I was there. It usually got less pronounced as the school year went on, but when I started at Sacred Heart I had just come back, and I'm sure I sounded like I just stepped off the boat."

"So this woman helped you through some of those hard times?"

"Yeah. She really did. We kinda became buddies," Ryan said wistfully. "I trusted her."

Jamie knew that few things were as precious to Ryan as trust, and she also realized that few things wounded her more deeply than betrayal. "I'm sorry this is so hard for you," she said softly, lacing their fingers together and giving Ryan's hand a squeeze.

"I know you are. It really helps to have you here with me."

"Do you want me to go in with you to see her? Or would you feel more comfortable talking to her alone?"

Ryan's head dropped a few degrees, and shy blue eyes peeked out through her long bangs. "Would you be willing to hang out in the library while I talk to her? I'd like you to be close in case I need you."

"Honey, I'd do anything for you, I hope you know that. I'll stay as close to you as you need."

Ryan laughed. "That might make Sister a little uncomfortable. I think the library is a safer bet."

As her fingers curled to rap on the door of the office she had entered so many times, Ryan cast a puzzled glance down at the strong, defined hand of an adult. She shook her head briskly, reminding herself that she was no longer an innocent young girl. Taking a breath, she knocked on the heavy wooden door.

"Come in."

Stepping into the room, Ryan was again transported back six years, amazed that the office looked almost exactly like it had the last time she had entered it and that the woman she gazed at had changed just as little. With a smile, she recalled her Aunt Maeve's motto: after sixty, change comes slowly to a woman's face.

Sister Mary Magdalene was a good deal more than sixty, Ryan knew, guessing that her former principal was at least seventy-five years old now. She had been past the usual retirement age when Ryan was in school, but Ryan had never heard a soul say that she was too old for the job. She had been the principal at Sacred Heart for almost thirty years and had taught biology for ten years before that, long enough to have been on the job when some of the current girls' mothers or even grandmothers had been in attendance. Taking the school from the troubled days of the sixties up to the current time was an enormous accomplishment, Ryan knew, and even today Sister showed no signs of age getting the better of her. "Ryan," she said with genuine fondness, coming around to the side of her desk to grasp Ryan's hand and squeeze her shoulder with her other hand. "It's marvelous to see you." Her eyes reflected her pleasure, and Ryan couldn't help but return her infectious smile.

When the older woman gestured toward a chair, Ryan sat down, finding that her posture was stiff in the rigid leather seat.

Sister laughed gently. "That chair seems to have shrunk a bit, doesn't it? Odd, since mine seems to have grown."

When Ryan gave her another studied glance, she noticed that Sister looked a bit smaller than she had six years ago. She still looked vital and healthy, but the signs of her age were a little more obvious now.

"I think you look great, Sister," Ryan said, meaning it sincerely.

The older woman folded her hands neatly on her desk, her pressed navy blue blazer exposing starched white cuffs. She had stopped wearing the traditional habit of her order almost thirty-five years earlier, but a navy blue or black suit with a below-the-knee skirt had taken its place immediately. The big change to her attire was the elimination of the elaborate headpiece that she had worn as a young religious, and that was an item of clothing that she had been more than glad to discard. "Your name has been popping up with startling frequency," the sister said forthrightly. "I assumed I was next on your list of interviews."

Her directness startled Ryan, but when she thought about it for a moment she realized that had always been Sister's style. "Can we do away with the preliminaries?" she asked, just as directly.

"No, I don't think that's wise," she said. "First I want to apologize to you."

Ryan cocked her head, waiting for the older woman to continue.

"After I spoke with Ms. Ratzinger, I spent a good amount of time and prayer thinking about what had happened with you, and I realized that my actions were wrong-headed and hurtful. I know it's too late to make an impact now, but I want to admit to my failings. I'm truly sorry, Ryan," she said, making eye contact with her young visitor.

"Why did you do it, Sister?"

The older woman shook her head, thinking back to the time in question. "I wasn't looking at the entire picture. I allowed myself to look at the issue with a very narrow focus. To me, it was a group of girls who no longer trusted one another. Some very vocal people wanted you off that team, and I honestly thought it would be better for everyone concerned if you just walked away. I knew soccer was important to you, but I had no idea that the coach at Cal would withdraw her scholarship offer just because you didn't play during your senior year. I didn't understand the gravity of the situation."

Ryan was shaking her head the entire time the older woman spoke. Her brow was furrowed and she seemed very impatient, speaking as soon as

Sister finished her sentence. "I think I understand what happened about the team, Sister. What I want to know is why you told other people about what happened between Sara and me." Her eyes were glowing with a determined fire, and the older woman blinked slowly, startled by their white-hot intensity.

"Told...told...why, Ryan, I swear I told no one! I would never do that."

This was the first time in Ryan's history with the sister that she had ever seen her stunned. Her normally implacable features showed the surprise she felt, and Ryan was quite disconcerted by the display. "Sister, that's what everyone tells me. But then they think about it, and they remember that they told just one person they thought was safe. Either someone else is lying to me, or you told someone."

The sister shook her head gravely, a determined look now filling her eyes. "No, Ryan. I told no one. I'd never spread a rumor about a girl, any girl. I admit I made a grievous mistake with you, but I did not betray you."

"Then who did?" Ryan was beyond frustration at this point, and her voice was much louder than she intended it to be. She scrubbed at her face with her hands, trying to get her mind around the ever-widening circles of lies or half-truths that someone was spinning.

"I can't tell you that. I don't know who would have done it. I can only swear to you that it wasn't me."

When Ryan shuffled listlessly into the library, Jamie immediately knew that she had not received satisfaction. They spent the next fifteen minutes talking over what Sister had related, finally agreeing that someone was lying, but not knowing how to determine who that someone was. "How much do you think lie detector tests for everyone would cost?" Ryan asked, only partially kidding.

"I have no idea, but I'll gladly pay for them."

"Shit!" Ryan stood and kicked at the heavy study table. "Maybe I don't really want to know. Somebody that I trusted screwed me over and then continues to lie about it six years later. Maybe I should just put it away and try to act like it didn't happen."

Jamie gazed up at her for a moment, seeing the roiling emotions reflected in her eyes. "Can you do that? I know you'd like to have a cordial relationship with Sara and her mother and Father Pender. Can you do that if you know that one of them might have betrayed you?"

Ryan flopped down into the wooden chair, dropping her head onto her arms. "I don't know. Maybe I can…" She trailed off, knowing that it would be difficult, but not knowing what else to do.

Jamie rubbed her back for a moment, then got to her feet when Ryan did. They linked hands and started to leave the library when Jamie was struck by a thought. "This is a school, right?" she asked, her eyes flickering with an idea.

"Uhm, right."

"What schools do best is make notes. There might be a note of some kind in your record that would mention the talk with Father Pender, or there might be something saying that Sister told the school counselor or someone. Come on." Jamie dragged her out through the doors, toward the principal's office. "We've got one more stone to turn."

Fifteen minutes later, the two young women were poring over the record of Ryan's years at the Convent of the Sacred Heart. As Jamie suspected, the vast majority of notes in the file had to do with scholastic honors, requests from various college coaches to attend a game to watch Ryan play, and other routine paperwork. Pulling out a score sheet from a standardized I.Q. test, Jamie read the score at the top right-hand corner and flipped it to her partner. "That's just sick," she said with a disgusted shake of her head.

"I.Q. tests aren't representative of people's intelligence," Ryan said, not bothering to look at the number.

"Uh-huh, tell that to somebody who's gullible." She continued to whip through the large file until her hands stilled on a neatly typed 8½-by-11-inch sheet of paper. Without a word, she handed it to her partner, and watched as Ryan's eyes darted across the words.

"Well, fuck me," she mumbled, getting to her feet to knock once again on the door to Sister Mary Magdalene's office.

This time Ryan was only inside for five minutes, but in that short time Jamie nearly wore a path in the carpet, pacing back and forth outside the closed door. When the door finally opened, Jamie was surprised to see an elderly woman holding Ryan in a fond hug. "Goodbye, Sister," she heard her partner say. "Thanks for helping me clear this up."

"Goodbye, Ryan," the older woman said, in a clear, full voice that belied her age. "I wasn't much help, but I'm glad that you feel better. Keep in touch, won't you?"

"I'll try to," she said, stepping into the outer office and grabbing Jamie in an emotion-filled hug. The door closed softly behind them, and it was all Jamie could do to keep her feet on the floor against the power of Ryan's embrace.

"Good news?" she gasped, nearly all of her breath squeezed from her lungs.

"The best!" Ryan's smile was enormous, and Jamie couldn't help but mirror it, even though she didn't know why they were smiling. "Nobody that I trusted screwed me."

"Huh? How can that be? That note…"

"Yes, that note was about the talk Sister had with Father Pender. She wanted a note in the file just for her own records."

"But it was typed…"

"Yes, yes!" Ryan cried. "That's who did it!"

She was still so excited that she could hardly talk, but Jamie had to know what was going on, so she directed Ryan to a bench in the long, empty hallway and instructed, "Breathe. Calm down a little bit and tell me exactly what happened."

Ryan closed her eyes and took some deep, calming breaths, finally nodding to show she was calm. "Okay. Sister took notes, and she put them in my file. Because they were confidential, she didn't want them typed. But her secretary took the file from her desk and typed them up. That's why the original was clipped to the back. There was a little sticky note that said "For your review" attached to the letter, but Sister obviously never saw it. The file got put away, so she didn't know that her secretary had seen the note."

Ryan still looked so happy that her face must have hurt, but Jamie didn't see how this solved anything. "I still don't get it. Are you saying that the secretary was the one who told? Are you sure?"

Ryan's arms crossed over her chest, and she nodded solemnly. "I'm positive. Not much of a deduction when the secretary was none other than Tammy Anderson's mother."

"Was she one of the girls on your team?"

Ryan nodded, a smirk on her face. "She was the all-star bitch, who was also a relatively poor back-up goalie." Her dark eyebrows twitched and the light went on for Jamie.

"Her mother told her, and she told the other girls so that she could force you off the team?"

A confident nod was Ryan's reply. "I'd bet the farm on it."

"But that still doesn't make sense," Jamie said, even though she hated to dampen Ryan's ebullient mood.

"What doesn't?"

"Why would your teammates believe her? It just seems hard to fathom that they would ignore what they knew about you."

"No, it doesn't," Ryan said. "Tammy was actually more popular with the girls who were left on the team at that point. They liked me as a player, but my friends had all graduated the year before. I didn't have any buddies left by that time. For all of her faults, Tammy was really the leader of that clique. It's not hard at all for me to imagine that the other players would believe her, especially if she told them that her mom had gotten the info from Sister Mary Magdalene."

"What does Sister think?" Jamie asked, assuming that she knew the parties involved quite well.

"She thinks it makes perfect sense," Ryan said. "I got the impression she isn't a big fan of young Ms. Anderson's. I think that's the closest Sister Mary Magdalene has come to cussing in a long while. She was just about purple with anger."

"I'm really glad that you think you found out who was behind this," Jamie said. "I'm just not looking forward to confronting two more people."

Ryan shook her head and got to her feet, extending her hand to lift Jamie to hers. "Nope. We…are…finished. I've got all the answers I need."

"Huh? But I thought—"

"Jamie," she said, "I only hurt this bad because I thought someone I loved or trusted had screwed me over. The fact that some prissy little snot tried to ruin my life doesn't bother me much. In fact, if she were here right now, I'd kiss her!"

Jamie beamed a smile up at her partner, tremendously relieved that her angst had been resolved. "I'm here," she said softly, batting her eyes.

"That you are," Ryan grinned and proceeded to kiss her senseless.

By the time they returned to Berkeley, Ryan's mood was lighter than it had been in weeks, and Jamie was grateful to see the lines of tension completely disappear from her face. That night they went to bed early once again, with Ryan falling asleep almost immediately, a sweet, innocent smile on her lovely features.

Chapter Fourteen

T he next morning Ryan wandered through the maze of offices in the under-construction Haas Arena, stepping over drywall materials and ignoring the not-so-subtle leers she received from a few of the workmen. She was planning on making a few changes to her fall class schedule to better accommodate her volleyball commitments, and she thought it wise to check with Coach Placer before she did anything hasty.

As she turned down the hallway toward the volleyball offices, she nearly collided with Coach Greene, who was balancing a large cup of coffee and a small brown bag in one hand, her briefcase under the same arm, and trying to insert one of the keys from a massive ring into her door. "Need a hand...or two?" Ryan asked and whisked the keys away from her.

"I'm happy to accept a spare hand, Ryan," she said, "although I'd prefer your feet."

"Still recruiting, huh?" Ryan observed, feeling the key turn roughly in the new lock.

"You're not the kind of player a coach gets over very quickly," she said wistfully. "It's kinda like having your heart broken." Her eyes were playful, and Ryan considered flashing a smile and taking off, but something inside urged her to stay for a minute and try to glean another bit of information from the woman.

"Do you have a few minutes to chat?" Ryan asked, cocking her head a bit.

"You bet," the older woman said quickly. "Especially if you want to talk about how much you hate volleyball."

Ryan gave a slight smirk and followed the coach into her inner office, waiting patiently while she got herself organized. "So what's up?" she asked while taking a sip of coffee, her eyes fluttering closed in pleasure at the first taste.

"I don't know if you know this or not, but I've had a very hard time letting go of all of the things that went on when I was a senior in high school."

Coach Greene cocked her head, and looked at Ryan quizzically. "No, I didn't know that. I assumed that you'd put that behind you. You certainly seem happy—"

"Oh, I am. I've just had some unfinished business. The good news is that I've learned some things in the past couple of weeks that have been helpful. Some people that I thought had betrayed me really hadn't, and it's been a tremendous weight off my mind." She shifted nervously in her chair and got to the point. "There's just one little thing that's still bothering me."

Coach Greene paused mid-sip and regarded Ryan carefully. "What's that?"

"I still don't understand why you gave up so easily. I was under the impression that Sara or Coach Ratzinger warned you to steer clear of me. But they both insist that they didn't do that. If that's true, it makes even less sense that you'd dump me so quickly."

The older woman nodded her head, looking thoughtful. "Would you mind if I got out your recruiting folder? My memory is pretty hazy that far back."

"No, not at all," Ryan said. "I'd appreciate it."

Five minutes later, the coach walked back into her office, holding the open folder in both hands. As she sat down, she began to thumb through the notes and memos that were neatly affixed to the manila folder. She paged through the notes, finally finding what she was looking for. Dropping her head into her hands, she carefully read the document, pursing her lips while she nodded her head. "I think I have it clear in my mind now. Do you have some particular question you'd like me to answer?"

Ryan shifted in her seat, staring thoughtfully at the coach. "I thought I already asked my question. If Sara and Coach Ratzinger are telling the truth, you dropped me just because I didn't play during my senior year…and I have a hard time believing that."

Pushing her chair back and grasping a knee with both hands, Coach Greene stretched in her chair for a few seconds, obviously trying to decide how much to reveal. She shook her head and confirmed, "No, it was more than that. I, uhm, I don't feel comfortable revealing who told me this, but someone did tell me about the trouble between you and Sara."

The look on Ryan's face was painful to watch, and the coach hastened to assure her. "It wasn't Coach Ratzinger or Sara. Rest assured that neither of them said a word about you."

"Sister Mary Magdalene?" Ryan asked, still looking heartbroken.

"No, Ryan, it wasn't anyone in a position of authority. To tell you the complete truth, it was one of your teammates. I don't want to reveal who it was, but it was someone who obviously had a bone to pick with you."

"I have a very good suspicion of who that was," Ryan muttered. But something about the story still didn't sit right with her. "It just doesn't make sense that you dropped me because of unfounded gossip. You're just not that easily influenced."

"No, no, I'm not." She got up and stood, facing the small window that looked out upon an expanse of dirt that had yet to be landscaped. "It was a number of factors, Ryan. When you quit the team, I was astounded, and I tried my best to get the truth out of Coach Ratzinger. The fact that she offered such a flimsy reason for your departure really had me scratching my head. I went to Sara, since I knew you two were very close, but she acted like I wanted her to give up state secrets." She laughed quietly. "As you know, Sara's a pretty open person, and her refusal to talk made me even more suspicious."

She turned and sat on the edge of her credenza, giving Ryan a long look. "I knew you were a phenomenal player, and I knew that your potential was even greater. But you'd never been soccer-mad. It came down to making a choice between you and Mindy Lau from Vallejo."

Ryan nodded, recalling the woman she had played against in an all-star game. "She was good," she said quietly.

"Yes, she was good. She was a starter for me for three years, and I was very happy with her. The bottom line is that I had to choose between someone who was dedicated to the sport, had fantastic grades, got along great with her teammates, and was highly recommended by her school administration…and you. I thought you had more potential, as a matter of fact, I'm sure you did. But something about your situation just didn't smell right to me, and I didn't want to go looking for trouble." Looking down at Ryan she cocked her head and said, "I'm sure it feels like I screwed you over, but that wasn't my intent. I just made the decision that I thought I could live with. If we'd been one player away from making the NCAA tournament I would have taken the risk and offered you the scholarship. But…we weren't."

"It would have been nice if you'd told me that," Ryan said quietly, still hurt by the complete snub she'd been given.

The coach looked a little uncomfortable. "It was a tough situation. Would you have felt better if I'd told you I was going with someone else because I had a hunch you were damaged goods?"

Ryan shook her head and said, "No, I guess not. It just hurt to be dumped. I always thought it was because you were afraid to have me on the team because I was gay."

Coach Greene laughed softly. "Nothing could be further from the truth. I don't have any negative feelings about your orientation. Heck," she said, a smile covering her face, "I'd be gay *with* you if you'd play for me this year."

Ryan joined in her laugh and observed, "I think my spouse and your husband would take a dim view of that."

"Oh, my husband's a pretty forgiving guy," she teased. "When you're married to a college-level coach, you learn that she'll sell her soul for a recruit."

Ryan stood and extended her hand to the coach, clasping it in a firm shake. "My partner wouldn't be so forgiving." She smiled. "Besides, I think volleyball is more my style at this point in my life. I had a very serious head injury a year ago, and it wouldn't be wise to go looking for trouble."

"Ryan, I've seen you play volleyball," the older woman laughed, getting up to sling an arm around her shoulders. "If everyone played like you did, they'd require helmets and face shields."

"I...get focused."

"That's an understatement," Coach Greene said. When they reached the door to the outer office she placed both of her hands on Ryan's shoulders, and looked into her eyes. "I wish you all the best. Rich Placer's gain is my loss, but I hope you enjoy every minute of your season."

"Thanks, Coach," she said, blushing a little under the scrutiny. "I'd like to come watch some of your matches this season."

"I'll definitely come see some of yours. Full-contact volleyball sounds like my kind of sport."

On the way back to the O'Flaherty home late that afternoon, they exited the freeway and headed toward the financial district. As they inched through the heavy weekend-bound traffic, Ryan once again expressed her reluctance to make the trip. "I just don't know if it's wise to take me with you to visit your trust officer," she said. "It's obvious that your dad isn't wild about my involvement in your finances."

"He doesn't dislike you. He's, well, he's acting like my father. He's very, very protective of me."

"Well, I can't fault him for that," she grinned as she reached over and squeezed Jamie's thigh.

Ryan was dressed in navy cotton pants and a crisp, white, oxford-cloth shirt with three-quarter-length sleeves rolled up just a bit. The shirt hung out, as was the style, but she still looked neat and businesslike. As they drove along in the Lexus, Ryan cast a quick appreciative glance at her partner. Jamie wore a light cotton sweater-set in mint green and slim-fitting chinos that accentuated her muscular legs. "You look really nice today," she said with a big smile. "I like you in sweaters."

"Thanks," Jamie replied with a matching grin. "You look pretty swell yourself, hot stuff."

"Good enough to meet a stuffy banker?"

Jamie snorted derisively as she considered the implications of that statement. "The question is, are the bankers good enough to meet you?"

H. Tucker Gray was just what you would expect, both from his last name and from his position as a vice president of a large trust department. His skin was so pale that it actually did seem to be tinted a fine dove gray, and his personality was similarly fiery. "Hello, Jamie," he said with a voice that was surprisingly sonorous for his diminutive size.

Ryan gazed at the little man and counted the number of chalk stripes it took to circle his tiny leg. Only five stripes showed on the front, and she mused that it would take a dozen to get around the same space on her own substantially larger leg. Jamie pulled her from her observations by saying, "Tuck, this is my partner, Ryan O'Flaherty."

He perfunctorily extended his porcelain-like hand, and Ryan wondered if the baby-smooth skin had ever done a day of manual labor. "Very pleased to make your acquaintance," he said cordially. Turning to Jamie, he inquired in his nasal, Eastern accent, "Are you partners in some endeavor that I should be aware of?"

Both women had to stifle a laugh, but Jamie rallied and said, "We're life partners, Tuck." His blank expression forced her to elaborate. "She's my lover."

It wasn't possible for him to grow any paler, so his skin did the only thing it could, it flushed deeply at the news. "I...I...I...I had no idea," he muttered as he groped blindly for his huge leather chair and flopped down into it. "I thought you were engaged," he said, thinking that he must have this young woman confused with one of the many similarly situated beneficiaries for whom he was responsible.

"I was, but I broke up with my fiancé a few months ago...mainly because I fell in love with Ryan." It wasn't the technical truth, but it was the emotional truth, even though she had not previously acknowledged it that way in public.

"I see," he muttered, folding his tiny hands neatly on his desk blotter. "I'm sure that you'll be very happy together," he managed with a voice that belied his sincerity. Turning to Jamie again he started over, "So, you came here today for...?"

"Two things," she said, businesslike as usual. "First, I can't find a copy of my trust agreement, so I'd like another. Secondly, I want to see if it's possible to give Ryan the authority to make withdrawals from my trust in case of emergency."

It was a tie for whose eyes bugged out more at the second part of this statement, but Jamie would have put her money on Ryan. "J...J...Jamie!" her lover said. "I don't need any such thing!"

"I want to make sure you could handle things if I became incapacitated or was unavailable."

Tuck immediately quashed any such talk. "That's not possible," he said firmly. "*You* are the beneficiary—only you. If you want to have a power-of-attorney drawn up, that is a different matter altogether, and I would think that your father would be able to help you with that."

"Okay," she said. "I'm just asking a simple question, Tuck. It's difficult for same-sex partners to protect each other legally. I'm just trying to determine the best way to handle my affairs."

"Of course," he said stiffly. "I'm happy to answer any questions you have." He looked anything but happy, but Jamie wasn't going to let him deter her.

"I have some general questions about the trust. Do you have time to answer them?"

"Certainly," he said. "That's why I'm here."

"Obviously, this trust will have a big effect on both of our lives. Ryan's not very familiar with trusts, so I'd like it if you could give her a general overview of the terms."

He raised one delicate eyebrow, but pulled the document in question from a file folder and spent a few minutes refreshing his memory of its provisions. "It's the Smith Grandchildren's Trust, but as you no doubt know, Jamie is the only grandchild. She is entitled to income distributions, but only on a discretionary basis. The only items that the trust will pay for without question are educational expenses. That includes tuition, books, fees, and supplies for any legitimate educational purpose. Jim and Catherine are both trustees, and they make all decisions regarding discretionary distributions."

Ryan scrunched up her nose and cocked her head at the little man, asking, "How does that work? Does that mean their decision must be unanimous?"

"Yes," he said, pursing his thin lips at her.

Ryan nodded, and Tuck continued. "The trust may distribute 25 percent at age twenty-one, 25 percent at twenty-five, and the remainder at thirty or upon marriage, although that will likely not occur now," he observed dryly.

"Are the distributions automatic?" Ryan asked, aware that Jamie had not received her distribution.

"The first two are not," he said clearly, a decided brusqueness to his tone. "The trustees can defer either of the first two until age thirty. I believe in your case you chose not to ask for your distribution at your twenty-first birthday, correct?"

"That's correct," Jamie said.

Ryan followed up, "If she changes her mind is there any problem with taking it now?"

"No," he said carefully as he glared at Ryan. "If her trustees agree, she may take that distribution at any time."

"What if the trustees don't agree?" Ryan asked, her mouth asking the question before her brain could override it. "Does she have any way to force them to make the payment?"

"No, Miss O'Flaherty," he said with his eyes narrowing. "She does not."

His attitude had begun to irritate Ryan several minutes earlier, and it was getting worse by the moment. "What if they're being unreasonable?"

"The standard of reasonableness rests solely with the trustees. Of course, you could waste hundreds of thousands of dollars of Miss Evans's trust on a court fight, but I'm confident you would not win." His eyes had turned into little blue steel ball bearings in his tiny head, and Ryan again wished that she had not accompanied her lover on this excursion.

"These questions are rhetorical, Mr. Gray," Ryan said evenly. "Jamie asked me to help her understand the trust more fully. That's all I'm trying to do."

Jamie considered jumping in, but Ryan was doing a good job of telling the pompous little man off, so she let her roll.

"Of course," Mr. Gray agreed with a thin smile. "I implied nothing more."

"Does Jamie have the ability to make investment decisions?" Ryan asked, determined to get through the questions that had been troubling her, no matter how irritating Mr. Gray was.

"No, she does not. The trustees have no discretion either. Mr. Smith trusted our very capable investment department to handle all aspects of the financial decisions."

"Do you have a list of what her current assets are?"

"Yes. Miss Evans gets a full report every quarter. That's how often we print that report."

"I keep all of those, Ryan," Jamie said. "They're at home."

"Let me make sure I understand one thing," Ryan said carefully. "Your investment department has full authority over all of the assets in Jamie's trust."

"Correct," he said.

"I assume that one person is really in charge of her portfolio?"

"Yes, generally that's true."

"How many accounts does that one person manage, if you have any idea?"

He looked a little uncomfortable, but he answered. "Probably about four hundred or so."

"Is his or her compensation based on performance, or is it straight salary?"

"Our money managers are paid very well, young lady. They are some of the best in the business, I'll have you know," he declared, with his ire starting to show.

"Did you answer my question?" Ryan asked pointedly, batting her big blue eyes.

He took a deep breath and let it out slowly, obviously trying to control his temper. "There are people in the investment group who study the market carefully and make recommendations on buys and sells. They are compensated according to their performance. However, the individual investment manager for Jamie's account is paid a very generous salary. We structure it that way so that they are not under the same pressure that an employee of a brokerage firm would be. It's not in their best interests to buy and sell stocks frequently just to move things around."

Ryan nodded her dark head, deep in thought. Finally the blue eyes peeked out through her bangs as she said, "But it doesn't reward outstanding performance either, does it?"

"It is a delicate balance," he said. "The investment world is a very complex one, Miss O'Flaherty. It's impossible to maximize return while providing safety. Mr. Smith was very happy with our philosophy and our performance. I think we have provided ample evidence that his choice was a good one."

"I'm not disputing that, Mr. Gray. I'm just asking questions to help Jamie understand this more fully."

He stood to his full five feet and said, "I hope that your influence leads Miss Evans to draw the correct conclusions about our performance. Now I must leave to meet a client. My secretary will bring you a copy of the agreement if you can wait a few moments." He indicated an elderly woman sitting at the desk just in front of his own. "It was a pleasure to see you again, Jamie." Turning to Ryan he extended a hand and said, "I assume we'll meet again, Miss O'Flaherty."

With that terse sign-off, he was gone.

"Do I just have a knack for pissing people off, or what?" Ryan muttered as she stared after his departing form.

"You must, although I don't understand it for the life of me," Jamie mused. "I think you're terribly charming, and you've yet to piss me off."

Ryan turned and caught the dancing green eyes gazing up at her. "I guess that's the only opinion I should care about, huh?"

"You betcha."

As soon as they arrived home, Ryan gathered the statements that Jamie had brought from their house and started to pore over them. She didn't hear the cell phone ring, nor did she notice when Jamie left the room for quite some time. A pair of warm lips upon her neck eventually startled her out of her concentration. "Yipes!" Ryan cried. "How did you come in without my hearing you?"

"You were so intent, I don't think you'd notice if I'd been chopping wood."

Ryan laughed at this exaggeration but she had to concede, "I get kinda focused."

"Kinda indeed." She started to strip off her golf clothes to slip into one of Ryan's big T-shirts, her normal lounging attire. "Mother says 'hi,'" she commented as she sat down on the bed.

"When did you talk to her?" Ryan was certain that Jamie had not used the phone located right next to her computer, so she was puzzled by the comment.

"She called just a few minutes after we got home. I went outside and played with your poor dog while I talked to her."

Scratching her head in puzzlement, Ryan commented, "I thought my hearing was really good. Maybe I should have it checked."

"Your hearing is excellent. You just get so into things that you're absolutely oblivious."

Playfully sparkling blue eyes regarded her as Ryan said, "You normally don't mind that I throw myself into whatever task is at hand…so to speak."

"I'm not complaining about your powers of concentration in the least, love. It's all good."

"I thought your mom would be traveling. Did she call you from the plane?"

"Nope. My uncle David came down with a touch of the flu, so the rest of the family decided to postpone the trip for a few days. She'll probably go next Friday."

"Cool," Ryan said. "She seemed kinda bummed that she wasn't going to get to see your father before she left. Maybe they can spend some time together before she has to leave."

"Yeah. I hope so, too. So, what did you find out about the state of my finances?"

"Well, the performance has been less than overwhelming," Ryan said. "I spoke with Brendan, and he explained that trust departments were often chosen back in the days when a return of 3 or 4 percent was very good. Your grandfather wanted to make sure that principal was maintained, and he obviously thought that was more important than growth. If you still feel that way, you may as well leave your distribution where it is."

"But doesn't that seem silly in this wild stock market? God, Mother has doubled her portfolio in the last four years."

"Obviously you could make a lot more money, but you have to realize that you'd be putting your principal at risk."

"I think we could strike a more moderate balance. I'd like to improve the performance while still being relatively conservative, and it doesn't sound like I can do that where my money is now."

"Well, it's clear that you have no ability to influence their decisions. If you want more control you do need to take your distribution."

"I think we should do it," Jamie said.

Ryan stood and stretched, unkinking her back after the long period of inactivity. "Why don't you wait until you have some idea of how you want to invest it? Get your ducks in a row, and that will prove to your father that you're competent to handle the money."

"As usual, you're the smart one," Jamie said sweetly, kissing her enthusiastically.

"Smart enough to have picked you," Ryan agreed, puckering up for the kiss that she knew her compliment would merit.

Chapter Fifteen

A fter dinner that night, Ryan gave her partner the high sign, and Jamie went back downstairs in accordance with their previous agreement. Ryan had decided that she might as well get a very unpleasant task out of the way, and she thought it best to do it alone. Conor was on a date, so it was just father and daughter left in the dining room when Jamie excused herself.

Looking at his daughter's carefully composed face, Martin cocked his head a bit and said, "If you were ten years younger, I'd guess that you'd either skipped school or broken something expensive."

"That bad, huh?" His daughter grinned. "I don't know why I'm so horrible at hiding my feelings."

"You know what I've always told you," Martin said calmly. "Get the bad news over with and then figure out how to fix it."

She nodded slightly, taking a breath as she observed, "This one might be beyond my ability to fix."

Seeing the very serious look in her eyes, Martin reached across the table and grasped her hand, his gaze penetrating. "There's nothing wrong with you, is there, Siobhán?"

You're scaring the poor man, Ryan, just spit it out, will you? "No, no, nothing like that," she assured him, pleased when his shoulders relaxed visibly. "Actually, in a way, it's good news."

"I presume that means that in another way, it's bad news," he guessed, nodding at the confirmation in her clear blue eyes. "Well, let's have it."

"Okay." Ryan exhaled heavily and said, "The good news is that I've finally figured out what happened to me in high school, and I feel immensely better about the whole affair."

"That's wonderful," he said, looking a little puzzled. "Tell me all about it."

"I will, Da, but there are parts of my story that you're not going to like one little bit."

Her ominous warning in place, Ryan began to relate her tale.

Nearly half an hour later, Jamie heard the dining room chairs scrape across the floor. Checking her watch, she considered, *Not bad. A half hour to get all of that out is quite a feat. And I didn't even hear Martin raise his voice. Maybe Ryan's better at keeping him calm than she thinks. I think I'll go up and check to make sure everything's okay.*

Opening the door, Jamie reached the first step when she heard Martin's rage-filled voice cry out, "Of all of the low-down, dirty, stinking things I've ever heard in my life…" *Okay, maybe she needs just a little more practice at this.* She grimaced, closing the door even as every instinct told her to go rescue her partner. *She wants to do this alone, I have to respect that. Damn, it's hard to respect that.*

"We've been friends with that man for twenty-nine years!" Martin cried, pacing back and forth across the living room floor. The small dimensions of the place made his trip very short, and the quick changes of direction he was forced to make made Ryan tenser than she already was.

"I know that, Da, and I agree that he made a very poor choice, but I think you have to give him credit for doing what he thought was right, even though it wasn't the best thing for me."

Martin stopped abruptly and glared at his daughter, and she had a brief flash of how the opponents of her great-grandfather's bare-knuckle fights must have felt right before they were knocked flat. "You're defending him! How could you, Siobhán?"

His blue eyes were nearly white with rage, and Ryan briefly regretted not letting Jamie handle this discussion for her. "Da," she said, as calmly as she could, "I was furious at first, too, but I think you have to at least give him the opportunity to explain his decision. He's been a very good friend to you. Don't let this ruin twenty-nine years."

"I've ruined nothing!" he yelled. "This is his doing."

"Okay, so it's his doing," Ryan said. "Isn't everyone entitled to a mistake?"

"Not when my daughter is involved!" He was breathing so heavily that Ryan feared he would pass out.

"Da, please don't do anything while you're this upset," she begged, afraid that her father would march down to the church and strangle the poor man.

"He made his bed, now he can lie in it!" With that he stormed toward the door, stopping only when Ryan dashed in front of him and placed both hands on his chest.

"Please," she said, her voice shaking, "I'm begging you not to confront him until you've had time to calm down. Please." Tears were streaming down her face now, and to her great relief they were effective at causing the irate man to stop and consider her request.

He was so angry that his entire body was shaking, and he finally took in a breath and nodded his head. "I'll be at your aunt's," he said, sidestepping his daughter and stalking out the door.

"Well, that was two tons of fun." Ryan flopped down on the loveseat in their room, looking quite the worse for wear. Her hair was mussed, probably from running her hands through it, and her eyes bore telltale signs of recent crying.

"I bet you have a headache, don't you?" Jamie asked softly, noticing the ungainly way that Ryan had moved about the room. Whenever she was very tense, she seemed to carry the stress in her neck and shoulders, and her posture reflected that fact.

"Yeah. A bad one." Admitting to pain wasn't something Ryan did readily, so her immediate acknowledgment indicated it must be bothering her a lot.

"Let me rub your back," Jamie offered. "I can help get some of the tension out."

Without a word, Ryan started to strip off her T-shirt and bra, her compliance causing Jamie to fret even more about how much pain she must be in. Ryan lay facedown on the bed, waiting patiently while Jamie retrieved the massage lotion from the bedside table. "We're almost out of lotion," she said as she poured the last of the vanilla-scented lotion into her palms to warm it.

"'Kay. I'll get more."

"It really upsets you when your father gets that angry, doesn't it?" she asked softly, beginning to stroke the long bands of muscle along Ryan's spine.

"Could you hear him?"

"I think the neighbors heard him," Jamie said. "I didn't have any idea he could yell that loud...or curse that much. Although I didn't understand most of the cursing...thankfully."

That merited a small chuckle from Ryan. "The worse it gets, the more he throws Irish expressions in. He was practically screaming in Gaelic there at the end—and he doesn't speak Gaelic."

"He's not angry with you, is he?" Jamie's fingers were probing deep into the rigid muscles along the tops of Ryan's shoulders, feeling some of the tension start to ease.

"No, well, maybe a little bit," she said. "He's angry that I didn't tell him some of this when it happened, but I think he's more frustrated with me than anything."

"So where did you leave things?"

"He promised he wouldn't talk to Father Pender until he calmed down. He's headed over to Aunt Maeve's right now. With any luck, she'll talk him out of strangling him. I think it's at least a double mortal sin to kill a priest."

"You really don't think Father Pender told Sister Mary Magdalene about you with any animosity, do you?"

"No, I don't. We've had our go-rounds, but I think he genuinely likes me. He knows I'm headstrong and that I have serious problems with the dogma of the Church, but I really think that he respects me and wouldn't go behind my back just to hurt me. He was misguided, and what he did was wrong, but when I think about it, I can understand that he was trying to help, even though it was ineffectual."

"Why do you think he went to Sister Mary Magdalene instead of talking to your father?"

"If I put it in the best light, he probably didn't want to tell Da if I hadn't told him yet."

"But you don't believe that, do you?" Her gentle touch was helping to relax Ryan, even though the subject matter of their discussion was very upsetting.

"No, I don't, and I know Da doesn't either. I think he did it because he thought I was the aggressor with Sara and that I might convince some of the other girls to go down my evil path with me."

Jamie's hands stilled and she paused for a long while. "Why on earth would he think that?"

"I've always been too headstrong for him to really trust, Jamie. Even as a kid we had our troubles."

The last of the lotion had largely disappeared, and Jamie's hands were starting to meet with some resistance. "I need to go into the bath to get a massage lotion substitute," she said, starting to slide off Ryan's hips.

Ryan grabbed her leg and held her in place. "No need. I feel a lot better now. Let's just cuddle for a while, okay?"

"Hmm, cuddle, huh? I hope you know that I'll never refuse to cuddle with you, so you really don't even have to ask. Just get into your cuddle position, and I'm there." She leaned over and placed some warm kisses on Ryan's vanilla-scented neck, breathing in the delightful scent along with warm skin and Ryan's shampoo. She waited until Ryan turned over and held out her arm, snuggling up against her chest automatically. "What could you possibly fight with a priest about when you were just a kid?"

"Haven't I told you about the big controversy about Michael's funeral?"

Jamie was quiet for a moment, finally saying, "I'm pretty sure I'd remember that discussion. I can't for the life of me think of how a funeral would be controversial."

Ryan's chuckle caused Jamie's head to bounce a bit on her chest. "You didn't know Michael." She laughed quietly. "I know I've told you about how ill he was during his last year."

Jamie nodded silently, her cheek rubbing lightly against the baby-soft skin of Ryan's breast.

"Months and months before he died, he asked me to do him a favor." She was quiet for a moment, obviously recalling the events. "He asked me to sing one of his favorite songs at his funeral." Her voice was barely a whisper, and Jamie cuddled up closer, providing warmth and support with her presence.

"Was the song controversial?" Jamie asked, knowing that Michael had an enormous love for all music and guessing that perhaps the song was inappropriate for a church service.

"Kinda," Ryan agreed. "It wasn't the content so much as the fact that it wasn't in our hymnals. Father Pender doesn't like to go outside the lines very much, and he was very reluctant to allow a contemporary song to be played."

"What was the song?" Jamie asked.

"It was a Stevie Wonder song from the seventies. Do you know much of his work?"

"No, not really. Uhm, was it really popular? Maybe I've heard it."

"No, I doubt it," Ryan said. "It wasn't a big hit, but Michael loved it. He said it summed up his feelings about religion in just a few verses."

"Will you sing it for me?"

Ryan nodded, "I will someday," then added, "but not now. I don't think I could get through it today."

"That's okay. No rush."

"I promised that I'd sing it, and shortly after that he lost his ability to recognize me." Hot tears started to fall, and Ryan wiped them away with the back of her hand as Jamie's hold tightened. "That was so hard," she whispered. "To have him lying there, wasting away before my eyes, and not be able to talk to him. It was just so hard."

Pulling out of Ryan's embrace, Jamie scooted higher on the bed and enveloped her in her arms. "Shh," she murmured, "don't cry."

Ryan sighed heavily and rolled over to get a tissue. "It's hard for me to talk about that time," she said. "I honestly think that was the hardest thing I ever went through. Harder even than when my mother was sick, because I knew what death was by then."

"I can't imagine," Jamie said, having never experienced the death of someone so close to her.

Ryan shook her head, trying to stop the images that still assaulted her memory. "Anyway, the bottom line is that when Michael died, Father Pender looked at his list of requests and said that the song couldn't be sung. I thought Da or Aunt Maeve would talk to him and set it straight, but Da sat me down and said that if I wanted to honor Michael's wishes, I had to make it happen on my own."

Jamie was aghast that Martin wouldn't go to bat for his young daughter, and her shock was clearly evident on her face.

"In retrospect, Da did exactly the right thing," Ryan said. "I was a wild little thing in most areas, but I was really, really shy when it came to expressing my opinion to authority figures. Having to do this myself was a wonderful lesson for me." She smiled slowly, her sadness still evident. "Years later, I found the instructions Michael had written for Aunt Maeve. He said he wanted me to handle everything concerning his musical requests for the funeral and that he knew it would be a tough sell." She looked at Jamie with her watery blue eyes and said, "Even when he was dying, he was trying to help me grow up. He knew I'd have to come out of my shell and make a scene to get Father Pender to include that song. For all I know, the song wasn't even important. He was just trying to teach me a lesson about standing up for things that were important to me."

"I can understand why you miss him so much," Jamie whispered. "He sounds like a wonderful man."

"He was," Ryan agreed. "He was everything I'd like to be."

"I assume you had trouble with Father Pender," Jamie said, continuing to lightly rub Ryan's belly and smiling when Ryan nuzzled even closer.

"I sure as heck did," she said with a very short laugh. "He finally gave in when I said I'd stand on the steps at the entrance of the church and sing it 'a cappella' when they were bringing in the casket."

"Would you have really done that?" Jamie could easily picture her lover pulling a modern-day Martin Luther-style protest as an adult, but she had a hard time envisioning a child taking a stand like that.

Ryan was quiet for a moment, finally pulling away from Jamie's snug embrace to sit up enough to look her in the eyes. "I'd have climbed up in the bell tower if I'd had to. There was not a person on this earth who could have stopped me."

Jamie blinked slowly, the fire and determination in Ryan's gaze so strong that it was almost hard to look at. "I'm so proud of you." Her hoarse whisper was accompanied by a few tears, which Ryan kissed away. They held each other tight for a long while, until Jamie reminded her partner of something. "We had a deal that you'd try to remember the happy memories of Michael too. Wanna give it a try now?"

Sniffling a little, Ryan rolled onto her back, slipping her arm around Jamie and cuddling her against her chest once again. "Okay. I mentioned earlier that Aunt Maeve let me read his instructions about the funeral."

"Yeah, I remember."

"Well, that was just one tiny bit of the volumes of writing he had." Ryan chuckled a little as she said, "He had diaries, journals, notebooks full of poems, essays on topics that interested him, a few short stories, and a good start on a novel that was really fascinating."

"Gosh, I didn't realize that he was a writer."

"Oh, yeah. I have some of his stuff here. I'll show it to you sometime. Anyway, the funny thing was that there were two notebooks that Aunt Maeve didn't show me until just a couple of years ago. They were both labeled, "Mam, for the sake of your sanity do not read these. Give them to Bryant, or Ryan when she's old enough to drink."

"What?" Jamie was completely puzzled by this warning, and she waited with rapt attention for Ryan to reveal the reason for it.

"One book was all of his poems that dealt with sex, and the other was essays and short pieces about his sexual experiences."

"Were they really risqué?" Jamie had a feeling that Maeve would be fairly easy to shock, so she reasoned that the material might not be too scandalous.

"Wow." Ryan fanned herself dramatically. "Bryant, Michael's lover, couldn't read any of his stuff for years. He couldn't even stand to have it in his apartment, so Aunt Maeve kept it all. Not long after I turned twenty-one, she gave me the notebooks. All I can say is that boy loved sex more than I do."

"Really? That's hard to believe."

"Indeed." Ryan's eyes were wide, and her head nodded slowly. "I'd show it to you, but you're still too young!"

"Oh, Ryan," she laughed as she slapped her thigh, "you're exaggerating."

"I most certainly am not," she insisted, jumping out of bed to go to her bookshelf. Grasping a cloth-bound journal, she flipped through the pages until she got to the one she was seeking. She crossed back to the bed and presented the open book to Jamie, watching with delight as her green eyes grew rounder and her mouth gaped dramatically.

Wordlessly, she handed the book back, shaking her head roughly, as if to dislodge the images that the poem had left in her brain. "Well, he certainly had the ability to get his point across in just a few words," she mumbled, a deep pink flush creeping up her cheeks. She cocked her head just a bit and asked, "Is that even possible? I mean...jeez!"

"I have no idea," Ryan laughed. "And since neither of us has one, we'll never know."

Much to Ryan's relief, her father did not commit mayhem against the parish priest. In fact, he agreed that he would wait a few days to talk to the man, although he declared that he would have to go to another parish for Mass on Sunday, since it was obviously sinful to wish ill to the priest celebrating the service.

Things were fairly calm on Saturday except for the low level of anxiety that Ryan had built up about the little excursion that she and Jamie were going to undertake that evening. After their dinner with Catherine, Jamie had called her father to apologize, and he immediately insisted they join him for a Giants game. Remarkably, Jim suggested that they invite Conor also, which surprised Ryan, but she was pleased that he was thoughtful enough to include a member of her family.

Even though she was pleased that Jim had made the offer, Ryan was still quite worried about what the evening would bring, and as they made their way to the stadium, her anxiety revealed itself when Conor seemed intent on driving her mad.

Ryan glanced into the rear-view mirror, a wry smirk covering her face. "Conor, if you don't put your seatbelt on and stop bouncing around back there, I'm not going to let you play with your new best friend." Conor was sitting in the backseat of the Lexus, and Ryan had already warned him three times.

"The Lexus is supposed to be so safe, I figured I didn't need it," he reasoned, continuing to bounce. "I can't help it if I'm excited. It's not every day I get to go to the ball game with somebody who owns all of my favorite cars. If we get to be buds, he might invite me down to hang with him sometime."

As Ryan pulled up to a stop sign she turned around and stared at Conor in amazement. "It's not a date, dude. Chill." Turning back to the road, she rolled her eyes, muttering to herself under her breath.

"It's okay, Conor," Jamie said, in her best placating voice. "He's the one who asked us to invite you. I think you have a real chance with him." She was taunting him mercilessly, but he was so invested in making a good impression that he didn't even notice.

"Do I look okay?" he asked in all seriousness. "I mean, I don't want to look like a culchie or anything."

Remembering that the term meant "country bumpkin," Jamie surveyed his look and was quick to reassure him. "You look adorable, Conor. You'll fit in just fine." He was wearing a sage green brushed-cotton shirt tucked into crisply pressed khakis, with a muted yellow cable-knit sweater lying beside him on the seat. The earth tones were very flattering to his dark complexion, and Jamie mused that even though her mother would be more impressed than her father, Conor would clearly pass muster.

"He's already married, Conor," Ryan added.

"I don't want to marry him," Conor scoffed, wriggling around in the backseat so that he could check his hair in the rear-view mirror. "I just want him to like me, so he invites me to hang around with him sometime." Satisfied that his hair was just so, he sank back into the leather seating and checked his watch. "You did understand that we're supposed to be there at seven o'clock, didn't you, Ryan?"

"Yes, Conor," she replied testily. "We've got twenty minutes, so you just sit tight and check your lip gloss."

After pulling up into valet parking, the tall siblings got out and stretched a bit, with Jamie smiling at them both for indulging in their chronic habit. "This is probably our last time to see the Giants at the Stick," Ryan mused, thinking of the many games she had attended with her brothers throughout the years.

"Yeah," he nodded somberly. "I think PacBell Park is a good idea, but I'm really gonna miss this old place." The Giants were scheduled to move to a new facility just south of Market for the 2000 season, and even though the park was reported to be well designed and was quite conveniently located, both siblings hated to say goodbye to an old friend.

"I'm not sorry to see them move," Jamie said. "I've been frozen stiff out here in July. The Stick is a ridiculously cold and windy place to put a baseball field. I still don't know why they chose this site." The park sat at the tip of Hunter's Point and was exposed to an always brisk wind blowing off the bay. Once the sun went down it could be downright nasty, even in the middle of summer.

They had not had time to stop by Jim's office and get the tickets, so they were forced to wait in a long will-call line to retrieve them. The line moved quickly, but Conor was still nervous about being late. To distract him, Ryan recalled, "Hey, remember the night we got the Croix de Candlestick?"

"You got one of those?" Jamie gaped in amazement. During a particularly bad period for the Giants, the team management had decided to capitalize on the cold, windy conditions in their marketing campaign. To that end, they instituted the Croix de Candlestick pin, given to everyone who stayed until the end of an extra-inning game.

"We sure did," Ryan laughed. "It was kinda raining and colder than all get-out. I think there were less than fifty people here at the end."

"Da was fit to be tied when we got home," Conor said, laughing. "The game lasted until about 1:00 a.m., and when we got home we were practically frozen stiff. To this day he fails to understand why we were so damned happy to have a little piece of metal to commemorate being frostbitten."

Much to Jamie's surprise, when they settled into their seats Conor displayed none of the nervousness that had been so evident earlier. The younger man showed his most confident side, speaking very knowledgeably about the Giants, the new ballpark, and every other topic that came up. He was clearly entertaining Jim, and Jamie began to regret the fact that they had invited him. It wasn't that she didn't want her father to know and like all of the O'Flahertys—she did. She just wished that he could warm up to Ryan before he was charmed by her brother.

Uncharacteristically, Ryan was quite low-key throughout the evening. Jamie realized that this was her way of playing it safe, but she also knew that her father wouldn't come to know Ryan if she remained this reserved around him.

By the third inning, Jim finally gave in to Conor's repeated offers to buy him a beer or a hot dog, and the siblings left to stand in line. Jamie moved back to sit next to her father in the box, and since she knew she would be grilled later she casually asked, "Are you having a good time, Daddy?"

"Sure am," he said. "I'm always happy to be with you."

Sharing his smile, she followed up on Conor's earlier wish. "You should think about inviting Conor down to hang out in your garage sometime. I think he'd really like it." Thinking about it during the game, she had realized that having Conor break the ice for the O'Flaherty clan wasn't such a bad idea. He and Ryan were quite a lot alike, and she reasoned that if her father grew to like him, Ryan might seem more palatable as well.

He furrowed his brow a bit and cocked his head. "Would he really? Why would a young guy like that want to hang out with me? I'd think he'd be out with some good-looking woman every chance he got."

"Oh, he does that, too," Jamie assured him, "but he's crazy for cars. Would you be averse to having him?"

"No, of course not. I like Conor a lot. He's really my kind of guy. I'll definitely do that."

She wanted to say, "Ryan and Conor are almost exactly alike, and if you like one, you'll like the other," but she thought that her father wouldn't appreciate those same attributes in Ryan at this point, so she held her tongue.

"I ahh, I had something I wanted to discuss with you, Jamie, but I wanted to do it in private," Jim said as he looked around at their neighbors.

"No one is listening to us. Go ahead."

Casting another glance over his shoulder, he leaned in a little closer and said, "I got a very interesting phone call from John Podesta yesterday."

Jamie's eyebrows popped up, recognizing the name of President Clinton's chief of staff. "What did he want?"

Now Jim's eyes lit up and he looked positively giddy. "He wants to know if I'd be interested in filling the remainder of the term for Senator Somers." The very senior senator from California had recently died after a lengthy illness, and speculation about his successor ran rampant. It was most common to offer the position to the wife of the deceased senator, but Jamie knew that the senator was a widower.

"Daddy!" she gasped. "Why...how...are you interested?"

"Yes, I think I am," he said, still unable to contain his excitement. "It would only be for a year or so, which makes it more attractive."

She sat in rather stunned silence for a moment until her civics lessons came back to her and she asked, "I thought the governor appointed people to fill positions like that."

"Oh, he does, but the White House is helping Governor Davis come up with a list of names. He'd make the final choice, but I think Washington has a pretty big say in who gets the nod."

"Would you have to run for office?"

"No, no, that I'd have no interest in. This is an appointed post. When the term was over, I'd come back home and return to the firm."

"Wow," Jamie said, still stunned by this development. "Why would you want to do this?"

"Contacts," he said as if he couldn't believe she would ask such a question. "I'd make very valuable contacts in that position. Lobbyists, big business...you name it."

I guess the public service thing is a thing of the past. "What do you think your chances are, if you decide to try for this?"

He pursed his lips, thinking for a moment about what he brought to the game. "I have no political aspirations, so that's a good thing, because there's no clear Democratic nominee for 2000 anyway. Senator Somers wasn't up for election until 2002, so no one's been gearing up for a run. Putting me in would let a viable candidate focus on running a good campaign. Plus, I'm well liked by Clinton's people and Davis's people. I've given substantial contributions to both of their campaigns, and they tend not to forget a friend. I also think that I have the kind of foreign relations experience they want from working with so many clients in Europe and the Far East. I know a lot of people who could help get a new trade bill passed."

Hmm, no thoughts about who would be the best person to serve the voters. I suppose that's another naïve concept. "If this is something that you want to do, I certainly hope it happens for you, Daddy. I'd certainly miss you and Mother if you were in Washington for a year, but I'll support your decision, no matter what you choose."

He looked a little puzzled at that and commented, "I can't imagine that your mother would go with me. I wouldn't think she'd want to give up her life here."

God, that's sad. I'd never let Ryan go off for a year by herself. Of course, Ryan wouldn't consider doing it, either. "Well, then we'll both miss you," she amended, wondering if her mother had even been consulted about this rather major development. "How do you think your partners would feel about it?"

"Oh, they'd be fully supportive," he said. "It would be very good for business. That's the important point."

"Of course, that's all that matters," she lied.

Ryan and Conor were slowly making their way back to their seats, and, as Jamie got up, Jim whispered, "Don't say anything about this to Ryan."

Her dramatically raised eyebrow quickly reminded him of the place Ryan occupied in her life and he amended, "I meant, don't say anything to anyone other than Ryan."

She kissed him on the cheek and whispered, "Thank you. I won't breathe a word."

On the way home, Ryan muttered, "I can't believe that Conor's going home with your dad. That's beyond weird."

Jamie slapped her on the thigh and said, "You make it sound like he's gonna get lucky."

"Hey, don't put it past Conor," Ryan said. "I know he'd sell his soul for a classic Mustang. He'd give up his body without a second thought."

"Well, I'm fairly confident that Daddy won't fall for his considerable charms. Besides, I thought it was sweet of Conor to ride with him down to Pebble Beach. That's a very long drive late at night."

"True, but there's no way Conor would give up the chance to drive the NSX back up to the city tomorrow."

"I thought his eyes were going to pop out of his head," Jamie said. "Daddy's been wanting to bring that car back home so it gets a little use, but Mother has never wanted to drive the BMW all that way alone. This really worked out great." She laughed softly, shaking her head at the persistent mental image that kept popping up. "I can't get the image out of my mind of the two of them in their jammies, playing CDs, making popcorn, and talking about all the cute new cars."

Ryan's head turned, making eye contact when Jamie spared a glance in her direction. "Conor...doesn't...wear...jammies."

"*Eeuuww!*" they cried concurrently.

True to his word, Martin attended Sunday Mass at Mission Dolores, since he was sure he would be unable to focus on the service at his own parish with his old friend presiding over it.

During their traditional Sunday morning brunch, Ryan noted that her father didn't display his usual spark, and she realized that bottling up his anger was taking a toll on him. When the dishes were finished, she went into his room and sat on the edge of the bed, gazing at him for a moment as he read the morning paper.

"This is really tough on you, isn't it?" she asked softly, reaching out to place a gentle hand on his knee.

"What's that, love?" he asked, folding the paper onto his lap, his gaze interested.

"Trying to stop yourself from making mincemeat of Father Pender." She tilted her head to maintain eye contact as his head dropped a little.

Martin folded his hands together and stared at them as he slowly nodded. "It's not my usual style," he said, in somewhat of an understatement. "But I keep my word." His gaze rose and locked onto his daughter's. "You don't ask me for many things, Siobhán. This is the least I can do for you."

"Can I amend my request?"

He nodded and waited, hoping that his daughter wouldn't make the already difficult task any harder.

"I know I asked you not to talk to him while you're still angry, but you don't seem much calmer about this than you were on Friday. Why don't we go over together and speak with him. If I can be there, I think I'd feel a lot better."

He didn't look very happy with this suggestion, but considered it thoughtfully before he replied, "I'd rather talk to him alone, but if it would make you feel better, I'm willing to do it together."

She sighed in relief and stood, extending her hand to help her father from his battered old chair. "Let's do it."

Blowing a kiss to Jamie along with a mouthed, "We'll be back in a few minutes," Ryan scampered down the stairs, trying to keep up with her father's longer strides. "Take it easy, Da," she warned. "We don't have to run."

He slowed visibly, albeit reluctantly. His hands were curled into fists, and Ryan wrapped her left hand around his right, asking to hold his hand. Martin immediately complied, and she felt reassured to have his large, strong hand clasping hers. "We haven't held hands in a very long while," she said. "It's nice."

"A certain green-eyed lass seems to have taken up permanent residence at the end of your arm," Martin joked, bringing his daughter's hand to his lips to kiss the smooth skin.

"True," she mused, drawing in a deep breath of the warm summer air. "I remember walking up this hill when I was little, holding your hand on the way to church."

"I had to hold your hand to keep you from darting into traffic," he laughed, only slightly exaggerating. "Your mother gave up the fight when you were around four. She decided to take the easy way out and keep track of Rory."

"Ah, I wasn't so bad," she scoffed, knowing that she had been every bit as bad as her father had indicated. "But no matter the reason, I have very fond memories of walking to church as a family. Sunday was always special, wasn't it?"

His eyes misted a little as he nodded. "It was, darlin'." Memories of his young family attending church together and then returning home for brunch flooded his mind, the sweet tableau causing a lump to form in his throat.

"I remember sitting at the dining table, talking about the sermon, and the scripture readings for the week," Ryan recalled. "I didn't understand most of it, but I have a really clear memory of how important it was to Mama that we live what we learned."

"That it was," Martin agreed, a sad smile covering his face as he recalled his wife trying to inculcate the lessons of their faith into their four young ones. "Her faith was truly her rock." Memories of the devastating pain Fionnuala had been forced to bear flooded his memory, and he wiped at his eyes with the back of his free hand as he said, "Thank God that she had it."

"She lived her faith," Ryan said softly. "Even though I don't have too many memories, that's one thing that I know." Martin gripped her hand tighter, profoundly happy that his daughter's memories included such a vital part of his beloved wife. "There's another thing that I know, Da."

He turned slightly and was greeted by a confident look on his daughter's face. "What's that?"

"I know that she wouldn't want you to be too harsh with Father Pender." Her words were soft, so soft that he had to strain to hear her, and his heart clutched in pain as he saw his daughter's face, but heard his wife's quiet, yet decisive voice.

Without warning, he threw his arms around his child and gave her a robust hug, whispering into her ear, "You're so much like her, Siobhán. You are so very much your mother's daughter."

"That's the nicest compliment I've ever had," she murmured, the emotion of the scene overcoming her. "Thank you, Da."

Releasing her, he pulled his clean handkerchief from his pocket and let her dry her eyes, then he did the same. Sniffing a few more times, he clasped her hand once more to continue their journey. "You sure do know how to take the fun out of a good shellacking," he muttered, his watery blue eyes belying his words.

"If it wasn't me, you know that Aunt Maeve would have put her foot down," Ryan said, knowing that her aunt was quite persuasive when she wanted to be.

He gave his daughter a full, warm smile. "Luckily, the good Lord blessed me with level-headed women to keep me on the straight and narrow."

"I'm proud of you, Da," Ryan said as they returned home after their visit with the parish priest. "I thought you handled yourself beautifully. You didn't even raise your voice."

He smiled at her, rather proud of himself, but still unhappy with the resolution. "I'm still angry with him," he said quietly, "but I suppose I have to let our twenty-nine years of friendship count for something."

"I think his explanation was rational," Ryan decided, even though she had her doubts as well. "I hadn't come out to you yet, and I don't think I would have been very happy to have him do it for me. I mean, ideally, he would have come to me first, but it's at least believable that he told Sister Mary Magdalene because he thought she would be the best person to control the situation if the rumors got out."

"But that one act caused you so much pain, Siobhán! It destroyed your dreams of playing soccer; it nearly ruined your academic career…so much happened because of it."

"All true," she said, "but you can't look at it like that. I've said this to Jamie before, but it bears repeating. Everything that happened to me culminated in my being at Cal last year. Losing the scholarship, being too depressed to play for Stanford, my reluctance to get involved in a long-term relationship—all of it led me to Jamie."

They were nearing the house now, and as they drew closer, Ryan could see a pair of sneakered feet resting on the ground, obviously coming from the stairway to her home. The owner's body was hidden, but the big black dog sitting patiently next to the feet gave Ryan a pretty good idea who they belonged to.

They were on the opposite side of the street, and as they crossed 22nd Street Martin said, "I'm going to stop at the Necessaries to pick up a few things." Seeing the longing in the deep blue eyes, he playfully swatted her on the seat and ordered, "Go on with ya. Your lass is waiting."

Ryan placed a quick kiss on his cheek and took off running, covering the short distance in a few long strides. As soon as Jamie caught sight of her, she stood on the second step, throwing her arms around the strong neck when Ryan approached. Duffy jubilantly jumped up and tried to finagle his way into the hug, and his human companions welcomed him, both of the young women rubbing his head affectionately as his big pink tongue peeked out in a happy doggy grin.

Martin paused at the door of the convenience store, unable to tear his eyes away from the scene. His daughter looked as happy as he had ever seen her, and he knew that the young woman who stood on the step, gazing at her with loving eyes, was a very large part of her happiness.

Ryan was speaking animatedly, her hands gesturing as they only did when she was immensely pleased about something. Jamie's arms were draped loosely around her neck, and she followed Ryan's words intently, seemingly hanging on every one. A small smile was firmly settled onto her face as she gazed into Ryan's eyes, and even from across the street Martin could see the love and affection that flowed between the two.

As Ryan finished her tale, Jamie released her hold and brought her hands up to gently cradle Ryan's smiling face, placing soft kisses everywhere. The look on the taller woman's face was nearly identical to the one on Duffy's when he was being praised for some particularly good bit of behavior, and when Jamie was finished she reached down and grasped Ryan's hand. They walked up the stairs together, their bodies unconsciously drifting closer. Their gentle laughter lingered in the air as they disappeared from sight, yet Martin stayed right where he was, letting the scene warm his heart.

The lass is right, he thought. *No matter what's gone before, she's terrifically happy now, and that's the important point.* Looking up at the sky in a familiar gesture, he smirked and addressed his late wife, a habit that had helped to keep him sane through his devastating grief. *I know you don't have the power to make the world turn, Fi, but knowing you, you've worked your charms on a guardian angel or two.* He laughed softly to himself, knowing that his wife could charm a celestial being as easily as a human. *There's just something that tells me that you used your influence to bring those two together.* He sighed heavily as he pulled open the door to the store, thinking, *Whoever is responsible, Fi, I think our little one has been blessed by the heavens.* Gazing skyward once again, he winked and asked, *Give my thanks to the proper authorities, won't you, love?*

The End